Irony and Influence:

A PRESUMPTIVE TALE OF PRIDE AND PREJUDICE

Riley St. Andish

A LAUREN LITERATURE PUBLICATION

Copyright © 2012 Riley St. Andish
All rights reserved.

ISBN: 1480022241
ISBN-13: 9781480022249

Chapter 1

*"Come now let us never bend to the will of fashionable thought.
But, think and act sincerely, thus being role models for all."*

-Anonymous

London, England
19 January 1803

Moving swiftly through the afternoon crowd, Mr. Darcy saw people on the boardwalk parting to make room for him. He was a man accustomed to having his way in all things concerning life, and he could have taken his progress as a matter of course. It may have been his authoritative and powerful bearing, or his expensive and exclusively designed clothing, yet he knew it was something more. It was more, because he had asked for more. This was the day that George Darcy would receive the supernatural help he had been asking heaven to grant him. He knew he would have that rescue, because it was a matter of life and death for his son, Fitzwilliam. He did not know the details, but he would recognise the answer when it was provided.

Darcy's handsome face was reflected in the shop window as he placed his hand upon the door and stepped inside. Looking at his pocket watch, he smiled happily to himself. Yes, he had time. For once he had plenty of time to spend in his favourite bookstore.

"Welcome, Mr. Darcy. It is always a pleasure to have you in our store, sir." A voice from behind the counter greeted him.

"Thank you, Mr. Banks. I am pleased to be here. I shall just browse. I shall call, if assistance is required." Thinking he was the only customer in the store, he relished the idea of secluded shopping. He was a man who greatly valued his privacy, and finding ample time in his schedule to leisurely leaf through more than three or four volumes in one visit seemed a heavenly benefaction.

Hearing laughter in the store, Darcy realised he was not the only patron. Gleeful voices blending together in merriment intruded upon his solitude. On any other day, this may have been an annoyance, yet somehow Darcy was instead basking in the joyful sounds. Listening carefully to their happy conversation, he began to interpret this disruption as an unexpected blessing. What he was hearing was actually most entertaining. It seemed to be an impromptu oration by a young humorist. Darcy felt his sullen mood lifting.

He felt lighter and desired to join them with alacrity. Yet, a man of his class must always use caution. Experience had taught him that eavesdropping could be most useful in this type of situation. He listened, quite carefully.

"Yes! That is exactly what I mean!" a melodic female voice was saying. Her tones were rich and expressive. Her cadence and vocabulary were fascinating. She was giving an amusing summary of the old play *Preicles, Prince of Tyre*. "Of course, we all know that it was partially rewritten by Shakespeare; so naturally it has much to divert and to entertain, even if a portion of the plot cannot be discussed in public! Shocking! Merciful Heavens!" Her parody was heaped with hyperbolism. Mr. Darcy was so engrossed, he was obliged to cover his mouth to refrain from laughing. Her delightful delivery was so comedic, Darcy soon found himself hanging upon her every utterance. Truth be told, he was forgetting himself, his problems, and even his surroundings.

Mr. Banks's carefree chuckles could also be heard bubbling up from behind his counter. As the laughter faded, she smiled and continued daringly, "Ah, 'tis a delightful comedy, contrived to enchant the audience. 'Tis set in strange lands, with even stranger characters. 'Tis a romance, a comedy, and has many twists. Oh! And, what is romance without agony?"

She put both of her open palms alongside her cheeks and sighed archly. Her two companions looked at each other, rolling their eyes, trying to control themselves. Unable to contain their levity any longer, their laughter flowed like water, cascading from falls.

"Lizzy?" a masculine voice snickered, "as your uncle, I must ask, and I am sure your aunt also, would dearly love to know: what does a young maiden, such as yourself, know of the agonies of romance? We had no idea you were so insightful, never having been courted." He chuckled, then, once composed, requested, "Pray, tell us of the agonies."

At this question, the girl lost her struggle to maintain her self-possession. She pursed her lips into a wavering smile. It held for a brief moment, then loosed, releasing a most pleasing laugh, which floated throughout the entire store. It was infectious.

Composing her face, and placing her laughter in check, she answered him. "Why, I supposed you knew, Uncle! I am constantly improving my mind with extensive reading! Is not reading of romance the same as being romanced?" At this response, they laughed again. "Well then," said her aunt, "pray tell us of these agonies, child."

She cleared her throat, "Ahem. In this improbable play, there are long separations, deaths, that are not real, but imagined,

Irony and Influence

then what?" she questioned rhetorically. "If the audience becomes confused, a chorus shall sing—'La!' Marina is saved from a murderer, by pirates, only to be sold to a brothel! Oh, Lord help us all! Yet, do not despair! She remains virtuous by talking each would-be patron out of their corruption.

"Now, you decide, Uncle and Aunt, is this realism? No, but it does weave a very fanciful tale, and an absolutely enthralling story, does it not?" Laughing again, they agreed.

"And," she said, tipping her head and arching her eyebrows, "all ends well. Leaving us with only one question…about the audience. Why does one sound so inarticulate when laughing?"

"Oh, Lizzy," her aunt cautioned, "the things you think of, child."

Mr. Darcy, a proficient eavesdropper, had now become transfixed. He could not resist watching them from the next aisle. Enchanted, he wanted to meet her.

Unaware of being watched, the trio continued their amusements. Obviously, they enjoyed each other's company, and they exhibited an astonishing ability to relate to one another with mutual respect and understanding. Their observer was intrigued. To George Darcy, it was wonderful to see a youth, about his son's age, finding joy in people of an older generation. He could watch and listen endlessly.

"Lizzy, which parts of the play did Shakespeare rewrite, do you know?" her aunt inquired. "Of course I do! He wrote all the good parts!" Tossing her long, spicy auburn hair back archly, she laughed with gusto, clearly enjoying the companionship of her uncle and aunt.

No longer able to deny himself the pleasure of meeting her, Mr. Darcy entered their aisle. He saw a couple of fashion with a very beautiful young woman. "Please excuse me," he directed, slightly tipping his head. "Hearing your amusement, I had to join you. An ungracious breach of propriety on my part, yet I must comment on your delightful discourse.

"I have not thought about that particular play in many years. May I please introduce myself and have the honour of knowing you? I am George Darcy." Reaching into his breast pocket, he drew out his card and handed it to the uncle who resumed the introductions: "Mr. Darcy, a pleasure, sir. I am Edward Gardiner." He removed his card and extended it saying, "May I present my wife, Mrs. Lucille Gardiner, and our niece Miss Elizabeth Bennet." Mr. Darcy bowed to the group; Mr. Gardiner returned the civility, and the ladies curtsied.

"Delighted!" Mr. Darcy smiled and continued in earnest, "Young lady, I have heard many lectures while at Cambridge, yet I assure you, none were as instructional nor were they as fraught with humour as was yours. May I ask your educational background?"

You are as witty and intelligent as you are breathtakingly beautiful. He mused to himself as he smiled at them. *What Providence this— Yes, you are perfect!*

Dropping a slight curtsey, she began, "I am, sir, the second daughter of a gentleman from Longbourn, Hertfordshire, Mr. Thomas Bennet by name. He is, I am sorry to tell you, a graduate of Oxford. He would have willingly sent me to that same estimable school if only I had been born male. I am, to my father's vexation, one of five daughters!" Training her bright green eyes on his blue ones, she pressed on: "It would seem that good King George III has no conventional objections to a girl being self-taught at home, using her father's textbooks. I have now completed all of those courses, and my most generous benefactors, Uncle and Aunt Gardiner have offered to celebrate by taking me on a self-styled tour, of sorts! I am, as always, forever in their debt."

"Well done!" was Mr. Darcy's genuine reply. "Congratulations! Pray, what ports of call do you anticipate?" *Self-studied Oxford courses! Remarkable intelligence.*

A dazzling smile delivered his answer. "What could be better or more beautiful than the Emerald Isle? We shall see sights of historical and architectural significance," she sighed.

"A lovely sounding trip," Mr. Darcy agreed sincerely.

"Yes," she continued, quite excitedly. "When it is concluded, I shall be filled with sights sufficient—which shall entertain me and keep a smile upon my lips! This is to help me hold my tongue. I shall keep a sober face. When confronted with questions or if ever I am asked for any opinions, I shall maintain denial that I have ever learned anything other than my music and needlework, suitable duties of piety and most Christian charity!"

With that, she dramatically lowered her lush eyelashes, placed her hand over her heart, and sighed theatrically.

Mr. Darcy threw back his head and laughed openly at this witty satire, intended to mock the current law excluding females from formal education! *My, but you are bright, and so beautiful, charming, amusing, and completely irresistible!*

Finding his voice, he queried, "If I am not being too forward, I have a daughter. Georgiana is two and ten years of age. Her mother left this earth whilst giving birth to her. I do my best on her behalf, yet I seem to be always in search of excellent role models for her."

Taking a breath, he regarded all three, "Would I be presumptuous to request your presence for tea tomorrow afternoon at three? We live at Darcy House just across the street from the Grosvenor entrance to Hyde Park. Meeting you, Miss Elizabeth would be a blessing to my child."

And a Heavenly rescue for my son.

Speaking for all three, Mr. Gardiner bowed, "Mr. Darcy, we would be delighted."

"I thank you, Mr. Gardiner," Mr. Darcy replied, smiling. "This is most gracious of all of you. I am in your debt."

Turning to Elizabeth, he nodded his head to her and asked politely, "and just one more imposition, if you would please, Miss Elizabeth? May I consult with you on your ideas for a book that I may give my son? He has just completed his studies at Cambridge. With the Continent in such disarray, he shall tour Ireland." "You do me honour, Mr. Darcy. Yes, perhaps a leather-bound journal would be welcomed. He would be the author of his memories. You could enhance the volume by having it embossed with 'Tour of Ireland 1803' and his name listed as the author. Would that suit him, Mr. Darcy?"

"Very much! While I may have thought of a journal, I like your idea for a personalized touch. Quite clever! My gratitude to you, Miss Bennet. Until tomorrow, then."

"Mrs. Taylor?" Miss Georgiana Darcy inquired as she followed the housekeeper around the first floor, "are you quite certain everything is prepared for tea? I am going to pour, and I need to know all is ready."

"Yes, Miss Darcy, all has been prepared just as you instructed. Now, if you shall wait in the sitting room, your guests shall be announced as soon as they arrive. Your father is prepared to join you immediately thereafter." Mrs. Taylor curtseyed and smiled to reassure the girl. All the staff was very fond of the Darcy family. Mrs. Taylor was happy that the girl had new friends coming to visit. She hoped these people would show kindness and true friendship to the child who was often so lonely.

Miss Darcy suffered from shyness, as did her older brother, Fitzwilliam, albeit, he was much better at masking this affliction with pomposity when necessary.

"Miss Darcy," Simmons announced, "Mr. and Mrs. Edward Gardiner and Miss Elizabeth Bennet."

Smiles and happy chatter filled the room as the little party entered. Their young hostess barely lifted her gaze above her shoes as she greeted them. She glanced nervously at the doorway, hoping her father would come to her rescue.

Elizabeth and the Gardiners went to work calming the young lady's case of shyness and nerves. Their smiles and friendly manners soon set Georgiana at ease.

"Miss Darcy," Elizabeth spoke first, "we are so very happy to meet you. What a cheerful room, and I must say, that is a handsome pianoforte. I can see that we have music in common, as I also play. Admittedly, I spend more time reading than playing. Do you enjoy reading as well, Miss Darcy?"

"Oh, yes I do." Georgiana managed a shy smile. Somehow she liked this older girl immediately. Perhaps it was her shining eyes and her irresistible smile. Most likely, it was because she was in the hands of an expert. Elizabeth could charm shyness away from anyone. At only twenty years old, she had learned to value cultivating friendships.

"What hobbies or pastimes do you enjoy, Miss Darcy?" Mrs. Gardiner inquired.

"Oh, I suppose I like to go for walks in the park, Mrs. Gardiner," she managed to reply.

"Lizzy here is quite a walker. Perhaps she may be able to join you some time for a walk in Hyde Park?"

"That would be lovely." Georgiana turned to Elizabeth, and asked, "Miss Elizabeth, is 'Lizzy' a family nickname?"

"Yes, Miss Darcy, you are correct. Do you have a nickname as well?" Elizabeth asked.

"I do. My family sometimes calls me 'Georgie,' I like it very much."

"I can understand that." Elizabeth smiled, "We seem to have quite a few things in common. Perhaps when we get to know each other better, we could play a duet, if you wish." Elizabeth offered. "We certainly do not expect you to play today upon our first meeting. I feel it is always so uncomfortable to be asked for the favour of a performance when nothing has been planned." Leaning forward and pretending to share something akin to a national secret, she whispered, "That sort of thing always makes me feel so nervous and shy. Do you not agree, Miss Darcy?" Upon hearing this, the younger girl melted. While having considerable talent at the instrument, Miss Darcy suffered from stage fright when playing for any company.

"Oh yes, Miss Elizabeth. I could not agree more!"

"Please call me, Elizabeth! We may dismiss the 'miss,'" she laughed. "I feel we are friends already." Georgiana laughed at the jest. She was beginning to relax.

"What hobbies and interests do you have, Miss, uh, I mean, Elizabeth?" Georgiana asked.

"I very much enjoy horseback riding, archery, and of course, just like you, I dearly love reading, music, and walking. I am a great lover of nature and the out of doors. I grew up on a small estate. It is the biggest estate in Hertfordshire. Of course, I must own to Hertfordshire being a very small place, indeed!" She pretended to hold a fan in front of her face to hide her giggles. Georgiana did the same.

Seeing that the girl enjoyed the joke, Elizabeth took it further. "In fact, Miss Georgiana, if we should go into the library and consult an atlas of England, we may very well find that Hertfordshire is indeed the smallest shire in all the realm! Or, the world?"

Laughter filled the room once more, and at that moment George Darcy decided to leave his place in the hall where he had been listening just outside the door. He had heard enough to determine the friendly and obliging characters of these kind-hearted people. He knew his daughter would be safe in their company.

"Welcome one and all." Mr. Darcy smiled at his guests, who had just risen to their feet. Friendly greetings filled the air. "Please, do be seated," Mr. Darcy offered, "what a pleasure to join your joyful little party, Georgiana!"

Nodding to his happy-looking daughter, he requested, "My dear Georgie, would you kindly pour? I am sorry to have been detained, Mr. and Mrs. Gardiner, Miss Elizabeth."

"Not at all, Mr. Darcy! We have been delightfully entertained by your daughter. Miss Georgiana is quite a wonderful hostess, sir," said Mr. Gardiner with admiration.

Elizabeth wanted very much to encourage the little girl. It was obvious she needed friends. "Indeed, she has been all that is welcoming, Mr. Darcy," Elizabeth added with a smile.

Looking at the Gardiners and Elizabeth, he thought, *I have not seen my little girl this happy in years and especially in the company of strangers. You people have known her less than twenty minutes, and you have set her at ease and given her all the credit!*

Thank Heaven! And YOU, Miss Elizabeth, I can hardly wait to see what effect you shall have upon my son! Yes. Indeed, I can scarcely contain my eagerness for that day!

"Mr. Darcy," Mrs. Gardiner drew his attention back to the room. "I should tell you that the name Darcy has been synonymous for fairness and integrity to me, my entire life."

"Indeed. I certainly do thank you, Mrs. Gardiner. Pray, how is that, if you please?"

"I was born and raised in Lambton, Mr. Darcy. Pemberly is well reported to be the most handsome home, yet your estate is best known for the careful consideration of your tenants."

"That is very kind of you to tell us, Mrs. Gardiner. Yes, my family has held that land since it was gifted to them by William the Conqueror. Of course, I grew up learning the importance of fair treatment to our tenants. It keeps me very busy, yet all is a labour of love."

"Have you visited Pemberly?" Georgiana inquired. "We would love to have you as our guests sometime, and perhaps we could give you a personal tour. Would we not, Father?"

"Of course! Please do let us know when you might be visiting Derbyshire again. We would love to have you visit." Mr. Darcy smiled and sipped his tea. "Perhaps it could be the last point of interest on your tour?"

"How generous of you, Miss Georgiana, and Mr. Darcy." Mr. Gardiner replied. "It would be an honour. We would enjoy that so very much."

"Are you at all interested in fishing, Mr. Gardiner?" Darcy inquired with a smile.

"Mr. Darcy, I must confess, there is nothing I enjoy more than fishing."

"Perhaps then," Mr. Darcy answered, "I may prevail upon you to fish with me. Pemberly has some very well-stocked lakes, and the fish are rarely disturbed."

"My! That would be such a great pleasure. How kind of you to offer, sir." Looking at his watch, Mr. Gardiner saw that the time for a proper visit was completed. He did not want to offend Mr. Darcy, nor tax Georgiana by staying beyond the limit. "My, this has been a pleasure. We must take our leave, yet it is with heavy hearts for we have truly enjoyed ourselves. Miss Georgiana, Mr. Darcy, would you both please do us the honour of allowing us to present a tea for you? Our address is number five, Gracechurch Street, near Cheapside, sir." Mr. Gardiner asked, as Mrs. Gardiner and Elizabeth both nodded their heads to Georgiana.

Georgiana looked at her father with bright eyes. He could feel her asking him to say 'yes' immediately. "How very kind of you all. Georgie and I would be delighted." Mr. Darcy responded, nodding towards his little girl, "Would we not, Georgie?"

"Oh yes, Father! And Mr. and Mrs. Gardiner, if I am not impolite, should my brother be available to join us, may we know if he would be welcomed, please?" she asked.

"Most certainly he would, Miss Darcy. We would be most honoured to make his acquaintance," Mr. Gardiner assured the girl with a smile. "You shall also meet our three children." Georgiana smiled, "It shall be a pleasure, Mr. Gardiner." The time was arranged for the following day. All parties were looking forward to the event.

As the Gardiner-Bennet party began to quit the room, Mr. Darcy stepped to the door. "I say, before you go, might we extend an invitation for dinner on Sunday? Nothing formal, just a family dinner. It would be our pleasure. I am certain Georgie would be very happy if you could include some time for a walk in the park as well. Shall we say two?"

"We thank you, sir. We happily accept!" Mr. Gardiner bowed, and each one showed the proper civilities, remarking upon the very pleasant tea and their charming hostess.

One hour later, George Darcy and his daughter were still excited about the very successful tea. Georgiana talked on and on about the wonderful Miss Elizabeth and her uncle and aunt. It had been a while since she had known such happiness! Both Darcys were eager for the visit to Gracechurch Street.

"Oh, Father, how I wish that Brother had been here to meet them. Do you not think he would have enjoyed them so very much? I do believe he would like Miss Elizabeth. Are they not about the same age, Father?"

As if an actor in a play, Fitzwilliam Darcy entered the sitting room.

"Oh, Brother!" Georgie thrilled, "we have just concluded a most wonderful tea." Looking at her father for agreement, she tipped her head and smiled, "Have we not, Father?"

"Indeed, it was a most entertaining and stimulating tea, dearest!" he concurred.

Georgie giggled, "We shall return their visit tomorrow at three. Oh, Brother, they have children I shall meet, and they kindly invited you as well. You could join us and meet Miss Elizabeth. Could he not, Father?"

Not waiting for an answer, and not looking at her brother's face, Georgie continued to speak about the new friends in her life. "I am happy to have new friends. They are so diverting. They agreed to join us for a family dinner on Sunday. Shall you not be with us, Brother? They are most amusing! Miss Elizabeth is exceptionally witty and kind. She is so delightful and wonderful!"

"Miss Elizabeth, another of the Ton's brightest, Father? No, I am afraid I have plans with my cousin on Sunday. It is an evening long looked for, so I would wish to be excused, dearest. Perhaps the very next time," Fitzwilliam placated. "Georgie, I dare say, I shall miss the tea tomorrow as well. It is not possible to commit myself to a tea. Besides, I am not comfortable in the company of strangers."

At saying this, the young man failed to look into the eyes of the older one. A man of the same stature, Fitzwilliam faintly resembled his father. However, his lifestyle did not at all reflect the man's character. In fact, the son's rebellious departure from his customarily honourable conduct had become most alarming. His father had taken note. It was painfully obvious.

Since his completion of Cambridge, he had begun steadily drifting away, further and further from his family, and their values. Sadly, his actions also failed to reflect his social class.

Fitzwilliam was irresolutely wobbling from all usefulness. Otis, his valet, was appalled at his lack of even a decent daily routine. He was spiraling out of control.

Protectively, the father had begun to form a plan to help his son out of this quagmire. He prayed and hoped fervently that it was not too late.

At four fourteen the following day, the Darcy carriage rolled away from Gracechurch Street near Cheapside. Mr. Darcy and his daughter were still remarkably happy with their experience at the beautiful Gardiner home.

"Father, was not the garden the most beautiful in all of London? It was like a fairyland, and their home is stunning with the most beautiful furniture. My, I have never seen so many things from faraway places. Would you say they had great value, Father?"

"Indeed, I would, Georgie. Mr. Gardiner is in the import-export business. I should imagine he is a man of substantial fortune," Her father concluded.

"And the children were so entertaining, Father. John is such a little gentleman at nine years, and Margaret at age seven plays pianoforte quite well. She told me Elizabeth is the best teacher. She has a master, Mr. Franklin, but she favours her cousin most of all.

"And, little Robert, called Robin. He is only five years old and yet he speaks so well. Does he not sound like a miniature adult, Father?" In her excitement she did not yield for her father to answer her questions. Georgie rushed directly into her next thought. "Oh, Father! Would it not be such fun to have little cousins to teach pianoforte, and help with their reading or just to play with them, as does Elizabeth?"

"I dare say, it would, my dear Georgie. Perhaps someday when your brother weds, you shall extend your family. I know all of your cousins are adults, my dear."

"Oh, Father, that would be so delightful!" she whispered, "and Father, would it not be most wonderful if Brother should wed Elizabeth?" She giggled, but she could readily see that her father did not smile. In fact, he almost seemed to be praying.

"Yes, Georgie," Mr. Darcy finally answered his daughter, "it was a most satisfactory tea in so many remarkable ways. I quite agree with you."

Sunday dinner at Darcy House was proving to be even more lively than the tea. All five were having a wonderful time, sharing memories of Derbyshire and Lambton.

Mr. Darcy remembered meeting Mrs. Gardiner's parents. He enjoyed hearing about her life as a young girl. Their meal had concluded when Colonel Rory Fitzwilliam was announced.

He joined their party just as they were leaving the table. Mr. Darcy made the introductions, "Mr. and Mrs. Gardiner, Miss Elizabeth Bennet, may I present my nephew, Colonel Rory Fitzwilliam."

Snapping into his sharpest military manners, the colonel touched his sword and bowed, noting Miss Elizabeth to be very lovely. Very lovely, indeed! *Well, well, well! Miss Elizabeth Bennet. You, my dear, are beautiful and quite delicious looking. What a delight it shall be to get better acquainted with you. Yes, much better acquainted. I must be included in more of these little dinner parties.* He was besotted! Yes, the battle-hardened soldier of His Majesty's Army was instantly besotted!

Rory joined the men as they parted from the ladies to enjoy a glass of port. He was eager to learn as much as he could about this exciting young woman.

"Elizabeth, would you care to join me at the pianoforte? I selected some duets that I thought we might wish to try. This shall be for our own enjoyment, not a performance."

"Of course, Miss Georgiana, I would love that!"

The two laughed, putting their heads together to read the sheets of music. Georgiana gave Elizabeth a serious look and told her she had a request. Then she said, "Please just call me Georgiana. We are friends now, and I am not really happy with formal addresses, are you?" Appearing relieved after delivering this thought, she smiled. Shy as she was, it had been difficult for Georgie to say the words she had rehearsed.

"Thank you, Georgiana. No, I do not relish formality. It can sometimes vex my poor head when I have to think, 'the oldest daughter is called Miss Family Surname, and all the others are called Miss Given Name.' But, what happens when the eldest marries? I often forget and continue as I did before the nuptials. It seems I am at times improper no matter how I try. Oh dear, oh dear! Perhaps none of the eldest sisters should be allowed to wed! That thought would make me most unpopular!"

"Yes, indeed, it would, Elizabeth!" Georgiana began to giggle and could hardly stop. "I should not want your own sister to hear you say such a thing! What is her name?"

"Oh, my eldest sister is Jane. She is the most fabulously beautiful girl you have ever seen. In fact, I dare say, you and she could be twins. You have her delicate classical features, beautiful blond hair, and lovely blue eyes. I am the second, then comes Mary. Mary has dark hair, as do I. A very quiet girl, given to reading sermons."

Georgie put her hand before her face and laughed loudly! "Sermons?" she squealed. Elizabeth smiled and arched her eyebrows, "Yes, sermons! Not only does she read them, she often shall quote their contents to individuals she regards as in need of her exhortations."

Georgie was quite taken with the giggles upon hearing this information. It seemed so far-fetched to her, and she looked to Mrs. Gardiner for confirmation.

"Indeed, it is true, Georgiana." Mrs. Gardiner assured the girl.

Elizabeth continued, "It can be quite inopportune. May I say, no one is safe? Some time ago, she delivered a short word of admonition to our very own pastor as our family was leaving the church after services!" Elizabeth concluded this intelligence with a smirk on her face and one slight nod of her head.

"Oh noooo!" Miss Darcy squeaked as she accidentally snorted her laugh, making her laugh all the more.

"Next is Catherine, we call her Kitty, and last is Lydia. I am sorry to tell you that Kitty and Lydia are very silly young creatures. When I am home, I try to give them assignments to keep them busy. But they always have other ideas. I dare say, they are a handful. Although Lydia is the youngest, she often leads poor Kitty astray. I am often chagrined by their behaviour." Elizabeth concluded, "Still, I love each of them."

Georgiana enjoyed the various descriptions of the Bennet sisters. She tried to picture what they might look like, and imagined the sound of their voices. She pondered what it would be like to have Elizabeth as her sister. She decided it would be absolutely wonderful! Regretfully, Miss Darcy wished that her brother had stayed home for the family dinner and met and fallen in love with Elizabeth. Georgie believed if they ever did meet, they would most certainly fall in love. She thought their children would be so beautiful, too.

Oh, but I hope she shall not fall in love with Rory and marry him. Oh dear, please no Lord. Let her fall in love with Fitzwilliam. Brother, where are you?

The music of a beautiful duet soon filled the house. The staff quietly lined up in the halls to hear. The door to Mr. Darcy's study opened, and the gentlemen filed into the salon to listen. The two girls played as if they had been born to play together. Both were amazed and enjoyed it so well. Georgiana asked Elizabeth to play and sing for them, and when she performed a beautiful Scottish folk song, everyone was touched. Her voice far surpassed even those who perform professionally on the stage.

"Miss Elizabeth, your beautiful voice and your sincere expression touch my soul. I beg a promise from you that after completing your tour you shall visit us at Pemberly, for upon my word, I absolutely must listen to you play and sing again when we have even more opportunity. Absolutely delightful, Miss Elizabeth." Mr. Darcy declared.

"Mr. Darcy, I must once more tell you that you are, indeed, far too kind. You do, however, make me feel all confidence, and I assure you that it shall be my pleasure to play and sing for you at your kind request. You do me honour, sir." Elizabeth blushed most becomingly, and her fine eyes shone even more brightly.

Turning to his daughter, he said, "Georgiana, how very well you played this evening. You were quite animated, dearest. I always love hearing you play."

The girl smiled shyly at her father. Mr. Darcy always tried to encourage his children.

Once again, it was Mr. Gardiner who announced that it was time to say farewell. "We away to Devonshire at first light. It is

Lizzy's fondest desire to learn some advanced trick-riding techniques, and our friend, an expert horseman, has agreed to teach her personally. A good night's rest shall certainly benefit us and help us to a good start." Mr. Gardiner expressed their gratitude for an evening much enjoyed, and the expected civilities were offered in their farewell.

After the company departed, Rory clapped his uncle on the shoulder and said, "Uncle Darcy where on this earth did you ever meet that dazzlingly beautiful girl, Elizabeth? She is as charming as she is lovely and talented. How wonderful that I came to visit. I can see I must invent even more reasons to visit you around mealtimes, Uncle."

Georgie froze. She could not breathe. *Oh no! I just knew Rory would think her to be beautiful. I am glad she is going away for a while. Please God. I want Brother to meet and marry Elizabeth. Find someone else for Rory.*

Turning to his beloved nephew, Mr. Darcy asked Rory to wait for him in his study. "I shall bid Georgiana good night, then I shall join you. I think we may need a little talk."

Wishing her father pleasant dreams, Georgiana went to her rooms to dream of Elizabeth becoming her sister. Jane, Mary, Kitty, and Lydia would become her sisters, as well. The Gardiners would become her uncle and aunt and then, John, Margaret, and Robin would be added to her as new cousins!

Mr. Darcy joined Rory in the study. Pouring two drinks, he delivered one to Rory, then studied his glass carefully before he spoke to his favourite nephew. He wanted to be fair.

"Rory, I love you like you are my very own son. I know that Fitzwilliam feels like you are his flesh and blood brother. You two practically lived together from the time my Anne died, until you enlisted. Even earlier than that if we include your years at Walton Prep."

Rory regarded the older man. His uncle continued, "Before I tell you what is on my heart, I feel I must solicit your promise of secrecy. May I? I am about to trust you with some very confidential information, son."

Rory nodded, "Of course, Uncle. I shall keep silent, whatever it is."

"Thank you, Rory. As often as you see your cousin, no doubt you have observed that he is undergoing some horrible changes. He has already compromised himself most shockingly. Much dark news is made known to me through very reliable resources. Many things we see here at home, and I am sure that through your observances, you would agree that Fitzwilliam is an inferior image of his former self."

Looking to his nephew for courage, he took another sip of his port. "Rory, it has been difficult raising my children alone. I have committed many errors. I realise now what a colossal mistake I made by giving so many advantages to George Wickham. I thought he might be a brother of sorts to Fitzwilliam, but I was in error. His father was my best steward, yet sending Wickham to Cambridge with my son was dead wrong! A fact your father continues to bring to my attention."

Rory studied his glass of port. It was too painful to look at his uncle and see his torment.

"I owe you my thanks, Rory. Had it not been for you, I would never have learned of the abuse Wickham perpetrated upon Fitzwilliam. You made me aware. My own son said absolutely nothing to me. Rory, I am at a loss as to why? Have you any ideas as to his silence?"

Rory shrugged his shoulders and shook his head sadly.

Looking at his shoes, George Darcy found the strength to continue, "I had to inquire of Fitzwilliam's valet, after the fact."

Uncle Darcy's embarrassment was obvious. Rory sat in the uncomfortable presence of his uncle. He felt he should say something to the suffering man, but what could he say that would help?

"I did not do anything unusual, Uncle. I only wanted to assist my cousin. Wickham has always hurt your son. I wish Fitzwilliam had spoken to you about it, years ago. It is true he suffered at Cambridge, but it started in our childhood."

"Yes. I wish to God I could undo my wrongs. I would like to make this up to my son. Rory, I would not like Fitzwilliam to hear what I am about to share with you. As his cousin, you should know I have it on the best authority that my son has chosen to go after the wrong things in life. I am praying for him to change his direction. I have formed a plan to help him. I shall tell him when he returns from Ireland. We shall attend Rosings for Eastertide, with your family, of course. Then, we shall go to Pemberly where I shall turn over all control and responsibilities directly to him, effective June first."

Rory looked as if he would interject—Mr. Darcy put up his hand and continued. "Oh, I shall be there to oversee his work, yet he must get his feet wet, and he must absolutely leave this useless life he has begun. Tonight, you met the girl I have chosen for him to marry."

He stood silently, watching the younger man. No objection came but he could clearly see his nephew's shocked and disappointed expression. For a battle-hardened soldier, Rory's face revealed so much emotion.

"Son, I tell you because I could clearly see your attraction to her. You may as well know now that I shall do all I can to influence them toward one another. This is a matter that I have put much prayer and effort into, and I shall not be denied.

"Oh, he has no idea and neither does she. Elizabeth is exactly the type of girl that Anne would have chosen for him. I know my son. She is what he needs to challenge him, keep him humble, and prevent him from becoming too gloomy. She shall keep him in his place! Fitzwilliam and Elizabeth have never met. In fact, it was just by a miracle that I happened to meet her, and her Uncle and Aunt Gardiner. Someday I shall tell you that story. For now, I have told you my plans and my hopes. I await Divine intervention. Time is the great revealer!"

Mr. Darcy poured another glass of port and then filled Rory's glass once more.

Sitting down again, he looked at his nephew and said, "Son, she does have sisters. No doubt you shall meet them. I hope it shall be soon!"

"Uncle George," Rory blurted, "I had no idea you were a romantic! I thought Aunt Catherine de Bourgh was the matchmaker, hounding Fitzwilliam his entire life to marry her daughter, Anne. Indeed, I thought it would really happen someday!"

"Never Rory! I forbid it! In fact, I now have some interesting family history that brings to light a situation that is sure to shake up your Aunt Catherine. Be at Rosings April ten, Easter Sunday and you shall see your aunt humbled and her voice stilled!"

"Uncle, I would not miss that for the world! Wild horses could not hinder my presence."

Bidding his uncle good night, Rory quitted Darcy House. He knew well just where to find Fitzwilliam. It seemed George Darcy was correct to be concerned for his son. "Damnable wretch. Darcy has always been blessed. I should hate him if I did not love him my entire life long!" He spoke his anger aloud.

Rory entered the exclusive upper circle club and spotted Fitzwilliam immediately. He was drinking quite a bit, and his man, Otis, stood in the corner with a somewhat sad expression on his face. This was remarkable because Otis, with his ten years of serving Mr. Fitzwilliam Darcy, maintained a practiced expressionless face.

"Rory!" Fitzwilliam yelled and waved his arm. "Pleeze join me, my most excel—excellent cousin," he slurred. "You just missed my most excellent friends from Cambridge. They are second sons just like you, and I wish you would meet them. But, they are not like you because they are not in the army. In fact, they are just like me, because they also do nothing at all. I am a first son, and it seems I have no importance. Except to drink this," he said. Then looking up at his cousin, "I say, did you know that I am your do-nothing- of- value cousin? My job at school is over and now I am—what? What am I Rory? I am at a loss to know what the devil I am." He tossed his head and looked down.

Looking at Fitzwilliam in disgust, Rory declared, "I would say that you are stinking drunk, Cousin Darcy. Why did you not bloody well stay at home tonight and join your family with their company for dinner? I happened by and met one very lovely Miss Elizabeth Bennet. Too bad. It is your loss Fitzwilliam."

"Aw, yesss, one of the Ton, nooo doubt! No, and I thank you. Not for me," Fitzwilliam mumbled as he drained his glass.

"You, Cousin, are a damnable fool!" Rory spat at him. "You have everything you could want, and you have not the slightest idea of how blessed you really have been. Come on, let me take you home. Clearly your brandy has done its job for tonight. I shall take you home, Cousin."

"Sod off, Rory! I have needs, yes needs. I am going to see any of those girls at the Bacon Street House. In fact, I shall see many of those girls. Tonight I shall count how many of them I can see in just one night. Do you want to come with me? I shall pay."

Reaching into the pocket of his coat, he suddenly remembered that Otis held all his money. "Oh, yes! That is correct. My man, Otis, shall pay." Looking at Otis in the corner, he waved and shouted, "You are a good man, Otis!" Glancing back at Rory, he demanded, "Cousin, wave at Otis."

Rory smiled at Otis and shrugged his shoulders. He put his eyes on Darcy and sneered, "Tell you what, Cousin. You go on without me. I shall just wait in the background. If you decide you do not want to meet a certain very delicious girl, then I may just step into the picture." *All I need to do is wait…*

It was nearly noon when Otis helped Fitzwilliam up the stairs to his room at Darcy House. His father watched from the hall and observed that his son was still drunk and smelled strongly of cheap perfume—the type that very cheap ladies would wear.

Yes, son. Your drinking and do nothing days are numbered, I assure you. Sober up Fitzwilliam, stay away from the opium you are offered and those women who service you for money. God help you, son, it is time to clean up and get on with the life you were born to live.

George Darcy went into his study. He sat quietly for a few minutes and then slid down to the floor upon his knees. He folded his hands and silently bowed his head in prayer.

There he remained for over an hour. Rising from the floor, the man felt a measure of comfort.

He began to hope.

Chapter 2

"Letters, once written have the power to live forever in the influence over the hearts of those who receive them."

-Anonymous

Mr. Darcy took out his handkerchief and blotted his forehead. He had laboured two hours over writing this letter to his son. It had to be perfect—he had to watch each word, each phrase. It was his one chance to say everything that must be said, yet couched in language that would capture the young man's mind and heart.

Taking one last look at the page, he folded the stationery, dropped the hot wax on the back, and pressed his signet ring down, sealing the letter. Pouring a glass of port, he sat at his desk and waited for Otis.

Stepping into the study, the fifty-year-old man bowed, "Good evening, Mr. Darcy."

"Good evening, Otis. Won't you please take a seat?"

The valet snapped his head up and looked very ill at ease. He had been a Darcy servant for two and thirty years. Servants never sat on the master's furniture, and they certainly never sat anywhere within sight of him or his family. It just was not done. To sit in Mr. Darcy's presence was unthinkable. Disrespectful! Disgusting!

Handing the sealed letter to his son's trusted valet, Darcy charged the man: "See that he gets this only after he has posted a letter to me. If over the course of the trip, no letter is sent to me, kindly bring this communication back to my study and place it in the drawer."

Otis nodded his agreement, "Yes, sir, thank you, sir." And then he added, "All shall be well, sir, I am sure, Mr. Darcy." He knew he should not have spoken in such a familiar manner to the master, but he had already violated his code of ethics by being seated.

Waving him out, Mr. Darcy reminded him to continue his reports. "I thank you for your help, Otis. Certainly you disdain providing me with this intelligence, and I am loath to ask it of you. Nevertheless, it has become necessary, if we are to have the young man we know and love come back to himself and to us."

"Very good, sir. Count on me."

"I am," was the sad reply.

George Darcy could scarcely believe his son to be in this sorry state. He hung his head in despair. For the first time since her death, he was actually glad that Anne was not there with him. Seeing their son slide down into a life of...could he admit it... debauchery was unthinkable! A lad who was always so proper, reserved, and religious.

How did this begin? What caused his otherwise self-disciplined son to shun duty and honour, sobriety and family, and turn to a life of sensual pleasure and intemperance?

His cousin Rory placed blame on George Wickham. It had been a mistake to pay for the man to attend Cambridge with Fitzwilliam. Insisting they share a room must have been a torment. It had been a grave error. Had Otis not informed him of Wickham's constant cheating on exams, and his theft of Fitzwilliam's work? Incurring large debts in his son's name? Yes, all that had been a mistake. He was at a loss to know why he had not stopped his support as soon as he became aware of Wickham's behaviour. He knew many were asking why, he, sensible George Darcy did such a thing? Why did he treat Wickham as a favoured son, even above that of Fitzwilliam?

He was aware of the gossip. There were still those who believed that George Wickham was the natural son of Mr. George Darcy. Had Fitzwilliam heard this rumour? If yes, could he believe it? Had Darcy not been paying attention to his son when he needed him? The only thing remaining was to change things now for the better.

Walking through the servants' hallway, Otis became lost in his thoughts. He was a loyal Darcy servant, and he knew it was not his place to sit in judgement on Mr. Fitzwilliam.

Can this tour of Ireland be the right thing for Mr. Fitzwilliam? Is it not a reward? Aye, the lad worked hard enough at Cambridge, sometimes doing his work a second time when that disgusting Wickham stole it, to submit it as his own. We all knew Wickham was not intelligent enough to accomplish Cambridge. He is a cheat and a thief! Lord knows how many others he has hurt, and all those innocent little virgin maidens he has seduced and ruined. Damnable fool, and bloody shame what Mr. Darcy's help has done for that evil man. But, to see Mr. Fitzwilliam now, spending his time drinking and chasing skirts, neglecting his father and sister, and shocked I was to see him turn away from his cousin's attempt to take him home! Tonight I finish preparations, tomorrow we away, and God help us. I hope the lad shall return a better man. If he does not it shall certainly kill his poor father...

George Wickham shifted in the old wooden chair, balancing a dirty paper upon his knee. It was messy, but it was all he had.

The chair lurched front to back with his shifting body weight as he wrote his letter.

Damn this chair, or maybe it is just the rum.

His heavy head was spinning now. He tried to collect his thoughts as he penned his message. It was getting harder to focus as he was spending more and more time drinking. He could not remember what his last meal was, nor when it had been eaten. He hated his circumstances and cursed Fitzwilliam Darcy as the source of all his miserable pain.

With a shaky hand he wrote to Wallet, a man whose 'fist could pen well':

Gates House

London, England

20 January 1803

Greetings Wallet,

You shall be happy to hear that I have a position for both of us, provided that you are still an artist with a quill and willing to travel a bit.

I shall contact you as soon as we are ready to go forward. We shall be bunce.

Regards,

G. Wickham.

He does not need to know that funds are a bit low right now. I shall get the cash required to do the job right this time.

The letter would need to wait until the next day to be posted. George fell from the chair and curled up on the floor, sleeping off his drink.

Miss Georgiana Darcy was filled with excitement as she held the letter from Elizabeth in her hands. The young girl carefully read the beautifully penned message:

Devonshire, England

6 March 1803

Dearest Georgiana,

We are having such a wonderful time on our tour. We have just departed Cornwall and are now touring Devonshire. It is beautiful. You would love the grand woods.

The trees are ancient and so very large. I can hear my sister Mary saying: "Oh what are men compared to rocks and trees?" 'Tis true, one feels quite small next to these silent giants. My, I am surprised that the birds are not too intimidated to build their nests in them. As far as trees are concerned, these are certainly most austere!

Have you visited Devonshire? The archaeological treasures are quite spectacular! With history reaching back to the Romans, Anglo-Saxons, Normans, and medieval times we have much to enjoy. There are so many artefacts from the Tudor era, as well.

I fancy my favourite place thus far is the Oliver Farm. Mr. Oliver is a friend of Uncle and Aunt Gardiner. He breeds horses. Most of their stock is working class, though some are very correct big moving jumpers. Oh Georgiana, you would fall in love with the many little foals. They are all so beautiful. How I wish you could be right here with me, daring to go out into the field and just jump up and ride. I have been doing just that, and Uncle is sore afraid I shall pick an unfriendly pony. Perhaps he is right. I should wait for a formal introduction before helping myself to an impromptu ride!

Tomorrow I start my special riding lessons from Mr. Oliver himself. I am very excited.

Can you determine that from my letter? I am afraid to read this before I post it, as it may be too enthusiastic to be sensible.

I know you are faithful to practice your pianoforte. I shall be unfit to play with you in that it has been so long since my hands have touched the instrument.

We shall end our tour in Kent. Uncle says we should arrive there by the first of April and stay until May seven, this shall include Eastertide, of course.

We are to be the guests of Aunt Gardiner's great uncle, Lord Claverstone. He is my own surrogate grandfather and the finest horseman and horse breeder I know. It shall be so wonderful spending time with him once again.

I do so love being out in the country. There is so much to do, riding, walking and archery.

I know not the geography, but if Rosings is near enough perhaps we may see each other. We could go riding, walking, or even shoot archery, if your father allows. At the very easiest, we would certainly enjoy tea, and perhaps playing pianoforte. I shall hope that we are close enough to visit. I shall ask Lord Claverstone of the proximity as soon as I arrive.

Please greet your father for us. Uncle and Aunt send their warmest regards and also wish to be remembered to Mr. Darcy. We all send our wishes that your brother is healthy, as well.

With Friendly Affection,

Elizabeth.

"Father! Father! I received a letter from Elizabeth! Is that not wonderful? Oh, I do wish you would please read it. She writes so wonderfully, and she sounds so animated that it is just like having a little visit with her, right here on the sofa."

"I would be delighted, Georgie. Now, just let me join you on the sofa, and we shall see what Miss Elizabeth has to share with us."

Otis stood quietly beside his master's trunk. His face was visibly aging, due to the stress and strain of the voyage.

Oh I do hope Mr. Fitzwilliam writes to his father today. A letter could so easily post on the morrow before we leave port. How shall I hint? I continue to hold Mr. Darcy's letter. At least I have nothing disgusting to relay as to his son's behaviour.

He drinks too much, but due to God, he has not touched anything stronger, and he has not visited any houses of ill repute. Thank Heaven. I can hardly tolerate such behaviour. 'Tis all such a shame.

Fitzwilliam entered his cabin and called to Otis, "Kindly post these before we leave port. It seems I cannot remember to ask it of you." Fitzwilliam handed his valet two letters for George Darcy. Otis smiled for the first time in at least two weeks. "Right away, sir," he said. After Otis took the two letters from his master, he quietly placed the one in his custody upon Fitzwilliam's desk.

Watching the movement in his periphery, Fitzwilliam went directly to his father's letter. There was no need to berate or question Otis about the delay of this communication. He knew quite well that Otis was precise in following orders. This had been saved by his father's directive. He sat down at his desk and opened the seal.

Darcy House

28 January 1803

My Dearest Son,

What can a father say to his son? I love and miss you. Yes, Fitzwilliam, I have for quite some time now. I suspect we have many things to say to each other. I know I have no few things to confess to you, and I would welcome hearing anything that is upon your heart. Perhaps we can arrange for a talk when you return.

Son, my primary reason for writing is to request your help. Immediately upon your return I shall require you to take over Pemberly for me. Oh, I shall be available to you for consultation. Yet, it is my desire that you be a hands-on manager, as have I.

I know you are stunned, shocked, and perhaps even a bit overwhelmed. I would have you think upon this but slightly as you travel, yet know how to plan your life once you return.

Your sister and I miss the very excellent company we once enjoyed. Perhaps you shall bring that bright and wonderful fellow back to us. We would certainly be most grateful.

Every day, we look to the calendar and consult as to April one and await the day when once again you shall complete our little family circle.

May God bless and keep you safe within His care,

Your Devoted and Loving Father,

G.D.

He wants me to take Pemberly from him? How can that be? Is he ill? Oh, God, no please, Lord, I cannot be without him. If not ill, what is he thinking? Me? What an overwhelming thought. Could I dare? Think man, think! Have I even spent enough time observing him as master? Yes, I could be manager of the household, but in truth, Mrs. Reynolds has done that to perfection. I might even botch that!

He threw the cabin door open and stepped out into the cold air. He had to walk. He needed to get off the ship. He needed to be in London so he could get to Darcy House and ask, no, demand, his father to explain this lunacy.

If I try to take Pemberly, we shall all end at Bedlam. I shall run everyone mad.

Standing at the rail, he shouted into the wind. "Father, oh my God, what are you about? No, Father! A thousand times, NO! I am not ready! I am not ready!"

In London, George Darcy stood to his feet and pulled the cord for Simmons. Fitzwilliam's letters had arrived. Action was needed.

When the butler appeared, Darcy placed a missive into his hand. "Simmons, please see that my solicitor gets this first thing on the morrow. Thank you."

Opening his appointment book, he suddenly thought of Elizabeth Bennet. He remembered their first meeting at the bookstore. *Yes, I am so fond of that journal entry, met Miss Elizabeth Bennet, my future daughter. Amazing. Perhaps next year we shall celebrate it as a little anniversary. Yes, that shall be a happy day! I shall make her a gift to celebrate. Jewellery? No, a book! May God haste to bring them together!*

Thomas Bennet looked at the letter in his hand and his heart leapt. He opened it quickly to read what Lizzy had to say to him.

Oliver Farms, Devonshire

20 March 1803

Irony and Influence

Dearest Papa,

I write to you from an area you know very well. I remember many times your telling me of the wonders of this place, and now I have seen it for myself. Yes, history does come alive here, and there is so much to see and to learn. How I wish you were here with us, Papa.

My true purpose in writing is to tell you that I know your action in giving Uncle Gardiner custody over my life, was done to protect me. Oh, how I thank you for standing by me when I needed you.

Is Mama still raving over my refusal of marriage to that fat toad, Mr. Collins? I think I can see you smile as I rightly call him a toad. He is your cousin, and heir, according to that dreadful entail, but I do see him as a smelly toad. I can still recall his foul breath as he demanded to take me for his wife. And, my own Mama attempting to force me to go with him!

Papa, I would have died with him. I know you recognised that as truth. Yes, it did hurt to be shunned by Mama and Lydia, but you and Jane, Mary and Kitty stood by me.

I do hope you understand how very much I love Uncle and Aunt Gardiner. It was Mama who sent me to live with them. Was I really newly borne, and only four days of age? I stayed with them until age seven because I was too lively for my own mother to raise. But, I was not too lively for Uncle and Aunt. They have loved me, Papa. And, I love them. They have been so kind. I owe them so very much. I hope someday to be able to repay them.

Papa, when my prince rides up to me on the biggest and most powerful stallion I have ever seen, I know that I shall recognise who he is, and we shall fall in love. He shall marry me and make me the princess of all his lands. We shall have an enormous library and expensive port. You shall visit us as often as you wish and be the happiest of men. We shall have grandchildren for you to love, and you shall love my prince as though he were your own son!

Until then, I shall continue to write to you, and to dear Jane.

Do not fret, dear Papa. I see you every day in my mind. I see you walking to Meryton, reading a book in your library, and trying to listen to five different conversations at once during dinner. Shall you try to see me, too? Here! Look! Here is your Lizzy waving her hands to you as she looks up at a mighty oak tree that once silently watched as Queen Elizabeth, my namesake, rode under its limbs on her new pony!

I shall write to you from London when we return. I believe I shall attempt to secure a position as governess, or perhaps a companion. I know I cannot long impose myself upon Uncle and Aunt. Upon my birthday, I must be prepared to make my own way.

Stay well, Papa. I shall continue to miss you and our very wonderful talks. Please let dear Jane sit in my chair and keep you company. Do embrace her for me, oh I miss her so! Please give my love to Mary and Kitty, and even to Lydia. I wish them well.

God bless you and keep you well and strong.

Your Loving Daughter,

Lizzy.

Bless my soul. She is a generous and forgiving girl. She is the very best of the five.
I shall begin praying for her prince to come and ask for her hand in marriage. Yes.
May God hasten that happy day for all of us. Oh, that I might see their wedding!

Lizzy dried her eyes as she finished the letter to her father. Why did she feel it was always her duty to cheer and comfort others when she herself was hurting? Sometimes she was more like the parent than the child.

'Tis for the best. I must smile and think my happiest thoughts, and I know I must think on the past only as its memories give me pleasure.

The hired carriage stopped at Darcy House. Two weary men stepped out and looked around. The house had never looked better. The younger man went very slowly up the steps and entered the house with dread. The older, using all his strength, bounded up the stairs, praying he would never be sent to sea again. He was grateful they could not go to the Continent for the grand tour, that would have meant a two year absence, not a voyage of mere weeks.

"Son! Bless my soul, Fitzwilliam, it is so wonderful to have you home." His father's affectionate welcome was heartwarming to the son.

"Father! "Fitzwilliam nearly shouted, "'Tis my greatest joy to return to you and Georgiana! I have been worrying so much over you since I read your letter. Are you well, Father?"

"Yes, Fitzwilliam, very well indeed," his father smiled as he embraced his son. "After you are rested, we shall talk. You are home, son. Go in and greet your sister. She has been watching for you all morning and shall be upset that you were able to come in without her seeing you first!"

After dinner, father and son retired to the study. Sitting face to face, each regarded the other with some reluctance.

"Fitzwilliam, as I told you, it is time for you to take complete control of Pemberly. I shall be there to help you, but you should be master. It is time for you to begin the position for which you have been prepared. You receive an estate that has been generations in the making. Now, you shall add your contribution. It is time, son."

George Darcy rose from his chair and refilled his glass of port. Turning back to Fitzwilliam, he continued to speak of his son's inheritance. "You shall make it your life's work. You shall train your son, just as I have trained you, and I shall say it is possible that when the time comes for him to take over, you shall know it in your heart, even if he is uncertain."

Fitzwilliam rose "Father, shall you not give me six months? Should I not observe you and your steward for six months?" Slowly shaking his head, George looked his son in the eyes, "Son, you must trust me in this decision. On the morrow we go to my solicitor. We shall make the legal change effective June one. I am not going anywhere. Once home, you shall select a room for your own study, and I shall continue to use mine to conduct my personal business. I shall have much to do as my own employment."

He reflected a moment, and then putting one hand upon his lower back, he said, "Honestly, I welcome the rest from the constant hours on horseback, and other duties that remind me I have had too many birthdays."

"But, Father—"

George Darcy sighed, "It is decided, son. Now, sleep well. We have business in the morning and in the afternoon we away to Rosings."

Mrs. Bennet was so angry her daughters thought she would be ill. The family had just returned from the wedding of Miss Charlotte Lucas to Mr. William Collins.

"Mama, it is rude not to attend the wedding breakfast. Please allow me to take my sisters. I shall explain that you are unwell and Papa has stayed home to assist you."

"No, Jane! I cannot allow you to go. Mrs. Lucas shall be expounding upon her good fortune. Charlotte has captured

Mr. Collins! Yes! Our, Mr. Collins! Oh that ungrateful child, your sister. I swear I shall never say her name again or look upon her insufferable face! We shall starve when Mr. Collins puts us out, and she could have saved us. No, we have seen to the church service, and now we shall stay at home."

Mr. Bennet followed along behind. He reached up and touched his coat pocket where he kept Lizzy's letter.

You are well out of this, child. The toad has caught his prey, and you are free to meet your prince. Oh, I do hope he is handsome, Lizzy. Poor Charlotte, she was always your favourite friend; now she is but a morsel for the toad. I shall away to my book room and try to avoid the censure of your dear Mama. Her voluble displeasure shall be rehearsed at least once more this afternoon.

Georgiana was all smiles during the carriage ride to Rosings. It was a perfect day, even though somewhat chilly. Her brother kept an eye on his very large stallion which followed along behind the carriage. He longed to be riding, but since he had been in Ireland so long, he did not want to ignore his family. He knew Georgie had especially missed him.

The girl could not force her eyes off her brother as he sat across from her. Always looking for pleasantries, she reached for Elizabeth's letter which she had been using as a bookmark, to keep it handy. It was possible she had read it fifty times.

Slowly and protectively, she drew it out and handed it toward her brother as a precious offering, saying, "Brother, I wonder if I may share a very pleasant letter from my friend? It is charming and quite diverting. I would admire it greatly if you would read it, please?"

His first thought was incredulous. He was a man with much on his mind and could not be bothered with insignificant children who wrote letters to each other.

Mr. Darcy watched the exchange with interest. "Oh, my! Georgie, is that the letter you shared with me? Yes, Fitzwilliam," his father agreed, endorsing the missive, "your sister is correct it is altogether lively. You might perhaps find it decidedly diverting."

Not able to decline now that his father had recommended the document, he reached out and looked at the elegance of the pristine handwriting. He began reading. Soon his thoughts were tumbling and his mind became greatly troubled.

Who is this who writes to my little sister of archaeology and history? And what type of person approaches strange horses in the field, leaps up and rides without tack? Archery? A lethal weapon in the hands of a youngster? What? Enough of this!

He stopped reading, looked up, and handed the letter back to his sister. "Father, I dare say I have concerns about this person. What kind of influence is this? Encouraging Georgiana to rush out onto an open field and jump upon a wild horse and ride without tack? Is she astride these animals and without benefit of a saddle? Has she no knowledge of propriety? No! I must say, whoever this Elizabeth person is, she has lost my good opinion, with reading just this one letter! And, my good opinion, once lost, is lost forever!"

Georgiana turned red. She opened her mouth to speak, but her father spoke first—"Now, son, if you had bothered to join us on the occasions when Miss Elizabeth visited our home with her uncle and aunt, you would not have reacted so violently.

"My, I must say, you certainly have formed an ill opinion hurriedly! Your cousin, Rory, has met her and formed a most positive opinion of Miss Elizabeth."

"I know Elizabeth is everything wonderful. Do you not agree, Father?" Georgie demanded.

It was astonishing that her brother could read the same letter and form a low opinion of the girl she wished to be her sister. *My, Brother, you certainly have changed. I remember when you were filled with adventure, and it was most pleasant to hear of your thoughts and plans. Now you seem so old, older than father, since you returned from your voyage, and somewhat insufferable.*

How could you read my wonderful letter and not have a good opinion of Elizabeth? The joy of life bubbles out of her and flows over onto everyone. I shall pray that when you meet her, you shall think better of her!

George Darcy watched his son with great care. He remembered everything about Elizabeth Bennet. He was most eager to speak with Mr. Gardiner again. That would happen in Kent. He had already sent a missive to Mr. Gardiner at his uncle's estate.

Yes, a meeting was urgently requested indeed.

Yes, son, I know you are thinking about that letter right now. What exactly bothers you about Miss Elizabeth? Is it because she is a thinking woman? Your instant mortification was most telling. It is a curiosity to see how one little letter can bring forth such opinion

Chapter 3

"If you have only the smallest interest to learn the truth of any matter, you shall not be thought supercilious."

-Anonymous

The keen blue eyes of Gerald Chatsworth squinted as he watched for the Gardiner carriage. Lucille Gardiner, his niece, had always been a favourite. Her husband, Edward, a very wealthy importer- exporter, continued to be a perfect match for her. Their one and twenty year marriage had proved to become stronger with each passing year.

Gerald and his wife were both very supportive when the newlyweds took in Edward's infant niece. Elizabeth Bennet, even at the age of four days, was exceptional. It did not take long before Gerald and Margaret also fell in love with the baby. He well remembered this event for it came during the same week he had been named an earl. That was the occasion of his formal name change as earls are compelled to adopt the name of their estate, thus Gerald Chatsworth had become Lord Claverstone the same week his little Lizzy was born.

Continuing to watch for the carriage, Gerald reminisced about Margaret begging him to take the babe for their own. He remembered his second thoughts. They were a couple in their forties, and the Gardiners' were just into their twenties. It broke his dear Margaret's heart when he had to deny her the child, but in view of her untimely death on Elizabeth's second birthday, it had been for the best. Fate had spoken against them.

Gerald could not stop his affection for the toddler. She held a very special place in his heart. He remembered how endearing she was at age five. He recalled how amused he was as he tried to explain to the little girl about being a peer of the realm. Lizzy's five-year-old mind could not understand his various names. Finally she was satisfied when he told her the only name she needed to know and remember was Grandpapa! He would always think of her as his own little child. She was exceptional-it was not just her intelligence—there was another, deeper quality about Elizabeth. She had a sweet, honest, forthright spirit.

Her friendliness made her irresistible. Especially to her Grandpapa. As Lord Claverston, he had tried to direct the House of Lords to pressure Oxford into allowing her to take correspondence courses directly under Professor Hale himself. All to no avail.

At least he could provide instruction of equestrian pursuits, advanced archery, and the study of herbs as medicine, which she chiefly acquired to be used as an intervention for equines.

Finally the carriage rolled into the driveway, delivering quite happy but weary travellers.

Gerald smiled to himself as he spotted Marigold in tow behind the carriage. He knew his Lizzy would not think of leaving her mare at home in town.

"Here am I, children, Lord Claverstone himself to hand you down and welcome you!"

After he had seen to their comforts, he took Edward aside and handed him a letter. "Edward, this arrived in the morning's post. I would point out the return which lists George Darcy as the sender."

"Yes," Edward responded as he drew the back of his hand across his forehead, "This is quite a surprise, Uncle."

Gerald looked confused, "Have you an acquaintance with the gentleman, Nephew?"

"Yes, Uncle. We met him and his daughter in January. We have been to their home on several occasions, and they to ours. Is he a friend to you, Uncle?"

"I have met him and his family many times over the years. We have attended the same cathedral on Easter services for the last five and twenty years. He is an honourable gentleman. Where specifically did you meet him, Edward?"

"It is quite interesting, really, I dare say. The three of us were in a London bookstore, and Mr. Darcy approached us, introducing himself and asking Lizzy many questions about herself. He apparently had been listening as she was expounding on literature, and he enjoyed her spontaneous lecture. He then invited us for tea with the express interest of an introduction of Elizabeth to his daughter, Georgiana."

"Oh yes, I remember now, Edward. He was made a widower as his wife died and left him with a baby girl. I see."

"Give me some time to settle in, Uncle, and I shall read the missive and disclose it to you."

Mr. Gardiner went off to find his wife and, taking her aside, the two of them opened the letter in privacy. They did not expect anything of a negative nature, yet protecting Lizzy was instinctual. She had suffered so much recently, it would be best to screen this communication and shield her if there were any bad news involved. Lucille wrung her hands.

Mr. Gardiner read the missive quietly to his wife:

Rosings Park, Kent

1 April 1803

Mr. Gardiner,

We have received a most informative and entertaining letter from your niece. Georgiana is eager to renew her acquaintance and visit with Miss Elizabeth. May I again impose on the good humour of your family and your uncle Lord Claverstone to apply for a morning visit tomorrow?

I should like a private word with you, Mr. Gardiner, and Georgie should very much like to spend some time with Miss Elizabeth. We should arrive at ten and stay no longer than one hour, if agreeable with you. I know this is extended time, but I am in need of your audience.

Most Appreciatively,

G. D.

"What could this mean, Edward?" Lucille wondered aloud, wrinkling her nose. "We must think of it as good news, my wife. Our new friend seeks our company. I cannot for the life of me think why such a powerful man would want to consult with me.

"I have absolutely no ill feelings about him, so I must think it is a social call, until he tells me otherwise." He smiled at his wife and lightly kissed her cheek. "Have no fear, dearest."

"Still, "Lucille said, exhaling loudly, "it is unexpected."

"Yes, dear," he agreed, "most unexpected." His voice faded as he became lost in his thoughts. *A letter from George Darcy. Never would I have anticipated such a thing. Time is a great revealer. We shall know about it on the morrow. No reason to speculate.*

They went together to tell their host that Mr. and Miss Darcy would visit on the morrow.

Then, Lord Claverstone went to join Elizabeth for a ride. He would inform her that her friend Gerogiana Darcy would visit next day at ten. He could not help but wonder if this visit from Darcy was regarding his little Lizzy. Time would reveal all.

❦

Mr. Bennet sat in his library, facing Jane who was sitting in Lizzy's old chair. Father and daughter sat in silence.

Jane finally spoke to break the spell. "Are you well, Papa?"

"Quite well, thank you, daughter. What is new with your Mama?" he asked with a mild curiosity.

"Now that you have asked," she answered eagerly as she leaned forward in the chair, "she is still very ill tempered. It seems now that everything that happens to her is Lizzy's fault. When she is unhappy, it is her nerves." Jane said.

"Then," Mr. Bennet declared, "there is truly nothing new, child. I have known this for thirty years." The man drew himself up, out of the chair and walked to the back of the room where he kept his port. Taking a glass, he poured out, nearly to the brim. Jane stared at the serving. He took only two steps with his long legs and met with his chair once again.

"I have had a letter from your sister," he told her, almost confidentially. "It is a private letter, just to me, but she says she shall write to you when she returns to London."

"Yes, I thank you, Papa. I shall look forward to her letter. I miss her very much."

"Yes, Jane, as do I." *Yet, it is my own fault she is banished, is it not? I have never stood up and taken the role as master of my estate and household. If I had, Lizzy would still be here with me. But, no need to tell you, Jane dear. You would not understand.*

At exactly ten of the clock, George and Georgiana Darcy were shown into the salon and announced. Lord Claverstone rose to greet them. He was happy to see the familiar face and held Mr. Darcy in high esteem.

"Welcome to Claverstone, Mr. Darcy, Miss Darcy. After all these years we have worshipped together on Easter, I do believe this is the first time you have honoured us with a visit."

"Yes, indeed, I have been remiss, Lord Claverstone. I ask your forgiveness. My sister Lady de Bourgh wishes to invite you and your family to join us directly after services on Easter. She and her daughter, Anne, would be honoured to have their good neighbour in their home. Lord and Lady Matlock and their children shall be there along with myself and my children. Your addition would be most pleasantly welcome. I believe you are well acquainted with my brother, Lord Matlock, are you not?"

"Yes, very well acquainted." Lord Claverstone's face warmed as he spoke of Lord Matlock. "We have served together many years. Wonderful fellow! I do indeed, count him as a friend.

"My thanks to your sister and niece, Mr. Darcy. Yes, on behalf of my family, we are very happy to accept this most generous invitation." Gerald bowed and smiled at Darcy.

Turning to Georgiana, he said, "Miss Darcy, Miss Elizabeth is most eager to see you. Phillips shall escort you." He smiled at the girl, and she returned his broad smile with a shy half grin.

Watching his daughter quit the room, Mr. Darcy turned to Edward Gardiner, "My dear Mr. Gardiner, if I may prevail upon your time and good nature once again?"

"Certainly," Edward smiled. His relaxed manner calmed the anxious-appearing Mr. Darcy.

Lord Claverstone turned to Mrs. Gardiner who was looking most curiously at Darcy. "May I escort you to the stables, Lucille? I know you shall want to see the new foal."

She nodded her agreement, and they quit the room together, leaving the two men to their conference.

"Mr. Gardiner, this is somewhat sensitive, and I ask you to trust me until my inquiry and story is made known to you. At that time, sir, I shall respect your wishes entirely."

Darcy was twisting his hands as he spoke. He seemed to be looking for a way to begin and was at a loss as to how he might make a start.

"May I ask a question that might be able to help you find your beginning, Mr. Darcy?"

"Indeed, that would be most helpful, my friend."

Edward looked the man in the eyes, blew out a long exhale, and asked, "Does this visit have anything to do with Elizabeth? Do you, perhaps have questions regarding her history?" Edward was blunt. He wanted the man to be able to come to the point, even if it had something to do with Lizzy.

"Yes, thank you. That is exactly the proper place to begin, sir." Darcy replied, relaxing a bit more. Mr. Gardiner drew a deep breath and thoughtfully began a brief history of Lizzy's life.

"Elizabeth is the daughter of my own sister, Mildred Bennet, whom I am ashamed to tell you has always been a selfish and very jealous woman. She was a fortune hunter who shamelessly chased and then finally married Thomas Bennet, who was extremely wealthy when they wed. But more on the story of their loss of fortune in a moment.

"When Jane was born, everything was wonderful. They had a beautiful little girl. Then came their second child, whom everyone thought was going to be a boy. Lizzy arrived, a female and her mother rejected her. She refused her own child at her birth. My poor brother Bennet wrote to us and let us know the terrible conditions of his home. He begged us to help with the child. We went immediately to Longbourn to take that beautiful, little four-days-old girl into our home and our hearts. She remained with us until age seven. At that time, poor Bennet felt guilty and asked that we might bring Elizabeth home and let them try again. By this time they had another three girls.

"I honestly do not know if it was guilt or jealousy, but my own sister began to mistreat Elizabeth. Every time we visited, the child would cling to us. God forgive us that we returned her at age seven years. She was a most pleasant little girl, and Mildred treated her ill.

"Brother Bennet took note of Lizzy's intelligence and began to act as her teacher. She learned to read and write quickly and that opened up many other fields to her. She could perform mathematics with ease and learned to speak French. Once she learned Latin, she seemed unstoppable. We believe if she had been male, she perhaps would have completed Oxford at about four and ten years of age. Learning is very easy for Lizzy. Uncle used his influence, but to no avail. His appeal for correspondence courses was denied."

Mr. Darcy was very moved to hear such a shocking background associated with this happy and vivacious girl of whom he had become so fond. It was difficult to listen.

The idea of her having to endure these insufferable assaults as a young child, made him feel physically ill. All of this abuse inflicted by her mother's hand, was unbelievable, intolerable!

"It is true we took the trip to celebrate Lizzy's academic accomplishments, but we also wanted to support her emotionally. Three months ago, a Mr. William Collins, a cousin to Mr. Bennet travelled to Longbourn. Because of the entail on the estate, Collins is to inherit. Using this relationship as leverage, the man descended upon the household and immediately sought Lizzy's hand in marriage. Naturally, she refused.

"Mr. Darcy, this annoying, insufferable, egotistical little man had formed an alliance with my sister! She told the man she would arrange everything, and Collins directed his request regarding Elizabeth only to Mildred. Thomas was bypassed and ignored. After Lizzy's absolute refusal, Mildred told her own daughter that she would disown her completely and forever if she did not marry Collins. Lizzy refused her.

"Next, Mildred demanded that Thomas turn Lizzy over to Collins to be taken to Hunsford, where he is curate for your sister, Lady Catherine de Bourgh."

The look on Darcy's face registered pure shock. "I am astonished, Mr. Gardiner!"

"Indeed!" Edward agreed. Maintaining eye contact with Darcy, he continued. "Bennet packed Lizzy's belongings immediately and brought her directly to us. He signed her custody over to me. This of course, broke her heart. Good natured as she is, she immediately thanked her father, telling him that he had protected her from that 'toad' as she refers to Collins.

Never once did she question why her father failed to stand up to her mother.

"She has written to her mother, telling her she understands and forgives her due to the extreme pressure about the entail. Mildred burned the letter and informed Bennet that 'his daughter must not attempt to contact her again as she shall never hear from her, nor look upon her face.'

"That sister of mine has been telling anyone who shall listen that Elizabeth is a wild girl. She claims that her long rambles are just excuses to climb trees and do all manner of ill behaviour. Using her youngest daughter, she bribed Lydia to bear false witness against Lizzy, forever setting sister against sister. Lydia was coached, and told the vilest of lies about her sister, and then she affirmed them to be valid. When Mildred shunned Lizzy, Lydia shunned her as well.

"Mildred broke Lizzy's bow and burned it along with her archery target and arrows. She has such hatred for her own daughter that we have told Lizzy it would be best if she never goes back.

"We are in hopes that the gossip of this selfish woman shall die out on its own, and that Lizzy shall not suffer any one thinking ill of her.

"Yes, Lizzy is spirited and admittedly a free thinker, but never wild, Mr. Darcy."

"Have you any reason to hope, Mr. Gardiner?" Darcy asked, his eyes nearly filling with tears. "Do you think she shall ever go home to her sisters and father?"

"We are not hopeful. Thankfully, her father and sisters may visit her in our home. I have tried to tell my sister that they would have no estate at all without Lizzy. That just serves to make Mildred all the more angry.

"Here is what happened to their fortune. Mr. Bennet is a fellow who would like to have reading be his world. He had no interest and no training when he took over his estate. His wife spends money without conscience, and he had a steward who was becoming wealthy looking after his estate's concerns. It was Elizabeth who took over all the accounts, estate and household, at just two and ten years of age. In fear of financial ruin, one day Bennet showed her the accounts and asked her what she thought was wrong. Mr. Darcy, that little girl found the deviously false accounting in a matter of minutes. Brother Bennet was astonished and told the child he would pay her a small allowance to keep the books. This she did up until the day Bennet brought her to us."

Darcy stood up, out of his chair, "Amazing!" He all but shouted his stunned response. "Absolutely astonishing that a child could discover what a villainous thief, who knew the workings of an estate, could hide from the owner."

"Yes, now you see why Lord Claverstone worked so hard on her behalf at Oxford. The girl has an extraordinarily bright mind. However, Elizabeth told her mother and her father that there would be dire consequences if Mrs. Bennet did not cease her elaborate spending immediately. Naturally, Mildred did not take kindly to her child giving her this particular instruction. It became just another thorn in Mildred's side where Lizzy was concerned."

"Yes, I can see that, Mr. Gardiner. This is an amazing story. I thank you for telling me. I shall keep this in confidence. And, now as to why I am here, in addition to learning more about Elizabeth. Her sad story is no reflection of her character, in fact, it is rather a confirmation of her steadfast ethics and her forgiving nature.

"Mr. Gardiner, I am a father who loves his children. It is true, I wanted Miss Elizabeth to be a role model for my daughter, but I also want my son to meet her. My wife, Anne, and I spent many hours talking of the type of woman we wished our son to marry. He was just two and ten when Anne died, and you may think he was too young for us to read his character, but we could, just as you know you own three children. While we could not know his nature with exactness, we were well acquainted with the magnitude of the duties that would fall upon his shoulders as master of Pemberly." He paused, and made eye contact with Mr. Gardiner.

"Fitzwilliam shall take control of Pemberly on the first day of June this year. He shall need a helpmate, a wife who shall grow with him into the towering responsibilities of this complex and demanding life.

"I have no way of knowing whether the two would even like each other. Your niece may have absolutely no interest in my son. I do not know. What I do know is this, the morning of the day we met, I asked God to show me Fitzwilliam's wife to be. Much like that faithful servant talked about in the Bible, who went to find a wife for Isaac. Do you remember that story, dealing with watering the camels?"

Edward nodded, and Darcy raced ahead with his thoughts. "I must say, for the first time in my busy life, I actually had ample time to spend within that bookstore. In fact, the crowds outside upon the boardwalks parted, to hasten me on my way. And, there you were with your niece. I was there, at precisely the right time meet you.

"Whether Fitzwilliam even takes notice of her, I would like to ask the three of you to come to Pemberly. Stay with us as long as you wish. Go to town, collect your children and when you arrive, we shall give you an entire wing as your accommodations. Or, if you trust us, allow Miss Elizabeth to be Georgiana's guest for two or three months. The girls are fond of each other. I shall leave all of this to you and Mrs. Gardiner. Your niece has had so much sorrow and turmoil in her young life. If you agree to even a portion of what I have requested, I shall guard her and promise you that no harm shall come to her.

"Even should my son have no real interest in Miss Elizabeth, he is a gentleman. He would not trifle with her. At any case, please keep Pemberly as a visiting destination on your journey home. We enjoy your friendship and shall be happy to have you as long as you wish to grace us with your presence. I know you shall do what is best for Elizabeth." At that, Mr. Darcy said his farewells and quit the room to call for Georgiana.

Edward set out to find his wife. *A very kind, Christian man, too bad his wife is not with him to advise him. I value Lucille's judgment. I shall be eager to watch her eyes as I tell her Mr. Darcy's story.*

Her eyes always tell me what she really feels. We both shall need to be most careful to make the right decision for Elizabeth. This could be a wonderful opportunity, or it could be filled with challenges. Extreme wealth may bring extreme problems.

Chapter 4

"The trouble with strangers is that we know nothing about them."

-Anonymous

Fitzwilliam hated being at Rosings. He felt it boring. Time dragged. The families had started the Easter tradition upon the death of Lord Louis de Bourgh. They wanted to support Aunt Catherine and Cousin Anne. It was a commitment to his mother's sister.

Walking briskly to the stables, lest anyone waylay him, he claimed his stallion and saddled the horse himself. Fitzwilliam was eager to put Rosings behind him for a little while. It would be unbearable until Rory could extricate himself from their aunt. She loved to hear him tell of the army. She had specific questions about the wars and, in short, he was her entertainment. Poor soul.

Mounting for a leisurely ride, he selected a country lane. It was large enough for two riders, or a small wagon or other such small vehicle. He walked his stallion, taking in the sights of the farmlands, marvelling at their painted splendour in the late afternoon sun. He was able to breathe freely and relax by himself. It felt good to escape the anxiety of thinking about June one.

In the distance ahead, he spotted a little phaeton and pony, driven by one who knew how to drive. He watched the vehicle corner the turns and admired the skilful hands of the man driving.

Fitzwilliam kept Percival at a slow walk, not desirous of returning to Rosings anytime soon. He kept his eye on the phaeton. It stopped and the driver disembarked, held up a recurve bow, and fired three arrows into a circular target posted upon a tree.

Fitzwilliam estimated the distance from the road to the target to be about one hundred yards.

Quite a respectable distance. Practice for competition?

The driver, moving very quickly, did not approach the target but simply reentered the phaeton and sped away.

As he watched, more closely now, it appeared to Fitzwilliam that the driver might be a woman, not a man. There was something about the swing of the driver's hips into the seat that persuaded him. The phaeton travelled down the road a good distance. This time, the driver stopped, did not exit the vehicle, but merely stood and fired three arrows, once again.

Just as before, as soon as the last arrow was sent in flight, the driver was seated and very rapidly departed, driving at top speed. Fitzwilliam watched in awe. He could not determine the gender of the driver. It seemed the archer was not concerned about the results, for the two targets were not inspected. Rather curious now about the marksmanship of the shooter, he decided to inspect both targets.

Upon examining the first target, he saw all the arrows were closely grouped in the centre of the bull's-eye. The second target was somewhat better in that the arrows actually shaved one another, vying for position in the dead centre of the bull's-eye.

Becoming more curious, he kicked Percival into a lope, pursuing the vehicle. It should be an easy task to overtake an archer using a little phaeton to move between targets. Looking into the distance, he suddenly thought better of the pursuit. The sun was quickly sinking in the west, and it would be very difficult to see the road after dark. Not knowing the area, and wishing to avoid becoming lost, he returned to Rosings. It was possible that Rory had found a way to extricate himself from their aunt.

His curiosity was piqued by the phaeton-driving archer who would remain a mystery. Even if the archer did exhibit a pleasingly slim figure and was an excellent archer and driver, all must be left unexplained due to the setting sun.

It was for the best, for in Fitzwilliam Darcy's opinion and experience, archers were not at all attractive, as a general rule!

"George!" Clayton called out as his brother-in-law Darcy entered the hall. "Join me in the library for a brandy?" Darcy regarded his departed wife's brother with fondness. As his neighbor in Derbyshire, George and his wife had been proud when her brother Clayton Fitzwilliam had been honoured to be named an earl-thus becoming Lord Matlock. Clayton's wife Nora was thrilled to become Lady Matlock. No doubt it had helped their son, Rory Fitzwilliam to advance to the rank of colonel in the army.

Entering the musty library, the two men sought chairs near the fire. For a few minutes they were content to speak of the family and the journey and even to disdain why Lady Catherine owned books when she never seemed to read or even speak of books. Finally Clayton spoke his mind.

"George, I wanted to warn you that Nora and I saw that scoundrel Wickham skulking around the house this afternoon. Best to alert young Darcy and keep an eye upon Georgiana.

"Honest to God, George, what in Heaven's name were you thinking to give so much financial assistance to that upstart? That rake got enough from you when you cared for him after his father's death. Did you really need to send him to Cambridge and insist that he room with your boy? Rory told us what a menace the man has been and the sorrow he continues to sow."

"Clayton, I misapplied my mercy. His father was a worthy man; I suppose I just thought the son would be as well. I clearly see my errors, and may God help me to make it up to Fitzwilliam. We are going to have a talk this evening, and I hope it shall begin a healing process for us."

"Darcy, I think you should have your solicitor put something in writing declaring that Wickham has received all he shall have of your funds. He should be warned off Pemberly and measures should be put in place to shoot him on sight at any of your properties, should he trespass."

"Clayton, you may rest assured that I have already put those directives into place."

"Please tell me, Darcy, that you are also aware of our circle, both in town and in Derbyshire, having long ill-reputed you as being the natural father of George Wickham?"

Standing to his full height, George straightened his jacket, as he wished he could straighten out the subject being discussed. He smoothed his sleeves, and then sat down again.

Looking Clayton in the eyes, he said, "Clayton, I absolutely deny such gossip! His father was my faithful manager. Those ugly rumours do his memory, and that of his wife, undeserved ill. My man, Simmons, assured me it was none other than Wickham himself who circulated those lies about his mother and me."

"Darcy, of course you have disclosed this to your children, have you not?"

"No, Clayton. I have no way of knowing that either Fitzwilliam or Georgiana have heard them."

Lord Matlock stared into his brother's eyes. He could be nothing but direct and unassuming in his honest assessment. Maintaining the usual civilities, he finally spoke.

"With all due respect to your judgment, George, how in heaven's name would it be possible for Fitzwilliam to room with Wickham and never hear the rumours, if indeed, it was actually Wickham who industriously spread them?

"George, you must make Fitzwilliam aware that these are lies. Your relationship depends upon his complete trust and respect."

Seeing his brother's mien changed, Lord Matlock softened. He would not press him further. He ended his appeal by saying, "Brother, you are a kind and gentle man. Your love for your son and daughter is very well known. I have no doubt that you shall be tireless in your efforts to support and reassure your children in this matter. Nora and I certainly defend you and continue to uphold your sterling reputation with all our mutual acquaintances."

At this, Darcy smiled at Clayton. Both gentlemen seemed gratified by the outcome of this discussion and were pleased with the sentiments which passed between them. The two had an enduring friendship. Each knew they could count upon the goodwill and support of their family connections and their longstanding friendship.

Fitzwilliam was pleased to see that his cousin had brought his swords. He was also well equipped and eager to assault.

The men elected to fence in an area at the back of the stables. They were accustomed to working out together at their fencing club in town. Rory taught fencing at His Majesty's Army Academy in London. He was always amazed at his cousin's skill level. He had the agility, strength, and endurance needed, but he also had an unexplained hunger inside him. He wanted, no, he needed to win. Something would not allow Fitzwilliam Darcy to lose; not the smallest and most insignificant wager, horse race, footrace or fencing match. The man was driven to be the best in whatever he was doing. The colonel identified this same drive in himself. They had been, after all, cut from the same cloth, so to speak. His cousin was a Darcy, but he was also a Fitzwilliam, through his mother's bloodline. A fact which many times demanded Rory's attention and respect. And which, no few times, had spurred Rory to help Darcy, even when he did not deserve help. It prevented Rory from being jealous of his cousin, and inspired brotherly affection in both men.

For Colonel Rory Fitzwilliam, fencing was about staying alive. He fenced to stay in the land of the living. Too many times he had fought the Spanish upon foreign soil, and his sword had saved his life. Yes, fencing was a lifesaving skill, not an exhibition. Not an exercise to maintain impressive muscles that would dazzle the ladies. The 'ladies,' of course, were of that variety who would regularly see men with their shirts and pants off.

Admittedly, Rory had his share of those 'ladies' as well, but his body had been so covered with scars that his muscles were of less interest. It was unfortunate that he had difficulty discussing the battle scars that earned him attention and admiration.

Always telling the family that they were using foils, the men instead used real and very lethal weapons. However, the weapons were employed with extreme care and used with the greatest skills and respect.

For the cousins, the best part of being at Rosings was fencing. Especially when they would ride into the forest to assault. The echo of steel and the crunch of an unpredictable forest floor gave their sport an edge that indoor fencing lacked.

Today's workout went as usual. Each man pushed the other as hard as he could, and each rose to the challenge. Fatigue always ended their match with mutual respect.

George Darcy sat down with his son after dinner. The two talked until three of the clock in the very early morning. Many things were confessed by the father. He began with his misplaced favours which were shown to Wickham, then he talked about the rumours in town, and in Derbyshire.

George Darcy poured his heart out to his son. Both men felt the experience brought them closer together. They agreed to speak again the next night after dinner.

Difficult as it was, Fitzwilliam felt a certain comfort that his father had opened the sore subject of George Wickham. He had listened to the older man, and told him nothing of his own feelings. He could not answer him when questioned. Not yet. He needed to heal. Wickham was a very painful topic to him.

He listened to his father deny the rumours, yet he still was uncertain of his father's innocence. What other explanation could there possibly be for his continuing to pay Wickham's debts, loaning him money, allowing his impersonation of Fitzwilliam, and providing financial support of his wild personal life? Upon reflection, the latter part of that question sounded quite a bit like his own recent history.

He began to see himself resembling George Wickham in character. Was it true that he was Wickham's half-brother? This would explain George Darcy's generosity. He was simply taking care of a financial obligation to his natural son. He sent him to the same university as his own legal son and heir, they even roomed together. What could be more fair? Is that not how all his classmates saw the situation? So they said.

Fitzwilliam began to form a decision about Wickham. If it was true and they were half-brothers, he was resolved NOT to act anything like Wickham. He desired to amend his ways before June first. God forbid any tenants make the connection of similar behaviours, or any other likeness between the two. Yes, Fitzwilliam Darcy held Wickham in the highest contempt. Whatever life George Wickham was living, he would take the opposite path.

Once in their rooms, neither man could find sleep. Fitzwilliam got out of bed and began making pages and pages of notes. He recorded his thoughts and some of the many things he wished to ask his father. In truth, he had not felt this good in years. In fact, it was possible that he had never felt this good about himself or his relationship with his father. All, but that nagging doubt about Wickham's parentage…

Perhaps Father deserves the benefit of the doubt. I myself require his forgiveness for my quite recent past. He has asked for my understanding; he deserves at least as much.

At last he laid his head on the pillow. He slept soundly for one hour, and awoke, feeling refreshed. He dressed without shaving and set off for the stables, wearing breeches, boots, and a linen shirt, open at the neck. He had never looked so improper in his life, and he had never been so self-assured about who he was and who he was becoming.

This April brought mild weather to Kent. It was still winter, but a warm spring-like morning greeted him. Entering the stables, he felt elated to have beaten the dawn. It was exhilarating to be up and out of the house before sunrise. He would start the day on his stallion. Percival travelled with Fitzwilliam wherever he went. At one and twenty hands high, the thoroughbred was a giant and could easily bear Fitzwilliam's large body. He had the ability to provide all the power and speed Fitzwilliam could long for, or need.

Waving the groom aside, he saddled his horse, mounted, and set off at a full canter. Setting his blue eyes upon the path, he did not see the dark figure crouching in the nearby shrubs. Had he seen then man in full sunlight, he would not have known him at first. Life's choices, made for ill, had sent the man into regressions which were now eroding his former good looks.

He had not the handsome face which accompanied him to Cambridge. He lacked even the colour and full vigour of health. George Wickham stood, watching the horse and rider disappear.

Bloody pup! Not enough time to jump out in front and spook his horse. Too bad. No matter, I came to see my generous benefactor, George Darcy, not that fool.

Fitzwilliam slowed his mount to a walk while entering the somewhat rocky area that led into the glade he remembered so well.

It was not so much the size of the clearing that drew him, but the romantic drama of the scene it presented each time he visited. He remembered the border of Sweet William that bloomed this time of year, surrounding the fresh, new, bright-green grass of the field.

Before entering the glade, he reined Percival, but it was without need, for something had already caused the horse to stop. Leaning forward, he saw what his horse was watching. The early sun beamed a ray of light upon a golden-coloured horse with a fair blond mane and long tail. Upon its back, stood a beautiful, barefoot girl with flowing raven hair. She was clad scandalously, in skintight buckskin breeches and a thin white linen shirt, which was open at the collar. Her feet and ankles were most improper as well, appearing as they had the moment they first arrived in this world.

The horse was bareback with a single thin rope fashioned as a bridle, which the rider held within her teeth. Even from a distance, her teeth flashed whiter than snow as she clinched upon the rope. This held her mouth in a perpetual wide smile, or perhaps it was a sincere smile.

Yes, it was a smile indicating her enjoyment of the unusual ride. The scene the two presented in the very early light, was akin to the grandeur of the natural setting. The girl, glowing with natural beauty which needed no enhancement; and the horse, healthy and well groomed, and obviously loving the work she did with the rider, made a scene worthy of highest admiration.

What in sweet heaven is this? Never have I seen anything of this, nor imagined its likeness. How is she doing that? Who is she? Where does she live? How old is she?

Though the glade was crisp, she wore neither jacket nor coat. She stood with both arms stretched out and kept her knees bent as she executed flawless balance. Amazingly, she took her horse in a circle, around the perimeter of the field. She held both knees flexed, her interior leg bent to a greater degree than the outer as she leaned inside. First circling right, then left, she built her speed into a rather rapid lope. Coming to a slow stop, she rode to the centre of the field and, with some caution, she started figure eights, enlarging their size as she increased in speed once again. He watched in fascination as she moved in perfect union with her mare. Her smile grew as she worked the horse with more and more control and solid determination. He fancied he could hear her saying commands to the mare. She was in a world of her own. She looked as though complete joy filled her. He watched as she gave herself over to the feeling.

After several thrilling minutes, she slowed the horse into a walk. To Fitzwilliam, it seemed the mare was as disappointed as he. Was the unique exhibition concluding?

Oh, please do not stop! Not now. Keep riding, oh please do not stop. Just a few more glorious moments of riding. You love this, do you not? What a joy to watch you.

She rode to the centre of the little glade and stopped her horse. Just then a bright ray of sunshine burst onto them. Rider and horse, were both bathed in a dazzling ray of purest light. Her hair was even more shiny than he first thought. Her colour seemed to transform under the brilliant beam.

He had thought her lush, flowing long hair was raven, yet now it looked a deep spicy auburn, and her ivory skin was covered in a most attractive and vibrant sheen. Her shirt, which was somewhat clingy under the influence of that sheen, was very obliging to the light, revealing a clear view of her firm, full, and beautiful breasts. As she turned in his direction, he was treated to a complete view of her chest. Even her delicious raspberry centres were displayed for his personal perspective. He became transfixed, forgetting to breathe. He had never been so enthralled.

I have not seen a more beautiful woman. Yes, she looks young, but certainly she is a woman fully grown. If only her performance could be unending.

The sun was more intense and moving higher in the morning sky. She continued to turn her head in a reconnaissance of the glade's border. Slowly she took the mare into a circle; her eyes were inspecting the brush and trees. She slid down astride her horse. *Oh God, she knows she is being watched. But we have been so quiet. Still. Steady.*

She began her quest with a walk, then quickly moved to a trot, and once again to a canter. Suddenly to his horror, she stopped and quickly spun around! Very slowly, she rode past him. Looking straight ahead with the sunlight in her eyes, she missed the frame of the big man, and his big horse. Still, she felt there was someone watching. Riding slowly around the glade, she continued to gaze into the darkness of the deep foliage. Passing her intruder again and again, the illuminating sun continued to affirm her physical perfection. Now, her full beautiful breasts were clearly visible through the sheer shirt, and he could see the dampness collecting around the crotch of her breeches.

All in all, she presented a most improper scene and her observer was having most ungentle-manly thoughts. Given his habits, it was understandable, given hers, she simply did not want curiosity seekers. Her thoughts and focus were solely to practice her skills, with her very valuable and most beloved mare.

How can I stand this beauty? Classical features, perfect bone structure defining her face, the likeness not even displayed as well in sculptures of Greek goddesses. Those fine eyes flashing with a fierce expression. Her beautiful and full breasts, bouncing and swaying, with raspberry centres. Her legs, displaying muscles which are so firm and yet decidedly feminine, as she rides her mare.

She stopped again. He froze. He was sure that even his heart stopped beating within that moment. He feared that she would end this amazing demonstration of masterful horsemanship. And, he dreaded the loss of the unforgettable vision of beauty and grace.

Does she truly see us, or sense us? Quiet. Do not breathe.

Too late! Taking a full headlong run, she reined to a quick stop, dead centre in front of him.

Frowning deeply, she shouted, venting her outrage. He was stunned! At first, he did not comprehend her words. He could not connect the anger she now displayed, with the most Heavenly vision she presented only moments ago. With great force, she hurled her verbal accusations at him. "You peeping, folly-fallen coxcomb!" It was obvious that she was disgusted with his behaviour, and she showed every sign that she would, most likely, never hold him in a favourable light. So plainly spoken was she, that her words needed no interpretation. In truth, her body required no words to emote precisely what she thought of him!

"Sir! What are you about? How long have you been lurking here? I perceive you are no gentleman! Certainly a gentleman would make his presence known to a lady!"

"I shall have you know I am most certainly a gentleman. I am riding, not lurking. You certainly do set quite a store for yourself when you do not own this property. This is not your personal glade. Others may ride past you at any time. What a temper! Control your anger, madam."

He watched her, listening for her reply. Hearing nothing, and missing the glare of her eyes and the set of her jaw, he dared to continue. "Besides, madam, by your appearance you are obviously no gentlewoman!"

She shook her head, sending her hair scattering across her shoulders, leaving her with an earthy, natural appearance. She had a uniquely sensual quality that he considered most desirable, enhanced by her complete obliviousness to her own appeal.

Effortless beauty. The closer she is, the more desirable!

The shaking of her hair also released a faint lavender and roses scent that wafted across the air and infused his senses with her sweet fragrance. This acted upon his body as a most intoxicating perfume.

She lifted her ribs upward so as to appear taller as she sat upon a horse a full six hands smaller than his horse. Squaring her shoulders, she tipped her head, and, piercing him with her eyes, she shouted in a harsh voice using great volume. "Indeed sir! I am a gentlewoman. A female offspring of a gentleman is called such, and I am telling you, I am a gentle lady both by virtue of my birth and my conduct. I would bid you a good day."

Her final remark was spoken with iciness, and yet she continued to emanate such a flow of warmth and exuded amorous passion. He wanted to make out her character. He already knew that her feminine charms were irresistible.

In a flash, almost too quick for him to see, she turned her horse. They moved as one. Horse and rider flew away in a wild run. It was neck-breaking speed, to which without thinking, he quickly matched. He could have easily out distanced her had they been racing. Rather he held her pace, and side by side they jumped two small hedges and a somewhat swollen stream before she slowed to a walk, then stopped. Without warning she slid from the animal, and he responded by dismounting.

Seeing him dare to dismount after chasing after her, she put up her hand in an authoritative and universal sign to warn the encroacher to stop all movement. She spouted at him:

"What is this? You chase me and then dare to dismount beside me? What wild nerve you must possess! I declare that I have never seen its equal!"

Fitzwilliam had never seen anyone like her. Any woman who could display this type of horsemanship was in a class by herself. He wanted to know her, but that seemed quite like taking honey from the midst of an active and angry hive! *A change must be made to help settle her, she must be charmed.*

Forgetting that his appearance was not well groomed at the present, he commenced to speak to her with his usual high toned and imposing manner. No matter about his attire, had he been well-groomed and expensively dressed, she would have paid it no mind. He had earned her anger and ill wishes. He daringly took up an opportunity to answer her.

"Now, I could see that your retreat was simply a short interruption of our earlier exchange. I wanted to present another opportunity for a better understanding and perhaps a happier outcome," he said condescendingly.

Outraged at this display, she stepped around Marigold. Wielding powerful words, she approached him with boldness saying, "You are more brash, sir, than anyone I have ever seen! How dare you give me a chase after telling me my appearance is improper!"

Purposefully wanting to tower over her, he looked deeply into her beautiful green eyes. Never could he recall seeing such a shade of green, framed with more lush lashes. Most vibrant were her fine eyes, and they deepened in colour as she spoke to him. Was it her emotions colouring them? *Um, do her eyes react the same way when she is in the depths of passion? Oh, to discover the truth of her darkening eyes!*

Pulling his lips into a tight line, he furrowed his brow and lowered his head as he spoke to her as directly and sternly as he could. He had chosen a few words and used them as curtly as if he were chastising a servant who had disappointed him.

"What can you mean? I did no such thing!" he raved.

Showing that she would not respond to his attempt to intimidate her, she blurted:

"In truth, you did, I dare say! I left the glade and you did indeed, give me a chase. Do you dare now deny it? How is that possible?" she inquired with sarcasm, while extending her hand to indicate himself and his horse, as the irrefutable proof of her argument. "For here you are, with your horse, on the very same space of ground which I now occupy with my mare!"

He was silent a moment as he thought of how best to respond to what sounded like a good point of argumentation.

Trying to soften his facial expression, he answered her as best he could without much time in which to think. "I rode after you, but just so I could set the record straight," he said, "and I see now that it was in vain, as you, madam, have no ability to listen when a gentleman speaks. I did not say that your appearance was improper!"

She was set for a quarrel. Pulling herself up to her full height, she squared her shoulders and tipped her head. Lifting one eyebrow into a high arch, she launched into a tirade which proved to ignite his anger.

"Do you not listen to your own words whilst you speak them? Are they not, indeed, pronouncements of your very thoughts?" she asked smugly, with her hands upon her hips.

Not willing to let this situation go on another minute, he wished to show her that her interpretation of his words was inaccurate. He would do it in a way so as to demonstrate his gallantry.

Looking into her eyes, he spoke slowly and clearly…"I declare most certainly, that at no time in addressing you did I use the word 'improper.' I did not allude to your appearance as being anything less than proper. Upon my word, you take offense easily, madam, and become hostile at no provocation, whatsoever, do you not?"

She rolled her eyes, "No. I do not! I am not hostile."

"Very well, angry, then," he said by way of appeasement, placing one finger along his cheek.

"Nor am I angry, sir," she declared folding her arms defensively in front of her chest.

"Very well, madam. If not hostile, nor angry, please acquaint me with this particular emotion. I should like to know the identity of that force which is propelling your words. Whatever it may be, it is a powerful thing." He exhaled slowly.

Not quite knowing what to do, she forced a slight smile. "It was embarrassment, sir. When I am embarrassed, I become frustrated and feel I am losing control of the situation. Then, that provokes—umm, a feeling very much akin to—ah, I would say, quite similar to what you might think of as anger. Some may equate it to hostility."

"Oh," he said, looking directly at her dainty feet.

"Yes. Oh." She looked down at her bare feet, wishing for her slippers.

Smiling at her, he nodded knowingly, "So, this is your apology then?"

Hearing these words, her green eyes smoldered and began to darken. She cocked her head upward, delicately arched her left brow, and spoke again. "Perchance you would wish to render the apology to me? You were indeed spying upon me, a maiden who was only out enjoying a morning ride."

"Well!" he spat with sarcasm, "a maiden I see you are, but your attire suggests a lad. Perhaps I thought you a male. I believed I was watching a gentleman's horsemanship."

This he stated with force, for he was now attempting to overwhelm her with his size and his authority. As a general rule, most people were impressed with his powerful influence.

She stepped closer to him, peering into his beautiful blue eyes. Her head was tilted upward as her stature rendered her just above his broad shoulders. "Clearly sir, I can now see that you are speaking purposefully to me, intending to manipulate me. I have just revealed that it was embarrassment that inspired my earlier words—yet plainly you wish to offend me in order to protect yourself!"

"Indeed!" he shouted throwing his arms into the air, causing his stallion to stomp the ground with force. He grabbed the reins to steady the horse. Then he looked directly into her green eyes, and was confronted with the fire currently at residence there. "Protect myself, from what? From you, a mere maiden, and a slight one at that! Shall I fear your strength may overpower me? Nay!"

At hearing the word "overpower" she stepped away to place some distance from him, for she had just become aware that she was close to him. Very close. Close enough to place her hands upon his chest, which she suddenly noticed was large, thick, very well-developed, and very strong looking. Dark, curly chest hair peeked at her from his opened shirt. His neck held her rapt attention. Suddenly she felt very uncomfortable. *Men have hair upon their chests? How does it feel? Does Jane know?*

"Nay—" she said quietly, using a much more subdued voice. "Nay, I meant you seemed to be making an effort to protect your obvious sense of superiority."

Momentarily his heart froze. His thoughts also began to stray as his eyes drifted to her full lips. She was biting her bottom lip now, looking at the ground which placed her lush lashes upon her lovely cheeks. Her thick and full eyelashes were long and black as night, perfectly framing her eyes. Her lips were so very luscious, full, and sensuous. He was enthralled.

Think fool. God help me. What do I say to her now? I do not wish to shout at such a beautiful woman. How do I defend a superior attitude? Words. I need words. Is argumentation an extravagance? An imprudence? Might we speak better words to one another? I am a man of honour, I shall demonstrate good intent and forfeit all claim to the right. Was I not peeping in a clandestine manner?

"Oh, uh, um," his eyes fell to the inside upper edges of her thighs. They were wet there. Her buckskin breeches clung to her crotch, revealing a delicious-looking paradise. Rational thoughts were lost to him. He was mortified as he heard himself actually groan aloud.

Quickly, he tried to cover this shocking sound coming from the depths of his soul. He could not remember a time when he had lost control. He coughed! Several times. Loudly and, he hoped, convincingly.

"Yes! Well, madam, I am afraid I am guilty of pride leading me to an unfortunate case of self-inflicted superiority." *Good. That sounded good. Watch her eyes to see if she accepted those words.*

His nearness still overpowered and excited her. Had she not just moved away a bit? "Take heart, sir. I understand that admission of a certain condition is the beginning of its cure."

Clearly she was softening towards him. Her voice sounded strange to her ears. *What am I about? Am I flirting with him? I do not flirt with anyone.*

In truth, neither one were quite themselves. Both their hearts quickened to racing. "In fairness," he admitted, "I should say, I did watch your display of horsemanship, for I have never witnessed such riding. I do suppose modern riding fashion for ladies would not support such riding as you perform. In addition, the use of boots would be very cruel." He watched her closely for any trace of anger or sarcasm. He saw only a sincere expression on her soft face.

She was staring at him. "Yes," she nearly whispered, answering slowly, "very cruel, indeed, I agree." Her voice faded toward the end of this statement.

His eyes seemed to drift over her without his ability to control his vision. He was looking her over from head to toes. *Oh God, that wolfish look shall not work with this vision of beauty and loveliness. Is this ignis fatuus, or is she a flesh and blood woman? I need to get to know her.*

"I quite lost my temper." They spoke in unison, to their amusement. Smiling, they did so again, "Excuse me." Lightly laughing, they stood just regarding each other.

She kept a safe distance away, which was still very close. *In truth, never have I stood this close to a man for this length of time. And those men were properly dressed. My, what I could say about his appearance. Does he always display chest hair? I must write to Jane.*

Looking briefly at the ground, she collected her thoughts, "Well, I thank you. Your words have removed the stiffness I perceived in your earlier discourse. Yes, you are correct, I must wear breeches. I had to fashion my own clothing for my riding." *Where did those words come from? Why did I say that to him? What has happened to my brain?*

"You?" he questioned. "You fabricated this riding attire? I thought these breeches might belong to another in your life, perhaps your brother or husband?"

"No. None such! Do you not know that all gentlewomen are expected to sew? We can and sometimes do make garments for ourselves. I ride early, leaving just before dawn to avoid being seen by anyone in the stables. I keep my gown and slippers in a bag which I hide in the bushes." Reaching into the hedge, she withdrew a cloth bag. Dipping her hand into the pouch, she pulled out her slippers. Tipping her head, she gave him a beautiful smile. It made him feel weak in the knees.

"Propriety dictates, sir!" she declared, tossing her wild-looking loose hair. *Oh God, when she tosses her hair, I can smell a lavender and rose scent. Her hair is so perfect in that untidy way. I should love to run my fingers through it, play with her curls, and put my face into it just to smell that sweet scent more fully…*

He nodded and retuned her smile with one that lit his handsome face, revealing his dimples and making him appear even more desirable. Suddenly she knew she would regret their parting.

"I must bid you adieu, as you seem to be standing in my dressing room, sir."

He stood there, planted to the ground. He knew she was speaking, but he had no idea what she might be saying. Her voice was so beautiful. Her sweet scent as she tossed her head, nearly unbalanced him. Oh, her hair, so beautiful, so sensual. He heard her voice clearly, but the words and their possible meaning were not available to him, for he was not listening. Other senses were acute, but not his hearing.

Instead of leaving as she requested with subtlety, he asked if she ever rode toward the sea.

He supposes me to be a local girl. I shall answer that I shall ride there on the morrow. "Aye. 'Tis my plan for my ride on the morrow. Perchance we shall see each other."

He responded quickly, "May I meet you here and join your ride? I have a feeling I shall be far less superior."

She laughed softly as she answered him. "As you wish, however, 'tis a necessity that we part if we wish to meet again."

He stood, spellbound, and did not move. She smiled again, arched her brow and tried once more. "I am at your mercy, sir, as I do require a costume change, and then I must saddle my mare. I am afraid that I must insist you leave me now, as I fear I may be late for my expected return. I pride myself on my punctuality."

He remained there, watching her. Exhaling loudly and looking up and to her right, she directed, "You must go, as my 'dressing room' has no walls, and I must change my clothing. Please leave me."

Understanding her at last, he turned to leave. Trying to recover his faux pas, he said, "Oh, I do beg your pardon. I was deep in thought about our ride to the sea. Please do forgive me, I shall meet you here on the morrow."

His return to Rosings began with a slow walk until he was out of her sight. He could not keep his thoughts from returning to the amazing sensual form of her exquisite body. The eloquence of her movements as she stood upon her mount, her faint scent of lavender and roses when she tossed her hair. All of this, caused his amour to grow. So much so, that he found the thought of a long walk or ride impossible. It would seem an erect membre virile was not compatible with a saddle, nor a welcome walking companion. No matter, his ability to relieve the distress was very well practiced on his part. Tying Percival to a low tree branch, he spotted a nearby copse. Moving toward it, he could see her beautiful bouncing breasts, firm tight legs, and her damp crotch. Reaching for the handkerchief in his pocket, he entered.

Heading back to Rosings, he mused on Shakespeare's eighteenth sonnet:

> Shall I compare thee to a summer's day?
> Thou art more *lovely* and more temperate:
> Rough winds do shake the darling buds of May,
> And summer's lease hath all too short a date:
> Sometimes too hot the eye of heaven shines,
> And often is his gold complexion dimmed:
> And every fair from fair sometimes declines,
> By chance, or nature's changing course, untrimmed:
> But thy eternal summer shall not fade,
>
> Nor lose possession of that fair thou ow'st:
> Nor shall death brag thou wander'st in his shade
> When in eternal lines to time thou grow'st:
> So long as men can breathe or eyes can see,
> So long lives this, and this gives life to thee.

Stone the crows! We do not know each other's names. Why did I not ask? Until dawn tomorrow, my sweet Goddess of Horses, I shall think of nothing but your free-flowing, glorious hair, your faint scent of roses, your fine green eyes, and luscious lashes. I shall revel in your sensual, full lips teasing me as you bite your lower one and your shape revealed in those buckskins, moistened as your sweet body glistened and glowed, leav-

ing you wet, just to torture me! The sight of your small waist and your strong legs wrapped around your mare, lucky horse! And, those delicious looking mounds topped with ripe raspberry treats! I am dead until the morrow! How can I think of anything but YOU, my beauty? Why would I desire to think of anything but you? You shall fill my thoughts, my dreams, my heart, and even my very soul until we are together.

He took his horse to a gallop. Never was there a more wonderful day.

Even your riposte thrilled me. Oh, for a woman who can speak and not talk of fashion! Yes! Offend me. Tear me to shreds with your clever words. I await the exquisite pain and long to suffer a violent storm of your angry words. You are beautiful when angry, irresistible when embarrassed! Oh, let us disagree again, soon. Or, even if we do not speak, if I could see you ride again, like you did this morning. I long to see you atop your mare.

Oh, that I could be your mount. Shall you ride me, someday, my Goddess of Horses?

⚜

With a great rush, Elizabeth Bennet put the tack on her sweet Marigold. She quickly dressed in her gown and slippers. Then mounting, they galloped to Claverstone. She was just in time. Entering the house a sweet new sense of well- being flooded over her.

Yes! At dawn's light we ride to the sea. Who are you, Handsome Man? Do you know the effect you have upon my person? My poor brain? Have you realised we did not exchange names? Without a formal introduction, we could not be introduced.

Marigold did not her job as my companion, neither was your enormous stallion of help. What a big horse, fitting for a big man. I make your mount to be one and twenty hands.

How tall are you, Handsome Man? Did you know I have never looked upon a man in an open shirt, nor been in so close company of a man who is not a relative? You took my breath away. You have hair upon your beautiful chest. Your chest is so thick, as is your neck. Ah, your neck is quite enticing, as are your arms, shoulders, and your back. My, I believe your body to be perfect, Handsome Man. And, so large! I have never seen so much of a man's body. Yes, you take my breath away. I hate propriety that would say we should not ride tomorrow. I shall tell no one. We shall ride to the sea. I shall wear boots, riding skirt, and jacket. No bonnet, I detest bonnets! Marigold shall wear a blanket and saddle. Marigold and I shall ride with a tall man, upon the tallest horse I have ever seen.

Later in the afternoon, Elizabeth took to the wooded path. She so enjoyed a long ramble in the forest. It calmed her and gave her peace. Her pace was swift, Elizabeth could not abide a slow walk. She always walked with a purpose and quickness.

Oh, to have the forest to myself. What joy. I do so love letting the forest wrap me in its tall trees and entertain me with the many calls of the beautiful birds that live here.

After about an hour, she stopped dead still. Cupping her hand to her ear, she listened.

What is that? It sounds like the clashing of steel upon steel. Could there be men fencing nearby? No! Fencing is a terrible sport. So unnecessarily dangerous, men foolishly risking life and limb, and for what? Entertainment? Male ego?

Turning back to Claverstone, she determined to spend time practicing pianoforte.

Chapter 5

"Understanding another's character is requisite to forming one's regard and esteem."

-Anonymous

George Darcy was enjoying a cup of coffee and reading the newspaper when a footman told him that a strange man awaited outside the house.

Instructing the footman to accompany him, Darcy headed out to meet the man. He suspected Wickham, and he was correct. "Mr. Wickham," he began, "I must ask upon what circumstance you are here at Rosings. This is most unexpected and unnecessary. Please state your business."

Very harsh way to begin, Mr. Darcy. Hum, what to tell him now? Why am I not invited inside? This is not what I had envisioned.

"Mr. Darcy, I am somewhat down on my personal finances. I would ask that you might perhaps give me a few pounds, so I may make my way back to London?" he begged.

"Wickham," Darcy cut him short, "I have recently had my accountant tally the amount of monies I have given you. The total is a staggering sum, I must say. I have been advised that not one additional shilling should be added to the already outrageous amount, an absolute fortune, which has been given to you.

"An order to restrain you from my person, my family, and all my properties has been issued through the courts. Should you violate this order, my men have been instructed to shoot you as a trespasser. Good day, sir." Having said his speech, Darcy nodded to the footman and returned to the house.

The footman, a towering man with a barrel for a torso, put his hand upon Wickham's arm. "I shall take you to a wagon transport bound for London. This is done to obtain distance between you and Rosings. Such is done for all first-time transients. Second offenders are jailed. No funds were paid by Mr. Darcy." Unable to argue, Wickham looked up at the giant and nodded.

I am not done with George Darcy. The wealthy hold all the good cards. I am not done!

It was late afternoon and young Darcy invited his cousin to join him for a leisurely ride. His plan was to talk, and, if possible, to watch for a little phaeton racing across the countryside. He only wanted to satisfy his curiosity as to the driver's gender. He had a feeling about the driver. The bonus was the wonderful scenery and time spent with his cousin, Rory.

Realising that the late afternoon hour was the same as the previous day, he kept his eyes peeled and was on alert. Ahead was a cloud of dust and the phaeton, moving with such speed one would imagine an extreme emergency! As he watched, he noticed that Rory was looking at the same object of interest. He had a wide smile upon his face.

"Cousin, do you see what I am seeing?" he asked, practically laughing. "A delicious figure of a woman driving that rig as fast as she can. Shall we come to her 'rescue'?"

They stopped their horses to watch the speeding vehicle go over a hill and disappear. As they waited to see the phaeton again, certain intelligence became available to Darcy.

First, the phaeton stopped, and a girl with long, flowing, spicy auburn hair stood up and fired three arrows into a target placed on a tree. Just as Fitzwilliam's brain registered it to be the figure of his very own Goddess of Horses, his cousin caused his heart to freeze and nearly stop beating altogether.

"Cousin Darcy, let us ride in quickly upon that lively little girl and make her acquaintance. She may after all need the help of a cavalry man, say a colonel in the army?"

"Cousin Rory," he replied, shifting in his saddle, "I am shocked at a soldier being more interested in the shooter than in the accuracy. Let us instead, inspect the target and see how she did."

Shaking his head in contempt, Rory laughed, "Darcy, no offense, but are you out of your mind? Be my guest and check the target, I shall meet the delicious young thing. She may need to be properly instructed with the use of a man's weapon." He laughed at his own clever play on words. Very pleased with himself, he put his head back and laughed again, so loudly that Darcy was afraid that his Goddess of Horses would hear.

"Nay!" Darcy shook his head. Frowning at Rory he retorted, "Archers are not attractive women, and the more accurate the shooter, the more homely the face and figure. I say we check the target first. There is plenty of time to overtake a little phaeton and pony."

"Either I have been away from my aunt's fabulous port for too long and I wish to return to Rosings and drink, or you just made an excellent point, using some very good sense. Let us have a look at those arrows."

Rory was appeased with Darcy's idea of viewing the targets. He was shocked at the accuracy and attempted to explain to Darcy just how rare a thing it is to find a perfect archer. He also expressed agreement as to what her looks might be, given her marksmanship.

"Darcy, I must say, you were correct. It is obvious the girl is consumed with archery. Between her shooting practice and driving that phaeton, she would have no thoughts of men."

Turning their mounts back to Rosings, Rory expounded, "Yes, cousin, a girl who spends that kind of time on sports would have no interest in men. There would be no time for courting."

Darcy, looked at his cousin with a big smile. "So, you think her a virgin, then?"

"Aye. And, most likely she shall die so, brother."

I think not, cousin!

The Darcy men met in the library again that night. Fitzwilliam began with many questions concerning his past love life. He asked his father if he should disclose his recent debauchery to any woman he felt he may wish to marry. What about health concerns?

George Darcy thought the question was more than just hypothetical. Remembering that previously, before the recent 'difficulties,' his son had spent large amounts of time in the company of Caroline Bingley, he speculated that she might be the girl in question. He decided to make an attempt to learn the truth of the matter.

"Son, do you now have a particular young lady in mind?"

"Perhaps I may, Father. It would not be one that you are acquainted with, I should say."

This put an end to the fishing for information. He knew his son would tell him about the woman when he was ready. He needed time.

Lord, I shall not try to influence him toward Elizabeth, I desire it to be Elizabeth, but you know what is best for both of them.

Wearing a stunning emerald-green riding skirt and jacket with a winter-white silk blouse, Elizabeth placed her booted foot into the single stirrup of the ladies' side saddle.

Hardly able to sleep for excitement, Elizabeth was happy to be outside. The air was sweet and full of the fragrance of spring flowers. She smiled as she told Marigold of their planned ride.

I wonder what my handsome man shall wear today? I hope a blue jacket to match his beautiful blue eyes. Shall he be clean shaven this morn?

Careful not to appear too eager, she walked Marigold back to the 'dressing room' area from whence they had parted. It was just beginning to be light, and she did not wish to be too far along on the trail so early.

Off in the distance the rhythm of a horse's gallop was heard. Fitzwilliam felt a rush of excitement as he entered the place he had left her just the day before.

Because we ride for pleasure she shall not wear her working clothes. No matter, she shall be beautiful. If she wears green to match her eyes, she likes me. If she wears a bonnet, she wishes to please me. If her boots are—oh! There she is—Ugh! No bonnet, but she does like me, she is wearing green.

"Greetings!" he called out as he took Percival to a walk.

"Good morning," she answered him, "Your timing is perfect. Are you set to start?"

"Yes. I packed a small knapsack with some few provisions." He patted his knapsack.

"As did I. 'Great minds think alike!'" she responded with a quote.

"Shakespeare!" he proclaimed with great aplomb!

"Nay, I am sorry to say—Dabridgcourt Belchier—1618." She corrected him sweetly.

"Are you certain? I seem to have given credit to Shakespeare," he declared.

"Yes. I heard you clearly," she retorted, with a fire building in her eyes.

He turned his head away so she would not see him smile. This is what he wanted. He wanted her to spar with him. He wanted to feel the sharp edge of her sword of a tongue. He enjoyed this feeling of contending with a beautiful woman. No other woman would face him this way and be combative!

"Indeed, Shakespeare!" he restated, officially, as if for the record. "Would you like a moment to think it through?" he cautioned her, "you are in error, you know?"

With these words, he regarded the colour rising on her neck and face. It was a very pretty addition to her natural beauty.

"Nay," she affirmed, smiling. " One who is correct has nothing more to think through!"

"You know, I strongly feel that Will Shakespeare is the author of that quote," he spat.

She shook her head, "'Tis a pity that feeling, even if one is feeling strongly, shall not make it so. Mr. Shakespeare had his time, and granted he wrote much, however, he did not say all that has been said, sir." She smiled upon finishing this thought. She would maintain her mind-set.

Oh, I love this, and it is a pity she is wrong. I shall be magnanimous and allow her to come around to my answer. I shall not wager with a mere woman. 'Tis unfair to her.

As they made their way upon the path at a nice walk, the sun was rising and bathing the countryside with golden streams of light. One beam shone upon her and made her appear luminous. Her classic beauty was incandescent. Her lips especially were moist and full, when she spoke they appeared to reflect the light. He was mesmerized watching them move as she spoke.

"You know," he began, trying to concentrate on their conversation, "I spent a number of years in the study of the Bard, and I have become an expert of sorts on his quotes. In point of fact, while at school, one of our favourite pastimes was actually a drinking game based upon favourite quotes. Someone would produce a quote, and we were to guess the author."

"Brilliant!" she said, mocking him, although he did not understand it to be so. She thought of her father, had he been there he would have caught her meaning.

"Indeed!" he responded, still ignorant of the fact that she was so diverted by his ego.

"And," she questioned, quite seriously, "how did you get along?"

"I am proud to say, undefeated during my entire time," he told her proudly.

"I suppose it was because you applied yourself to practice," she suggested smartly.

"Are you mocking me?" he asked angrily, his own eyes darkening with emotion.

"No, not at all, I was just thinking that the way to proficiency is to practice."

She was making sport of me in some way, I just know it. I shall show no mercy, I shall make a wager with her, and she shall lose. It shall be a good lesson for her.

"Madam, I am so certain, that I would like to make you a small and friendly wager. Are you game? Are you so sure of yourself that you would risk betting with me?"

"Aye. I am certain. Yet to be sure, I should wish to hedge my bet, if I may?"

"A pleasure, what would you like to know?" he asked, earnestly.

"Where did you obtain your education, sir?"

Ah, at last. I shall try to watch her eyes when I tell her.

"Cambridge!" he said proudly.

That shall impress her; she shall ask about my languages and my courses of study!

"Excellent, then. What shall be the prize to the winner?"

She is not impressed. Perhaps she has not heard of Cambridge.

"If I win, you shall teach me to ride standing upon my mount. If you win, and I do emphasize the word 'if'—you shall name your prize, madam."

"A generous offer, Cambridge scholar. Yet, you are expecting to win. 'Tis a wager!"

The sun was now well risen, and they looked at each other with eager eyes. Their eyes were stunning. Together they made a striking pair. Both smiled and felt pleased at the idea of spending the morning together.

"Other than attributing quotes to authors, what do you like to do?" he questioned.

"I enjoy reading. Shall we talk about books? Would that suit you?" she tipped her head and smiled at him.

"Brilliant!" he shouted. " I shall start. What type of books do you read?"

She frowned at him, and then held her lips in a tight line to avoid smiling. She asked directly, "Is that your start? 'Tis not a game of questions, in that you start with the first question. 'Tis but a friendly discussion about books, in that you tell about the book you are reading first. The one who starts tells his book."

Jolly good start, this! Just what I wanted to happen. "I am simply using good manners. You are a lady, you shall tell your book first."

"Forgive me, but I do not understand why I am to be given special consideration in this. Do you think women inferior, or perhaps less well read? My book is smaller, and therefore it shall take less time to remark upon my book?"

He wisely answered, hiding his smile. "No, I am just eager to hear of your likes."

"Very well then, I enjoy history; poetry; and sometimes, just to lighten the day, I read novels. Architecture interests me greatly," she said," but those books are hard to find."

"Aye. What poetry are you reading now?" *Did she say architecture? Nay, it must have been arts and other cultures. I need to listen as she speaks She would not mean architecture.*

"Cowper. And you?"

"Shakespeare's sonnets," he said and smiled at her.

"Oh yes! To brush up on your quotes, I presume?" she teased. But as soon as the words escaped her lips she wished to retract them, for he seemed wounded.

Oh, so you wish to tease me now, fine eyes? Oh yes, very well then...

He feigned that she had hurt his feelings from his previous bragging. He was quiet, but it was all in jest. He wanted to enjoy seeing her think she had done him damage.

"Ahem!" she offered to apologize by saying, "Please do forgive me, I also like the sonnets. I regret that I did not inquire as to your favourite."

Still, he stayed to his tease and answered her not one word. He kept his eyes on the trail.

"Favourite number? Let me guess, eighteen?" she offered, using her own personal favourite.

"Sonnet number forty-two," he finally responded to her question.

Ugh, my least favourite... She lifted herself from her ribs and smelled the fresh sea breeze, and declared, "Ohhh, look at that view! And the fresh smell of the sea breeze. So beautiful."

I do not think he heard me. He does not seem to hear very well. He does miss a good bit I say to him.

"This looks like a good spot to stop for a while if you wish. Our horses can graze on the grass, and we have a good perspective from that rock!" he suggested shyly.

With that, he dismounted. She started to dismount upon a large flat rock. Immediately he met her and reached up to lift her from the saddle. She smiled at him, and their eyes locked for a very long time.

"Thank you—" she whispered nearly into his ear.

One moment after he let go, her right boot slid from the rock, propelling her quickly forward. She began to fall, instinctively putting her hands out in front of her. He quickly stepped in front, encircling her slim waist with his arms. Her hands came to rest firmly pressed against his chest. In seconds, she reached up and put her arms around his neck.

At first, they staggered a bit, then she slid her arms down to place them around his waist, and he lifted his arms higher upon her back. They took on the appearance of two ice skaters, trying to steady one another simply by holding each other. At last, they stilled.

It was an amazing moment. The air itself was charged around them, and they both became fully aware of their mutually hypnotic and very sensual feelings. For several minutes they stood there, locked in such an innocent yet tantalizing embrace. Neither wanted to step away, both wanted time to stand still.

"Thank you even more," she said, yet they did not move.

"My pleasure, are you well?" he continued their embrace.

"Yes," she answered in a whisper, "I cannot remember ever feeling more well than I do at this very moment."

"I would have to say the same thing," he admitted. "I believe I know exactly what you mean."

Both were fully aware of their wildly beating hearts. Each could sense the growing intimacy of the embrace. Each moment brought more desire, greater longing.

"What are you feeling, if a gentleman may ask a lady?"

At this, he felt her tremble. She was breathing with very shallow breaths, and he felt her swallow. He knew very well the meaning of these obvious signs. She, on the other hand, having no experience in the arms of an attractive man, had no idea what had come over her, and she felt troubled.

Pulling her wits about her, she attempted to answer his sincere questions. "Because I always try to say only the truth, I shall tell you. I feel, safe, protected, and welcome," she whispered. It was straight forward and directly to the point. There was no attempt to impress him with a flowery speech, no poetry brought to mind.

"And you?" she asked, redirecting his question. She listened very carefully as he spoke, wanting to remember his every word. She intended to memorize his answer.

"Extremely comfortable—happy—content and also welcome," he whispered. His reply brought a deep sigh from her depths. He could feel her relax. Surrender? That sigh from her soul had a profound effect upon him. She was so open with her feelings. There was no guile in her. So unlike other gentlewomen he had known. He noticed that she could be very sweet and quiet. Gone for the moment was her sauciness and sometimes impertinence. And, in addition, she felt so good. Her size was perfect for him, and he could feel her delectable curves. He smiled. It was so wonderful to hold her in his arms.

This remarkable girl, horsewoman, phaeton-driving and target-shooting archer, and God knows what else, was perfect for him! "I thank you for this," she was saying plainly.

Her shocking innocence and purity, was now eliciting an incredible response in him. One that he did not want her to feel. Reluctantly he began to step away. She caught his arm and begged, "Oh, a moment longer, please?"

Regretting the disappointment he knew he was causing her, he turned toward Percival.

"Come with me," he offered with a very polite voice. Without taking her hand, he took his knapsack down from Percival's saddle and motioned her to follow him.

He led her to the flat face of a large rock and put his wool blanket out for them to sit down together. He then put his arm around her and, to her surprise, drew her across his chest and wrapped his other arm around her shoulder. They sat there silently, watching the sea as a gentle breeze caressed their faces. Sitting side by side, neither of them spoke one word.

They simply watched the sea.

What is she about? I have known women intimately and have never had such an erotic experience as that embrace. God, I want her to be mine. Have I not been in her company for more than eight hours? Is it too soon for love? She is honest to a fault and says what she means. She does not fawn over me. Refreshing. I love her sparing spirit and firm opinions. Her hair smells of lavender and roses, it is so wild and so beautiful from the ride and the breeze. I would love to put my fingers into it and inhale her scents and kiss her head, and her lips and…

There they sat. Two perfect strangers. Two hearts desiring so much more from life and from each other. They sat, happily entwined in each other's arms, yet side by side. Their horses had grazed and were now sleeping in the warm sunshine. She placed her head upon his shoulder. He reached out and took her hand in his. No words were needed for them to communicate what they were experiencing. They felt peace.

Clarification—this is not a romantic novel—I need clarification, what am I about with him? Where am I headed? I, who have a life that feels akin to dancing on the point of a pin!

No home, no employment, and no prospects. I just told him I felt safe and welcome in his arms. No matter. May seven I shall away. I shall never see him again. Best I never see him again, this is so improper. He probably thinks I am unfit.

He broke the spell. "I have some refreshments if you wish. I have wine, some cheese and bread and some fruit. Shall I get it?"

"That sounds wonderful. I have nearly the same, if I can manage to stay upon my two feet whilst I fetch my knapsack." She chuckled softly as she walked toward Marigold.

In a few moments they returned to the blanket and laughed when they saw the same fare. Neither admitted to being a houseguest and at the mercy of their hosts' cooks. The sun was warming and the wine relaxing. The sea was calm, the weather beautiful. Their picnic was perfect. They were beginning to feel as if they had known each other for years, rather than hours.

"May I ask a question?" she wondered, as he lifted his head up to her. He had just finished eating and was relaxed, lying upon his stomach, holding his head up with his hands, supported by leaning on his elbows. He had been watching the horses, and her words startled him.

"Certainly, if my answer does not cause you anger and distress," he teased, smiling.

"Humph!" she smiled back at him. "Does it bother you that society's rules would condemn us for our illicit behaviour? May I be so bold as to say, that if it does not give me guilt, then it is permitted by God? Is it not He who gives us power to convict us of our own sins?" she concluded with a slight frown on her brow.

"My, you are a theologian, are you not?" he said, sounding surprised at the depth of this sincere question. He thought about the question, but he did not know the answer. "I would not disagree with you, but then I know very little of these deep questions. Do you ponder such things often?" he asked with sincerity.

"Nay. Do you think I often see men alone on private picnics and sit with my arms about them upon a private rock, in front of a very silent and private sea, and in the company of two equine chaperones?" she asked him.

Somewhat sorry that she felt he was meaning to decry her behaviour or her question, he rushed on to defend her character. He wanted to respect her intellect as well. "No, I dare say, I know you do not. I think I simply wondered your thoughts on religion."

"Oh." She smiled at him, and he felt weak and suddenly did not want to talk of God or the church anymore.

He quietly asked her, "Was I the first man?"

"Heavens, yes! Until yesterday morn, I have not even so much as stood still in so close a company of a man who was not my relative. Save for dancing a set with a gentleman, and that is, as you know, very limited standing, or touching."

"Do I embarrass you with all my inquiries?" she asked with such innocence that he had to smile at her as he answered that he did not mind and in fact, he enjoyed her questions.

"There is something about you that makes me feel I have known you for such a long time," she said, as if just stating a fact. There were no implications and no teasing or playing of games as he was accustomed to when talking with women. She did not trifle.

"I was the first man to embrace you?" he asked again, as if proud of what her answer would be and wanted to hear her affirm it once more. He looked deeply into her beautiful green eyes. They were filled with peace.

"Aye. But, I shall not ask the same of you," she said, then she looked down. Her thick lashes rested upon her cheeks, shielding her expressive eyes from him, as though they wished him not to read their secrets.

"I do not wish to anger you, nor embarrass you," he spoke his response very slowly.

"Thank you, for we know what I do when THAT happens," she said, laughing at herself.

"Yes, indeed," he also laughed. "And, I shall not wish to see that demonstration again! You seem such an innocent young girl, and yet, I know you are fully grown. You are, petite?" he asked as he turned onto his side, propping himself up on one elbow.

"*Oui!*" she smiled.

"So, not a child, but innocent? Do not be embarrassed, I cannot tell you how, but I know you are an honourable maiden. You are so beautiful and yet, no suitors? No one has made you an offer that you have accepted? You are obviously accomplished, and does that take your time and interest in that you have not been married as yet?" he asked, nearly blushing. He had never before questioned any woman, thusly.

"My, what a varied question, or should I say questions, but I understand what you are asking me. No, I have not accepted a proposal. Yes, unfortunately I have had one, and I wish never to discuss it, as it makes me ill-tempered when I even think of him! Of them!" she spouted, becoming upset with the reminder of her mother's actions.

"Yes, I spend large amounts of time in study and other pursuits. No, I do not seek the attentions of men." Here she stopped and looked at him in a way he had never seen her look. She acted as though there was more to add, but nothing more was provided.

"I want to know more, but I shall not invade your privacy," he said. "I have already done that thrice, I am afraid to tell you." At this statement, his face turned red!

"Excuse me?" she asked in amazement. "Pray, explain yourself."

"Well, the one sin you know about, that was yesterday, watching you ride."

At the same moment, unbeknownst to one another, they each had the very same thought. *Good Lord, was it only yesterday? I feel we have known each other much longer.*

Could it really be only four and twenty hours of their acquaintance? To both, the duration seemed much longer, months? Years?

He continued his confession, with a second transgression. "The evening before last, I was on a leisure walk with Percival, and we took a narrow country path, just big enough for, say a little phaeton and pony?" As he said this, he watched her face. She coloured, and he saw a storm in her eyes. He feared the worst. He looked down and away from her and waited.

She sat straight up. Anger arose in her face. She looked at him in unbelief and cried, "You saw?"

Putting one finger across her sweet lips to still them, he held it there and said quietly, "Now, please do not say something that shall take you a long time to recover from your ire. Yes, I saw, but I did not have any possible way of knowing it was you. You, madam, drove like a bat suddenly released from a cave! Do you crave speed? You shot your arrows as swiftly as possible. In fact, that is what I watched. I checked two of your targets after you drove away.

"I only followed for two. One, when you got out of the vehicle to shoot, and the other whilst standing upon the phaeton.

"Again yesterday," he was speaking rapidly now, "I and my cousin observed you whilst on the same route. I recognised you yesterday and knew it was you. There I have confessed my sins, and now I ask for your forgiveness. I shall tell no one."

"Very well, then. That puts an end to it. I was simply looking for a way to add some excitement to my target practice." They both laughed.

He nodded his head in understanding and added, "I am glad you are an expert shot; it may serve you well someday."

Too soon, it was time to leave the enchantment. The horses were ready to go, and she wanted a run. The ground was flat and obliging. Run they did. They managed to stay side by side.

Glancing back and forth, neither could remember having a better time riding in company.

Returning to her 'dressing room' area, once again they parted. She indicated that she could not get away in the morning but offered a walk in the early afternoon. He agreed and suggested meeting at the same place. They smiled at one another, regretting their parting, and then went their separate ways, back to their lives.

Upon my word, we still did not exchange names! Certainly it must be fate. I wish I knew what dear Jane would say. "Lizzy," she might say, "everything works out for the best. It is for the best that you do not know his name, nor he yours!"

"Percival, we did it again! Another meeting with that beauty and still no name! Bollocks! I want her to know my name. What say you, Percival?"

Upon his return to Rosings, Fitzwilliam saw his cousin Rory standing outside the front door. He appeared to be hiding.

Waving his hand, he got the colonel's attention. "What in blazes are you doing outside the door? I would like to think you were waiting for me, but I know better."

"I am hiding, cousin! Have you met that, that, little man?" Rory asked.

"Apparently not, I have no idea to whom you refer. What little man?"

"There is a decidedly annoying cleric inside. Collins by name. He is new and insufferable!"

Colonel Fitzwilliam had little tolerance for obsequious men. He preferred men who were audacious, bold, and brave.

"Would Aunt Catherine have any other kind, cousin?" Darcy reminded him. "She would have no one that would not venerate her, would she? Let us go and see how many times he bows to her, shall we?"

"Cousin, it is not good to make sport. He is a clergyman with the Church of England."

"Yes, Rory, but there is port inside. Shall we go quietly into the library and partake?"

Inside the library Fitzwilliam's eyes searched the books thoughtfully. "I have a need to check a quote," he muttered.

Rory served the port. "Cousin, you seem in good humour today."

"No more than ever," Fitzwilliam answered, not taking his eyes off the books.

"Then why the big smile?"

"Happy to see you, cousin." He took a drink, set his glass down, and stretched out his long legs. Closing his eyes, he crossed his arms, in front of his chest, remembering how it felt to hold her. He could still feel her curves and smell the lavender and roses. Opening his eyes, he looked at Rory and asked, "Cousin, tell me. Have you ever loved a virgin?"

"Well, I do not like to brag," Rory started, "but of course. Several I should think." The colonel lifted his head upward and to the left, as if trying to count the number.

"No, Rory, that is not what I am asking. I am asking if you have ever fallen in love with one. Perhaps back in school, or your early army days?"

"Cousin," Rory said, "I am proud to tell you that I have loved no woman. It is a sign of weakness. I have seen it make perfectly sensible men lose their minds. Love? No, virgin or otherwise." He was quiet a moment, and then inquired, "Why on earth do you ask, Darcy?"

"Oh, just trying to make out your character, cousin." Fitzwilliam answered him simply, "You could say, I am sketching you, I suppose."

"Darcy, I understood you better when I collected you from your club, and you were completely in your cups." Rory said, amazed. "What a question!"

Darcy closed his eyes again, crossed his arms in front of his chest, and once more remembered how good it felt to have her arms wrapped around him. He had held her hand; it was so soft and small. She did not seem to want anything more. Stunning! Most shocking how an act of such innocence would bring him such desire. It was positively erotic in the highest sense. Making him desire her, even beyond the moment, beyond the pleasure of having her, right there on that rock. An experienced woman would not enjoy his closeness without showing her arousal and demanding more from him. Here was a girl who had never even had her hand held before, he could tell that for certain. She did not flinch, but he knew it was a new experience.

She told me I made her feel safe, protected, and welcome in my arms. I want to do that for her. Even without knowing her name. Does it matter? I want to take care of her.

What of her family, her connections, her fortune? All these things matter to a man of my class, but is not love more important? Do I love her? Is it possible to love her so soon after…well, not meeting her, for we truly have never been introduced. So soon after discovering her?

Meeting his father again after dinner, Fitzwilliam asked for help with the author of the quote. George Darcy gave the correct answer: Dabridgecourt Belchier.

With that, their nightly meeting commenced upon a gloomy note. Fitzwilliam hated losing. Climbing the stairs at midnight, he passed Rory. The two agreed to ride in the early morning. *We shall ride, cousin, and stay out of that glade.*

⚜

Just before noon Elizabeth finished her bath and put on her pale blue gown. She pulled on her half boots and called for the maid.

Although the girl had no experience as a ladies' maid, Elizabeth asked her to help with a loose braid. It turned out well, and the maid tied a pale blue ribbon on to secure its weight.

Passing through the halls, she said a cheery greeting to her grandpapa. It was just about time to meet her friend. *Our third meeting and still no names. I rather like it, perhaps it is for the best. I away May seven. His life is here…yes, it is for the best.*

Entering their meeting place, she saw his long legs striding toward her. He was handsome in buckskin breeches, brown boots and a white shirt, blue plaid waistcoat, and blue jacket. His hair was attractively windblown. She thought him very fetching.

"Hullo," he waved and smiled.

"Greetings! It is good to see you again. Did you have a pleasant morning?"

"Quite pleasant, I thank you. It would seem I lost the wager, but then, you knew that, did you not?"

"Aye. 'Tis character building, I dare say. An opportunity for growth?"

"Dabridgecourt Belchier!" they said in unison. Then they laughed.

She delicately arched her eyebrows and asked, "And now, may I name my prize?"

Oh God, let her ask for a kiss, or another lengthy embrace or—

"Have you realised that this is our third visit, and we do not know each other's names?" she was saying, "I blame it on propriety. We have been too conditioned to the social norms in which a third party performs a formal introduction. I am quite ashamed of myself for falling in line, rather like a lemming."

"Yes," he agreed. "Somehow I forgot to introduce myself and inquire for your name. I do hope you shall forgive me."

"I feel I should tell you that I am merely a visitor in Kent," she stated rapidly. She did not want him to interrupt her and tell his name. She wanted to forego that intelligence.

"As am I!" he declared with his eyes shining. He could hardly wait to hear her say her desire for a prize.

"Then, knowing that, makes my prize even better for both of us. My prize is this, and I hope I do not disappoint you with what I shall request," she looked into his eyes, "because, I away May seven, perhaps it is best that we never know each other's name.

"Please do try to see it my way. You can forever be the most handsome man who shall ever make me feel welcome. Therefore, I shall call you, 'Handsome Man,' and I shall simply be 'Horsewoman.'"

Bloody hell, my name would impress her. Now I cannot tell her who I am?

As she said this, she noticed him looking very upset, so she quickly added, "Without names, we are also without expectations. For example, you need not fear that I shall chase you, seeking to trap you as a husband. And, in addition, I shall have no worries that you are after my fortune!"

He laughed, although his face continued to wear a frown.

Suddenly she stopped on the path, turned, and dazed him by searching deeply into his blue eyes. She seemed to be penetrating his very soul. Silently, she sought his emotion. Now he, just as suddenly, was studiously reading her face. Was she hiding a sly smile? What was this? How he wanted to know her name, and her to know his.

Why this downturn? I need to impress her with the Darcy name.

She quickly continued before he could speak, "Without knowing names, we can be completely honest with one another. For example, I can tell you one thing openly, decorum disgusts me!" Her eyes flashed. "Yes! I have said it. I detest being dictated to by propriety! And, this is most important. Please note this fact about me: I abhor a palfrey and its insulting, ambling gait!"

He threw his head back and laughed for some time. She added her melodic laugh. "I see what you mean. It shall be freeing. However, I do most ardently object to my calling you 'Horsewoman.' If I am to be 'Handsome Man,' I shall call you my 'Goddess of Horses!'"

She laughed at that, curtseyed and proclaimed, "I thank you, sir, and that is absolutely my last disagreeable curtsey!" Pleased with herself and feeling giddy, she stopped once again.

She tilted her head and proclaimed with great dramatic effect: "To honour you, Handsome Man, I would much rather boldly take your hands in mine thusly—" she took both his hands in hers immediately and squeezed them for emphasis.

"Is that not better than a curtsey?" she asked.

"Indeed!" He laughed again. "Yes! Well done!"

"While enjoying this liberating experience," she added, "I should also wish to disclose that I absolutely detest bonnets, hats, and feathers worn in the hair!"

"Brilliant! Shall we outlaw them entirely?" he offered.

"Oh," she added, "and if I wish to write a letter to a gentleman, I, a single gentlewoman, shall do so!"

She looked at him and saw he was lost in thought. "Ahem! 'Tis your turn, I believe, or perchance you already miss the tedious adherence to the demands of decorum and propriety?"

"No." he said simply. "I just found myself hating the thought of May seven."

She moved around to the front of him on the path. Her eyes were fixed upon his, her sensual mouth slightly parted.

"That is the best thing anyone ever said to me," she looked upset and unhappy.

"If you would forgive me this transgression—may we break the rules and kiss each other?" he suggested, hopefully.

She nodded and smiled, "I am in agreement, yet I should like to establish the rules for the kiss."

"Is this to be a 'privileged kiss'?" she inquired, "the type serious lovers enjoy, or more a sudden and sweetly spontaneous, natural, born of the moment kiss?"

"'Tis," he stated," a mutually agreed upon, prior to the kiss, type of kiss. With or without an embrace. Your option, Goddess of Horses."

"As you have already observed, I do have quite a fondness for embraces, provided they are quite lengthy and one is held firmly enough to appreciate being held." She smiled.

"Yes, I must say, I have a newly acquired affinity for those as well. May I please consider my options?" His eyes sparkled as he saw the opportunity of tasting those luscious, delicious-looking lips, at last. Maintaining a serious expression, he continued, "I have given thoughtful consideration and have decided that I can deny you nothing, Goddess of Horses."

Suddenly shy, she smiled at him and stepped forward, straightening to her full height. She reached out and placed her hands upon his chest. Not expecting that, he felt a burning heat where she touched him. He closed his eyes nervously and slipped his arms around her.

He lowered his lips to hers, and then, halting there, he kept his lips just out of her reach. She encircled her arms around his waist. "How does this feel?" he asked her.

"Better than yesterday, and I did not think that possible. In all honesty, I could do this more than just once a day," she murmured.

"Please allow me to still your mouth with a kiss," he whispered with his voice trailing off.

She signed softly. Tension building, her knees went weak, and he was obliged to hold her up.

Their lips met tenderly, gently, and very lightly. In fact, she was not at all certain that they were touching. His lips moved unhurriedly over hers, and as lightly as a feather. She moaned.

Without planning it, he lifted his hand to her face and stroked her cheek. She ran her fingers through his hair. Their movements were light and very gentle, their lips sweetly caressing each other. He felt her tremble, and very slowly he lifted his head away from her. Using one hand, he gently pulled her head against his chest and was surprised to feel tears upon her cheeks.

"Are you well, Goddess of Horses?"

"I hardly know."

"Why are you sad? Am I so terrible at this tender expression of affection?"

"Nay. You are most wonderful," she answered him softly.

"Well, what then?"

"'Tis not for you to know," she whispered. "Please do not ask me. Remember what happens when I am embarrassed."

"Yes, but is there anything I can do?"

"Please just hold me like this. I so like the feeling of being safe, protected, and welcome."

"May I see you tomorrow? Perhaps for an early ride?" he begged.

"Yes," she answered him, with just one syllable.

"I shall look forward to it, my Goddess of Horses. About this kiss, did you not like it?"

"I liked it too much, Handsome Man."

"How so?"

"I have always told myself, I would kiss none but the man I shall marry. But, May seven I shall away. We are not promised tomorrow. Because neither of us perform to propriety, I could not miss this opportunity. The tears, however, are still private."

Intending to comfort her, he pulled her tighter to his chest. A sweet feeling of joy flooded over them. And, astonishingly, they indulged once more in a kiss. This kiss betrayed a deep longing in both, as he gently brushed her lips with his, and slowly stroked her jawline. His moist lips softly caressed hers. She closed her eyes, and he slightly opened his mouth. She moaned deeply as she felt his soft tongue gently touching her lips. The feel of his velvety tongue moving slowly just inside her sweet mouth was more pleasing to her than the tempting elegance of melting chocolate. Yielding to an impulse, she relaxed her body into his, and began gently touching the tip of his tongue with hers. This accepting gesture ignited a flame of passion in him.

He tightened his hold on her and deepened his kiss. All of which, she welcomed. She could not breathe, and did not care. She was lost to all the world, except his tender embrace and this kiss, which had captured her heart and soul. For the first time in her life, she felt a deep passionate affection and longing for a man. This man, this stranger…

Both felt a desire, an amorous fancy, and a mounting strong sexual need for the other. Love? It was an enthusiastic liking, a mutual need to obtain the affections of the other. A need to gain an intense and exclusive relationship with the other. A desire to give affection and to please the other. A need to be attached to the other. Love.

Shaking, she placed her hands back upon his chest and slowly pulled away from him. Breathing hard, with her chest heaving, she felt her heart racing. Her lips were burning.

"Oh, my," she said, looking into his eyes. "So, *that* is a kiss?"

"Yes, it is," he whispered slowly. He, himself needed to recover.

"I suppose, to a man of the world, it was just a kiss, one, in say thousands?"

"Umm, what are you asking of me, Goddess of Horses?"

"I simply need you to rate the second kiss, with the probable millions you have had."

"I do not know," he searched her eyes. Suddenly he wanted to protect her. He wanted her to stop talking. She hunched her shoulders somewhat and suggested, "For instance, is it insignificant, such as one glass of water compared to another?" Nervously, she bit her bottom lip.

It was more than he could stand. He wanted to comfort her. He could sense her pain, but he could not define it, and she would not reveal it to him. Taking her hands in his, a look of adoration flowed from him. "Our kiss—or, do you wish me to say, your kiss—is the finest of wines, and all others I have had were stale water." He said this hoping to bring her comfort. He failed.

"Oh," was her only response.

"My Goddess of Horses, did it escape your attention that I was overcome with emotion? I tried to keep our initial kiss chaste, realising it to be your first. But, it became more intense than I intended. In our second kiss, my thirst for you over powered my senses.

"I declared myself in that second kiss, Goddess of Horses. What perchance do you think I was saying to you and to myself?

"Little Miss Goddess of Horses! Are you a blind, girl? Can you not see what you are doing to me? I have never lost a bet to a girl. In fact, I have never wagered with a girl before you!

"You bested me in knowing a quote. No one does that! You ride better than I, and I pride myself on being an excellent horseman. You called me on my superiority and told me when I was overpowering you that I was protecting myself. Protecting myself? No one talks to me like that, ever! You are honest to a fault. You actually told me what my embrace meant to you, then, you asked me to hold you longer! And you felt so good! Your green eyes darken in your passion, in which you could easily be lost, yet you trust me.

"You impaired my hopes by not telling me your name, then you crushed me by not asking mine! I cannot take my eyes off you; you move with a sense of elegance. You are well read. You loath vacuous talkers. You are modest, punctual, and thoughtful of others.

"You face an uncertain future, as we all do, with realism, and even though I suspect you are feeling somewhat fearful, you shall face it, whatever it may bring. I enjoy nothing better than having you spar with me, and I cannot wait to see you again, even before we have parted.

"You, phaeton-driving archer, modiste of your own riding clothes, you dazzle and amaze me. Heaven only knows what other things you do well, and I should only hope to someday discover them. When we are apart, I can think only of you. I allow the world to go on without me.

"I want only to keep you safe, protected, and feeling welcome. I have no pity on the man who marries you, in that you just gave me your first two kisses. I shall always treasure the memory of them.

"You call me a man of the world? Little Miss Goddess of Horses, I fear the first of June. I scarcely know what day it is, and I care not. I want only to see you, to listen to whatever it is you wish to say to me. I love to watch you ride in your breeches and linen shirt. My day begins when I am with you, and ends the moment we part. I am, madam, a lost puppy!"

"I have always loved puppies," she said quietly.

Later that evening the Darcy men were holding their nightly conference in the Rosings library. Fitzwilliam had a question for his father.

"Father, I would like to ask a personal question, if I may? You may chose not to answer, and I shall understand."

"Ask anything, son."

"Did you fall in love with mother immediately? That is to say, when did you know you loved her and wanted to spend your lives together?"

Mr. Darcy sighed and lowered his eyes, thinking of Anne. "Yes, I believe I knew I loved her from the first moments I met her. She was right for me. Does that make sense to you?"

"Yes. You had a love match. I know as a Fitzwilliam, she brought great wealth, and her influence was exceedingly powerful, was it not?"

"Yes. I would agree on both points. My advice to you, son, would be to marry for love. You have great wealth, and an exceedingly powerful influence. If you care not about a match with a peer of the realm, then look for love, with the right woman, of course."

Fitzwilliam changed the subject, and they concluded early. Entering his rooms at midnight, he discovered a message on his bed. He knew this writing well. It was the careful hand of Georgiana. Smiling broadly, he tore open her message:

Rosings Park, Kent

7 April 1803

Dearest Brother,

I miss you. As you told me in the carriage, you are much too busy to worry about children's affairs. I would, however, wish to invite you to attend tea with me. Elizabeth and Mrs. Gardiner shall call for me at 2:30 tomorrow. I am most excited and would be very happy to share their wonderful company with you, if you desire to join us. Please let me know if you wish to attend, and I shall send a message to Mrs. Gardiner to tell her that you shall come with me.

Yours With Great Affection,

Georgiana Darcy.

He sat down and penned regrets.
She is an adorable sister, but I care not for her friend!

It would have been difficult to determine which one was more eager to reach the glade. Arriving at the same moment, both were excited to spend time together in the pre-dawn morning.

She was dressed in her breeches and linen shirt, with bare feet, and his heart skipped a beat when he saw her. Upon seeing him, she smiled, noticing the expression of approval upon his face. He was happy to see her in her working clothes.

"Good morn, Handsome Man! Shall we both dismount and be very improper?" He practically jumped from Percival with anticipation. She joined him as they met between their horses.

She gave him a quick hug, and he kissed her cheek. He set his jaw, wishing for much more. He consoled himself by recalling that he enjoyed her breasts being crushed against his chest.

She, sensing his disappointment, hid her grin.

"I know you lost our bet," she called as she stood beside Marigold, "but I thought I would like to teach you a riding trick anyway, if you fancy learning one."

He nodded his agreement and kept his eyes upon her.

"Have you ever performed a rescue mount?" she quizzed. She explained the useful skill, and he was very interested to learn. It was decided that he would ride Marigold to perform this trick.

"Have you ridden without a saddle?" she put the question to him, supposing his answer. Learning that this was his first time, she encouraged him to try. Mounting the mare, he was delighted with the horse's smooth gaits. After a few circles in the glade, she deemed him ready for the rescue mount.

He watched her joy as she told him how to extend his right forearm for her to wrap both hands firmly around. She explained how to approach her and when to lift and swing her up. Finally she deemed him ready to perform the trick.

This felt strangely wonderful to him; she had released herself into her teaching, and it was endearing.

"Now, let us try the rescue," she directed. "Go to a quick walk, please."

Excitedly she stood in the field. When he came close to her, she grabbed the extended forearm, gave a fast skip and jumped while he pulled her up and swung her around behind him. His strength made it easy, and it was delightfully entertaining for both! After several rescues, she pronounced him perfect in his technique.

"This is so wonderful. Thank you so much!" he called back to her, as they galloped around the glade on their final rescue. Noticing that she held onto him very tightly, he began to enjoy the pressing of her breasts onto his back. Her arms stretched around him with both hands holding onto the top of his thighs. Her grip was very close to his groin. He was dazzled by the sensations it was creating in him. He loved the scent of her hair blown by the gentle breeze. She was so sensual; he could not remember ever being so excited by a woman. He felt his amour rising. He thought he could hear her humming, or perhaps it was sighing. Lost in his sensual diversions, he failed to hear, she was speaking.

"I say again, I am coming over in front of you."

"No! Do not do it!" he shouted, wanting to keep her from seeing the evidence of his excitement.

Too late! She had skillfully moved around and was now riding immediately in front of him, with her thighs swung neatly over his. He was hardly able to think. What to do? Too late to worry that she might see the large bulge in his breeches, for her crotch was being firmly pushed into his arousal by the force of the gallop.

Quickly he reined the mare to a walk, and tried to pull himself away from her. She looked straight into his beautiful blue eyes, and lacing her fingers into his hair, she pulled his head forward and kissed his lips! Marigold stopped. His heart was racing wildly. She brushed the sides of his face with the backs of her hands. Then she pulled slowly away, and rested her forehead upon his forehead. Their bodies remained firmly pressed together.

"That is for being an excellent student," she purred. Smoothly she pulled her right leg back and away, then slid gracefully down from her horse. Slowly leading Marigold to Percival, she intentionally turned her head away from him as he dismounted. She wanted to give him space, and some measure of privacy.

He walked around to the far side of his stallion, then looked over the horse's back and smiled at her. He feared it was a foolish-looking grin, but it was the best he could offer. She announced that she had to leave early for she had to go prepare a tea for a very special friend.

"May we meet tomorrow, early morn, at our usual meeting area?" he asked with a shy smile.

"Yes, but may we walk, please?" she wondered.

He agreed, and she turned Marigold as she began to quit the glade. Smiling, she called, "Until then, Handsome Man," and she took off at a dead run!

God, what a woman! I am shaking. I could not have fantasized about anything that exciting. What torture. Her lack of experience is killing me. How can I forget the feel of her, and the two of us on a moving horse! Help me Lord, I think she is almost too much for me. Of course, if I had the privileges of a husband…I must find a way to make her mine. Who is she? Answering that question is the place to start!

Georgiana reached the front door of Rosings just as the carriage arrived. Her friends were on time, and a happy Georgie boarded. Elizabeth and Mrs. Gardiner greeted her warmly. As the carriage door was closing, Fitzwilliam came around the corner of the house.

As he smiled at the sight of his excited sister embarking upon her tea party trip, two images filled his eyes. One was the Claverstone Crest on the door, the other, to his complete bewilderment, was his Goddess of Horses riding inside the carriage! A beautiful young woman, her spicy auburn hair swept up in an elegant French twist, and looking exquisite in a bright ruby-red gown. She smiled at Georgiana and said something that made his sister laugh loudly. He was stunned! Elizabeth Bennet? He squinted and tried to get a better look. His mind entered a dense fog.

Could it really be? She said she was preparing tea for a very special friend. The very same Elizabeth Bennet I said I loathed meeting and so carefully avoided for months! Fool! I, the king of fools! My very own Goddess of Horses, so well-known to my family. Sharing books, music and, oh, no! Surely she would not share secrets with a little girl? No! She would not, but what might a dear little sister tell of her brother, or my father say of his son?

He laughed aloud. He whistled, and he had never before whistled! He enjoyed it! He was so happy he felt he could kiss Rory, or even Aunt Catherine! Taking the steps two at a time, he dashed inside. His father would be the first to know! He was in love with Elizabeth Bennet, deeply in love! He wanted to shout! He loved Elizabeth Bennet, most ardently!

Entering his aunt's reception room, he heard his father's voice. George Darcy was angry. Very angry. As he listened, he could hear two voices that were unknown to him. Taking a place in the back of the room, he watched and listened.

"I am afraid, sir, that I shall need you to repeat that story." His father was questioning the man, "Please start at the beginning. I do not want to miss one part."

Recognising the cleric, Collins, from the night before, Fitzwilliam wondered how the man had managed to make George Darcy more angry than his son had ever witnessed.

"Ahem, I, ah, Mr. Darcy, may I say, sir, that I did not expect such a celebrated gentleman—"

"Collins! I demand you repeat the story I heard you telling my sister just now."

"As you wish, Mr. Darcy. I was sharing a letter I have recently received from the esteemed wife of Mr. Thomas Bennet, from whom I am to inherit an estate in Herefordshire. She tells me her second daughter by birth has gone mad, and due to that unfortunate fact, she had gone wild. Miss Elizabeth Bennet has been taken by relatives for evaluation. Perhaps she shall be installed at Bedlum. Now I—"

Fitzwilliam wanted to rush in and pulverize the man. Instead, he held his peace and stood quietly to listen to his father's examination.

"Mr. Collins, have you any idea what you are talking about?"

"Well, indeed, yes—"

"Sir! I inform you that you owe my sister, Lady Catherine, a profound apology. Thanks be to God that I overheard you and stopped your damaging mouth! I tell you, sir, that Miss Bennet is a close personal friend of my own daughter, Georgiana. Miss Bennet has only just now arrived in Lord Claverstone's carriage to escort my daughter to tea!"

George looked as though he could harm the cleric. Fighting his anger and disgust, he continued, "Answer my questions, sir. Did you go to the Bennet estate with the idea of marrying one of the five daughters? And did you single out Miss Elizabeth of the five?"

"I did, but you see, it had all been arranged by Mrs. Bennet who assured me that the girl would accept me, gladly."

Of course you wanted my Goddess of Horses out of the five. You earth-vexing boar-pig. Fitzwilliam could scarcely maintain his place and hold his tongue and temper.

"Mr. Collins, you were improper, sir, at the very least. It fell to you, to be required to ask her hand of Mr. Bennet; he is the master of the estate and the household. He is the father! Insufferable!"

Mr. Darcy narrowed his gaze, "You are a miserable coward. You should be very thankful it is against the law, or I would call you out as a cad and an improper coward. For so you are, to use your leverage with the entail to procure a beautiful woman to wed. It would give me great pleasure to run you through, sir!"

"OH!" an unfamiliar female voice shrieked.

Mr. Darcy looked at the corner of the sofa and saw Mrs. Collins. In his anger, he had forgotten she was in the room. Bowing to her, he said, "My dear Mrs. Collins, forgive me. I quite forgot your presence. Your delicate ears should not be forced to hear any of this conversation. May I offer my son, Fitzwilliam, to escort you to your home, please."

At this invitation, she rose, as if numb, and took Fitzwilliam's arm, and quietly the two quitted the house. They did not know, but each of them held Elizabeth Bennet in high esteem.

Ending the conversation, Mr. Collins agreed to Mr. Darcy's demands that he write letters of apology and confession of his conduct and commission of his sins. Recipients of these were to be Mr. Bennet, Miss Elizabeth Bennet, Lady Catherine de Bourgh, and any others to whom he might have repeated slander and false witness against Miss Bennet.

Fitzwilliam nearly raced back into the library. He was most eager to tell about his relationship with Elizabeth and to hear all that he missed as he escorted Mrs. Collins home.

"Father, I cannot wait another moment to tell you that I have met Elizabeth Bennet, and we are in love. I know, you must be thinking it has been too few days, and I would agree, under usual circumstances. Father, our acquaintance has been most unusual." Fitzwilliam then told all that he could recall to his father. He praised the man for his treatment of Mr. Collins and thanked him for his defense of Elizabeth!

Mr. Darcy was thrilled and thankful to God! He invited Fitzwilliam to listen to his unusual story of Elizabeth and the Gardiners, starting with his prayers, and the meeting in the bookstore. It touched Fitzwilliam's heart to hear how God had heard and answered his father's prayers, especially when he recalled that he was determined not to meet the girl in London.

Lastly, George Darcy told his son of the story Mr. Gardiner had shared about Elizabeth's early life. He related Mrs. Bennet's shunning of Elizabeth upon the girl's refusal of Collins.

"Father, upon our very first encounter, I felt she would be my wife. I have had flashes of the two of us at Pemberly. Now that I know her history, I know she shall be such a help to me in all things about the estate. This may shock you, but even without knowing her name, I was going to propose to her. Oh, what a fool I have been, had I only met her months ago!"

Mr. Darcy's eyes grew wide as he listened, and he held his lips tightly together to keep from laughing for the pure joy of this news!

Suddenly emotional, Fitzwilliam shifted in his chair. He was on the verge of tears. "Advise me, Father, do I tell her all that I have been doing?" He stood now, and began to pace the room.

"Do you think it possible I have contracted a disease that I might pass on to her? And, what of my confession? Do I tell her all I have done? Shall she ask me? She is intelligent and intuitive. She may surmise my past. She is scrupulously honest, and shall demand the same of me. If I lie to her, it shall destroy our relationship. Please tell me what to do; what you would do?"

Standing to his feet, George Darcy put his hand on his son's shoulder. "You shall have some difficult times, I fear. I can only offer you this, stay in front of trouble. Be honest and treat her as you would wish her to treat you. If she asks you, son, tell her, and never lie to her."

Chapter 6

"Sometimes a healthy dose of impertinence is required to allow persuasiveness to achieve the desired effect."

-Anonymous

Arriving at the agreed upon location, Fitzwilliam leaned against a large ash tree. It was just beginning to show its green leaves. Somehow it encouraged him with the promise of new life and starting over, fresh and clean.

His wait was brief. As he watched, she approached through the early mist. The sun was just about to rise in triumph. She looked lovely in her yellow gown. Her half boots were just visible under her skirt as she walked. Her gait was strong and determined. Elizabeth did not stroll. She moved like someone with a goal and destination in view.

Stepping away from the ash, he spoke, "Good morning, my Goddess of Horses! What is your pleasure for our walk today? You are so elegantly adorned; we should be riding in a carriage to spare the hem of your gown."

"Handsome Man, good morrow. I thank you, but I dare say, no mud shall trouble me. You certainly look well, very rested and quite relaxed. Either you have spent more hours in sweet slumber or you have found the key to happiness and shall use it to unlock all the mysteries of your future. Upon my word, you appear quite worry free!"

"Indeed! You are amazingly correct on both assumptions. Yes, my slumber was very sweet, because just yesterday, was I given a heavenly key!"

"Pray," she urged, studying him thoughtfully, "do tell me, what is this heavenly key that assures your future peace and happiness?"

"'Tis a gift that gives me power to answer riddles and questions. I have been granted one guess, my Goddess." He bowed as he supplied the intelligence.

"For what purpose shall you use it, Handsome Man?" she inquired dramatically, placing one hand over her heart.

"On this you must advise me, my Goddess of Horses."

"Let it be as you desire, Handsome Man. What advice may I offer you?"

"'Tis akin to the riddle of *Pericles, Prince of Tyre*; a bride was offered for the correct answer to the king's riddle, or death to the one who answers wrongly."

"Aye—" she spoke, somewhat reverently.

"You judge, Goddess. Shall I solve a puzzle I have been at for several days?"

"Speak plainly, Handsome Man, so that I may understand." She gazed into his blue eyes, which were now darkened with emotion.

"Plainly stated, you, Goddess, are at once the puzzle and the prize. What say you to that?"

Beginning to realise he wished to guess her name, she fought back tears. She did not know what to expect. She felt herself begin to blush as she considered what she needed to say.

"Sir, I do not have the pleasure of knowing what to say to you. Shall your desire be to unlock the secret of my name? If you fail, how then should that be death to you? Yet, if you succeed, shall it be your wish to wed?" Casting her eyes down, she bit her lower lip.

"My Goddess of Horses, you are so very correct. I should desire to wed this very day, yet, if I fail, then I shall die. I shall find life without you to be the same as death.

"May I guess your name, and shall you be my wife, if I am correct?" he asked trembling, for he was very nervous.

She did not expect this turn of events. Unsure of herself, she began to examine her boots, as his gaze became too intense. "Handsome Man, if I say yes to your drama, and you are correct in your guess, is that, indeed, meant to be a yes to your proposal?"

Fearing she thought it to be a jest, he took her hands. He had to make her understand that this was a real proposal of marriage. "Say yes to my drama. I wish never to be parted from you."

Slowly he turned each hand palm upward and kissed them. Leaning closer to her, he smiled and held her eyes. Her heart beat wildly, and her eyes nearly brimmed over with tears.

"Sweetest and most intuitive Goddess of Horses, I wish to wed quickly, and not to delay our honeymoon. No doubt, there would be many wonderful embraces and kisses to be enjoyed."

He slid his arms around her waist and pulled her so close that she could feel his breath on her face. The passion in his eyes was not to be mistaken. His voice, now a whisper—"Shall I tell my Goddess of Horses what is written in her heart, for I see it in her eyes. Those green eyes, which are now darkened in her passion, tell me that she desires the one she knows as Handsome Man to speak her name aloud. Shall he?"

Tears were falling from her eyes. She began shivering, "Very well then, yes! Take your one and only chance and guess my name. Risk it all for me." She closed her eyes and said softly, "I pray your tongue finds the right name, Handsome Man."

Gently placing his fingers along her jawline, studying her lovely face, he took his time, wishing to remember forever the tender expression she wore. Her brow furrowed. She slowly began to chew her bottom lip. Her breathing was shallow, and her eyes bore a soulful expression. Tenderly he placed one arm around her waist, and the other behind her head. He bent down, just until his lips lightly rested upon hers. Very slowly, he whispered, "My Goddess, your true name is Elizabeth Bennet." So saying, he kissed her, briefly, tenderly.

There was a reverence in his tone and manner that captured her heart. She gasped. Her eye lashes fluttered rapidly, and it was evident that she could not speak for a moment. Upon her face could be seen the evidence of a deep peace and joy.

The sun was just now risen, and her colour was also rising with a deep blush spreading from her neck to her scalp. Her appearance had never been more beautiful.

At length, she exhaled—she looked up at him, and holding back her tears she murmured, "And you, my Handsome Man? Are you then, Fitzwilliam Darcy?" It was her best guess. She waited.

He smiled, silently. He locked his blue eyes upon hers. Without warning, he picked her up in his arms and spun her around and around. He laughed and demanded she say his name, again and again.

She, laughing and crying at once, answered, saying, "Fitzwilliam Darcy!" over and over again. He stopped turning and kissed her. Firmly at first, then gently, their joy became their private world. When he set her feet upon the ground again, he looked into her eyes.

"Oh, my love," he said, brushing her tears from her cheeks, "I was so hurt when you did not wish to know my name! I thought I might not survive. It is music to my ears to hear it spoken from your lovely lips. I shall always love to hear you say my name." Wrapping his arms around her, he kissed the top of her head.

"When did you learn? How did you discover my name? Oh, Fitzwilliam, I am so stunned, and so very happy, my love."

"Yesterday, when you and your Aunt Gardiner came to call for Georgiana, I saw you in the carriage You were smiling at her and looking so beautiful in your red gown. Shall you allow me to tell you that I love you, most ardently, Elizabeth Bennet? It has been only a few days, yet I know it is meant to be!"

"Yes, I do love you, strange as it may sound for having such a short opportunity to make out your character. You see, we have spent scant hours together, yet your father and Georgiana have revealed so much about who you are. I have learned of you for four months."

He looked embarrassed and studied his boots for a few moments before he spoke. *Bollards-here it is, I cannot tell her I detested the whole idea of her. I avoided her like the plague and even ridiculed her letter to Georgiana. Words. I need words she shall believe and sentiments that shall not hurt her nor sully me.*

"Yes," he said, "and I have laboured under several errors about you. First, I thought you to be one of the Ton, on a hunt for a husband. Next, I thought you did not have an interest in meeting me, as neither Father nor Georgie tried to introduce us. They both avoided any mention of wanting us to meet. Lastly, I believed you to be a child, about Georgie's age." She laughed at this last confession.

"I shall always be thankful that our lives touched on our own, not as Fitzwilliam meeting Elizabeth. I would have fallen in love with you either way, but to meet as we did! My, shamefully peeping at you and desiring you. You, calling me down on my pride and ego, and my lack of manners!

"For me, it was love, respect and admiration, and it is growing, Elizabeth! I was so in love with you from the first moment I saw you.

You dared to challenge me; you spoke to me as I needed to be spoken to, directly, harshly, and without flattery. You had no idea of my wealth, nor my holdings, and I got the sense that you simply did not care about such things." He rushed on, with so much that he wanted her to know. "Elizabeth, you have made me so very happy.

"You said yes, you shall marry me!"

Getting down on one knee, he asked her again, just so they could tell their children that their father got down on his knees to plead for their mother's hand.

Hand in hand they walked to Claverstone. She explained that her Uncle Gardiner had her custody, and it was his consent and the blessing of her uncle, aunt, and even her grandpapa that she desired him to secure. As they reached the house, he hoped they were awake.

The couple sat side by side on the sofa facing the Gardiners and Lord Claverstone.

"In ordinary circumstances, we would feel this is much too soon to be sure of affection. However, Mr. Darcy—"

"Please call me Fitzwilliam, sir."

"Thank you, and I shall be 'Uncle,' as I was saying, we have had a close understanding with your father for some months now. And, through a continuing relationship with your sister, Lizzy has known your character for quite some time. Lucille and I have discussed this topic many times. We agreed that when you did meet, events would move rapidly."

No one noticed Elizabeth's eyebrows shooting upward as she heard her uncle speak. She kept silent and listened to everyone very carefully.

"Uncle," Fitzwilliam replied, "I realise some would be shocked at how quickly things are happening for us. I thank all three of you for your support and understanding. We shall always depend upon your wisdom and your guidance."

Edward smiled at the couple. He liked the young man immediately. "We are also aware that you shall become master of Pemberly upon the first of June. You must be thinking that you would like to wed very soon, indeed."

Elizabeth was stunned! This intelligence met her as a shock. She had not been told, and now she was very much shaken. She looked at her uncle and aunt in disbelief. Seeing her shift in posture, her fiancé became alarmed. He began rubbing her back, very improperly. "Elizabeth, dearest, are you well? I did not intend to conceal anything from you. As soon as we have an opportunity to talk, I shall disclose everything to you. I meant no ill, dear heart."

"I did not believe that you did, Fitzwilliam. I suppose I need to understand many things. Uncle and Aunt, you appear to have had more information than I. Pray, enlighten me!" She squared her shoulders and folded her arms in front of her. It was a posture they knew well. "Do you think I am fit, and, if fit, am I ready to be mistress of Pemberly? I know nothing of this estate. What of its size and greatness?" Looking at Fitzwilliam, she pled, "I need you to tell me of your home."

Lucille was perhaps the only one in the room who could read the near panic state of her mind. She spoke to calm her, "Lizzy, dear, you are more than prepared. You have knowledge and experience that few young women have attained. You are educated and poised. There comes a time to step into life's role and fulfill that for which you have been prepared. This is a call, dearest."

"Mrs. Gardiner, excuse me—if I may, Aunt, that is so eloquently spoken. I myself have been filled with so much discomfort that I could hardly sleep at night. Meeting and falling in love with Elizabeth has brought me peace." Turning on the sofa to face her, he spoke from his heart.

"Oh, Elizabeth, I begged my father to postpone this installment. I pled to have six months to shadow him and his steward, but he refused me. He said it was time for him to step down, and my duty to provide my contribution. It is a certainty with an ancestral home, like Pemberly, that the son and heir shall become master. I am blessed to be assigned before my father's death. Many heirs are not as fortunate. Father has promised to help and guide me. He already loves you and has every confidence in you. Having you by my side as mistress shall be so wonderful for all our tenants, and for the increase of Pemberly. I need you so much, Elizabeth. You feel you are not ready; I know I am not ready, but Father shall help us. We shall have our family to guide us."

He turned and smiled at his new uncle, aunt, and grandpapa. "Together we shall grow in our roles, day by day. Is this not what marriage is, no matter what occupation or profession?

"Please let me add this, if I may? Elizabeth, I feel this is an arranged marriage. God has put us together. He has given us mutual affection and set our minds as one. This is what he does for those who ask his help. I need his help, and I need you."

She looked into his earnest face and his loving eyes and smiled. He touched her cheek and returned her smile.

Lucille raised her voice, somewhat surprised at his public display of affection. "What remains is to settle the date, and, of course, the place of the wedding. Lizzy, what is your vision for your wedding?"

"I desire a small wedding, Aunt. Family only would be my vision; however, I know not what the Darcys' would want. Fitzwilliam?"

"We are already in Kent. My Aunt and Cousin de Bourgh, Lord and Lady Matlock, and Rory are here. It is possible my additional cousins would be able to be here by the seventeenth.

The only one I would add is my dear friend, Charles Bingley. We can marry in the cathedral. Lord Claverstone, I am sure Mr. James, the cleric, would agree. My godfather, the Archbishop of Canterbury shall provide us a special license consent. We may away to Pemberly the same day. I desire we have as much time together at Pemberly as possible, before June first."

"Son, it would be a pleasure to host your wedding party. Claverstone could also host your wedding breakfast, and you could away to Pemberly immediately following." Gerald smiled as he offered his home and his heart to the young couple. It was very special for him to do this for his Lizzy.

"Sir, we both thank you." Darcy said, "Yes, that would be wonderful. My father and I are planning to host all of you and your family at Pemberly on or about May ninth…as soon as you can reach Pemberly after you away on the seventh. We wish you all to stay as long as you like. It will be our extreme pleasure to have you as our guests for at least six months, please."

He smiled at Elizabeth. "I told Father of my planned proposal yesterday, as soon as I determined your name."

Looking at his new family, he said, "When we met, there was no one to introduce us, so we did not know one another's names. At Elizabeth's request, we continued without the benefit of names. Only yesterday when you called for Georgie, in the Claverstone carriage, did I see Elizabeth and realise it was she!

"This may shock all of you, but I was prepared to propose to her in any case, even without knowing her name. I wished to build a future with her as the person I had become acquainted with, and upon our relationship."

For a few magical moments they were alone, whilst in the company of their family. She smiled at him and said, "Fitzwilliam, I would have said yes, had you been a wood cutter living in a cottage deep in the forest!" Everyone laughed, but she was not saying it in jest.

Fitzwilliam's excitement returned once he was assured of Elizabeth's devotion to him. He was eager to press on with their plans. "Beloved, I hope your father, Jane, Mary, and Catherine shall come to the wedding, and then on to Pemberly. We wish for everyone to stay as long as they desire." Elizabeth was so happy to hear him say the names of her sisters. "Father and Georgie shall want to assist us, my love, in planning events for our guests. We shall plan wonderful entertainments, something for everyone to enjoy. Lord Claverstone, as an avid horseman, I know you shall enjoy a few hunts."

"Oh!" Elizabeth nearly giggled, "Are ladies invited to the hunts, as well?"

"Certainly. I would never again ride in a hunt, anywhere, without my Goddess of Horses!"

They looked at each other and smiled, then laughed loudly. Lord Claverstone shrugged and mused, "Oh, to be young and in love again!"

Turning to Lucille, Fitzwilliam suggested, "Last night, Father and I discussed arranging a trip to town. Perhaps Rory and I could travel on horseback and accompany the Darcy carriage. I shall obtain the special license and the settlement papers. Perhaps, Uncle, you would have some business to conduct; Aunt, you could call for your children and their governess and see to your needs for the visit to Pemberly. Elizabeth, you shall need your wedding gown and wedding clothes. You shall be in need of a good winter's wardrobe for the Derbyshire weather, and an array of costumes for your role as mistress of Pemberly. I am in hopes that your father and sisters would wish to meet with us in London. We could spend three days there in which your sisters and Georgiana and perhaps your aunt as well, may help you shop. I would be most happy to purchase whatever needs your sisters may require for our wedding and trip to Pemberly.

"If this sounds agreeable, I shall send a missive to Georgie's modiste and reserve her time for you.

"Should you wish the trip, perhaps Georgiana may accompany you and Uncle and Aunt in the carriage?"

All agreed this plan sounded as if it would meet their needs. It was decided that all the Bennets would stay at Darcy House, and therefore, Mr. Bennet and Elizabeth's sisters would be able to spend time in the other home, of which she would soon be mistress.

After these arrangements were settled, the entire group awayed to Rosings to see the Darcys. They were all looking forward to seeing Georgie's reaction to the engagement.

Knowing that Elizabeth had a close relationship with his sister, Fitzwilliam wanted to wait until they could tell her together. He knew it would be a splendid surprise for the girl. He also wished the surprise to be very diverting for the family.

***

Georgiana sat on the bed at Rosings. She was considering writing in her journal, even though the day had just begun. Life at Rosings was so boring; there seemed to be nothing special to write.

A knock at her door alerted her to a maid in the hall, who told her that her brother requested her presence in the library. Georgiana was jolly now, thinking that perhaps he wanted her to join him for a walk. No matter what he wished to do, she would welcome the time spent with him.

Pulling the door open, she peered into the somewhat dark library. Waiting a moment for her pupils to adjust to the limited light, she slowly stepped inside and tried to look around. She finally saw Fitzwilliam, but he was not alone. Looking at silhouettes, she could only make out her own brother's features. The others were either masculine or feminine and all with seemingly dark hair. His face she saw clearly now, although still quite dim. He was wearing a big, silly grin.

He was looking with fondness at someone facing him. It appeared to be a dark-haired girl.

Oh no, he has found a wife before he has even met my Elizabeth! I shall not meet this girl.

Giddy with joy, he decided to jest with his sister. "Ah, and here she is now. What gentleman in all of England could have a better sister? Miss Georgiana, please come and greet the wonderful woman who shall be my wife!"

She shut her eyes tightly! She did not want to look at that dark-haired woman. Wishing to cry, she did not want to enter that room. She could sense, not see, that others were sitting in the room as well, but in her grief and sorrow, she did not realise it was her father, with the Gardiners and Lord Claverstone. To Georgie, it was only her selfish brother, who had formed an ill opinion of Elizabeth and would not allow her to recover from his violent disregard.

He spoke to her again, "Dearest, here is the woman who shall be my wife and your new sister. Please come and greet her."

Georgie was dazed, and a lovely melodic female voice was speaking. "Oh, but we are already so well acquainted!" The familiar and beautiful voice was saying. "What could be better than having her as my own sister! Are you as joyful as I, Georgiana?"

"Elizabeth, oh, Elizabeth!" Georgie cried out as she whirled around and flew into Elizabeth's arms, nearly sending them both to the floor. Recovering, she kissed her over and over again.

Then she stood upon the sofa and began kissing Fitzwilliam's cheek. "Brother, thank you! Thank you! You have made me so very, very happy! I have longed to have Elizabeth as my very own sister. I have prayed for it for months, and now we shall be sisters indeed! Father, our prayers have been answered, have they not? You told me to pray and believe and I did."

Laughing, Fitzwilliam looked at his beloved and said, "I think she somewhat approves the match, do you not?" The room filled with laughter. The servants who overheard them remarked that they had never seen such joy at Rosings!

"Oh! But how did you ever meet? You must tell me, please?" Georgie begged and giggled with pure joy. She planted herself next to Elizabeth, took her hand, and would not release it.

Fitzwilliam told the story of how they met and how he learned that his love was actually Elizabeth Bennet.

The soon-to-be-united families discussed the proposed ideas and within a small amount of time refined the plans to away to town on the morrow.

Aunt Gardiner requested that Fitzwilliam tell them somewhat of Pemberly.

"Thank you, Aunt. I shall tell of the house, if I may. The grounds around the home total eighteen point five miles in its circle. Near the house, we have installed the invention of William Murdoch's coal-oil lamps. The home uses natural landscape to its full advantage with several lakes and beautiful rolling knolls.

"Our gardeners have designed very special gardens, with many walks which you shall enjoy, my love. A work of many generations, the house is four wings, four stories high. The total number of rooms is over three hundred. The basement is headquarters for our footmen, a large wine cellar, and storage areas. The ground floor has three kitchens, a large ballroom, a large dining room, and a large music room. These are useful for sizable events, say five hundred guests. There is a grand library, an art gallery of statuary, a gallery of paintings, and a special music room.

"We have two all-inclusive rooms for hobbies and games, a billiard room containing six tables, and of course, various guest rooms.

"The second floor also has some guest chambers and an additional library. Two studies and two grand salons are on this floor. The third floor is for private family use with family rooms, a remarkable private library, a music room, a grand salon, a grand sitting room, and private solarium. Three studies are on this floor, along with Father's private study. Near the house are hothouses for growing out of season and hard to obtain fruits and vegetables, and greenhouses for ornamental plants to maintain the grounds.

"We have two house farms. These grow crops for our use. We also have two dairies, two poultry farms, one mill, a candlestick maker's shop, leather saddle and harness maker's shop, a blacksmith shop and six carriage houses. You shall be happy to hear we have four stables. One stable is for value animals and family horses and pets.

"On the outer grounds, we raise red and black angus cattle, sheep, and goats. We have at least one herd of wild horses. Those are animals that have strayed or run over the years. When you see them, they shall take your breath away!

"I am sure I am forgetting something. I cannot tell you the number of servants, but we do employ shepherds, cattlemen, husbandmen, grooms, stable boys, butchers, bakers, cooks, weavers, a gunsmith, leather workers, mill and dairy workers, farmers, grounds-men, maids, scullery girls, valets, housekeepers, footmen, drivers, messengers, butlers, and," looking to his father for assistance, he shrugged, "well, perhaps I shall do even better with that list after June first."

Elizabeth looked as if she would faint. Aunt Gardiner held her hand as she listened to her fiancé give the recitation. "Lizzy, dear," Aunt Gardiner squeezed her hand, "you shall learn all of this as you go along. You shall see, it shall be as natural as can be once you are in residence."

Grandpapa saw this as an amazing opportunity for his little girl. "Lizzy, my girl, remember how you thrive on a challenge. You shall rise to this one. Fear not!"

"Yes, Grandpapa. Clearly it is a good thing that I am deeply in love with this man! While others may plot and scheme for the position of mistress of Pemberly, I approach it with fear and trembling, and a healthy dose of caution. I am determined not to make mistakes. I shall do my best."

Both Darcy men agreed, "That is all we ask of you!"

At that, they quit the room, knowing that they would share Easter services and return to Rosings.

As they entered the hall, Fitzwilliam pulled Elizabeth into a closet. He wrapped his arms around her and kissed her passionately. It surpassed any of their previous kisses, and Elizabeth nearly became dizzy. "Beloved, I shall ride beside your carriage and escort you home. I shall stay until Grandpapa throws me out into the stables."

As they quitted the closet, they met Rory in the hall. He, not knowing of the engagement, smiled broadly and greeted Elizabeth with baited breath. Wisely, she offered her hand to him saying, "It so pleases me to tell you that we are to be cousins, colonel. May I suppose that the army shall allow me to call my new cousin, Rory?"

Rory was obviously overwhelmed, and not pleasantly, for he himself had designed a plan to court her when his uncle released the idea of her marriage to his son. Yet, trying to recover himself, he took her hand and kissed it lightly, saying, "Congratulations to you both, and much happiness to you, Miss Elizabeth! So, you shall be a Darcy? Well then, are we not all blessed?"

Over his shoulder he whispered to Darcy, "You dog, Darcy! We shall need to talk later. I believe you have some information you failed to gift me with, my cousin!"

The three walked to the driveway and met the carriage. The trip to Claverstone greatly amused the Gardiners and Lord

Claverstone. Everyone in the carriage enjoyed talking to Darcy, who rode Percival and chatted through the open window. They liked Darcy a great deal and were eager to know him better.

Entering the grand salon at Claverstone, Darcy spotted the pianoforte. Seeking a private conversation with Elizabeth, he requested of his new aunt that Elizabeth should play for them. Lucille thought it a wonderful idea and encouraged Lizzy to open up the instrument.

As she began to play, Fitzwilliam stood and offered his services turning pages. Smiling, she agreed.

"Would you think me a rake, if I told you that I am dying to hold you in my arms and kiss you?"

He could see her smile, and she whispered that she desired the same. After playing one half hour, she rose and asked her uncle if the two of them might sit on the chairs on the far wall, just to talk. Edward granted the request, and they spoke tender words to each other softly enough as not to be understood by the others.

Fitzwilliam discovered her age, and told her his and that his birthday was June one. They spoke at first about general information, then, he asked her very personal questions— each one making her blush violently, and each one more probing than the previous. Strangely, she found that she enjoyed it, and that she wanted to tell him everything of herself. Using a comparison of a set at a ball, he asked her about previous boys or men she might have had an interest in, and then he regretted it and worried that she might ask the same of him. To shock her, and throw her off the subject, he used the steps in a dance to ask how much education she had received about sex. Laughing, she told him that it was difficult being a country girl, for her ignorance of male anatomy left her halting between an image of a stallion's great pendulous length and the enigma of a newborn kitten's ambiguous genitals. Nothing vexed Elizabeth more than lack of knowledge on any topic. Her lack of information about sex was making her nervous.

She blushed bright red when he asked at what age her menses began! He wanted to know what days in the month she had her courses, and how many days they lasted. She boldly told him.

Then, he asked if she knew what the last step of the dance included. She was so shocked she turned white. Even so, she told him that she did know.

With that, he took pity upon her maiden's brain and reached out and gave her hand a squeeze. He thanked her for answering his questions and told her she was right to trust him, reminding her that he would be her husband in a matter of days. He whispered that he was thrilled with the idea of teaching her all she should know and reassured her that their marriage bed would be filled with felicity!

Finally, he was forced to take his leave, because it was turning dark and there was no moonlight.

She felt some relief from the intensity of his inquiries, but at the same time she mourned his leaving and dreaded the balance of the evening without him. *Yes, we shall indeed, be the happiest couple in the land...*

Chapter 7

"Spoken vows have great influence and power, once uttered their fulfillment shall carry the speaker to a final destiny."

-Anonymous

The cousins waved the footmen away from the incoming carriage and personally attended to the arrivals.

Once disembarked, Elizabeth was greeted by her very eager fiancé. Rory suddenly stepped in, took her hand, and bowed, kissing her hand. Walking her very quickly into the house and away from Fitzwilliam, he told her that his Aunt Catherine, being French, and speaking French, kept a very formal household. He said this planning a jest at Elizabeth's expense. He had devised this plot partly for jocularity and partly to punish her for her betrothal to his cousin. It was his hope that Lady Catherine might drive a wedge between the couple. Knowing Catherine's contrary nature, he wished her to have a negative reaction toward Elizabeth and create a rift between the pair.

To succeed in the scheme, he needed to keep Fitzwilliam ignorant of his plan. But, in so doing, he created an appearance of familiar and secret conversation with Elizabeth. Seeing Rory close to Elizabeth, Fitzwilliam scowled fiercely at him. Becoming jealous, he began asking when and where they had met, and how many times they had been in each other's company. Elizabeth stepped close to her fiancé, smiled, and whispered into his ear. He relaxed and gave her a glorious smile. From that moment, the couple maintained eye contact and began a communication with their eyes and facial expressions.

Everyone gathered in the main salon. Lady Catherine always loved to make a grand entrance. She walked with the bearing of a monarch and took her receiving chair. It was her daily practice, whether there was audience or not made no difference to the woman who held her rank and position with tenacious and greedy fingertips. Having married a wealthy man of title, eight and ten years her senior, she had devised a plan. A selfish scheme, invented by this self-centered woman. She sustained the import of her strategy by saying it had been a pact between herself and her late sister, Anne, Fitzwilliam's mother. This could never be confirmed as truth.

Catherine had claimed that she and her sister, the late Anne Darcy, had wished their children to wed. This Lady de Bourgh pursued, not for her daughter's happiness, but to make her daughter a wealthy woman, with homes and security. Such a marriage for Anne would permit Catherine to retain ownership of Rosings, and allow Lady Catherine to avoid living in the dowager's house. Even though the Darcys never took this to heart, George was eager to put an end to the matter. He was prepared today to offer documentation to quiet Catherine's rants and calm her poor daughter's nerves, and then offer a toast to his son and future daughter. Mr. Darcy offered his arm to Elizabeth, and the two walked toward their hostess. "Sister, I present Elizabeth Bennet," he offered with great drama and a happy smile. Upon hearing her name, Elizabeth presented a low curtsey, smiled and, as naturally as can be, proclaimed, "Je suis, heureux de vous rencontrer. C'est un honneur pour moi pour entre dans votre maison."

Georgiana smiled as she listened to her new sister speaking French like a native. However, Lady Catherine had no such pleasant response to Elizabeth. She reddened, for in truth she spoke no French, and comprehended far less! Believing she was being deliberately upstaged by this slip of a young girl, Lady Catherine started a stream of stammering insults. Once begun, no one could stop her. Everyone looked stunned! The Fitzwilliams' blanched, but Rory, working hard to stifle laughter, stood innocently beside his father, Lord Matlock.

"Are you French?" Lady Catherine barked at her. Making a very good recovery, Elizabeth pled, "Oh! I do beg your ladyship's pardon. I am afraid the fault is entirely my own. I was ill informed."

Smiling, she looked sincerely to Lady Catherine and then diplomatically lowered her eyes.

After a few seconds, she made eye contact and continued. "Wishing to make an excellent impression upon your ladyship, I sought the finest information. It was my error believing you to be French. My formal greeting was misplaced, yet my heart's desire was to present a favorable introduction to your ladyship and your ladyship's daughter."

Overcoming the embarrassment of her lack of knowledge of the language, and her fear of mockery, Lady Catherine decided to use the opportunity to appear gracious and forgiving. She relaxed and attempted to offer a smile to add legitimacy to her attempt at a great-hearted resolution of the misunderstanding. "A perfectly innocent and understandable error, Miss Bennet. We are delighted to make your acquaintance."

Her family stood amazed at her magnanimity. None had ever witnessed as much on any occasion. Rory decided to leave well enough alone, and the introductions continued with every possible civility. Drinks were served to all. When everyone seemed more relaxed, George stood up again and spoke. "Upon purchasing additional lands in France, my solicitor in Calais has sent me a most shocking document. This instrument was discovered during the process of my purchase. The original is filed in Calais, I, however, have a copy and one for you, Lady Catherine. It is of a very unusual nature, as are nearly all ancient declarations. It shall be most interesting to all of us."

Clearing his throat, he started to read *en Francais*. His audience became annoyed very quickly. Finally, Rory stood to his feet and said bluntly, "Uncle, we shall all concede that Elizabeth is the most fluent in French. Please allow her to translate so that we might have our dinner sometime today!"

"Here, here!" The crowd agreed.

Unfolding the scroll, Elizabeth began: *Sang Rivalite de Henri de Bourgh avec Jean Luis D'Arce*

> *Dans l'annee de notre Seigneur* 1418 AD... Marie Elise D'Arce fell in love with Henri Paul LeFevre, a handsome young man. A large dowry was demanded and amassed by the head of the D'Arce family. However Phillipe de Bourgh was secretly in love with Mlle Marie Elise D'Arce. To prevent her marriage to another, he and his kinsmen stole the dowry. Unable to replace the fortune, Marie Elise was not allowed to marry the man she loved. In torment and agony of grief, she threw herself off the roof of their castle to her death.
>
> Two of her brothers Jeorge Formion D'Arce and Henri Damion D'Arce went to the de Bourgh castle and attempted to recover the stolen treasure. Feigning insult at the accusation, de Bourgh went wild over the denouncement. Covertly, he ordered the deaths of the

two D'Arce men. Now blood was shed from three D'Arce family members. There was outrage and a Sang Rivalite, Blood Rivalry ensued. It was most serious and violent and numerous deaths were counted from both families. It was so fierce that the de Bourgh family priest attempted to repair the damage, but to no avail. A resolution of the matter was reached in 1679 when both families took vows that neither would mix blood with the other. It was sworn that never would a de Bourgh marry a D'Arce and therefore, the peace would be instituted and maintained.

Upon reaching the conclusion, she handed the papers back to Mr. Darcy. The room was so quiet it seemed that no one was breathing. Rory looked as though he would explode; he wanted to laugh and shout at the scene. Fitzwilliam was pixilated on the inside even though he had not imbibed, but, not wanting to give offence to his aunt, he kept his eyes on his hands, which were clasped in his lap. George gazed at his sister-in-law, Lady Catherine, and the Matlocks fixed their eyes upon the same, fearful of an outburst. Georgiana sat with tears in her eyes, and her mouth open. She feared her aunt. The four visitors simply sat waiting for someone to speak.

It was Anne, quiet, little Anne, the girl who was always so ill, who stood promptly to her feet and gave a happy sounding shout at the top of her lungs! She put her hands high into the air and waved them about, and nearly singing she exclaimed, "Hallelujah! Thank you Uncle George!

"This one beautiful document sets me free. Oh, how at ease I shall remain forever!" Looking at Fitzwilliam she nearly shouted, "Oh, cousin! I dearly love you as a family member, and I know you have a face that has driven dozens of ladies of the Ton into raptures, yet was it not fantastical that we should ever wed? Yes, the entire idea of our engagement was so far-fetched as to offer nothing but entertainment as a fairytale. You cannot know my relief!" At that, she sat down, looked at her mother who gave her an icy stare, hung her head, and maintained silence.

Lady Catherine blanched. She had held her breath throughout the presentation and concealed her anger at her daughter's outburst. How she wished she could simply block out the last half hour and destroy that hateful document. She was beaten. Drawing herself up to her full height, she stood and said, "Brother, I thank you for revealing the truth for all of us. So the vow has been spoken, and even written long ago, never shall de Bough blood mix with D'Arce!" This put an end to her imagined engagement which she had planned for her daughter Anne and Fitzwilliam Darcy since their births. Rory exchanged glances with his uncle. He thought the man had never looked younger or healthier. Even his father had a glint in his eye that made Rory want to laugh! He knew Lord Matlock had been privy to this intelligence prior to its revealing. What a coup to keep it under wraps until Easter. The men were glowing!

Lastly, Rory looked at his cousin. Fitzwilliam was staring at Elizabeth with a sparkle in his eyes; she had apparently just given him a type of sign language that made him obviously *very* happy. It was a difficult thing to observe.

Wanting to remove attention from the devastating news, Lady Catherine indicated that dinner should be served. Formal seating was observed, with the exception of Anne who was hastily reseated between Rory and her uncle Darcy. Following the meal, George requested champagne. When all was quiet, he stood to his feet, lifted his glass, and smiled at the couple.

"It is with such joy that I salute my beloved son, Fitzwilliam, and his fiancée, Elizabeth Bennet. I should like to drop formal civility and simply speak from my heart as a father who has prayed much for his children. Anne and I spoke often of this day, and I wish she were here. It has been a joy watching God bring these two lives together, as only he can. I should like to say, it is as their Creator intended, for they were formed for each other from their births." Upon hearing this well- turned phrase, Lady Catherine reddened. "The wedding shall be hosted by Lord Claverstone, Elizabeth's surrogate grandfather."

At this Gerald smiled and raised his glass to the couple.

"Mr. James shall conduct the ceremony in the cathedral at ten in the morn of the seventeenth. The wedding breakfast shall be immediately following the service at Claverstone. We are in hopes that the entire Fitzwilliam family may be in attendance. Of course, everyone is invited to Pemberly on or after May seven for a lengthy celebration of the nuptials."

The betrothed couple looked exceedingly ecstatic, as did Anne de Bough! Later, Fitzwilliam was not disinclined to relate the story of Aunt Catherine's belief that Anne and he should wed. It had been his constant mortification, as she repeated the arrangement to him upon every occasion of their seeing one another. Having an end of it was wonderful!

Elizabeth found the story very amusing, and she took particular notice of his awkward and halting account of the years suffered at his aunt's obsession of him as her son-in-law. She made a mental note to console him, when it could be done privately.

Miss Caroline Bingley sat across the table from her brother. She was petulantly lecturing him on his lack of interest in her martial goals. She felt him lacking brotherly affection and attention to duty.

"You, Charles, have continued to ignore me. If you had taken me to Darcy House and Pemberly each time you visited Mr. Darcy, I would have extracted a proposal by now. Honestly, if Mama and Papa were here they would skin you alive for neglecting me!"

Reading his paper, Charles managed to block out the monotone drones of her voice. He did not even lift his eyes in her direction. Caroline was always saying the same things to him. Lies and tales of Fitzwilliam Darcy.

"You had better listen to me. I swear by all that I am, that I shall be a wealthy woman. I shall find a way into Pemberly. I shall risk everything. Charles, I am not afraid to dare. Do you hear me? I shall do anything to put myself forward."

Easter dinner for Wickham was bread and a bottle of wine. Stale bread and cheap wine. Disgusted, Wickham hung his head and whined. It was always Fitzwilliam Darcy's fault.

This is the last of my funds. I shall get what the Darcys' owe me, if I must die trying. No more waiting for what should be mine. Wallet and I shall act; my plan is worth the risks.

I shall reap what I deserve. I grew up on that estate, why am I out in the cold now? Am I not entitled to a share? My father made them what they are today. It is the fault of that Fitzwilliam. Why does he inherit and take all?

Claverstone's carriage departed Rosings, and the happy party returned home. With a full moon, the cousins rode escort, just as Fitzwilliam had done the night before, and as they would do again on the morrow's trip into London town.

Arriving at Claverstone, the party began to feel the fatigue of the day. Entering the house, Lord Claverstone and the Gardiners asked to be excused. Mr. Gardiner admonished the young couple they should have twenty minutes to say their farewells in the company of Rory.

Elizabeth reminded Rory he was in her debt. Accordingly, he quit the house and went out to the stables, as the couple disappeared into the library. They fell into each other's arms as soon as the door was shut.

"You were spectacular tonight. What beautiful French, perfectly spoken, like a native."

"Thank you, love. I have worked very hard on that tongue."

A very low, husky voice she had never heard before growled at her, "Umm, and I should like very much to work hard on a certain tongue, myself. It is a privilege of our betrothal."

"Ah, it took me several years to perfect my tongue, I sincerely hope—"

He pulled her closer, and, holding her head, he caught her still-moving lips and drew them into his. Her knees weakened. He caught her by her hips and pressed his pelvis against hers.

She sighed deeply and pressed back. Sweeping her off her feet, he sat on the sofa, placing her accessibly in his lap. Putting her head upon the upholstered arm, he brushed her lips lightly.

She ran her fingers through his hair. He moaned. She sighed deeply, and both closed their eyes.

He reached his hand up to her face and stroked her cheek with his fingertips. Lightly they traced her jawline to her ears, then ever so slowly down her neck onto her *décolleté,* where he allowed himself to stop only at the neckline of her gown. She shivered at the newness of this explorative touching. His brushing lips began a slow smoldering kiss, with such extravagancy of mutual desires that could not be gratified, nor even slightly indulged, on the strength of an engagement. Granting satiety to such passionate demands would certainly be presumptive of the marriage vows and require an action never to be performed in the grand salon of Claverstone.

He reluctantly and slowly pulled away from her lips. His lips were still tingling, and the sweet taste of her mouth remained fresh on his breath. He began to whisper in her ear. "Beloved, I am overjoyed at our engagement. I can barely wait for our wedding. In the morn, we away to town where we shall receive your father and sisters. This shall be an honour for me. I confess I cannot wait for us to spend time together in your new home. You have visited on many occasions, but this time we shall select our rooms." He continued his kisses, "It is my desire to share one bed. I see no reason for lovers to separate, do you not agree?"

His zeal aroused her own ardor with a hunger she had never known. He consumed her every thought and desire. He possessed her heart. "I could not envision any reason to sleep otherwise, my love. Why marry if a couple does not share a bed? I could not sleep without your arms around me. I am so happy you feel the same, beloved." He smiled at her answer.

"I should have a request, I think," she murmured softly, almost to herself, for she felt very shy and uncertain.

"Name what you require, my love. Whatever you need for your comfort shall be given you. As future mistress, the entire staff at Darcy House shall serve you."

"Oh, I thank you," her brows knit together, and he knew she was thinking it over.

Kissing her again, he stopped a moment, "Umm, depend upon it, sweet Elizabeth. Whatever makes you comfortable and happy shall be done for you, beloved. Would you speak your mind to me; what is your request?"

She bit her bottom lip, "'tis not a request of your servants, but of you."

"Go on, please."

"Since our ride on Marigold, I have had an intense curiosity about your body. I wish to see you, my love." She kept her voice at a whisper, and smiled bashfully at him. "You see, books and museums have been my only resources and I have many questions . . ."

Her eyes were increasing their expressions of passion for him. "I have some concerns, perhaps. There is much I do not know, shall you teach me? I am feeling such lack because no one has instructed me." Her voice was barely a whisper. "Ohhhh, my love—" she slowly stopped talking, as he kissed her passionately. Slowly he lifted his head away and smiled at her.

"Shall we spend large amounts of time together in town?" she questioned in a whispery voice.

"Yes," he answered, while placing kisses around her *décolleté*. She shivered at the thrill of his lips on her chest. He daringly hooked one finger in the neckline and drew the gown down as far as he could. His kisses followed the finger downward. She arched her back, and asked, "Is the room I shall occupy close to yours?"

"Practically the very same room, my love." He responded between kisses upon her breasts.

"So you may visit me, and stay as long as you wish?" she inquired nervously, as his lips were daringly approaching her nipple.

"As many hours as you desire my company; shall that please you Miss Bennet?" He thought about licking her areola and then reaching to her nipple, but he decided against it for the sake of her innocent sensibility. Looking into her eyes he promised her that they would not presume upon their marriage vows.

Once again he kissed her lips. Their breathing was short and irregular. They kissed deeply, longingly, and almost without reserve. He placed his hand on her neck, then lowered it, again exploring her breast as far as the fabric of her gown allowed. She arched her back permissively, melting under the newness of his sensuous touches. He watched her, smiling at her responsiveness.

Reluctantly he rose, took her hand and assisted her as she placed her feet upon the floor. Lifting her hand as she stood, he softly kissed the top of her head. Saying farewell, he awayed with the intelligence her body had supplied to him. She was ready to give him anything he desired.

Immediately following breakfast, the trip to town commenced as planned. Two riders stationed themselves alongside the carriage. Time flew for the passengers and the riders. The trip was pure joy!

Turning onto Gracechurch Street, the carriage stopped at number five. It was a beautiful, large home, with a lovely, well-maintained garden. Georgiana had visited several times with her father, and she loved the home and the family. All went inside. In moments they were met by three very happy and well-behaved children. What a sweet reunion. John, Margaret, and Robin were happy to see their mama and papa and cousin Elizabeth again. They remembered Georgiana much to her delight!

She told them she was to be their new cousin and introduced them to Fitzwilliam who would marry Elizabeth and become their cousin, too. It was a thrilling day for Georgie, the children began calling her 'cousin' and insisted she call them the same.

The once lonely Georgiana, now had three new little cousins, and four new sisters. When Edward and Lucille took the girl aside and bid her call them uncle and aunt, her eyes filled with tears of joy. Aunt Gardiner assured her she could visit as often as she wished and stay as long as she desired, with her father's permission naturally.

The Gardiners were more than happy to be left in their own household. Biding adieu to the Darcys, Rory, and Elizabeth, Mr. Gardiner promised to accompany the Bennets to Darcy House upon their arrival. The group from Longbourn was expected before nightfall.

Upon reaching Darcy House, Rory went to the rooms which his aunt Anne had given him years prior. Georgie called for a bath, hugged Elizabeth, and promised to join them for tea later.

Fitzwilliam took Elizabeth's hand and led her to a main floor suite. It was lovely and very well away from all the other bed chambers. Four rooms were connected in the suite. An enormous floor to ceiling fireplace occupied her complete attention as she entered the largest bed chamber she had ever seen! Very beautiful furniture was most tastefully arranged with a huge bed dominating the space. The canopy and draw curtains of the bed matched the counterpane in shades of blue. There were three large chests, two bed tables, and a small desk with an intricately carved chair, all situated upon the most beautiful carpet she had ever seen.

Quietly leaning against a wall, Fitzwilliam silently watched her taking in the space. He was smiling sweetly at her obvious approval of all she viewed. He wanted to let her assimilate.

He realised it would take some time for her to soak up the environment as well as mentally absorb the idea of their marriage bed and the concept of mutually sharing rooms as a couple.

He watched her initial reactions knowing that her eyes especially would tell him all he desired to know. It was almost as if he could read her very thoughts. He knew that her adjusting to Darcy House's opulence would help ease her into the grandeur of Pemberly.

He followed her as she entered the large sitting room with a smaller fireplace, and she smiled at him as she sat upon the comfy sofa, then tried out each of the matching chairs. "This is a cozy place to relax," she said, smiling her extreme approval of the cheery room. A small bookcase offered space for about one hundred books and a sideboard provided a nice area for meals to be taken in their rooms. There were fruits, meats, and breads set out, along with several bottles of wine and pitchers of water. She walked to the sideboard, poured a glass of water, and held it out to him. He gladly received it, then she poured one for herself. Without a word, she turned and continued her self-guided tour. Two dressing rooms were attached to the sitting room. She smiled as she spied one already filled with Fitzwilliam's clothing and shoes. Lifting her brow, she turned and looked at him briefly. She walked through his dressing room, looking at his clothing and then, closing her eyes, she inhaled, gathering in his scent. It was highly recognisable to her and very desirable. Fitzwilliam stood watching her, a huge smile upon his lips. He was very pleased at her natural responses to him and her acceptance of their future living areas.

"Do you like these rooms, love, or should we look at others?" he offered, slipping behind her and threading his arms around her waist. He put his head on her shoulder. "Of course, I love these beautiful rooms!" she answered. "My, what a large bed. It is absolutely perfect for two. It is immense," she declared and turning to face him, she put her arms around his neck.

They smiled at each other, and she placed her head against his chest and sighed deeply. "I am so pleased that you approve, my sweet Elizabeth. And," he said, nibbling upon her ear, "about the size of the bed, beloved. I confess, I sent Simmons an express missive and had him move my things into these rooms. You may redecorate all or any part you desire. In fact, we may purchase all new furniture if you wish."

"No. One does not change things that are already perfect, Fitzwilliam."

Upon his subtle signal, Elizabeth's trunks were brought in and placed on the floor. A maid appeared to shake out the clothing. Items were either hung or set out to be pressed. Within minutes her personal items were placed into the dresser, and her grooming articles were neatly arranged on top of the dresser.

An older woman of one and forty years came into the room and was introduced as Jeannette, her ladies' maid. Jeannette was selected because Elizabeth had requested a French-speaking attendant. This she did for reasons of confidentiality. Elizabeth liked the older lady very well and was impressed with her qualifications. Speaking French, she thanked her saying that she would very much appreciate her assistance. As she turned from Jeannette, her gaze dropped toward the floor of the sitting room.

Spotting a chest of about three feet in height, five feet in length, and four feet in width, she felt a curious rush. Looking at Darcy, she raised her eyebrows and teased, "Pray, Mr. Darcy, what secrets are lodged within? What resides within that coffin? Is this a haunted mansion?"

It was clear that he was not going to be a player in her happy little game. Seeming somewhat cross, he tried to brush quickly past her jest wish a sharp answer. "That is an arms, chest, love. Nothing for you to think about."

Elizabeth did not know what 'arms' meant to him, but in her world this answer only spurred additional questions. Darcy saw an opportunity to divert her and rushed beside her. Bending his head down, he began to kiss her neck and with great passion. Surrounded by his arms, she sank downward allowing him to hold her upright. "Beloved, that always sends shivers down my spine and weakens my knees."

"I know," was the welcomed response. At that, she turned around to face him and kissed him tenderly. Slowly drawing away from him, she put her head against his shoulder.

"I love you so much, Fitzwilliam." He affirmed his love to her as well, and then silently thanked heaven that he prevented her from looking into that chest.

What was I thinking? If Aunt Nora's hatred of fencing is matched by Elizabeth's, she shall surely bring strong opposition to the sport. That chest shall be moved.

"Elizabeth I am so pleased that our rooms are to your liking. I want you to love Darcy House."

She smiled at him, thankful for his thoughtfulness. "I already do love Darcy House, and I would also adore a wood-cutter's cottage deep in the forest if you were there with me," she murmured.

She could hardly contain her joy and excitement. His exuberance was displayed in his body and his conduct. He enfolded her in his arms and drew her shamelessly into him, letting her feel his arousal. He deeply inhaled her lavender and roses, then kissed her head. Paying close attention to her, he watched for signs of acceptance. Slowly he began to press himself onto her, and turn her face upward. He wanted her to look into his eyes. The invasion of his soul-penetrating stare was met by hers. Encouraged, he moved his hands to her bottom and began unhurriedly rubbing her firm, round sensual buttocks. He sighed profoundly. "How I love and adore you, my beautiful Elizabeth."

"Umm, I deeply love and adore you," she arched her back and purposefully pushed herself against his very full arousal. Kissing him, she drew his lips into hers, and prompted by a natural impulse, began to rub her mound against him. Clearly enjoying this, she moaned.

Her visceral responses to him were enough to demonstrate that she was not capable of denying him anything he might ask of her. Learning all he needed to know, he kissed her twice, whispering that he had many responsibilities to meet. He invited her to enjoy all the amenities of the home which was soon to be hers. They would meet for tea when she was ready.

Elizabeth and Georgiana reached the sideboard in the main salon at the same moment. As they filled their plates, they laughed about the trip making them both very hungry.

Fitzwilliam and Rory filed in moments later, the former in very good spirits. Rory jested with the group in an effort to improve his own attitude. It was increasingly difficult for him to be in the presence of his cousin and his intended. Everyone laughed at his easy humour, but no one saw his raw emotions.

Realising he had another attempt to set Elizabeth at odds with Fitzwilliam he said, "Cousin, have you time to go to the club and fence today? I have a new rapier and I am eager to use it."

Rory did not heed the cautionary looks Darcy had been throwing his way, in an effort to quiet him, but those looks were easily read by Elizabeth. "Fitzwilliam, what is all of this? We must talk, now, if you please?" Darcy followed her into the hall, trying to think of what he might say.

Once outside the salon, Simmons approached to inform him of the Bennets' arrival.

"Excellent, do bring them into the salon right away." Turning to Elizabeth, he placed his hands upon her shoulders, and looking deeply into her eyes he whispered, "I believe it is best if we see to our guests, do you not agree?"

Stepping back into the salon she said, "Make no mistake, we shall discuss this later." Kissing the top of her head, he whispered, "I love it when you speak like a wife, my darling!"

"Sir: Mr. Thomas Bennet, Miss Jane Bennet, Miss Mary Bennet, and Miss Catherine Bennet."

They entered and began to bow and curtsey, but Elizabeth rushed into her father's arms. "Papa, you look so well! Dear Jane! Mary and Catherine!"

Fitzwilliam, Rory, and Georgie waited for her to greet her family. At last, she took Fitzwilliam's hand and led him to her father. "And here you two meet. Mr. Thomas Bennet, I am honoured to introduce to you, my own prince! Mr. Fitzwilliam Darcy!" It was just the ice breaker the two men needed. All of the appropriate introductions followed the normal course. Rory decided it had been a very long time since he remembered seeing so many beautiful girls in one room.

Georgiana secretly delighted in suddenly being surrounded by so many new sisters! She looked forward to knowing each one. There was such felicity in their easy company.

The visit that followed included the enjoyment of the delicious food. The gentlemen took port in the library. Fitzwilliam was made aware of his future father's love of books. Mr. Bennet was amazed at the vast library available at Darcy House. He would certainly visit his daughter and son quite often with the proximity to Longbourn so very close. He made the decision to spend as much time in this glorious bookroom as possible during the current visit.

In truth, Mr. Thomas Bennet had more interest in books than he did serving as chaperone to his virgin daughter under the same roof as her intended. Mr. Bennet was decidedly disinclined to attend any duties of fatherhood. His plan was to read, eat and sleep. If absolutely necessary he would converse with others. Had he been questioned on the topic of his daughter's delicate situation with her fiancé, he would have spoken in favour of the calendar. Their wedding was only days away.

The ladies all made themselves comfortable in the large sitting room. Their excited conversations sounded much like those of Longbourn. Georgiana felt at home with each of the girls. Gone was her shyness. Soon she would learn the rituals of sitting on each other's beds, giggling and brushing each other's hair. Each girl was charming although their personalities varied, just as Elizabeth had originally told her. And, just as she had claimed, each sister was wonderful in her own way, deeply loved and appreciated by the others!

Finally Elizabeth announced she was going to retire for the evening. Jane also stood and walked alongside her into the hall. "I shall go with you for a while, if I may," she said sweetly.

Elizabeth suddenly realised that her own private life was on a different plane. "Jane, I feel I must rest this evening. We shall have hours to share tomorrow, in fact I shall see to it."

Jane accepted this as Lizzy's new wisdom as an engaged woman.

At last Darcy House was quiet as each guest was made comfortable in their appointed quarters. Sleep came soundly to each inhabitant except for those who needed more than sleep to find rest.

Fitzwilliam waited until the maid left Elizabeth's room to enter the hall. He tapped the door lightly once, then entered. The room was bathed in candlelight. Small candles surrounded the bed, and some larger ones had been placed upon the dresser and tables. The flowers he had ordered were there, just as he directed. A large silver tray bearing a bottle of wine with two glasses had been placed upon the dresser closest to the bed. The delicacy of the silk sheets and pillows was of a refined quality that few subjects in England had ever seen. An attendant had turned these down and folded the counterpane at the foot of the bed, leaving a soft blanket for a cover over the sheet. The manner and form of the bed prepared for the evening was reflective of the station and refined taste of the household.

The room in general offered a splendid grace and polish which contributed to a lavishly comfortable night's rest for its occupants.

He smiled approvingly as he surveyed the room. Feeling he had chosen their rooms well, he noted a satisfying perspective of the room. It had been prepared as he instructed. He was very pleased with his staff and with the result of his own design.

He sat in a chair and removed his jacket, and boots and stockings. He opened his shirt.

Suddenly he saw her. His breath caught in his throat as his eyes rested upon his beloved.

She was magnificent. Her beautiful hair flowed in long, thick curls and cascaded gracefully across her shoulders. A single gardenia was pinned back just above her left ear. Her perfect face was radiant, and she bestowed a full smile upon him. Her fine eyes sparkled with desire for him.

She was clad in a bright red silk robe, tied loosely at the waist. Her shapely legs reached out beyond the fabric as she walked toward him with her arms outstretched. He strained to see the outline of her dark pubic hair, just barely visible. One of her *seins*, peeked out at him, revealing part of a raspberry. She encircled her arms around his waist. He could not think.

Her gardenia filled his senses with its perfume. The intoxicating feel of her bare flesh, as close as the thin silk, numbed his brain and teased his fingertips. He wanted more. So much more than to stand there, holding her. *I did not plan for this. What have I been doing lately? Put the woman on the bed and take her. I cannot do that with Elizabeth. I need to lead her gently. I am not prepared. How can I not take her, after seeing her like this, yet I promised. How can I sleep with her and not join with her? Think! I need to think!*

"Beloved," she began, "I should think I may be nervous on our wedding day, as you see me naked for the first time. Therefore, it seems a good idea to me, for you to look upon me now. I desire you to satisfy your curiosity in advance, so that I may relax. I shall remove my robe and then replace it."

In rapt attention, he watched as she pulled the sash and allowed her robe to open. Then she slipped it down over each shoulder, nervously. She held it in place for a few seconds, just to build her confidence, then allowed it to flow into a rich pool of red silkiness around her dainty feet. He did not see it fall. He did not so much as look at her face; if he had, he would have seen a shy smile as she bit into her lower lip.

Fitzwilliam Darcy groaned loudly. He bit his lower lip hard in hopes of maintaining control over his emotions and his body. "Ohhhh, Elizabeth, I dare say, you are the most beautiful woman I have ever beheld. The Italian sculptures have not rendered anything near your actual likeness. "None of the masters have painted a woman with your perfection! I am undone! My beloved, you are so perfect. Oh, you are so much more than I could yearn for, or imagine. Oh, just to behold you for a moment in time; yet, here you are, my darling. Wonderful, sensational, loving, and affectionate Elizabeth, you are mine! What a fortunate mortal, to have a goddess fall in love with me!"

He did not see her smile at his words of praise. His eyes were elsewhere. She turned around for him. When his vision fell upon her beautiful back, he moaned again. She stopped and stood still. He murmured something she could not hear about her derriere. When she turned to face him, his arms were quickly winding around her, and he began ravenously kissing her neck. It took her breath away and sent shivers down her spine. Both were startled! He, to a passionate reception of her physical attributes, and she to a realisation of his commanding control over her passion and emotions. She felt it! And, she rather enjoyed his dominance. It was more to her than the air she breathed.

He released her from his tight embrace and she quickly scooped up her robe and donned it once more. "Now, shall we lie together, my love?" she innocently asked him. He made no response.

"Darling? Are you well? Fitzwilliam? Fitzwilliam?" she spoke with concern. He was dazed. Had she been talking to him? Finding himself, he had a sudden thought to ask for help.

"Elizabeth, I am undone. I have been so looking forward to this, but I did not plan on you being so—so perfectly desirable. So voluptuous! I am not sure how to say this…I need a moment to compose myself."

Something in his manner told her it was not a jest. She was not sure how she could help him.

"Shall I pour a glass of wine for you, Fitzwilliam?"

"No. I thank you," he said slowly shaking his head.

"The bed is turned down. Shall we lie down, beloved.?" She led him to the bed, but he sat down. He could not take his eyes off her.

Silently he stretched his long frame atop the bed. He was clad in his breeches and linen shirt, just as he had promised. She draped her body over his, rubbing his bare feet with hers. "Ummm, this is nice," she whispered, threading her hand through his shirt to feel his chest. "And, this is very, very nice," she murmured, rubbing his chest seductively, "do you not agree?"

Reflecting a playfulness, he closed his eyes and answered, "Ah, Elizabeth, when shall I become accustomed to your beauty? Your body is so perfect, so consummately prepared for mine. Take pity on me, my love; the sight of your perfection is a detriment to my willpower. Oh, God, Elizabeth, I desire nothing more than to join with you right now. I hate my own self-restraint and the promise I made to you. It is painful."

"What may I do to ease your suffering, sir?" She reached to his breeches and began to unbutton them.

Alarmed, he grabbed her wrists, as if to stop her. Tipping his head, he furrowed his brow and squinted, silently inquiring as to what she was doing.

"Do you not remember?" she questioned, "I asked to look upon you?"

She waited for his response. His brain was inadequate. His blood supply was elsewhere.

"I thought you did agree at Claverstone. Do you not intend for me to do so? I wish to see you. May I remove your breeches? I may require you to open your legs, and I want you to retain your dignity."

At this, he struggled to sit upright. Obviously, this was news to him, and he was more than a little alarmed. His concern was not that his beautiful fiancée wanted to remove his breeches, but that the request came from one completely inexperienced! "Excuse me?" he responded.

"Yes," she nodded, "I think these are best removed." He was at her mercy. Somewhat wary, he tried to read her thoughts as to this request. Failing that, and seeing that she had a plan, he decided to inquire of her. "Elizabeth, do you remember when I asked about the last step of the dance?"

"Yes," she answered with passion.

" Is that what you are asking me for tonight? Do you wish us to join?" he asked, to be clear.

"No," she answered plainly. "Do you not remember that I told you I was curious about your body since our ride on Marigold? I said I had unanswered questions about your male body and asked to see you for myself." She waited patiently for him to comply with her request. Seconds later his breeches were gone.

At the sight of his erect *membrum virile*, she lost her thought and gasped at him!

"My, oh my! You are enormous! Well…you are tall, and very well built…so I, suppose I should have known you would be—um? That is to say, I should have realised that, ah, you would be—" She swallowed hard as she continued her stammering declaration of his manhood. Her mouth went dry. She bit her lower lip and for the first time raised her eyes to his. Blushing wildly, she whispered, "My! But that bulge in your breeches certainly does not tell half the story, does it?" Fitzwilliam squinted one eye as he beheld her. He was half amused at her befuddled attempts toward exactitude, and half fearful of what this issue of the size of his erection might mean to her.

He watched her face carefully. She was thoughtful and quiet, as if pondering a question.

"You must be much larger than most men, pray by how much?"

"That, I would not know," he answered, holding back a smile.

"No. Of course not. I am just—that is to say, I am wondering now if the dimensions are regulated to scale? Does length go by height? And, what of thickness?"

"Once again, I must claim ignorance on this subject," he replied, trying to sound matter of fact.

"Please understand me, Fitzwilliam. I am at a disadvantage. Now I am feeling that it is possible I shall not be able to, ah, accommodate you. Or, is this something that I shall eventually, um, ah, possibly 'stretch' my way into? Somewhat like growing taller as I did when I was a child?" Her face revealed serious concerns. He reached out to touch her cheek.

Trying not to laugh, he forced a frown and bit down hard on his lip. Although amusing to him, he could see and sense her fears.

"Please have faith, my dearest Elizabeth. All shall be well for us, have no fear."

"Yes, I am sure you are correct. Umm, let us not think on it at the moment." This she said to lighten the mood and to lift her own spirits. She smiled at him. "May I touch you, Fitzwilliam?"

Merciful heaven, what is she to do? Lord, help her to have good instincts and not to hurt me or make me laugh.

Reaching her fingertips to stroke his *membrum virile*, she noticed her hand shaking. His size was intimidating, yet the important thing to her was the way he felt. As Elizabeth wondered at the mysterious organ, she was stricken with such tender feelings for Fitzwilliam.

She considered that this much maligned body part, created by God for his sons, had suffered defamatory slurs. As soon as she received her courses, her mother began to instill fear of the unending pain inflicted by this one organ. She, and other ladies of Meryton, coached and warned girls of the sinister evils done to women and young girls of all ages by the penis. Yet, Elizabeth could clearly see that this was her beloved's body. It was suddenly beautiful to her. She could not divide her beloved; this part of Fitzwilliam was still Fitzwilliam. And, as she was beginning to learn, this is was what her own body was calling for, longing for, and desiring.

Looking into his eyes, she stroked him and confessed, "All my life I have been taught such fearful and terrible things. Yet, now that I am better able to deal with your size, I realise that God has designed you, for me. I think your size is befitting you, my love."

Surprising him, she bent her head down and inhaled deeply of his manliness. His scent was so very pleasing to her. He watched her with great interest as she took her time inhaling, placing her nose nearly upon his *sac velouté*. It was as if she wished to commit his scent to memory.

He had never felt such a closeness with anyone in his entire life. Mesmerized, he observed her with intensity and, undeniably, very great interest.

Rubbing his inner thigh with her right hand, she lightly rubbed over his *sac velouté* with two fingers of her left hand, then gently kissed it. Looking into his eyes, she asked, "Is there great sensitivity here?" Keeping her eyes level with his, she searched his face.

"Yes, indeed."

She watched his face with such concerned innocence. She had been told, to hurt a man, kick him there. She began to fondle him ever so gently; he found it endearing. Her kiss was fetching, and her total focus on *that* part of his body was licentious. Although he favoured *sexe oral*, it had only included his *membrum virile*, no one ever touched him *there*. His *sac velouté* had never been given any attention. This act of love was completely new to them both.

It was not premeditated, she just followed her desire to demonstrate her love. It was a gift. He awaited her wet attentions, and then realised she did not know what to do beyond the gentle kiss to his testicles. Sensing his desire for more she said, "Please tell me what you wish of me."

Softly he whispered his desires. She smiled at him, and slowly she began to kiss him again. At once, as if overcome with affection, she pressed her cheek against his length, and then began licking him. Following his instructions she became lost to her acts of love and devotion, and moaned at her own pleasure as she became more, and more aroused. Her wet adorations were exquisitely passionate. She wished him to receive all she had to give.

He had obtained oral acts before, rendered to him with as much feeling as a bar maid wiping ale from a counter top. No matter how frequently he requested it, even paying additionally—receiving it was always the same. Quick and impersonal, seemingly an inconvenience, at best. Never was it anything like this!

"Oh, Liz-Beth, my God, do not stop, I beg you, Liz-Beth!" The sound of his voice, so thick and husky, and revealing such extreme enjoyment, acted as an aphrodisiac upon her amatory energies. Her youthful sexuality was increased, promoting an even more amorous experience for Fitzwilliam. His heart beat faster, and his breathing was more ragged than he had ever encountered. "Oh my God, Liz-Beth, what are you doing to me? Um, I have never—Oh, yes! Yes! Ahh, my Liz-Beth, yes!" He placed his hands on her head, and his eyes were closed. "Oh, my sweet girl, you are so wonderful, and this is SO GOOD, please, do not stop this!" Elizabeth was in her own paradise. Fitzwilliam's eyes were now fixed on her, and he watched her as she swallowed again, and again. She continued to draw all the precious nectar from him. Slowly she lifted her head, and told him how much she enjoyed loving him in this manner.

Taking her in his arms, he began to kiss her hair, and wet it with his tears all at once. "God, Liz-Beth, how I love you! You, loving me in this manner is my fondest desire. This is my ardent sensual pleasure. You generous, loving, and kind creature. I hunger and thirst only for you, your love, your kisses, and your attentions! How I love what you do to me! Thank you for loving me."

She placed her fingers lightly over his ears and began to play with them. Then, she kissed him, the way he had taught her to kiss him. Putting her head down upon his chest, she sighed deeply.

He gently rubbed her back and said, "Pray, Liz-Beth, try not to kill me with your love making. This being your first attempt at pleasing me, how shall I survive as your husband once you are practiced?" Her only answer was to sit up and help him remove his shirt. They settled down between the sheets, their bodies curving around each other snuggly within each other's arms.

Both were tired.

"Are we now lovers?" she whispered.

He tightened his grip on her and smiled, "Yes, my own true love. First we were friends, then betrothed, and now we are certainly lovers. We shall always be lovers!"

"And, always friends," she added, squeezing his arm. Almost as an afterthought, she sighed, "Tomorrow I shall need to look closely at your muscles, my love. Your body is most fascinating." Elated and exhausted, sleep overtook them, and it was the slumber of those who had found fulfillment. It might even be called, peace.

Fitzwilliam awoke with Elizabeth's head on his chest and her hair fanned out upon him. He could feel that her silk robe had opened during the night. Her arm was gracefully stretched over him, and he enjoyed the feeling of her breasts pressing firmly onto him. One leg was extended over his thigh, and he was startled to realise that her *mon veneris* was fabulously resting upon his accommodating flesh. He could feel that special part of her lying upon his upper leg. Her beautiful profile was turned upward, and those luscious lips were moist and slightly parted, as though inviting his tongue to play with her mouth.

The sensation of waking with her nearly atop him, and the sight and feel of her, had much appeal. This surpassed his best fantasy! It was most stimulating to him, as his body was always obligingly *pret a faire l'amour* in the morning. He moved his arm, and she stirred, and said his name in her sleep. To his delight, she pulled him closer. Lying there, watching her, he felt so blessed; he thought this was what love was meant to be in marriage. She was everything he could ever want. He was content. He watched her sleep. She stirred and he hoped she would wake up, wanting what he wanted.

"Fitzwilliam, is it morrow?" she murmured, sounding so seductive. She blinked her eyes.

"Is it even possible that you get more beautiful by the morning?" he asked, kissing her forehead.

"I do not know the time. Shall I look at my watch for you?" he offered, smiling at her.

"No. Let us pretend that it is early evening. I should like to repeat loving you. Is it possible?"

He smiled proudly at her. She sat up and lifted the covers and smiled wildly! "Oh yes, Fitzwilliam—yes. Umm, thank you, beloved. Last night in your passion you called me Liz-Beth, I should like to hear you say it again, just the way you did last night, with all the same emotions…"

The Gardiners were up early in preparation for attending the day. Edward's new connections would very likely bring much prosperity, yet along with that would be additional work. Lucille's work with and for Elizabeth's preparations would demand her time all day long, and then there would be the dinner tonight.

Lucille was making ready for her trip to Darcy House. She would join the happy party of nieces in shopping for Lizzy's wedding clothes and Pemberly wardrobe. In addition, there would be planning and preparation for the wedding trip to Kent, and then on to Pemberly.

At Darcy House, Fitzwilliam and Liz-Beth were giddy in their newly acquired expressions of love. Their focus was their love.

"About my fencing?" he inquired, quietly.

"Yes, I want to be fair. I know how I would feel if you told me I could not drive a phaeton as I pleased, nor practice my riding, and jumping bareback, nor shooting. However, please note, I strongly object." She tried to look stern, but her eyes were filled with love.

"Kiss me, I must prepare for the morning and then farewell."

She threw her arms around him and bid him stay.

"Liz-Beth, pray, help me. We must face the world for a few more days, and then we shall honeymoon. We shall stay abed as many days and nights as you desire, I promise. I need your help now. I need you to maintain proper behaviour. How shall I face your father this morning at breakfast? 'Good morning, Mr. Bennet, Lord, but your second daughter is glorious when nude! Her mouth was made for loving me, and I cannot wait to worship her with my body!' You are his daughter, I ask you only to be ready when I am ready, so I do not face him alone. I fear that my newly found convivial state shall be exposed upon my face! I would be mortified for him to have this personal intelligence.

"Also, pray, do not be so beautiful and enticing with your eyes. I need to control myself, especially around him. Good Lord, I live to be with you, and I thrive on our loving each other. I would do nothing but be naked and abed with you every moment of the day, and soon, I shall arrange it to be so. But for now, I do not need everyone to know that we are enjoying our engagement with such vigor, my lovely Liz-Beth."

"Have no fear, love," she said, kissing him. " If the *London Topics* has arrived, he shall not even look at us. He is lost to that newspaper! He has been thus all my life," she said, reassuringly.

As planned, the two reached the breakfast room at the same time. He allowed her to be first to greet her father. Mr. Bennet was drinking a cup of coffee and reading the *London Topics*.

Fitzwilliam and Rory entered at the same moment. Mr. Bennet had no suspicions about the new intimacy of the betrothed couple. His thoughts on intimacy were altogether long in the past. The very distant past. Rory on the other hand, took one look at his cousin and saw the profound change!

Good God, Fitzwilliam, you lucky bastard. You have had her, and she was delicious was she not? I knew she would be. How can I talk to her now, knowing that you have taken her as your own? If I did not love you as a brother, I would hate you.

All the men stood as the sisters filed into the breakfast room. Mrs. Gardiner joined them, and they mapped out their day. Rory wanted to escort the ladies all day with their shopping, and it was decided that the handsome son of an earl would be welcomed. Fitzwilliam would take care of his business, starting with a letter to his friend Charles Bingley, and Mr. Bennet would enjoy the library.

The letter to Bingley was quickly completed. It simply invited him to a very private family dinner at Darcy House that evening. He was under strict orders to tell no one, most especially his two sisters and his brother. Fitzwilliam sent the letter with no return information and under a plain seal.

Next Darcy met with Mr. Simmons and Mrs. Taylor. He told them of his wedding plans, and the two allowed him to think they had not guessed. Miss Bennet was well known to the staff and quite beloved. In sharp contrast was Miss Bingley who had been trying to trap Mr. Fitzwilliam Darcy into marriage for quite some time. Had that happened, the two would have tendered joint resignations.

Shopping went happily along with Colonel Fitzwilliam. Everywhere they went rumours grew. At the modiste, it was whispered that Fitzwilliam Darcy was to marry Lord Claverstone's granddaughter. The wedding was to be a secret; however, it was learned that the event would be in Devonshire on June one.

Inside the exclusive shop, Elizabeth and Georgiana spoke only in rapid French. Upon overhearing them, a slender and elegant female hand pulled the back curtain. A beautiful pair of lavender eyes peered out at them. Finally the sultry, fashionable woman appeared. She introduced herself as Juliette Marie, the famed *couturiere de Paris*. Now living in London for political reasons, she was excited to hear what she believed was two Parisians speaking in her fitting room. Continuing their conversation in French, the three ladies conversed. It was a thrill to speak with the talented designer. Elizabeth liked her instantly.

Excusing herself to consult with Aunt Gardiner, Elizabeth exited the workroom. Just before entering the front of the shop, she overheard two clients who had just entered. They had evidently just heard the news of Mr. Darcy's engagement, and they took the opportunity to depart from their elegant breeding and uncommon education to speak quite disparagingly of Fitzwilliam.

Stunned and instantly in tears, she fled back into Juliette Marie's workroom. Finding the woman alone, she burst into sobs and fell into the near stranger's arms. In fluent French, she related what the women had been saying. Calling him a 'skirt chaser' and a 'womanizer' they laughed at the idea that some poor girl would actually marry him. Without knowing her they scorned Elizabeth and called her a fool …

To Elizabeth's surprise, Juliette Marie laughed! She explained these bitter and disappointed women were upset that they had not landed such a wealthy and handsome gentleman. It was, Juliette Marie told her, *aigre raisin*, 'sour grapes.' Elizabeth protested. Asking the older woman how she could handle the idea of him bedding so many other women, Juliette Marie laughed again. She asked Elizabeth if Fitzwilliam was a good lover. Answering in the affirmative, she slowly smiled. The older, wiser woman explained the French attitude regarding the experienced lover. She said that Elizabeth should be thankful to the other women who taught him how to touch and bring her pleasure. The world was filled with men who had no idea how to touch and make love to a woman. They were, *pas bon au lit!*

She thought it over. She was a woman of logic. Imagining herself with a man who had less interest in amour, she suddenly felt she understood. She hugged Juliette Marie and thanked her.

Taking her hand, Juliette Marie warned her. You must never take him for granted. He has tasted many. You must stay fresh and keep him interested in you. Should you refuse him, he shall know where to go to find someone who shall show an interest in him. Thanking her for more than fashion, she kissed her new friend on the cheeks and quitted the workroom.

After their entire party awayed, the mysteriously reclusive Juliette Marie Mille de La Porte emerged from her workroom. She looked at the patrons in her salon and declared in perfect English, "There goes a true Parisian woman. It shall be my honour to design for the new Mrs. Fitzwilliam Darcy. She is an amazing lady and French to her very core. I am so proud to dress such a beauteous, perfect, and stylish lady!"

All the customers wondered about the beautiful, and mysterious Elizabeth Bennet.

With the wedding gown and wedding clothes taken care of, and over one hundred other items ordered, Madam Juliette Marie Mille de La Porte prospered greatly, and as the highly valued modiste for Mrs. Fitzwilliam Darcy, her future was secure! All of London would want her services.

The joyful group made it to Darcy House in time for tea, after which Fitzwilliam escorted his fiancée and his sister to their family jeweller to purchase a wedding ring. No news item appeared in the newspaper; no gossip columnist had leaked the intelligence; there was no knocker on the door at Darcy House, and the staff had kept mum. Yet, 'tis a well-known fact that one clever merchant can generate word of mouth news quite effectively. Gossip spread through the Ton like wildfire. The long illusive Fitzwilliam Darcy, known to be one of the ten wealthiest men under age thirty, had been taken off the market. The coup accomplished by the ravishingly beautiful Elizabeth of Devonshire. She, the granddaughter of Lord Claverstone, also of Devonshire, and heiress to a mysterious French fortune, was of French and English heritage. It had been reported that the wedding gown designed exclusively in Paris would be constructed by *Maison Mille de La Porte* of London. They said the value of the gown shall be in excess of 5000 pounds. The veil was to be delivered from America directly to Devonshire where a very private wedding would take place on June one.

These delightful rumors reached Fitzwilliam, Elizabeth, and Georgiana while they selected the wedding ring. Elizabeth and Georgie conversed in French about the *Sang Rivalite* of 1418.

They looked at several jewels and speculated if those had been like Marie Elise's. Completing their transactions as quickly as possible, Fitzwilliam guided the ladies by the arms as they quit the store. "I am afraid," he said very seriously, though mocking his ladies, "by nightfall Elizabeth of Devonshire's wedding ring shall rival a queen's!" The three could not contain their laughter!

Entering that same jewellry shop, Miss Bingley inquired as to the identity of the three people just leaving. She could not quite recognise their faces. She thought one was Mr. Fitzwilliam Darcy.

"Yes! Quite. No doubt you are also hearing of the marvelous Elizabeth Bennet of Devonshire who has captured the very wealthy Mr. Fitzwilliam Darcy. Yes, I am well pleased to inform you that the actual wedding ring was purchased here, not minutes ago. I shall certainly need to inform the *London Topics*. Shall I disclose the enormous amount settled on the ring? Nay. That would be crass and a breach of confidentiality toward such imminent clients."

"I have not yet been informed." Caroline puzzled, "Please enlighten me, sir."

He gleefully told her all he knew. What he did not know, he willingly supplied. He did manage to keep to the story as it was told him, in spirit, of course.

The ring's value? Yes, it did rival a queen's, nearly. Of her beauty? Yes! The most exquisite young woman he had ever seen. She spoke fluent French to her sister, Miss Georgiana Darcy. It is presumed that she is at least one-half French. Yes. Raised partially in Paris.

Her wealthy parents immigrated to Devonshire before the unpleasantness reached them.

Their fortune? Intact, of course!

Elizabeth's surname is, or may be LeFevre. Related to Henri Paul LeFevre, fiancé of Marie Elise D'Arce in 1418. An ancient event prevented the marriage. At last a Darcy shall wed a Le Fevre. It was cosmic, was it not?

Miss Bingley had heard quite enough. She burst into tears and quit the store, post haste! She needed to find Charles immediately!

Darcy House was filled with mirth! Rory, Jane, Mary, and even Aunt Gardiner laughed until they cried! Mr. Bennet felt that gossips deserved to be lied to and saw no problem with allowing the subterfuge to continue.

By the morrow the entire family would read the Ton's lies. There was not one Darcy, Matlock, Fitzwilliam, de Bourgh, nor even Claverstone who had not been the victim of the vicious *London Topic*'s writers at one time or another. Fitzwilliam sent a missive to his father informing him of the versions of the stories they had heard. He asked if the family should print the truth. At Rosings, George Darcy considered the point with their Lordships' Matlock and Claverstone. It was decided that privacy could better be obtained if the press printed the June first wedding story. All agreed nothing could be done to shut down the gossip. There would be time for a correct story after June one. If the truth would be believed by anyone who reads the *London Topics*. But, the gentlemen of the press would not be put off for long.

Marshall Topper, reporter for the *London Topics* sought the servants of the house next door to Darcy House. It cost only three shillings paid to the cook to learn that the guests at Darcy House were Thomas Bennet's family, of Longbourn, Hertfordshire.

Mr. Topper was surprised to find Mrs. Bennet at home. He told her he wanted an interview for a story about mistresses of Hertfordshire. When asked about her children, she swore she had four daughters; Jane, Mary, Catherine, and Lydia. She had but four daughters!

A reporter in Calais confirmed that Mr. George Darcy recently received authorized copies of *The Sang Rivalite* dated 1418 AD. After establishing these facts, the *London Topic* printed every fantastic story on Elizabeth LeFevre.

No one was fooled by the Bennet ruse. No, they had the truth. Her surname was now established to be LeFevre, descended from Henri Paul LeFevre. The *Topics* reported the entire ancient tale. The tragic story with the happy ending which took over two centuries to complete! The story had everything, theft, suicide, murders, love denied. The *Topics* made money; merchants made money; and even the families concerned increased in influence.

Arriving at Darcy House, Bingley looked his very best. It was difficult leaving his sister Caroline, but the message was most specific. He would not cross Fitzwilliam Darcy.

Bingley did not wait to be announced; he bounded into the room, forgetting the bow, and he blurted, "Darcy! I have not heard from you in nearly a year! I was so thrilled to receive your invitation. And, today, all over town I have been hearing the most delightful stories of you. You? Getting married? Perhaps, I, to be sure, but you?"

"Bingley, so happy to see you again, old chap! Yes, it is true. I have never been more elated in my life! You must meet Elizabeth, she is a goddess, old friend! I am still in shock that she actually said 'yes' to me!"

Rory heard Bingley's voice and ran into to the salon to join the young men. "Bingley, it has been an age since I have seen you! Darcy never mentions you. I thought you were dead!"

"No. No. I just suddenly became persona non grata. I was overjoyed to receive an invitation to Darcy House, once again."

"Yes." Fitzwilliam answered slowly. "I am afraid I grew quite weary of your ever-present sister, old friend. Do forgive me, shall you not?" Remembering the shameless way Caroline pursued Darcy, the three enjoyed a good laugh.

"Bingley, we seek to wed in a very private ceremony. Allowing that, we need to swear you to secrecy, or Rory shall have to run you through with his sword. I would like you to attend me. I cannot spare you, old chap. The wedding first, then an extended visit to Pemberly, with the finest people you shall ever meet in your life!

"One consideration, if you please. In no way do I want your sisters or brother anywhere near us. You must come absolutely alone this time."

"I understand, Darcy. Caroline has done nothing to recommend herself to you."

"Bingley, I do not even want her to know you are with us, at any time. What say you?"

He thought this over for a few minutes, and then a possible solution came to him. "Perhaps," he reasoned, "I could manage a business trip north. I shall invite Caroline. She loathes anything to do with the family business, Darcy."

"Excellent! Plan to be gone for six months, at the least; yet we wish you would chose to stay longer if you desire! Now, come and meet my beautiful future wife!"

Dinner for twelve at Darcy House was a smashing success. It was the very best dinner party in the history of the home. After dinner the gentlemen enjoyed cigars and port in the library, and the gentlewomen went into the main salon.

Soon the gentlemen rejoined the ladies, and Georgiana, Elizabeth, and Mary began to play the musical arrangements they had practiced.

A true and trusted professional, Simmons skillfully declined the visitor at the door. He informed Miss Bingley that Mr. George Darcy was very firm about allowing absolutely no visitors who had not been specifically invited per his own written invitation.

Simmons was more than willing to place Miss Bingley into her own carriage, or should she prefer, she would be charged with trespassing and delivered to the London magistrate.
Mr. Darcy would gladly prefer charges against her in that case. Caroline departed in her carriage, and Simmons went to alert Mr. Fitzwilliam Darcy as to the caller and the nature of the call.

Young Darcy had just rejoined his guests when Elizabeth stepped to the instrument. She performed an Italian love song. Just as his father told him, she was better than any professional on the stage. He knew her melodic voice was singing the words just for him. Her green eyes looked at him with the same expression she used that morning as she loved him.

Finally the evening was over, the Gardiners awayed to Gracechurch Street. Bingley went to his guest rooms, as Darcy did not trust him to be alone with his sisters and brother without telling them all he knew. Caroline must not learn a word of their plans. His man should pack for him, and then covertly come with his carriage in the morn.

Elizabeth had never experienced anything akin to the act. So much happened to her, so quickly, that she was not certain what actually did occur. It had been more pleasure than she could understand. Sensations had engulfed her beyond her mind's ability to comprehend.

"My love, you are very quiet tonight," she spoke into the darkness. "Your silence is starting to frighten me, Fitzwilliam. Have I displeased you?" Closing her eyes, she hoped for his reassuring response. There was no response, only silence. He made no answer.

Fitzwilliam held Elizabeth in the darkness, but he did not speak to her. He had just loved her in total silence, and now he was not speaking. She was trying to cope with unsettling feelings. She wished to speak with him about his attentions, but he was silent. Her spirit was crushed.

Dark thoughts now invaded her mind.

His attentions to her very private parts were quite foreign. Without a word of affection or comfort he had fondled her, and she loved it, but he quickly changed his position and replaced his familiar fingers with his very inquisitive mouth! With the right introduction, it would not have felt so strange. Unaccustomed, certainly, but not so borderline uncomfortable, and possibly improper? Wicked? Was it sinful?

My you certainly exercised your prerogative in an exploration of my body. Is that a privilege of our engagement? I suppose it was fair. Did I not the very same to you? I must admit when all is said and done, I did quite enjoy the pleasure I felt.

"Fitzwilliam?" she whispered. "I have so many questions for you. I enjoyed what you did tonight, but I am confused. You hardly spoke one word to me, did I do something wrong?

She waited. There was no response. Fearing he was disappointed with her, or possibly even tired of her, she began to feel rejected and humiliated.

Fitzwilliam feared she would ask him about the women in his past, and he wanted to avoid all questions. He was awake, of course, but wished to avoid a deep conversation.

This is it, I never want to hear the questions she shall ask. If I lie, she shall hate me, if I tell her the truth, she shall hate me.

"Why would you deny me the comfort of your words of love, or refuse even to explain what you were going to do to me. Is this anger, or are you disappointed in me and wish to annul our engagement and send me back to Uncle and Aunt Gardiner?

"In all the years of my life, I have not known the body parts you stroked and kissed. One part was so powerful, it took control of my body and caused me to jolt so forcefully that it was nearly frightening. You said you would teach me all I need to know. Shall you not help me understand, please?"

Fitzwilliam made no response. Looking at the corner of the room, she imagined herself sitting on the floor, and crying into her hands. She knew from past experience this would provide a strange sort of comfort. But, as she watched the light from the fireplace strobe across the chamber, the image faded, and she decided against becoming his victim.

Had this been a mistake? Yes, that is what it had been. What could ever make a girl like me think I could belong with a man like this, living in such a home? I, a turned out girl from Hertfordshire. I shall not allow myself to wallow in my pain. Perhaps now I am disappointed in my papa's failure to be my chaperone. Truth be told, it was up to me, how could I have let this happen? What am I about with Fitzwilliam Darcy? How did he become my world so quickly? Why do I so desire him? Now I am wanton. Still an intact virgin, even though I am no longer naïve, nor innocent. I shall leave him on the morrow-but, how shall I survive without him?

Rising from the bed with determination, she grabbed her pillow and snagged the corner of the soft blanket which had been covering the lovers. Without looking back at his supposedly sleeping form, she set her jaw firmly and guided by the candlelight entered the sitting room. That fire was nearly embers and she felt it fitting with her mood. Throwing the pillow forcefully in her anger, she aligned herself along the beautiful sofa and pulled the blanket around her body as tightly as possible.

Watching her leave their bed, Fitzwilliam's heart filled with a cold fear and dread. He was fully awake, of course, and had heard her every word. He felt cowardly and ashamed. He well knew that her pain had been escalating and the discomfort he had caused her was now swollen into a great suffering. He had made her feel rejected. His continued silence and disregard of her anguish had seemed a disaffirmation of his love. He hurt her, and he hated himself. The one thing he wished to prevent in her life, he had now caused. Had he not vowed to protect her so that she would never suffer humiliation again?

He knew her discomfort and unhappiness was now greater than his greatest fears of exposure. He had been trying to protect himself and now it was quite possible that he had destroyed their relationship.

How could he help her without exposing himself? How could he make amends without confessing his embarrassing past? He had no opiate to assist him through this anxiety, not a snort nor even a glass of strong port to take the edge off. Only the empty bed could motivate him. The fear of losing her forever compelled him to rise and go to her on the sofa.

He took her up into his arms and carried her back to their bed; the soft blanket still wrapped tightly around her body. "Pray, let me be, Fitzwilliam. Can you not see I would rather you leave me alone?" She began to struggle to free herself from the blanket. "Please, I beg of you, just show me to another room, or I shall dress and find a servant to take me to Jane's rooms. Tomorrow I shall go to my uncle and aunt's home.

"Tonight I was in your arms, thinking I belonged there, but your shocking, cold silence told my heart that you no longer love me. I learned from your silence everything I need to know of your true feelings. I can clearly see that you no longer desire me for a wife. I certainly do not wish to wed someone who has no feelings for me."

He knew he had to do something immediately, but what? He continued to keep her close to him. He sat on the edge of the bed, holding the greatest treasure he had ever been given. Slowly he began to rock back and forth and stroke her hair softly. He tried to console her crushed spirit and give answers to her accusations.

"No, for God's sake, no Liz-Beth. I have not changed my mind, I could never change my mind concerning you. Oh God, I love you more than I love my own life! I did not mean to hurt you with my silence. I do not understand my own taciturn episodes,

I beg you to forgive me, please? Do not allow my failings to lay waste to our love. I am so very sorry, my darling.

"You are an innocent and should not suffer like this. Oh my, sweet girl, Elizabeth. What have I done? Please never feel shame nor embarrassment during nor after any of our acts of love. You have done no wrong at all. Your behaviour has only been correct, and you could never disappoint me. I dare say, your body is flawless, even upon very close inspection. You, my darling, lack nothing! I love and adore you and completely worship your body. Pray, let me kiss away all your disappointments. Oh, how shall I make amends to you?

"Yes, I was silent tonight whilst I loved you, because I was afraid. The fault is mine. You are too bright for me. You were perfect tonight. I used my knowledge of the female body to bring you extreme pleasure. I knew you would experience ecstasy and would develop a predilection for that particular expression of love. When you were so incredibly responsive to my loving you, I put aside your innocence in the heat of my passion.

"I feared what I might say to you whilst loving you, that is why I said nothing at all. I know it was a colossal error on my part. How could I think it was correct to refrain from telling you I love you, whilst loving you? What a disaster!

"I was afraid I would say something like, 'I have pleasured many women with this'— or, perhaps I might have slipped and said, 'you enjoy this more than anyone I have ever…' You would have been crushed with a broken heart, and I mortified! Yet, look at what I have accomplished, you were crushed with a broken heart, and I now am afraid of losing your love forever."

After several minutes of insupportable silence, Elizabeth spoke. "Fitzwilliam, are you telling me that you kept silent whilst loving me because you were afraid you would speak of women you have been in love with, and you feared your sexual encounters would be disclosed to me? Why did you not speak to me of them before this? Do you not trust me at all?"

Bloody hell. There is her legal voice again. Most men would not tolerate questions or comments like these, and most women would not dare to ask.

For the first time, she smiled, looked deeply into his eyes, and said, "Fitzwilliam, I asked you to tell me what pleased you. You could have given me an idea of the act, but that was not what brought my despair. It was your coldness to me, your cruel silence. You said not one word of love, and yet you performed acts upon my private part without so much as telling me you loved me. Not before, during, nor after. No words from you, just a complete invasion of an area that took all my self-control and restraint not to fight you off or at least try to clamp my legs shut tight! I knew nothing of the act, and even so, we would not be having this conversation if you had only told me you loved me. Three words would have satisfied me.

Your hushed performance, followed by grave silence and indifferent treatment of me when I begged you to speak to me, filled me with self-doubt. This is the first time you have loved me and left me completely heartsick! How could you turn a deaf ear to me? Can you not understand that communication is necessary in relationships? You cannot hope to know my thoughts on any matter. Am I an unreasonable woman?"

She is correct. When shall I stop my selfishness and begin to care for her first? How do I answer her and keep her respect? Do I deserve her respect?

"Fitzwilliam, do you think me so dull that I do not recognise that you have five adult years over my lifetime? You are a man, a wealthy man, with women throwing themselves at you. Why should you pretend that you have no past experience? If I said your past does not matter, I would be lying. But, I have no moral right to question you about how many women.

"I do ask this of you. We shall be living in London and Pemberly. If there are women with whom you have had a romance, or other encounters that could be thrown into my face, I ask you to tell me about them, right now. I do not want to be at dinner and separated with the gentlewomen who wish to slice up the new bride from Hertfordshire whilst you have cigars and port. I am a very jealous person. If I see you after our wedding showing too much attention to another woman, I would be tempted to put an arrow through her heart.

Or, possibly through both your hearts.

"Does your silence mean that you are thinking it over, and you are not sure if you wish to tell me? Or, does it mean you have nothing to tell me.

Tomorrow I shall send an express to Mrs. Reynolds and order the dismissal of Mary Simpson, Alice Owens, Polly Jensen and Martha Hill. Yes, and I shall tell Simmons to dismiss that new blond girl, Dawes, Margaret Humphries, Carole Carmichael, and Sara Henson. Six months' severance pay? I have failed to think this through.

So many servants. Bloody hell, what was I doing with my life?

"Fitzwilliam, are you going to be silent again? Are you thinking that the situation shall never arise and I shall not need to know?"

After a few minutes more, he responded, but he did not answer her questions. He finally spoke saying: "Elizabeth, I have been about many things since a quite young age; most of which, I am not proud. I did not ever consider that someday I would meet a woman like you, and wish I had your purity. But, Elizabeth, I do wish to God I had your purity. When I fell in love with you, I wanted everything to be the first time with you. But it is too late for that. I do not even know that I could have waited for you, if God had shown you to me, and told me to be chaste and keep myself only for you, and wait for you.

"I must tell you this. The amazing way you love me is so very different from any other experience. Even the same act is completely different with you. You are so generous to me. In every act of love, you give yourself to me. Every act of love, is a gift from your heart to mine. I have never been loved like this in my entire life. I tell you that I have loved no woman in my past. You may ask Georgie or Father. They shall tell you that no one has even been special to me."

"Fitzwilliam, I shall try to remember that. Feel free to remind me, now that you are no longer protecting yourself from your past. If that is your final word to me on the subject and there are no names I should know of women who might suddenly appear in our lives and try to stake a claim upon you, then let us go to sleep. I need to tell you that I am not good at pretending.

"You may as well know that you have hurt me deeply. I very nearly left you tonight. You need to begin to trust me. We are to be married. You may tell me anything, and I shall always try to see your side and understand your point of view. Good night my love, sleep well."

She kissed his lips quickly, arose from his lap, and got into bed. He climbed in and put his arms around her. She did not turn away. He could barely breathe. He knew she still loved him, yet she was deeply hurt. He made her cry in an effort to needlessly protect himself. She knew what he had been doing. Protecting himself. Had she not called him on it the first day they met?

Fitzwilliam slept very little. Long before dawn he determined that he must try to bring their relationship back to where they had been when they arrived in London.

Offering up a silent prayer, he began to kiss her hair. She stirred and to his complete relief, she said his name and moved closer to him. She was still sleeping.

Oh God, how she loves me, and seeks me even in her sleep!

"Good morning, sweet Elizabeth!" He kissed her shoulder. "Do you wish an early start on the day, or shall I let you slumber?" She opened her eyes, and smiled at him. It was a very hopeful sign. To his relief, she kissed his lips. She allowed him to deepen the kiss, if he chose to do so. With a deep moan, he abandoned his fears and caught her sensual mouth in his.

It seemed that her ardor replaced all rational thought, and the experience of last night was put behind them. His tender attentions to her mouth became wildly passionate within moments. With the kiss, Elizabeth felt her fearful, angry thoughts of doubts and insecurities begin to melt away. Caught up in their own sensual appetites for each other, they soon became unrestrained. "Trust me, please, love?" Fitzwilliam pled.

She nodded, and he smiled.

Their hands reached out for one another. A touch, any touch, anywhere. His fingers invading those senses of her body again. This time, she welcomed him. "Oh, yes, do it again, pleazzee!" Suddenly she felt him throw the covers from the bed. He moved her body with force, she atop him, facing down, toward his feet, his erect *membre virile* was touching her lips. Her breasts smashing into his stomach, she felt a pillow being placed under her hips, and his hands firmly parting her legs. His soft lips began kissing her inner thighs and his fingers stroking that place of amazing sensations. She heard him saying how much he appreciated her love and devotion and that he wanted her to know how much he loved and adored her. He wanted to bring her pleasure, and asked her if this was well with her. He said he wanted to do what she wished, and he loved her very much. He told her that every part of her body was beautiful. She said she loved him, and then began by kissing the blunt end of his fully erect *membre virile*. Instinctively she drew him into her waiting mouth and lavishly stimulated him with beguiling ministrations. She lapped and sucked while drawing her fingers slowly over his inner thighs and scrotum.

Her overwhelming responsiveness was far better than he had hoped.

They released themselves into their own cravings, passionately finding that their indulgence was rewarded with mutual gratification. Their joy and their expressions of love to each other were freely and exquisitely performed. Each lavished the other with simultaneous ecstasy! When they had done with each other, there was a delicious explosion of words.

She spoke of her undying love for him, and of their future. He told her that he had never been so satisfied and happy. He wanted her to know that he had never before performed the act they just experienced. He had read about it, but he never had an intimate relationship where such mutual attentions were possible. In fact, it was important she understood that he never had, ever in his entire life, been in love with anyone else. It was only Elizabeth who had ever taken his heart.

She asked her questions. Where is the hymen? Does it fall out when you break it? Shall it dissolve? What about the time she fell from her horse? The doctor told Aunt Gardiner her hymen might have broken. At age seven, Elizabeth thought the hymen was a bone!

He did not know the answers. He had never been with a virgin. She shall be his first, his one and only.

She told him he had the ability to bring her pleasure she had never known, but at times it was so intense it almost felt like torture. She wanted to know if she did that to him.

They talked about what they had both just experienced together. They talked about it until they both wanted to do it again…

The news reporters were stationed outside Darcy House. This made the process of leaving for Kent very involved and time consuming. Carriages had to be sent in stages. Otis and Jeannette were sent as decoys for Fitzwilliam and Elizabeth.

Fitzwilliam rode Percival, leaving from the rear of the livery. The Bennets took a road to Longbourn, then doubled back to Kent. Charles Bingley was met with his carriage by his man, Parker. Georgiana and Elizabeth left in the second Darcy carriage. Colonel Fitzwilliam left on horseback from the front of Darcy House and rode to his barracks, before turning to go to Kent.

Once again Lord Claverstone met the Gardiner carriage. He was so pleased to see the children again. Bingley and the Bennets were next to arrive, and lastly the carriage with Georgie and Lizzy rolled up.

Elizabeth sent a message to George Darcy requesting the company of Georgie. She wished her new sister to remain with her until the wedding. Her help was much needed. This pleased the girl very much!

Fitzwilliam had much work to do, and used Lord Claverstone's library daily. He wanted to be near Elizabeth. Jane spent nearly every moment with Charles Bingley. It was obvious to everyone that they were falling in love. Lizzy spent large amounts of time with her Grand papa. They rode, and he taught her of bloodlines and horse breeding.

The servants at Claverstone, declared that it had been years since the gentleman had been so joyful. It was a blessing to have his enormous home filled with happy, lively people. He further looked forward to visiting Pemberly for the same reasons.

At last the morning of April seventeen arrived. All the guests had entered the cathedral. Everyone took their places for the service. The first to stand up was Charles Bingley. He was wearing a grey suit with a pale blue shirt. He looked wonderful across from Jane who was wearing a blue gown trimmed in white. The pair looked stunning.

Next Fitzwilliam entered. He wore a very stylish suit of the newest fashion, with long trousers. It was deep blue, with a slightly lighter waistcoat. His silk shirt was a light shade of blue that nearly appeared to be white. He looked most handsome and very happy as he joined his friend and waited for Elizabeth.

At last she appeared. He thought she had never looked more beautiful than at that very moment. She was fabulous in a cream-coloured silk gown with an empire-styled waist. It was cut away in a scoop neck, yet with long sleeves forming a peak at the mid-point of her hands.

Her face appeared so fresh and lovely through the delicate lace of her exquisite veil. It reached her fingertips at the front and lengthened toward the back. It was the same soft cream colour as the gown and a perfect match to the long cathedral-length train which was made of matching lace and silk. She carried a bouquet of white roses surrounded by Sweet William from the glade. For her herb, she chose dill, as everyone knows it increases sexual desire. In keeping with tradition, the bride and groom would nibble on the dill throughout the wedding breakfast and keep eating it until it was gone.

Elizabeth looked astonishing in the marvelous gown, veil, and train which had been exclusively designed for her. The style, combination of fabrics, and rich colour set a new trend. The overall appeal of her wedding ensemble, and even the popularity of her bridal bouquet, spread throughout the realm, Europe, and even to America.

Weeks later, Mrs. Bennet and Lydia would read and see sketches of the fabulous Fitzwillliam and Elizabeth Darcy's stylish wedding in a special addition of the *London Topics* exclusive issue! The source who leaked the details, including the design sketches, was never discovered.

For several moments, everyone awaited the cleric, Mr. James. His arrival was well planned. He wished to allow proper time for the family to observe the precious scene before them. Mr. James felt that strong family support of the marriage helped to safeguard the success of the union and promote happiness for all. He wanted the guests to reflect upon the lives which were soon to be united, forever!

The bride and groom locked eyes as Mr. James began the service, proclaiming "Dearly beloved, We are gathered here…"

Elizabeth listened to the first admonishment: marriage is ordained for the procreation of children to be brought up in the fear and nurture of the Lord. Fitzwilliam heard the first and the second: marriage is ordained as a remedy against sin and to avoid fornication that such persons as have not the gift of constancy might marry and keep themselves undefiled members of

Christ's body. The third: marriage was given to support and help each other throughout all of life's trials.

It was difficult to concentrate when all they could think about was being together, always.

Mr. James invited anyone who could show just cause why they may not lawfully be joined together, to speak or else hereafter forever hold their peace.

Next were the vows: "Fitzwilliam Darcy, wilt thou have this woman to be thy wedded wife, to live together after God's ordinance in the holy estate of matrimony? Wilt thou love her, comfort her, honour her, and keep her in sickness and in health, forsaking all others, keeping thyself only unto her so long as ye both shall live?"

"I will."

"Elizabeth Bennet, wilt thou have this man to be thy wedded husband to live together after God's ordinance in the holy estate of matrimony? Wilt thou obey him, serve him, love, honour, and keep him in sickness and in health and forsaking all others, keeping thyself only unto him as long as ye both shall live?"

"I will."

"Who giveth this woman?"

Thomas Bennet beamed. He was here, giving away his Lizzy. Stepping forward he proudly said, "I do—" then he took her hand and placed it into Fitzwilliam's hand, turned with great pride, and took his seat.

And now, here comes the part where I promise in public that I shall have sex with my wife.

"I, Fitzwilliam Darcy, take thee, Elizabeth Bennet, to be my wedded wife to have and to hold from this day forward for better, for worse, for richer, for poorer, in sickness and in health, to love and to cherish till death do us part, according to God's Holy ordinance; and thereto I pledge thee my troth. With this ring I thee wed, with my body I thee worship, and with all my worldly goods I thee endow. In the name of the Father, and of the Son and of the Holy Ghost. Amen."

"I, Elizabeth Bennet, take thee, Fitzwilliam Darcy, to be my wedded husband to have and to hold from this day forward for better, for worse, for richer, for poorer, in sickness and in health, to love, cherish, and to obey till death us do part, according to God's Holy ordinance; and thereto I give thee my troth."

Mr. James finished by saying: "God the Father, God the Son, God the Holy Ghost preserve and keep you. May the Lord mercifully with his favour look upon you and so fill you with all spiritual benediction and grace that ye may so live together in this life, and that in the world to come ye may have life everlasting. Amen."

With great joy everyone attended the wedding breakfast at Claverstone. Grandpapa told Mr. and Mrs. Darcy that he could not remember having such joy in his life as the two of them had brought. They gave him their thanks for everything he had done.

After spending the required time at the breakfast, the couple, very eager to be gone, said their goodbyes, telling everyone they would see them at Pemberly. They left in the second Darcy carriage with Percival and Marigold tied behind them. A groomsman watched over them throughout the trip. Atop the carriage was an expert driver, and a very big footman.

Chapter 8

"We are all subject to life's hazards. Some, more than others are placed within danger's cross hairs.

Only the very wise understand the placement of targets, and their avoidance."

-Anonymous

Elizabeth Darcy noticed a subtle change in her husband. She observed him carefully, trying to determine exactly what it might be. Whatever it was, she found it quite fetching!

Looking out the window, Elizabeth was enchanted with the village they had just entered. "Oh, husband of mine, just look at this charming little place. It is so romantic, is it not?"

"Indeed," he agreed, as he put his head next to hers to see the village again, "I have always loved stopping here for the night. It is called Swan's Creek."

Their carriage pulled into the inn. The servants' vehicle was already there, and their horses had received care. Darcy smiled. *All seems to be going to plan.*

Elizabeth remarked that theirs were the only two carriages. The inn seemed empty. He made no comment. Stepping out to hand his bride out of their carriage, he smiled as he looked at the pristine condition of the inn. It looked better than he remembered. Taking Elizabeth's hands, he helped her down, whispering that he wanted more dill from her bouquet. She gave him a quick kiss on the cheek, and smiling, whispered that they both should have more. Elizabeth looked around at the inn as they walked to the desk. "What a charming and romantic place. It has a very special presentation, and the interior is so tastefully decorated. Thank you for bringing me here, darling, this is absolutely lovely." Fitzwilliam smiled broadly and patted the hand which was on his arm.

Mr. and Mrs. Thompson stood behind the desk. "Oh, Mr. Darcy, how wonderful to have you here and to meet Mrs. Darcy. We are so very excited that you are spending such a special time with us. Everything you have requested has been seen to, and your man, Otis, has assured me that you shall be very happy, indeed, sir."

"Mr. Thompson, I am so pleased to see you again, and we are looking forward to a long, rewarding relationship with you and Mrs. Thompson." While Fitzwilliam chatted, Elizabeth continued looking around at the inn. Everywhere her eye fell, she found new enchantment, but she was becoming concerned for the success of the inn, "Mr. Thompson, I do hope your business is brisk. I fear I see only workers present. If I may, where are the other guests?"

"Yes, business is wonderful, Mrs. Darcy. I thank you. I assure you, all have arrived, Mrs. Darcy. Please enjoy your stay. Otis has insisted upon showing you to your floor." He bowed and stepped beside his wife. The couple smiled brightly at them, and seemed quite pleased.

Climbing to the top floor, Elizabeth could not shake the feeling that the inn was nearly empty. She inquired of her husband, frowning as she listened for his response. He simply stopped at the top of the stairs, squeezed her hands, and beamed at her.

Otis and Jeannette opened the door to their suite. Elizabeth stared! It was magnificent! The grand sitting room was elegantly furnished. A lovely dining room that could seat twelve was attached. She looked at her husband and giggled as they entered a fabulously appointed bed chamber with a bed as large as theirs in town! There were two dressing rooms which were equipped with all of their favourite and necessary items. Anything they, or anyone else, could possibly desire was contained in this suite.

"Oh, Fitzwilliam, have you ever in your most fantastic dreams seen such an amazing vision as these rooms, available at an inn, located in such a charming village? That they should be situated here, is more than fortunate." He leaned against the wall as she went from room to room and inspected their accommodations. He watched her closely, with an engaging smile emerging upon his face.

Elizabeth continued, "Darling, did you say Swan's Creek is the name of the hamlet?"

"Yes, Liz-Beth. You seem taken with our rooms. What of the inn overall?" he asked, smiling.

"I dare say, it is very romantic, is it not? This is the most beautiful inn I have visited. It is quite past my understanding of inns. Do you not think it to be the finest inn in the realm? Or, perhaps the entire world? Swan's Creek Inn. Lovely."

Fitzwilliam's face was glowing, his smile had spread in a most delightful fashion. His dimples were clearly visible, and he looked quite handsome. His bride could scarcely keep her hands off his person.

"Indeed. I agree, beloved. It does look accommodating. Suitable for a couple wed only this morning." he murmured, watching her closely.

"Oh!" she swooned, "'Tis a dream come true, I dare say, I could never have envisioned anything as wonderful. It is more than accommodating. Who would not want to start their wedded bliss in rooms like these? Such an immense bed, in a beautiful chamber. It is most inspiring of romantic love, do you not agree, beloved? Are you not inspired?"

"Yes, my beautiful minx! I am most salaciously inspired. With you, and the inn. I desired our first night together would be very private and luxurious. We could not be in a public room, with others listening behind paper thin walls. How could we love on just any bed, or just any linens? No. Nothing but the finest for us, my love. That is why I bought this inn. Just for us, Elizabeth. I am so glad you are pleased."

"Did you indeed buy this inn, just for us, Mr. Darcy?" she asked him, while rubbing his derriere seductively.

Smiling at her, he lowered his voice to a husky sound and crooned, "Of course, I did, my wife. I wanted you to be comfortable when we spend our first time joining as one." He stepped behind her and slipped his arms around her waist. She rested her head back against his shoulder.

"Are you, quite comfortable, Mrs. Darcy?" he whispered into her ear, and then nibbled on her earlobe.

"Ummm, I am deliciously comfortable, Mr. Darcy. I thank you."

"I cannot tell you what you just did for me when you called this room most inspiring!" He pulled her closer to him, and she slid around so they could be face to face, and feel each other's body better.

"And so it is!" she declared. "So comfortable and inspiring. What if we desire more than one night of comfort and inspiration, Mr. Darcy"

"Hum, what would inspire you so, Mrs. Darcy?" he lifted his eyebrows and leered at her.

"Perhaps, my lover shall keep me so supremely excited that I fail to notice what day it is, or we are so blissfully engaged in love-making that we care not what day it is?" she murmured.

"Are you confident that your lover can satisfy you and keep your interest, Mrs. Darcy?"

"Aye, I am intoxicated for life, and I have not yet fully imbibed," she responded, while letting him know she was eager for them to join. "I am so filled with love and desire for my lover," she continued playfully, "that even the thought of his touch thrills me greatly, and my body hungers for him, day and night."

Darcy's dimples were fully displayed as he enjoyed this little game with his bride. "My! But you are so young, perhaps you are only enamored with 'love' and not your lover?"

"Nay! I cared not for love, nor gave it a thought until I met my lover. He is love, to me. He is the only lover on earth. Only he can satisfy me. I am greedy for him, and obsessive in my desires. He shall quench my thirst, and in my lust for him, I shall wish to be abed more than one day, I dare say," she whispered, softly stroking his jaw.

"Then, the matter is settled, Mrs. Darcy. We shall stay abed for as many days and nights, as we wish."

Something in his manner thrilled her. She contemplated the change in her husband. His continence was the same, yet he seemed straighter, stronger, more sure of himself. What was it? Dignity? Self-assurance? Whatever it was, she found it quite fetching. Yes, she felt it was very irresistible indeed.

Everywhere they looked, the evidence of Otis and Jeannette's attention to detail was apparent. Platters of food were placed upon the table. Trays of wine and champagne were found in the bed chamber, pitchers of fresh water abounded in each room.

Elizabeth told Jeannette to take the evening for herself. She quickly freshened her face and breath. Then, still in her wedding gown, with her veil in her hand, she looked for her husband.

He, dressed in his wedding clothes as well, was on the bed, looking very relaxed. He had been watching her with intensity. It made her somewhat nervous.

"Mrs. Darcy, you are a vision. I wonder, how does a vision appear under her gown? What, I ask myself, does the modern bride wear as undergarments?"

"Ohhh, I am scandalized, Mr. Darcy! And amazed that you did not lift my gown to see for yourself."

"I would rather you do it," he said, lying on his side, with his elbow bent and his head resting upon his hand. He had been observing her closely. She met his gaze and boldly lifted the gown, revealing her stocking and slippers.

"Madam, I see a shocking lack of undergarments. Did you go to church as such?"

"Aye. I wanted to prepare for this moment. For, I thought you might wish to see,"

"Come here, virgin. I would have a closer look at you." As she moved, he jumped up, grabbed her, and threw her upon the huge bed. Her veil flew across the room, as did one slipper. They kissed and rolled upon the bed as two people without a care in the world!

Finally, they stood and slowly disrobed each other. At his insistence, she stood still before him, wearing only her veil. He found it exquisitely alluring and beguiling.

"Just let me look at my bride, attired only in her beautiful veil." He stood staring at her. "Turn around, please. I may have missed the full effect earlier today. Ahh! Yes, I can clearly see how it accents your beautiful back. Perfect for your purity, beloved."

At that, he fastened his arms around her and ran his hands up and down her back. He was totally relaxed and in absolutely no hurry to take her. He was determined to go slowly.

"What is it about you that is so very different, my love? You are my Fitzwilliam, yet you are somehow quite changed. I cannot decide what the difference may be. I fancy it, my love!"

He was loving this type of tribute and attention. Especially from his bride wearing only her wedding veil. However, all he did was smile at her, in that new and very fetching way. It was beginning to cause a burning desire deep within her. She was feeling an urgent need for him to love her, and this time to completion!

He eased himself behind her and placed his hands around her waist. She turned around. He began to run his hands up and down her back again, comfortingly at first, then more amorously. His palms rubbed over her firm, round buttocks suggestively and lingered there, indulging in the curves of her delectable derriere. He smiled to himself as he marveled at the absolute perfection of his wife's young body.

Suddenly she pulled away from him, interrupting his preoccupation of her posterior. She looked up at him, and boldly declared, "I have it! You are self-assured, calm, confident, Yes! I have been trying to figure it out all day. Fitzwilliam Darcy, you are now a married man! As such, you are your own man! You make your own decisions, chart your own course, and plan our future. You are head of our household. Your father is a wonderful man, and a loving man. But, he is just your father now, not your boss, nor your authority figure. You are making your own decisions, are you not?"

He smiled at her, and embraced her again, and commenced his fondling of her buttocks.

"When did you buy this inn?" she asked him, in a hurry to make her point. "And organize these rooms, and their contents?" He gave her a squeeze as he answered: "April third, when I knew I would marry you and take you to Pemberly. Whomever you were, I loved you deeply from the start. I wanted everything to be perfect for us. This inn is the finest down the coast leading into Kent.

It is on the best traveled road. The architecture is perfect; I just added the furnishings. The staff is well seasoned, and efficient. Everything just aligned. I knew it was perfect for us to add to our holdings." Ending with an engaging smile, he began to kiss her.

"Brilliant! What a wonderful business opportunity. You are a visionary, my love. These accommodations are fit for those of your class," she said, " Nothing like this exists but here."

"*Our* class, darling!" he corrected her.

"Yes, yes, *our* class. And, these rooms shall rent for—how much for the night? What of the other rooms? What of the annual profits and losses? How long shall it take to recover your initial investment, love?" Her voice showed her excitement and pride in him.

"No, no, Liz-Beth, you do too much thinking. I have other plans for your right now. Trust me, you shall not need to use your brain at all. Just relax and enjoy yourself."

He slowly removed her veil, kissed her gently and promised, "Elizabeth, this is a very special time. We are going to go very slowly. I want your consent in all we do together.

"Tonight only, I am a virgin of sorts. This is my first—and my only—time to make love to a very beautiful virgin maiden, with whom I am deeply in love. It is my first time to bed my wedded wife, to worship her with my body. And, the first night we shall spend in our new inn."

She arched her delicate eyebrows. "My, my, Mr. Darcy, you have been a very busy man. No wonder you would like to slow down. I am all enamored of you, darling. My, you can act quickly and decisively. Your excellent business acuity and your intellect must be added to the long list of things that cause me to go wild with sensual desire for you!"

He straightened to his full height. "Yes, I certainly have been very busy. And just for you. I intend now, to keep you a very (kiss), very (kiss) busy (kiss) woman (kiss) Mrs. Darcy." His voice trailed off, and he applied his full attentions to kissing her. She welcomed his velvety tongue, and sweet soft lips. His kisses began to make her feel a wooziness she had never experienced before, and she held on to his shoulders. Elizabeth put her complete powers of concentration upon his very sensuous and thirsty mouth.

How he led her to the bed and placed her upon the many propped pillows, she would never know. As she so reclined, her lush dark hair spilled over onto his head. He saw it, and enjoyed the feel of it as he continued kissing the hollow of her throat. His scent was intoxicating, just as the touch of his fingertips became hypnotic. He was drawing his fingers slowly from side to side over her stomach.

She responded by running her fingers along his neck. Now aware of his arousal pressing into her thigh, she groaned, loudly. It was the first time she heard herself groan aloud. At last she was at liberty to vocalize her pleasure without the fear of being discovered.

Upon hearing her groan, he stopped and looked up at her, as if to determine the cause of her outcry. Realising it was pleasure, he smiled. Suddenly he wanted to smother her with kisses, to lick every beautiful inch of her ivory skin. Lowering his head to her bosom, he began to accomplish his desire, as he alternately kissed, licked and sucked, right, then left. His fingertips began an invasion of the secret places of her pleasure, known only to him. He became relentless in his slow stimulations. For Elizabeth, it was a mixture of torture and euphoria. Over and over again, he repeated his acts of devotion. Her desires caused her to beg him for more and more!

She was shocked at the sound of her own voice in its urgency. The boldness of her demands shocked her as well. "Oh, I am wanton," she whispered in his ear, but she could not stop begging. He was happy to bestow his attentions, but at his own pace. He would not be rushed.

It was a tumult of pleasure and pain. Her desire mixed with his delay. At his touch, waves of sensuality crashed over her, causing her to torque her back. Her body convulsed into a contorted frenzy as the powerful storm he was creating in her went on and on without mercy! He watchfully stroked her breasts, only to desert them as he pacified her by gently rubbing her inner thighs. She could not breathe, yet she found that voice which demanded more! He did not disappoint her. Pleasing her was the centre of his desire. He began to moan as he continued to feel and kiss every curve of her body.

She was the sole object of his love and passion. He had just promised before God that with his body he would worship her, and he intended to fulfill that vow. Frequently! His only quest was to draw them into a life of sensual, mutual marital felicity and bliss. He went deeper and deeper into his own desires. He took her with him. He watched her closely as her muscles contracted sporadically causing her back to arch, again and again. He smiled to himself as her hips began to move of their own accord, undulating to a pulsating rhythm he was directing. He was taking his cues from her body. He loved it! Never had he enjoyed loving a woman as much as this, their first time.

Her head was now moving rapidly from side to side. She had fallen deeper than ever before; her physical and emotional sensations peaked again and again and again. Using only his hands and mouth, he kept her in a place of continuing pleasure. He wanted her at the pinnacle of voluptuous delectation. She had never known such sensations, and had never thought of the ways she could receive from him. He counted her orgasms until he lost himself in their sublime enumerations.

He liked watching her closely. Observing how his storm was overtaking her. It thrilled him. Her every move confirmed that he was her desire. Yet, his desire now was to love her and teach her body to receive all her sensual pleasures from him. Always.

His delight was giving her the kind of pleasure only a husband can give his wife.

He whispered her name and told her of his ardent love for her. He said he wanted her to be comfortable with him, yet he relentlessly played on and on with her virginal maiden's body.

He appeared not to regard the wild sensations he continued to create in her. His hands and mouth became more and more familiar with her curves. He was intimate and insistent with her body. More demanding than she had imagined. She had vowed before God to obey him. She would always obey him. She closed her eyes. His fingers lightly stroked over her forehead, and he spoke lovingly to her. He was coaxing her into complete relaxation. He was beguiling her to release all her fears.

He traced her lips with his tongue, moistened them and opened them to enter her mouth again and again, and all so softly and gently. He controlled her mouth now, just has he did her body.

She wanted to beg him to enter her and become one flesh with her, but his mouth would not allow her to speak. She could not free her mouth, and she did not want it to be freed.

She wanted him to do more and more of whatever he wanted to do to her. She wanted to be taken further into his storm and experience more of his depths. She craved this new freedom of sensuality he was creating. She loved being more than compliant and yielding. She felt herself becoming unfettered. He sensed the changes in her and found this freshness delectable. His stimulations now incited a new intensity in her responsiveness. Her hands and fingers became ravenous. She was now matching his touches in an exploration of his body. They both shivered in raptures, as she began to deliver intricate attentions to his *organs genitaux*. He was enthralled as she stunned his senses again and again. Over and over she lavished her wet favours in a coterie of devotion. He was mesmerized at his own increasing arousal.

His hands began slowly stroking her inner thighs and gently urging her legs apart. Her mind now found the reality of the time for their joining. She heard a voice above her calling her name. Telling her something about her readiness. She felt his familiar touch within the apex of her legs.

His fingers invading and teasing her senses. His voice sounding like a gentle breeze. "Ahhhh, dearest, darling Lizzz-Bethhh, you are soooo wet. You are soaked. Your body is ready. Are you ready for me?" she became aware of his knees prompting her legs further apart. Her heart beat wildly, realising it was time. *Dear Lord, I want him to fit inside me. Please.* Allowing her legs to be moved further apart than they ever had been in his company, she closed her eyes and waited to feel his flesh touching hers. She felt him moving around her, and sensed him, rather than saw him kneeling between her legs. At last she could feel his tip rubbing against her, collecting her lubricant. "Ohh! Do you feel that, love? Our first flesh upon flesh touch. Is it not wonderful?"

"Yesss, my lovely wife. It has been dreamed of, and imagined, and yet it is so much better than the dream. It is so intimate and so precious. How I love and adore you, Elizabeth Darcy! You, my darling are so beautiful. Are you ready, beloved?"

"I am," she smiled. She lifted herself up to see as much as possible.

His heart was telling him to go slowly and be gentle. He began to enter her, very slowly, so gently, and with just a shallow placement. He also was unsure of his large size entering such a petite girl.

She felt stinging pain in her skin, yet she heard herself saying, "Fitzwilliam, I want you inside. Yes! Please, yes!" a wild sounding voice encouraged him. She was stunned to hear it. It was a shocking sound, too loud and too course to be her own voice. Yet, it would not be silent.

"Oh, dearest, darling Fitzwilliam, hurry, oh please hurry, love. I need you now! Please, now!"

At her urging, his instincts took over his body. He kissed her deeply and thrust into her nearly as hard as he could. Again and again he plunged her depths.

What was that? A sting? A pain? It shall most likely pass. Perhaps it was some kind of stretching. She started to grind into him with an effort to capture more of him. She wanted to be sure she had all of him inside her.

Who was in control of this marionette that had become her body? Who was moving her hips and pelvis like that? Who was pushing against his thrust as hard as possible in an effort to possess more and more of him? *Pain! Yes it is pain, it is still here and somewhat searing.*

"Did it break? Tell me, did you feel it?" she demanded answers as she tightly clutched his arms. Her husband answered her. "Your childhood fall from your horse did not break your hymen, my love, I just did! Are you well, my sweet girl? Do you still love and desire me?" Secretly he took great pride in its destruction. He had taken virginity from that gorgeous girl in the glade! *Oh God! Such satisfaction! I cannot wait to see the sheet. At last I shall know the truth of the matter. Everyone I know has bragged of it. Now, I could, but I shall not. Otis should box up the sheet, I shall keep it.*

"Yes, I am well, darling. It was a brief pain. Of course I still love and desire you! More than I can—Oh! Fitzwilliam, more, I need more of you, now! Please do not stop, my love. Oh, yes, that is so wonderful, oh my love." Sooner than she wanted, he slowed and stopped. He allowed his body to cover hers and rested atop her. She found this part of their joining so sweet. He used all of his energies, his love, devotion and undivided attentions on her. His desire was to satiate her needs and longings. He had used splendid stamina, and was spent. She whispered, "Did you find pleasure, or were you too concerned about your virgin?"

"Yes, of course, my first thoughts were of you, but it takes little to satisfy me, love."

"Husband, I love the feel of your exhausted, sweaty body covering mine. I have never felt more safe, protected, and loved. Thank you so much Fitzwilliam."

"Thank you, wife. And do you also feel welcome?"

She chuckled softly and squeezed him. "Very, very welcome, indeed."

"I am a man of some weight, and I do not wish to smash you, beloved." She held on to him tightly. "No," she begged as she clutched him, "I am perfectly wonderful and do not even feel your weight. I suppose it is the same miracle that allows us to join. You are enormous, and very hard, yet somehow quite soft. You fit inside me! That is to say, I believe all of you fit inside me. Did you, love?" She waited anxiously as he answered her.

"Yes, my darling, we are a perfect fit. Does that please you, Mrs. Darcy?"

"Naturally, everything about our joining pleases me, my darling. I love the feel of you, inside and out. I can feel your power. It is I think a miracle. I shall not wonder if I am unable to walk for a few days, yet I care not!"

"No matter, my wife. We have no plans to remove ourselves from this wonderful bed for days, perhaps." Moments later, he started to withdraw from her. "Please stay as long as you can, I love having you in me and on me, Fitzwilliam. I feel so very close to you. Closer than I have ever been to anyone in my entire life. You, my husband are my home."

"Oh, Elizabeth, every time you speak to me, my heart melts. I adore you."

"Fitzwilliam, shall you make a promise to me, before God?"

"Ask anything of me, dearest one."

"Please promise me now, that you shall be with me the entire time I labour and give birth to our children? Each time? Every time? Be right there in the room with me and help me? I shall need you," she pled.

"Yes, Elizabeth, my wonderful wife. We shall go through our babies' birthing together. I shall stay by your side, I promise you before God. If you must endure it, so shall I."

"Fitzwilliam?" she asked. Her breathing was now fully recovered.

"Yes, my loving wife?"

"I know we just loved, but is it really too soon to desire loving you again, now?" She asked this while placing wet kisses over much of his neck. "I find an overwhelming need building in my ring. I fear it shall not be denied."

"But, I thought it was painful the first time," he teased.

"Yes, but in a beguiling way. It did not diminish the sensual raptures you gave me."

The newly wedded couple did join again and again. They counted four times and, happily, two other mutually agreed upon acts of love.

※

Elizabeth enjoyed multiple soaks in the tub. She did not tell her husband why they were needed. It was enough that her manner of walking was altered for the first three days.

Fitzwilliam Darcy took more than a little pride in his wife's unusual gait. She did not speak of it, yet, he knew she was sore. She did not allow that fact to alter her passionate participation in their lovemaking, nor did it keep her from instigating coitus. They continued to count, another ten times in the next two days!

Bright and early on the morning of April twenty, the couple approached their carriage.

Fitzwilliam delayed their boarding to speak with Mr. Thompson. Elizabeth's strict attention was drawn to two young men in their teens and a poor unfortunate horse. The pair were cruelly prodding the animal into a walk. Unsuccessful in their efforts, they began to abuse the horse. She followed them afoot and rounded the corner of the inn as they turned. She approached the animal and stilled him. Then she spoke harshly to the teens, admonishing them sternly about animal abuse and horsemanship.

Frightfully, she felt her body being abruptly lifted up from the ground! Strong arms snared her from behind and within seconds carried her with uncomfortable force into a waiting carriage.

She felt dizzy, discombobulated, and confused. The skillful driver took off at a rapid gait and the horses did not slow their gallop for several miles! She cried out, turning her head to see who had perpetrated such an injustice upon her personage! It was her husband. His face was a storm cloud. He remained silent and stared at her with a deep frown between his brows.

"Why ever did you do that?" she demanded indignantly. "I have never suffered such humiliation in all my life! In addition, I was so frightened, I nearly lost my water!"

He spoke not a word but simply continued his brooding stare. Silence was her answer. After the space of half an hour, he began, "Elizabeth, I realise you are not accustomed to your new station. I believe some fault lies with me in this regard. You have neither seen your new home nor do you comprehend the extent of your wealth. Because of our station, influence, and most certainly our great wealth, I must explain my inexorable position on personal safety and security.

"Indeed! I do feel some explanation is required, given my very rough treatment. I thank you, husband."

"You did not know the dangerous position you allowed yourself to enter, my darling. Yes, to you it seemed only two youths and a poor unfortunate horse. But, did you feel how suddenly I caught you up into my arms and spirited you away into our carriage? You were powerless against my size and strength. I had you in seconds."

"Yes, but I—"

"That entire scene might well have been prearranged in order to kidnap you, love. What better bait than a horse needing your rescue? It takes very little to learn about Mrs. Darcy, soon to be mistress of Pemberly. And, stories of you have been widely circulated, have they not?

"As my wife, you would be worth a considerable ransom. But, as a beautiful woman, your fate would make the experience far more devastating than either of us could face."

He began to educate her on the true purpose of the footmen. He told her of the large number of men, hired arms, who were loyal to the Darcy family. Their sole purpose is to act as bodyguards for the family. They are to keep trespassers out of Pemberly. Their presence alone maintains order and peace.

Elizabeth moved to the seat beside her husband. She laid her head on his shoulder. *What have I done? I am Mrs. Darcy, but who is Mrs. Darcy? What of my freedom? These dangers have been completely unmentioned until now. Why did we not discuss this at Rosings when he told me of Pemberly? How shall we ever have a normal life? What shall this new world hold for me?*

"Fitzwilliam, I honestly care not for your wealth—"

"*Our* wealth," he corrected her.

"Our wealth, yes. Although I care not for the wealth, power, or position, I do love you with my whole heart. I can see that I married you without knowing exactly what that entailed. I shall depend upon your instruction, and I promise to obey you in this matter. I want to be safe at all times, and I want your peace of mind, as well. I shall learn the rules for my security in and around Pemberly, and everywhere else I go, it seems.

"Please tell me something, dearest? The footmen at Claverstone, are they—?"

"Of course., Elizabeth. Lord Claverstone is a member of the House of Lords, and a peer of the realm. He must have bodyguards."

"In all the years I have visited him with Uncle and Aunt, I always thought they were, just, oh, I do not know? Attendants?"

He smiled at her, "Sweet Elizabeth, keeping you safe and protected shall be a full time job for all of us, I believe. Yet, it shall be much easier with your assistance. I am gratified to remember what a good student you can be, when you desire such!"

As they drove to the next inn, Holy Cross Village, he gave her more details of how the footmen watched over them, in the house and on the grounds. He assured her she would begin to see the workings of the security when they reached the entrance of their estate.

George Darcy was alarmed when he read the missive from his banker. In vivid detail, Mr. Marshall outlined the recent attempt at fraud against one of his accounts. It seemed George Wickham had attempted to draw on a draft signed by Mr. Darcy.

The ever alert Mr. Marshall foiled the plan when he signaled his clerk to call for the magistrate. The diabolical Wickham, however, managed to extricate himself from the bank's security men and elude those officials who were in pursuit.

Most troubling about this event, according to Mr. Marshall, was the authentic look of the document and even more disturbing the high quality of the forgery that displayed Mr. Darcy's signature. Mr. Marshall knew that Mr. George Darcy never used such transactions. It was Mr. Marshall's quick thinking that prevented the loss.

Mr. Darcy decided he would away to London immediately to confer with the authorities. A ruse of this level was not to be ignored. Action must be taken. Mr. Darcy's personal detective took the case. He would determine who in England was capable of such a remarkable forgery.

After six days of intensive investigation, it was narrowed to two persons. The first with such talent was a Mr. Edwin Wallet, the second, Mr. Charles Robert Easterly. Mr. Easterly was determined to be abroad. Mr. Wallet was found to have ties with Wickham. A countrywide search for Wickham and Wallet ensued. If they were in the realm, they would certainly be found.

Caroline Bingley was obsessed. She wasted not one waking moment as she searched for her brother, Charles Bingley. He had been last seen entering Darcy House. No one remembered when he departed. Simmons refused to speak with her. The authorities would not approach the Darcy family.

Caroline wished she had paid more attention to Charles when he explained the two to six month journey he would make for business. He often would away to the West Indies to check on their holdings. No one she contacted would enlighten her. His office was no help to her. It seemed no one paid much attention to her brother. She could hardly blame them. He was such a bore. At the moment, bore or not, she needed him to access Mr. Fitzwilliam Darcy. She must stop that sham of a wedding!

Edwin Wallet was deeply disappointed that the attempt at the bank did not yield results. Funds were very low. He needed money. If this forgery business would not profit, how about kidnapping the old man?

Waiting for Wickham at the Dirty Tavern, Wallet looked nervously at his watch.

"Wickham where have you been? You took your bloody time, lad. I have a new plan for the Darcy funds. We must kidnap the man! By now every business and solicitor in London has heard of us. I am guilty with you. I say we nab the old goat and get the ransom from his family. You know Pemberly. It should be easy to get on and off the estate." Wallet wanted Wickham to listen to him and follow his plan.

"A plan, to be sure, Wallet. What if we cannot get at him? He is getting older, and he may not get around outdoors as he once did. Why not just nab the next person we see of the family?"

"Aye," Wallet said drinking his ale, "I read in the *London Topics* that the pup shall wed a wealthy woman. Let us nab her, shall we not?"

"I need to raise a stake. Let me have a few more nights of cards at the gentlemen's club," Wickham urged, "With those winnings, we can away to Lambton and get to the Darcy fortune."

The couple spent only one night in the Holy Cross Village Inn. Otis had bought all the rooms so they were the only guests. By morning they went on to Pemberly's countryside. Elizabeth certainly had no idea of the size, beauty, and import of her new home. She was amazed. Fitzwilliam loved seeing it through her eyes.

Their carriage was entering a mountainous roadway. Clearly they were climbing now, and the countryside appeared much more lush and green. It was breathtaking! Upon the top of the mountain, a complete stop was required. They had reached the first Pemberly guard station.

Once Fitzwilliam had been identified, they made way, and behind them, one of the guards fired a weapon into the air. Fitzwilliam explained that this was a signal to the next station. They had been alerted of a vehicle which had been cleared as welcome upon their property. This was the case at each consecutive station. Elizabeth was jolted with each shot. She was not accustomed to the use of firearms. Thus, their trip continued for miles and miles after entering the estate. It was vast.

How is it possible that one family owns all of this? How many years has all of this been in the Darcy family? Pemberly must be much larger than all of Hertfordshire. Three such shires could easily fit inside the area we have just traversed.

As if reading her thoughts, her husband squeezed her hand and smiled at her. "Darling, Pemberly is an enormous estate. It may seem overwhelming at this moment, but after you fall in love with it, the idea shall sit easier with you. I promise. As you know, each generation has the responsibility not just to take care of it in stewardship, but to add to its wealth and beauty.

"All of our children shall be taught the duties of stewards. Our firstborn son shall be especially schooled in the steward's responsibilities. It shall be our job to instill the love of this land and its preservation into his heart and mind. Oh, my beautiful wife. That thought fills my soul with love for you. To me, you are the future of Pemberly, as much as I. Father has told me these are his feelings, as well."

"Oh my," Elizabeth sighed, "I feel the need to sit quietly and watch and learn. 'Tis a new feeling for me."

He laughed out loud and kissed her. He was filled with excitement at the thought of sharing his home with this most wonderful woman. As with any new marriage, the two had much to teach each other, and both were eager to learn.

She was beginning to see that each manned station observed their progress. It would be difficult to penetrate the estate through this road. The mansion had been visible as they approached. Fitzwilliam explained that the roads were planned so that the house would appear and then suddenly disappear from the traveler's view. It was designed as a sort of mystery for those approaching. This information enhanced her trip. She now watched closely for sightings of the mansion. It was to her, so beauteous! The closer they came, the larger the home appeared. It was so very enormous. Evidently each generation had added to the estate. Not only had they added to the house, but lands, too. There was the pasture of green trees and grassy landscapes, the river and the numerous lakes and streams which supported more wildlife than she had ever seen.

Leaving the mountainous curves, they entered the pasture lands. This land now had gentle rolling knolls dotted with black and red angus cattle. Next, she saw only sheep, and then goats occupied the land.

Once again the giant mansion dominated their perspective. It was magnificent. The architecture took the best advantage of all the natural surroundings. The additions Fitzwilliam had mentioned were not noticed at all. It was as one building, complete, as if so planned. The natural grace and beauty was perfectly symmetrical and altogether pleasing. The exterior was grey stone, all of the outer buildings were of the same. A perfect blend of style and materials. Viewed from any angle, it was a most graceful and lovely home; pleasing, harmonious, and well-balanced with the environment.

"Yes, love. It is larger than St. James's Palace. It shall take some doing, but you shall learn the wings and levels. I shall be with you and help you understand the flow of the home. 'Tis easier to navigate than Rosings or Claverstone. The rooms and their purposes have a more natural arrangement. Soon you shall understand.

"Tonight we shall abed in my chambers. On the morrow we shall tour our home. We shall select the rooms we wish to adopt as our own. We shall visit the attic and other chambers to see furniture options available. Should we not find items to your liking, we shall purchase them.

"I would prefer we both occupy the same bed chamber and large sitting room and have two separate dressing rooms, just as we have in town. When you see the amount of clothing I possess, you shall shame me, I fear." At that she laughingly squeezed his arm.

"Yes, I would want us to share the same rooms. Shall your staff be scandalized?" she asked.

"*Our* staff, sweet Elizabeth! No, of course not. They shall be happy for us. Liz-Beth, where is that vibrant girl who hates decorum, and defies propriety? What has happened to you, my love?"

"Coitus." She said shyly.

He laughed and hugged her. "Oh, and now that we are home, you do not wish the servants to know that we love each other? How shall we have an heir if we do not copulate? What of the sounds they shall hear? Your shrill giggles and our moans and sighs at all hours of the day and night? They shall know, Elizabeth. They shall appreciate doing laundry for only one set of bed linens."

At last the carriage stopped in front of the house. Elizabeth was speechless to see all the servants lined up along the driveway to greet them. To Elizabeth, there were more than one hundred, yet she was not sure. At the head of the line was Mrs. Reynolds. Fitzwilliam stepped out, and handed Elizabeth down. She made eye contact with all she saw, and smiled. He took her hand, and led her to the back of the line. One by one, they walked and greeted their staff. She was amazed at how many names he knew. He spoke to each one as they moved along. She remembered the final group which appeared to be standing apart from the others. There was Fleming, the head butler; Clovis, the head footman; Parks, the steward; Mrs. Reynolds, the head housekeeper; and Gram, the stable manager. Each wanted to greet the newlyweds.

After a personal greeting to each, Fitzwilliam spoke to the group. He thanked them for their very warm welcome and told them how much they were appreciated. Elizabeth surprised him by speaking next. She wanted them to know how very much their reception meant to her. They put a friendly and smiling face upon her new home. She was looking forward to getting to know them. Their reputation for excellence had already been made known to her by the Darcy family.

It was apparent that these words were highly valued. Heads were held up, and all eyes were upon their new mistress. At their dismissal, she won even more friends as she slipped to the back of the carriage and gave special pats to Marigold and Percival. She learned the names of the two groomsmen who came to take their horses.

Then, she approached Mrs. Reynolds again and took her hands, thanking her for arranging such a warm and splendid welcome for them. The older woman softened.

It was difficult for Elizabeth to see the inside of her new home. Fitzwilliam walked her through at such a rapid pace. He was eager to get her to his rooms. It had been a long ride to Pemberly, and he needed her closeness. He craved her sweet love.

An informal selection of more cold foods awaited them in their rooms. Fresh milk and lemonade was offered with pitchers of cold water. Two baths had been drawn, and clothing was set out in minutes. Otis and Jeannette had once again thought of everything for their care and comfort. Not waiting for food or bathing, Fitzwilliam picked up his wife and tossed her onto his bed. It seemed she could not wait either!

Later in the evening, the couple exchanged their wedding gifts. Elizabeth presented Darcy with precious oils, aromatic waters and pomades that she made from a process called enfluerage.

She had been trained in the use of herbs and plant extractions. She told him of the exotic uses she had planned for a later time. He enjoyed the scents. Learning he did not own a hunting knife, she purchased one in London and had it engraved with his name and their wedding date. Other gifts she bestowed were a new jumping saddle, a horse blanket, and a braided bridle like Marigold's. The bride had plans for them to ride, very soon.

Fitzwilliam presented his bride with a signet ring with her initials, stationery, and a gold and diamond cross on a gold braided chain. Elizabeth was thrilled. He was happy to tell her of the archery ranges. One had been built into their interior game room for her use in poor weather. Other archery supplies for tournaments, and practice were ready to be set up outside for coming activities with their expected guests.

The last gift was in a large box. She opened it to see the finest deer bow she had ever seen. She also found a leather quiver, with razor sharp arrows, and arm and finger guards. All had been imported from America. Elizabeth was thrilled. She strung the bow immediately and donned the quiver and protective wear. "How do I look, darling? Like a fearsome huntress, but with both breasts?"

"Oh, I had quite forgotten reading about the Amazons, indeed. Why do I not reserve judgment until we remove your robe? You can don your regalia again, and then I shall tell you how fearsome you look!" he said, as he began to slowly remove her robe. She smiled at him with a sly gleam in her green eyes. "I was hoping you would say something like that, my love…"

Caroline Bingley tried in vain to interest her sister in the quest to locate Charles. Mrs. Hurst had more interest in staying with her husband, Mr. Hurst. If Caroline wished to hire a public carriage, and roam the country for their brother, it was no loss to Mrs. Hurst.

Caroline considered the cost. She was always in debt. Each month her fashion requirements far exceeded the meager allowance she was permitted. Charles had threatened to cut her off entirely unless she could keep her expenses under control. The cost of a hired carriage and footmen would be more than she could withstand. Perhaps she would write letters. It was only the final week of April. She had plenty of time to stop the June one nuptials.

Fitzwilliam and Elizabeth were having more amusement than any two people should be allowed. They toured the mansion three times. Then, Mr. Darcy would tell Mrs. Darcy to locate him in a certain room, giving her only an allotted amount of time to reach him.

The staff speculated on the 'reward' she received for finding him in the correct room within the time allotted. It was thought among the servants that the ballroom was too frequently selected. She was, after all, trying to learn her way around the entire house…

"Liz-Beth, stand in the corner with me. Look upon our images in the mirrors. Does this not allow for perfect viewing of us, my darling?" She put her arms around his appealing neck and then laced her fingers together. Smiling a satisfied smile, he began to undress his wife.

Once naked, they beheld their embraced image from the doubled perspectives at the corner of the ballroom. Slowly he began to caress her curves; their sighs were especially audible in the vastness of the empty cavernous room. "You did lock the doors, did you not?" she asked nervously. He nodded, not wanting to let her know that the footmen in the hall understood perfectly well what they were about in the ballroom. He smiled reassuringly and led her to the blankets and wine basket. "You got here in half the time. What shall be your prize, my love?"

Whispering in his ear, she related many things she desired them to watch together. He smiled. Nodding in agreement, he opened their bottle of wine. Blushing, he began to fulfill her first request.

George Darcy sat in his study at Darcy House. He glanced at the calendar, April twenty-nine. In less than a month, he would be on his way back to Pemberly. Looking at the tray upon his desk, he saw two letters in the afternoon's post.

>Pemberly Park, Derbyshire
>
>27 April 1803
>
>Dearest Father,
>
>With great joy I write to you of my admiration and love of my new home. Your son and I have settled on rooms at the back of the second floor, within the second wing. It is our wish to use a single bed chamber, with a very large sitting room and two dressing rooms.
>
>The furniture within the former decorations shall serve very nicely for our sitting room, and the bed chamber furniture shall be swapped with Fitzwilliam's existing furnishings. This shall result in zero cost to Pemberly. The walls are being refreshed with forest green paint for the bed chamber; the sitting room shall be a cheerful yellow, and the two dressing rooms are already to our liking.
>
>We have likewise selected a room very near the library to use as a joint study. The future master tells me he wishes our desks to be arranged facing each other. I feel quite sure he shall tire of the arrangement, yet there is no dissuading him of it at present. Mrs. Reynolds informs me that you have requested a dinner on the evening of June one, to celebrate Fitzwilliam as the new master and his

five and twenty birthday. I wonder if I may intrude upon these plans?

Would this not be a wonderful opportunity to host our tenants upon the larger lawns of Pemberly? This celebration would be to introduce and welcome the new master. We could offer families venison roasted upon outdoor spits, ale, and produce of the season. Perhaps corn could be roasted outdoors, just as it comes from the field? A slice of cake would be a wonderful treat for the tenants and their children, would it not? Perhaps we might offer a reel or two after the meal is consumed. I hear Lambton has some wonderful musicians.

The crowd would be dismissed to their homes, but advised to watch the sky over the lake just after dark. Fireworks could then be displayed.

Might our private party, including our family's guests, be offered a spectacular viewing of the fireworks and a late birthday dinner upon the roof of Pemberly? I have inquired of Mr. Clovis and am told that the roof is secure. No harm would be done to the structure and no injury to our guests.

Father, I suggest this rooftop party because your precious son has told me in confidence that it was one of his guilty offenses to sneak up to the roof when Rory or other cousins would visit.

Father, I depend upon you to be candid with your daughter Elizabeth upon these important points. It is my sincere wish to blend in with the plans of Pemberly, and not to disrupt and standout as a misfit. I shall await your wisdom before I even think of approaching Mrs. Reynolds. Poor soul, she is a wonder in all she does. It shall pain me to burden her with the celebration should you approve my plans. Yet, I shall work to shoulder as much of the burden as she is willing to release to me.

Father, we have been very much enjoying our carefree time as newlyweds. It has been bliss.

Please understand, however, this is, after all your home. We hope that you and our sister shall return upon your own desire and not willingly delay for a day in May upon our account.

We are sending letters to Georgie in Kent, knowing that she is enjoying her sisters and cousins.

Love to you,

With Christ's Help May You Remain in Health,

E.D.

Oh Anne, she reminds me of you, in your youth. She is a treasure. See how she considers the cost of their rooms? Even you, did not that, my darling. Pray, what would you have thought about sharing one bed? Now that you are gone, I wish I had found the courage to suggest as much for us. I could not guess that our time would pass so swiftly, my darling.
He ran his finger across the seal of the second letter.

Pemberly Park, Derbyshire

Riley St. Andish

28 April 1803

Dear Father,

I pray this letter finds you in good health. I must say your son has never been better! I have married the finest woman in the realm. No! Make that the world!

If you had seen her response to Swan's Creek Inn! She could not praise everything enough. And, when she learned we were the new owners, her brain immediately calculated the income of said rooms, and she began to accost me for the length of time required to recover my outlay.

In great relief, may I tell you she heartily approved the investment. The woman never stops thinking. Father, I have met my match. We had some tense moments when some of my past nearly caught up with me. My wife sternly put me in my place. She has a mind full of debate and her memory complete with textbook learning. In truth, sir, I fear our next conflict and pray that it shall never occur. I would sooner die than hurt her again.

We have been riding the estate daily. Elizabeth has now met nearly all the tenants. She has been memorizing their families' names and even the crops they shall harvest. I should shock you and tell you that she prefers to ride bareback. She loathes the sidesaddle, although she willingly uses the same, and dons ladies' riding attire when we visit tenants. Your new daughter is most forward thinking, and her thoughts for the most part are unconventional.

She regularly talks of earning enough of her own money to open the very first women's university in England. This is, of course, far in the future. She does acknowledge the fact, but proudly adds that our own daughters shall attend.

Perhaps I should prepare you and Georgie. I have a devil of a time keeping my hands off her person. I have already lost myself to her, and she occupies all my thoughts, day and night.

I am so filled with love and devotion to her that I frighten myself. She simply says she shall enjoy it until our children arrive. She knows full well that I shall abandon her and apply all my affections to them. I do not think this possible.

Father, I thank God daily that you prayed for me to have a better life. He sent you into that bookstore. Now he has filled my heart with nothing but love for this remarkable woman. I feel I have a future, indeed. Never have I had such dreams for Pemberly!

Keep us in prayer, Father. We still face June one and beyond.

God keep you and Georgiana,

Your Devoted Son,

F.D.

May was full of mild weather at Pemberly. The Darcys spent their days riding, and Elizabeth attempted to teach Fitzwilliam archery. He could not best his wife, and therefore had little interest.

The couple established a daily routine. Their correspondence was reviewed just after dinner. At present, there were two letters to read. Seeing her letter from her father Darcy, Elizabeth wished to hide the contents in order to save the surprise. She slipped it into her pocket.

Darcy took his letter and rang for two glasses of wine. He sat upon the sofa in their study and stretched out his long legs. Extending his hand to his beautiful wife, he said, beguilingly, "Allow me to read to you, my love." Offering his lap, she smiled sweetly and settled seductively onto him. He opened the letter from his father and read it aloud. It was filled with good humour and without any mention of the Wickham fraud attempt. Their second was from Kent. Georgie had written to tell of the wonderful time she is having with her new extended family. She was requesting that Mary and Kitty be allowed to live at Pemberly. She feels she cannot be without them.

Dropping his letters, he kissed Elizabeth. She responded in full surrender to him. Within moments they became lost in their kisses. Before she knew what was happening, he stood, took her in his arms, and carried her into their rooms. Unseen by him, she took the letter from her pocket and placed it on the dresser.

Hours later, Fitzwilliam called for Otis and Jeannette. The Darcys would dress for dinner. Elizabeth planned a striking gown and a diamond choker, bracelet, and ear bobs.

Meeting Fitzwilliam in his dressing room, Elizabeth was a vision. Her hair was fashioned into a French twist; her daringly low-cut gown fit with precision, and the jewels stood out with eye-catching appeal.

"Mrs. Darcy, you are a vision of grace and beauty this evening. What is the occasion, my love?" he asked as he traced the neckline of her very low-cut gown, with one finger, while his other hand squeezed her mound through the elegant fabric of her skirt.

"Today is the one month anniversary of our first morning in the glade. I was going to wear my breeches and linen shirt this morning and beg for a ride, but you were ready for another type of ride. I must admit, I enjoyed riding you so much more than Marigold. You, my husband, I am so happy to say, are an insatiable lover. How I adore you for it."

With this said, she seductively allowed her hand to brush him, as she lifted it to lightly trace his jawline. She notice that his eyes were in bondage to her bosom.

"We had better have this conversation in the dining room, beloved. I do not trust myself so close to our bed." Offering his arm, they went to dine upon their favorites. All their meals were now served in smaller amounts than was fashionable. Elizabeth favoured more practical meals.

During dinner, they discussed their plans for the following day. He would meet with Clovis in the morning and she with Mrs. Reynolds at the same time. Following these meetings, they agreed to ride.

After dinner, the two went for a walk around the grounds. The air was sweet and so was their time together. Looking around the gardens, Fitzwilliam mentioned the seclusion being somehow reminiscent of their glade. Holding her close, he reached around and began to unbutton her gown. Looking into his sensual, sparkling eyes, she was having a hard time trying to tell him, no, yet she feared the area lacked privacy.

"No? I just want to take the gown down to your waist. It shall allow me to admire your chocker and to stroke your lovely breasts, darling. You shall enjoy it so very much, I promise you."

"That is all you desire? Just to look, touch, and to feel? That and no more? Can you not do that around the low neckline, sir?"

"Liz-Beth, may I please lower your gown? In a few weeks the house and grounds shall be thick with our loved ones, and we shall not have the luxury…"

He looked so young and innocent and sweet in the moonlight. His eyes, which pledged his love to her pled his case. Her resolve was weakening.

"Well…I suppose, it would do no harm here in the dark corner." She had barely spoken the words when his nimble fingers had opened the gown and folded it down past her waist. His eager hand reached her mound to squeeze it. He began kissing her breasts as his fingers started to play in her silky curls. Her heart skipped a beat in anticipation of them teasing her flesh.

Once they did, she began to moan. There was no telling when he had opened his breeches. She knew only the feeling of the cold stone wall behind her, and the oh, so welcomed thrusts that took away that demanding and urgent longing, deep within her. Only he could satisfy her needs.

They loved fiercely and with great passion. Neither spoke a word; their rapid panting and frequent grunts and moans did not allow for talking. With glassy, dilated eyes, they held each other's gaze throughout their lovemaking. Neither one blinked.

She adored the cold marble wall that held her firmly in place, while her lover pushed into her, hard! It felt so good to take in all of him. She loved his urgency and the exciting force he was using to penetrate her. She loved the sweat on his face.

Fitzwilliam loved the power and control he could command by keeping her in place while he pushed powerfully, nearly as hard as he could. She loved it when he dominated her this way.

This unyielding pressure he used increased her excitement. She often told him that she took comfort in his potent strength. His seed exploded into her as she bore down hard on her muscles that squeezed his *membre virile*. They were elated at their heights and their timing.

"That was—" she tried to exclaim, but he stopped her.

"Yes. I know. I said all I wanted to do was to touch, feel…I suppose I should say I am sorry, but I am not sorry—I loved it, Elizabeth!"

"Husband, could you not sense that I loved it, too?" she cried, much louder than she intended.

"Oh, my" she continued now nearly whispering, "I scarcely noticed that I was on my feet, save for the few times you actually lifted me off my feet! I loved your power!"

He brushed a few strands of hair from her forehead. "To what may we compare that, love?"

"What was it?" she asked, "perfectly wonderful? Magnificent? Exciting? Enjoyable beyond imagination?"

"Better than all my daydreams? Oh Elizabeth, I saw stars! Can you believe it?"

"Oh Fitzwilliam, we must do that more often; it was wonderful. I have never felt you so forceful. You plunged into me so hard…it was amazing. You were vigorously incredible! You were tempestuous—Pardon, love? Did you not just say you saw stars? I do not doubt you."

"Yes, my lovely bride. I, your husband, for the first time in my entire life, saw stars! I saw stars whilst reaching an orgasm during coitus with my sensual young wife! I have read of such things, but I doubted the validity of such an experience." He took her hand and led her into the house through a seldom used door, stopping to kiss her briefly.

"I dare say, I do not have enough knowledge on the subject to ask an intelligent question." she said, scarcely able to contain her joy.

"Liz-Beth, we must have more such frolics, and spur of the moment interludes."

Entering their sitting room the next morning, Fitzwilliam saw his wife reading her letter and smiling.

"You look happy, Mrs. Darcy. Do you wish to share?"

"I had not intended to do so, but since I am caught, I certainly shall."

> Rosings Park
>
> Kent
>
> 6 May 1803
>
> Dearest Daughter,

Your letter made your new father and sister very proud. We have decided that your birth made you a Bennet, but God designed your heart, long ago, to be a Darcy.

I marvel at how much you are like my Anne. You have a kinship with the land and a love for people that she also possessed. You are so kind and also such an intelligent manager to see June one as a holiday for our tenants. I and your sister took quite readily to your idea of the picnic in honour of Fitzwilliam taking on the role of master of Pemberly. Your ideas on the open spit cooking of the food ties us even more to the earth. No doubt our tenants shall see the connection. The use of wild game from the estate along with our farm's corn is excellent. Cake is festive also, and Georgie absolutely loves the idea of each one attending receiving a piece. It shall be a special treat for all, especially the children. Engaging the musicians from Lambton, shall provide employment for some of those gentlemen, and they are, as reported to you, very skillful players.

As to your other celebration ideas, I have taken it upon myself to make arrangements here in London. All shall be done as you requested. I think it a marvelous idea and quite fitting.

Yes, I am covert, son. I imagine you are reading this at Elizabeth's side.

As to your fitting in rather than standing out, your plans are so much more than I could have thought about, very creative and wonderful. You and Mrs. Reynolds must see to them at once.

Kindly tell her that I, as well as you, rely upon her expert help. She shall no doubt give you little to "shoulder' as you put it. Although she shall love that you asked to help. Georgiana and I shall arrive with the rest of our family, on or near May twenty-nine.

Our Love and Best Wishes in the Power of our Lord,

G.D.

Darcy picked her up in his arms. "It sounds like you have made an excellent impression on your father and sister. Am I to determine that we shall have a tenant picnic on the first of June to announce the installment?"

She cast her eyes to the floor. "It would seem so, Mr. Darcy. Are you angry?"

"Indeed, I am! With myself and father in that we did not think of it! I need to punish you for being an excellent thinker and planner!" Turning around as they looked at the room, his face lit up. He walked her to their bed chamber.

"And what shall your punishment be? I know. You hate to have your feet tickled. So shall it be. I shall tickle both feet until you cry and lose your water!" He tossed her upon the bed, then stretched out next to her, and rising up above her, he pinned both hands upon the bed with one of his. But, rather than touch her feet, he started under her arms and then became lost to her breasts.

George Wickham entered the Dirty Tavern and found Wallet waiting for him, dressed in his finest clothes. Wickham patted his pocket and declared himself 'bunce'!

"Wallet, tonight I did it! The little turtledoves left their tail feathers on the card table, and Gerogie boy swept them all! We are bunce and ready to take any or all of the Darcy family."

"Brilliant Georgie! I suggest we go to the estate and try to snare that new little Mrs."

"We certainly shall go to the estate, but we must get the old man. He is the one in control. Nothing on the estate shall be done without him. They shall be mad to get his freedom. It shall be our gain as they shall pay whatever we demand!"

Wallet nodded his head in agreement.

"Tonight we away to Lambton, Derbyshire. We shall take our rooms and then scout the area for a secure place to sequester the old man. We shall hold court, and Mr. Darcy shall be separated from his property. We shall judge him!"

Caroline Bingley hired a carriage. she was en route to Devonshire. She would stop the wedding long before June one. It should be no problem locating a lord in Devonshire. After all, was it not mostly sheep and cows?

Registering as a guest at the Rose Hill Inn, she elected to stay for just one night. Her desire was to reach Clavertsone in the morning. When the magistrate and Lord Claverstone heard what she had to say, she was sure they would bow to the just cause she could present. Fitzwilliam Darcy must marry her.

Sitting on the edge of the bed, she opened her money bag and poured the contents onto the counterpane. She had but few remaining pounds. No matter, soon enough she would be mistress of Pemberly and have unlimited wealth.

Exhausted from the dirty trip, she decided to lie down atop the counterpane. She loathed the acts of intimacy committed in public rooms. She dared not touch the sheets. As she drifted off to sleep, she wondered if Mr. Darcy would demand sex with her. He did not seem to enjoy her, so he would probably have a mistress. No matter to her.

Elizabeth met in the salon with Mrs. Reynolds whilst Fitzwilliam sat with Clovis in their study.

"Mrs. Darcy, I must say you were generous to share this wonderful day with the tenants. Many of them are my family, and this holiday shall be a blessing to them. 'Tis a joy for me to bring this about just as you suggest. Mr. Fitzwilliam seems so changed, completely grown and fully responsible. We are so proud of him and it is wonderful to honour him."

Details were completed. The hunts and fire pits were scheduled with the grounds; the farm was to be alerted to their produce needs, and the bakers were to be notified. Each woman had her list.

The roof top party was planned as well.

Just as they completed their meeting, Clovis asked Elizabeth to come to the study.

Entering the room, she was somewhat surprised to see Parks, Gram, and Fleming already seated across from her husband. They appeared to be waiting for her.

They rose to their feet as she entered. She nodded to them and took the chair her husband offered. He then signaled Clovis to begin.

All eyes were on Elizabeth.

"Mrs. Darcy, your husband asked us to brief you as well on this urgent matter of security."

"Please, Mr. Clovis."

"Thank you, madam. I shall begin with the matter of a legal restraining order against one George Wickham. This is a legal document filed with the courts that names Mr. Wickham as a clear and ever present threat to life and limb to Mr. George Darcy, and his family. This includes yourself, of course. I am sorry to inform you."

"Yes, yes. Go on, please," she directed with authority.

"It has been realised that the level of threat has increased as there was a recent attempt to commit fraud and theft." The man continued with the detailed story of the recent events in London. Elizabeth was surprised to learn of it, as their father had avoided telling them.

Mr. Clovis was near his conclusion, explaining of the kidnap threat. "It is believed that George Darcy is the intended victim, yet with all the news featuring yourself, there may be a threat to you, as well. Wickham is a special risk because he has actually lived here at the estate during his childhood and into his early adult years."

She shifted her eyes to her husband. "I am so sorry, he what—?" she asked in Fitzwilliam's direction with a frown. It was Clovis who answered, "Yes, madam, I can see it is upsetting to you. I regret the discomfort, Mrs. Darcy."

"Not at all, excuse me, Mr. Clovis. I wonder, as such, is it possible that there might be a likeness of Mr. Wickham here at the house so I could become familiar with his facial features?"

"Excellent idea, Mrs. Darcy." His likeness was found in George Darcy's study and shown to Elizabeth at once. She wondered why her father-in-law would have and retain such a drawing. She said nothing of her questions, saving the puzzle in her mind. Perhaps one day she would inquire more about this dangerous man.

Elizabeth studied the likeness. She had never seen the man.

"I thank you, gentlemen. I shall remember that face. What of his height and weight, please?"

"Yes, nearly as tall as your husband, not as well built. Somewhat stooped at the shoulders."

"Pray, tell me, and please do not spare me, what is the action taken upon his person if he trespasses?"

He looked to Darcy, who nodded.

"Yes, Mrs. Darcy, the court orders us to shot to kill the man."

"And what of my behaviour, please? May I continue to ride about the estate, or do you wish to restrict my movements?" she asked.

Again the man looked to Darcy and awaited his release.

"Madam, we thank you for your willingness to cooperate. We shall attach two men to follow you when you ride about the estate. Mr. Darcy has told us of your love of riding and shooting. He has expressed confidence in your equestrian skills, and as such it has been decided that should you wish to ride alone, two footmen shall follow you. It shall be at close range. Our men shall be armed and skillful in caring for your safety."

"I thank you, sir. If it would be possible, I should like to meet them. I had planned to ride only with my husband and have no plans to ride alone, yet I should desire to meet them and know their faces." She looked to Fitzwilliam again.

"One more question, if I may? Pray, does he act alone in this forgery attempt? Might there be two or possibly more involved in this plot?"

Darcy was smiling, though he was looking at his desktop thoughtfully while she asked her questions. *She must attend more of these meetings, she thinks better than they.*

"An excellent question, Mrs. Darcy. At present we do not know. It is possible he works with a man called Edwin Wallet. We do not know how many may be involved. Yes, I should have made mention of the possibility of more being involved. Thank you, Mrs. Darcy."

Having concluded their talk, the men quit the study. Fitzwilliam rushed to her side.

"Darling, I hope this does not distress you too much. It is unfortunate we have planned the June one picnic and all our guests' events. Perhaps we should cancel?"

"Nay. God shall care for us. We shall pray, and all shall be well for us. Now, how did such a one as Wickham come to live here in this wonderful place?"

They walked outside to enjoy the sunshine as he told her of Mr. Wickham the steward and his son, George. He told of the boy Wickham, who had been older and bigger than Fitzwilliam.

He revealed being bullied and injured many times as Wickham pushed him down stairs, out of trees, and merely beat him for enjoyment. He recounted the old man's death, and George Darcy's misplaced benevolence and of Cambridge. Even though difficult for him to expose the pain, he told her of his embarrassment and humiliation of being forced to room with a man who impersonated him as he gambled, secured debts, and all other manner of vile deeds in Fitzwilliam's name. He avoided telling Wickham's sexual exploits, as they were somewhat like his own.

Elizabeth had heard enough. She would remember the facial appearance of Wickham and his physical description. She would be alert and if necessary take action to protect herself. Never again would she allow herself to experience that feeling she had when the two young men with the horse made her a possible victim. She would never forget the lesson her husband had taught her that morning!

Caroline Bingley was prepared to break her fast in the dining room. Her bags were packed, and she was nearly ready to call for her hired carriage.

Picking up her greasy fork, she wiped it again and again on her napkin. Staring at the ham swimming in grease and the runny eggs, she began to eat. It would not do to become weak.

She was in Devonshire and soon she would see Mr. Darcy.

Edwin Wallet and George Wickham stepped down from the post wagon they had hired to take them into Lambton. It was cooler in Derbyshire than in town. Their clothing was thin, yet looked good enough to avoid negative attention. Clearly they needed to take care of business soon!

Walking into the Rusty Gate Inn, Wickham stepped to the desk and registered. He paid for one week, in advance. Walking slowly up the stairs, he could hear Wallet as he registered.

The two did not have a look of prosperity, yet there was nothing about them to cause concern.

Wickham disappeared into his room. It had taken him only moments to determine that Mr. Darcy could not be brought to either of their rooms.

"Wickham," Wallet whispered, as he lightly tapped upon the door. "Are you there?"

"Of course, where would I go?" he shook his head as he opened the door to admit the man. He began speaking as Wallet entered his room. "We can accomplish more if we split up. I shall go to Pemberly and scout the house. Knowing so many of the staff, it shall be easy for me to get close to the house." Wickham loved to brag about his connections to the estate.

At last our plan is coming together. I shall most likely find a little virgin today. Pemberly grows them lush and easy. It shall be good to break a maidenhead or two today…

At last the day of arrival was at hand. The couple showed their excitement. They were eager to greet and settle their guests. Having just enough time for a relaxing ride, they headed to the stables hand in hand. She wanted to talk about her business idea.

"Darling, I cannot wait for Grandpapa to see the horses. Have I not told you, he is the best selective horse breeder? He has amazing knowledge of the first English Thoroughbreds from the early 1700's. Have you heard the story of the three Arabian stallions who were the source of our racehorses? He shall thrill you with his understanding of the breed, and also of the Warmblood carriage horses. You may want him to examine all our stock. He is a fountain of information.

"Darling, you are making me dizzy! I am sure you are trying to tell me something very important, yet remember I am but a dull Cambridge man, without benefit of your Oxford studies." He smiled archly, then chuckled, waiting for a reaction. She gave him a little swat on the buttocks, then looked around quickly to be sure they were unobserved.

Elizabeth squinted up at him, and gave him a very seductive smile. "Oh, did I forget to tell you? Yes, I have a secret all my own. I intend to finance my women's college with the money I earn as a breeder of fine horses. It shall be the work of a lifetime, love."

"Husband, as my head of household—"

"Yesss?" he raised his eyebrows.

"I promised before God to obey you and I shall," she said, pressing herself against him in broad daylight.

"Uh-huh, I am aware of it" he said, giving her a smile from one side of his lips.

Watching his lips, she licked her own. "We have just been so very busy with, umm, so many, ah, other things. It may have slipped my mind." She slowly licked her seductive lips once more.

"Hum, I shall wager it slipped your mind. I know you well enough, wife of mine, to realise that nothing gets past that sharp trap you humbly call your mind."

He stood close beside her and discretely placed his hand on her buttocks and rubbed them hard.

She looked into his blue eyes and smiled, mouthing the words, 'I desire you' then she winked. He laughed to himself, keeping his lips in a straight line to stifle a smile. Tilting his head to one side, he nearly whispered, "Tell me your dreams, love. I want to know all your dreams."

"I wonder if you shall share them, Fitzwilliam?"

She talked rapidly of English hunters, American Quarter Running Horses, and Virginia farmers who send their mares to England for studs to improve their lines.

She told of the stock at Pemberly which she believed would be a good start for them. As she spoke, she turned slowly into his waiting hand. He grabbed her mound firmly and began to pulsate little squeezes into her as she continued to talk.

If he had the interest she would put together the financials. When he had the time, she would be happy to show him her plan. Of course, Lord Claverstone must evaluate the stock first.

"Tell me more, my wife," he offered, as he now began to push his palm into her centre through her gown. They kept a close eye, to be sure they were not watched. Her heart was pounding, and her breathing was now ragged, clearly her ardor was rising. "Well," she tried to continue, adding little moans of pleasure at his attentions to her crotch. "As you know, some mares stay fertile from spring, summer, and even into late fall. So I was thinking that if Grandpapa should write to Sir John Standish, and advise him of our studs," she rolled her deep green eyes at him, "and here is where it gets personal for you, beloved. Especially since Percival is exceptionally large, in hands, I say, ah, hum, I feel that he might make a good beginning for us, should you use him for stud. What do you think, love?"

"My, Mrs. Darcy, you make me dizzy. I believe I shall have no peace, and you shall not allow me any idle time, shall you? Your business ideas take me by surprise!"

"Well, I do sometimes have *other* ideas, have I not?" she reached up and traced his ear with her fingertip. "Your ears make soft, gentle targets, love. I could trace it also with the tip of my tongue.

Are they not a special and a most sensitive surface of your masculine body?"

He quickly drew his hand away and lifted it to playfully swat her hand from his ear, "Liz-Beth, I see you shall be a handful today."

She laughed. "Oh, that is very good, love, considering what you have been doing to me. Indeed, you have certainly taken a handful, have you not? Oh, and I love it!"

"Come on my frisky little filly. Let us ride before the morning leaves, and we miss our opportunity. We have only hours before the first carriage arrives. Perhaps we shall find a secluded little copse, and I shall be blessed with a mouthful."

Hurrying to catch them just as they mounted, Mr. Gram rushed out with a message from Mr. Parks. "Mr. Darcy, I am pleased to reach you before you departed. I am sorry to interrupt. Mr. Jenkins has arrived from Sanderson Ridge, and he has an urgent matter concerning his cattle. Shall I have him wait while you ride, or would you like to interview him?"

"Yes, Gram. I am eager to hear about the condition of his stock. " he sighed audibly. "Please take him to my study to wait for me."

Turning to Elizabeth, he smiled wistfully. He hung his head for a brief moment. Looking up, he asked, "Is the date today June second, my Liz-Beth?"

She laughed. "Cows have no calendar, my darling Handsome Man. Is it my fault you are not a wood cutter sharing your cottage with me? Go on. Do your duty to assist Mr. Jenkins, love. May I ride with my escorts?"

"Of course!" his answer was somewhat terse. He was regretful of their loss of more outdoor frolicking, to which he was looking forward.

"Where is my coltish stallion? Attend your business, darling, but retain that playful spirit you were blessing me with a few moments ago, please. You shall need it when we meet again!"

She laughed and tossed her head, walking toward Marigold. Caught in the moment, he matched her stride and grabbed her waist. Drawing her near to him, he pressed into her body. Kissing her, he drew her lips into his and gently sucked. The suddenness and lustfulness of his gentle assault thrilled her. Her knees weakened. Pulling his lips from hers, he pressed them to her ear and probed it with his tongue. Then he whispered, "I am a very thirsty man; I so enjoy the juices of life that flow in you, my sweet Liz-Beth. I shall be waiting for my Goddess of Horses." He left her delightfully dazed, and desiring him to stay with her.

It seemed that the master of Pemberly intended to do as he pleased with her, when and where he wanted. He had a wide smile upon his face, as he set out to join Gram and Jenkins in his study.

After a few minutes to compose herself, she thought to look around the barn. They had been alone. Servants were beginning to learn to keep a wide distance from the Darcys wherever they may be on the estate.

Elizabeth donned her leather arm and finger protectors, attached her quiver over her shoulder, and strung her hunting bow, then pulled it over her head. She squinted toward the groomsman.

"Bobby?" she asked the young man. "Would you please tell Roberts and Finch that Mrs. Darcy is riding alone this morning and shall wait for them near the lake. Oh, please let them know Marigold does not like to be kept waiting. Thank you."

She cantered Marigold out to the lake. She felt safe there, within clear view of the house.

Her escorts delayed. She took the time to remove her boots and stockings. Tying them together she placed them over the horse's back. Just for fun she began to shoot. Just three arrows, out to the tree line. Pleased with the bow, she smiled and looked at the yellow and white feathers in the distance.

She felt, heard, and then saw the two riders approaching. She lowered her body down to sit upon the mare. Waving to the men, she cantered off toward her arrows.

More than two men were watching Elizabeth as she stood upon her horse and shot. George Wickham had made his way onto the grounds and was skulking amongst the trees. He had been reminiscing about the number of virgin maidens he had sweet talked into that part of the park.

Those pretty little maidens. They were so ripe, and pretended they did not like it, but they did. They only cried to excite me. What is that? A girl in riding clothes, but with no boots?

Too poor for a saddle, she must be a groomsman's daughter. I could teach her to shoot. I could show her how to sit on Georgie's saddle and let her ride me! Yes, bring that maidenhead right here. Let Georgie teach you about life...

He thought his wish was coming true, as she did indeed ride toward the tree line. "I am getting my arrows," she shouted over her shoulder, "Come if you wish," The lazy men had little motivation to ride anywhere. They were footmen, and they found it disgusting that she did not use a proper saddle. Why the bow and arrows anyway?

Marigold headed for the arrows. She could anticipate Elizabeth's movements.

Elizabeth searched the shadows of the rich growth for the white and yellow feathers. Finally she spotted them, although a sudden movement caught her eyes away.

Stretching up to her full height, she saw a man coming out of the shrub. He was stooped at the shoulders and was at the right height and weight. Slowly, she drew an arrow from her quiver and loaded the bow as Marigold slowed to a walk. In her peripheral vision, she checked for her men. They had stopped and were talking together. They did not see him, nor were they looking at her.

Marigold moved closer and closer to the intruder. Elizabeth became convinced that she was about to be within speaking distance of George Wickham.

She held her weapon down against her thigh and dropped Marigold's reins. Using her legs, she told the mare to keep walking straight.

Wickham stopped.

"George Wickham!" she shouted, sounding determined. "Stand still! You are trespassing upon Darcy property!"

"What is that you, saucy wench? Come to me from that horse, I shall give you the ride of your life! Ask any little strumpet here. I shall show you a real man. It shall be a joy to break your little maidenhead, miss. I shall help you down from—"

"Wickham! I have warned you!"

He kept advancing toward her, laughing. "I shall take you by force, if I must."

Quicker than he could take his next breath, she lifted her bow, sighted her target, and pulled the string back, letting the arrow fly to its full weight and strength. It took flight, with the sound of a thick rush of air through a large straw. Elizabeth loved that sound. It reassured her every time she heard it. Her keen eyes watched the arrow fly into its target, the right upper thigh of the insulting, vile man who had just threatened her with rape! *I shall not be your victim!*

The missile hit its mark, with a splattering sound. Remarkably, he stood still, perhaps because it is shocking for one to see an arrow embedded within one's own flesh. Very little blood trickled at the site of entry. Shock had delayed the sensation of pain.

Thus he was not able to determine that the wound would be mortal.

This first arrow struck the upper end of the shaft of the femur along with fibrous tissues. It nicked the femoral artery. It was a painful wound, to be sure. Entrance of the bladed tip was painful, yet later it would be the removal of that small, razor sharp, triangular arrowhead that would cause the most destruction.

Elizabeth was amazed to see the man turn to hobble up a small embankment to hide. She loaded another arrow, and warned him to stand still, by law, he was not at liberty to depart. After a second warning, she lifted her bow, took aim on her target and fired.

Women everywhere who heard this story knew that she had indeed aimed at the man in this particular manner. It was a victory for so many ruined girls and young women. Her second shot was to a posterior target. Wickham offered his buttocks as he turned uphill.

His threats were still ringing in her ears. Watching him present his arse as he scrambled away, she decided upon her next target. Lifting her bow to sight, she took her time, allowing for his movement. She sent this shot upward into his coccyx. The blade tip shattered the first three segments and then sliced the lower end of his rectum. It spiraled into the scrotum. And with a slight rotation, the blade twisted, lodging the tip in the centre of the right testis.

Even a layman could see that the removal of this second arrow would obliterate his scrotum entirely.

Within seconds he was down on the ground, writhing on his side, and howling as a man experiencing intense pain. This wound was bleeding into the ground. Her footmen had observed her by now and were riding towards her. They seemed confused as to what should be done. With their lack of action, Elizabeth took charge. "Fire your weapons! Fire them now!" she commanded. They simply sat and stared at her with their mouths open.

She loaded and lifted her bow. Pulling into firing position, she inquired, "Must I shoot you both as well as Wickham? I clearly told you to fire. We must signal for help! If you do not, I swear one of you shall die on this spot! Roberts, fire one shot!"

The men believed her. Her voice was level and calm. She kept her weapon trained on them.

Roberts began firing as she instructed. One shot every three seconds. They must send Clovis a signal for assistance and give their position.

Keeping her bow trained on them, she waited until their weapons were empty. Then she forced them to dismount, she took the reins of their horses, and kept the men with their hands upon their heads.

"Now we shall wait for Clovis. We shall see what he has to say to the two of you."

She heard hooves approaching. Many. They were urgently riding toward the tree line. It was easy to spot Fitzwilliam. Percival and his rider were tall and could be seen from a great distance.

She wanted to cry when she saw him coming for her, but she knew she must remain strong. It would not do to cry in front of these footmen, and even though Wickham would not know of her tears, she would not cry in his presence.

In seconds, the riders were upon them. She did not relax her bow. Darcy jumped from Percival and ran to her. He put his hand upon her back and looked at her face.

You are my Fitzwilliam but you look...angry? Fearful? Shocked? Puzzled?

Imagining the footmen had just shot Wickham, he was confused. "Elizabeth," he said, calmly rubbing her arms, "tell me which man shot Wickham? Did he fire upon you first? You may put your bow and arrow down now, my darling. You are safe now."

"I cannot release these men. It is possible they are part of the plot for they did nothing to come to my aid. I was forced to shoot and kill Wickham. They fired their weapons because I forced them to signal for help. I question their loyalty to the Darcy family."

Clovis had joined them and heard her brief account. He knew there was much more to this story. Looking at Fitzwilliam, he nodded toward the bow.

Placing one arm around his wife, he gently and quietly said, "I am so proud of you, beloved. You took care of yourself. You did the right thing. Now, let us give this to Clovis, he shall take it to the house for us." He took the bow and arrow, then helped her remove her quiver, and wrist and finger guards. She stood mutely and passively next to him, allowing him to give her protection away.

Elizabeth knew she had just killed a man. She knew she had inflicted pain and suffering upon him. It was strange that she did not care. What was wrong with her? Would the church excommunicate her because she could not confess this as sin? Would her husband hate her now? Would he fear her? She had taken a human life. What should she be feeling?

"Elizabeth, what has happened here? Tell me. Are you well?" he was asking with concern.

Wickham was still writhing in pain on his side. He no longer yelled with agony. No one went to attend him.

Clovis was standing next to Darcy, but she saw only her Fitzwilliam. She maintained eye contact with her husband, looking only at him as she spoke to the footman. "Mr. Clovis, I am sorry to report that your men had little interest in watching over Mrs. Darcy. They halted their mounts and sat talking as I spotted Mr. Wickham skulking in the tree line.

"Wickham presumed me to be Mr. Gram's daughter. He propositioned me, telling me he would have me ride him, and he would show me a real man. Then he told me he would pull me off my horse and rape me. I did not respond to his threats.

"I informed him of his legal violations against Mr. Darcy, and made sure that he knew he was indeed upon Pemberly land. I warned him I would shoot him. He seemed amused at the idea. He moved toward me, and I raised my weapon and sighted his right upper leg. Then, drawing back full strength, I shot him, as promised.

"Whereupon, Mr. Wickham turned to retreat. I informed him he was in violation of the law and was not free to go. So I took aim once again and shot him in the tailbone and scrotum."

Looking at her husband, she added, as if for his ears, "It seemed appropriate. I am sure if I had not been mounted and armed, I would have indeed been in real danger of him."

Squaring her shoulders, she looked at her husband and said, "Mr. Clovis, your men did not assist me at any time. I had to demand they signal you. They fired only as I demanded them. That was why you saw them under my arrow.

Three men threw Wickham's body over his rented horse. The gelding was led slowly back to the Pemberly stables.

Slowly everyone departed the scene. Fitzwilliam held her in his arms, "Darling, are you well? I should never have left you, nor should I have allowed you to ride without me. I am so sorry this had to happen to you, my dearest love."

God, if Wickham had gotten Elizabeth down, and especially had he known who she was, he would have violated her terribly. Lord, thank you so much for taking care of her. Help her now, as she deals with this. I have never killed a man, maybe Rory could be of help. June one, and now this-if I only had some opiate or even that medicament liquid they make from opium. Surely there is a vendor in the countryside somewhere with just enough to help me take the edge off.

She looked up at her husband and gave him a slight smile. "I am so relieved that you came for me. I knew you would come with your men. This is not our fault. You could not have known Wickham was anywhere near us.

"God was with me, my husband. Just like David with the sling shot. He made my aim sure.

"I am very troubled about Roberts and Finch. I fear evil from them. They were either with Wickham, or they have a plot of their own. I feel it."

Clovis approached them. He knew he should keep it short. They wanted and needed to be alone.

"Mrs. Darcy, my men shall see to everything. I shall get to the bottom of the actions of these two failures. They are my men; their fault is mine. I shall give you both a full report when I get it from them. I take full responsibility for their lack of attention and assistance, Mr. Darcy, Mrs. Darcy.

"There shall be some work involving the Wickham situation. He shall be taken to the undertaker, and the magistrate shall want a sworn statement from you, Mrs. Darcy."

"Thank you, Mr. Clovis," they answered.

Mounting up, she wanted to ride, but could sense he needed to talk. They rode to the stables. They brushed their horses. Elizabeth led Marigold to Bobby and asked him to give her a bath. Then she threw her arms around the mare and kissed her neck. She held her sweet face and looked into the big brown eyes and muttered her love and thanks for the horse's care.

Wickham left Pemberly in the back of a wagon with a black cloth over his head. He did not see the lofty trees, or the blue sky. He did not hear the birds celebrating with their songs. Mr. Smiley, the undertaker, had George Wickham in hand.

When Wallet returned to the inn, he was filled with excitement. He had found the perfect place to take their hostage. He was feeling very satisfied with himself, then he heard the news.

The inn was abuzz; one of their guests, a George Wickham, recently checked in, was shot dead as a trespasser at Pemberly.

Everyone in Lambton was telling of his death. Many young girls were feeling that justice had been done, at last.

Approaching the clerk, he asked, "I understand Mr. Wickham has been killed?"

"Aye, and well enough as I heard. It would seem Mrs. Darcy was accosted by the man, and she, being armed with a bow and arrow, shot him stone dead. Can you imagine? I just told my wife, what would women be doin' with those dainty little bows and arrows? Can they not just play croquet as well?"

"Do you know Mrs. Darcy?" Wallet asked.

"I cannot say anyone in Lambton has seen her. Not yet. They are newlywed. But, if you stick around you shall see her. The Darcy family comes into to Lambton regular."

Word of the shootings and the details of the wounds made the gossip rounds as well. It was not long before everyone in the kingdom heard the story.

Walking up the staircase, they held hands. Her eyes were straight, his were on his wife. They entered their rooms, and he called for a warm bath to be drawn quickly.

Jeannette came into the dressing room and softly asked Mrs. Darcy what gown she wished to wear to greet her guests.

"Oh! I completely forgot they are coming today. I am sure they shall arrive at any moment. Please select something for me, Jeannette. I value your judgment, and your knowledge of my belongings exceeds my own!"

Elizabeth spoke only French when speaking with Jeannette. Even Fitzwilliam could not keep up with their conversations. They spoke too rapidly and often used words he did not know. Some servants complained of an unpatriotic atmosphere created by this language. It was certain, after today, no one would dare speak a word against Mrs. Darcy or her ladies' maid. All ladies and young girls who worked in the mansion greatly admired the actions of their mistress. Any language she desired to speak was perfectly wonderful to them.

The bath was made ready in record time. By the lowered heads and the preparedness of the staff, Elizabeth's actions were already known to all the servants. Elizabeth was heralded a heroine. Wickham had no friends at Pemberly. He was a menace in the truest meaning of the word.

"Let me help you, my lovely Liz-Beth." Fitzwilliam began removing her riding clothes. He was very gentle with her. "I would like to bathe you, if you consent."

"Thank you, beloved. I should like that very much."

He lifted her up in his arms and kissed her forehead. Then he gently placed her in the tub. Using her lavender soap and a new sponge, he started washing her shoulders. He carefully examined her arm for any sign of injury sustained from using her bow with such force. He was relieved to see that she was perfectly unharmed.

"Do you want to talk about it?" he asked her, sounding shy and uncertain of himself.

"Yes. I think we should. I know you probably need to, my silent Handsome Man."

"I just need to know that you are going to be well. It was a terrible thing to happen to you, Elizabeth. I have always told you that I would protect you and keep you safe. Where was I? In my study hearing about cattle. What was I thinking to let you ride?"

"You were thinking that Pemberly had the very best of footmen," she said. "Mr. Clovis has the best reputation the kingdom. Your men are completely trustworthy. Except this morning Roberts and Finch were not loyal. They did not do their job. It was not your fault, and not mine. God was faithful and did not fail us.

"Marigold did a better job than Roberts and Finch. She saw Wickham and sensed danger. What an amazing horse. She deserves better care. A bigger stall, more carrots and oats. Perhaps we could place a young retriever with her for company?"

"Yes, Liz-Beth. We shall let Gram know to get started on that right away. Whatever you wish to be done for Marigold, shall be done. My God, I love that horse! I quite agree!"

"She took such good care of me. She saw my arrows and took me to them. This allowed me to see Wickham. She saw him and knew he was dangerous. Oh. That gives me chills. He was watching me and had evil plans for me. Fitzwilliam, his words to me were course and so vile. He was capable of anything."

"But God prevented him, beloved. He would not allow you to be harmed." he reassured her.

"Fitzwilliam, could I tell you what troubles me most?"

"Yes. I want you to tell me everything, Liz-Beth. I desire to be of help to you."

"I am worried that you shall not love me as you have loved me. I have taken a human life.

"Oh, they have not told me, but I knew I inflicted mortal wounds upon him. That was my intention. I was not going to become his next victim! I could not let him defile me. How could you ever make love to me again, if he had?

"Yes, I knew it was necessary to kill him. I did what was necessary. And, then I inflicted a second wound because I was so enraged. I could not stop myself. Even though I knew full well that the first shot would take his life, I was so furious that I shot him again, just for my own well-being!

"Can you still love me? Shall you trust me with our children? What shall I teach them? Shall you worry about my fitness to be a mother?"

He could see that the price she was paying was great. She now began to doubt her own values, and perhaps her own self-worth?

Her words were pouring out now, and she could not stop herself. "Now I have blood on my hands. I must tell you I do not think I regret it. I am glad for Father that there can be no more Wickham plots of kidnapping. He can do no more mischief. He shall never rape another girl," she declared.

"I would have rather that Roberts and Finch had been doing their job as well as Marigold. Their eyes should have been scouting the tree line for Wickham. They should have shot him before he had the opportunity to speak one word to me! But you taught me the lesson of staying safe with those two youths and the horse. I knew he must not touch me. I would have rather taken his life, than give him my flesh to torture. I knew I must kill him. There, I have confessed all of my darkened heart to you.

"What I do not know is how you feel toward me now. Can you trust me? Shall I kill someone else? Am I cold blooded? What kind of woman am I, Fitzwilliam? Oh—"

She finally started to cry, at last allowing her emotions to flow from her.

He helped her out of the tub and wrapped the towel around her. He carried her to the sofa in their sitting room, and sat with her in his lap. She rested her head upon his shoulder.

She stopped crying.

"You, my wife, are the kindest, dearest person I have ever known. You are sweet and so loving. You have a love of people and a love and fear of God. You are caring and so gentle.

"I trust you with my life, in fact, you protected my life today, along with all our family. You did what you had to do. Darling Liz-Beth, you could have done no less. I am proud of you, love.

"It is very unfortunate that Roberts and Finch did not protect you. Clovis shall deal with them. We shall learn more about them in the coming days. I am sure.

"I rejoice that you are well and sound. You were unharmed. God gave you the strength to do what was needed.

"Oh, Elizabeth, love of my life. I cannot bare to think of what might have happened to you. That evil man was capable of unspeakable things. You are safe, that is all I care about.

"I want you to continue with your archery. You must, my wife. It is a God-given talent. You were shown how important talents are in protecting our lives. You never know when you may need to defend yourself or your family again." He smiled at her as he finished telling her these things and held her tighter to him."

"Are these your true feelings, or are you telling me what you think I need to hear?" she asked him, frowning. She studied his eyes and waited for his reply, "Liz-Beth. You shall tax my brain too severely with your logic and debate approach to your husband. I am a simple man. I say only what I feel and what I mean."

"Then, all I need now is for you to love me. Right now. Perhaps on the rug before the fireplace? I need to inhale your private, manly scent, to touch your strength and feel your power and then your protective weight on me. Do you understand why?"

"I believe I do. You need to know that you and I are well. You need assurance that our love is strong enough for you to suffer the pain of being required to take a human life and that I can separate you from the actions you were required to take."

She smiled for the first time since that morning at the stables. "You are not too dull, for a Cambridge man."

Caroline Bingley could not believe her ears. The clerk at the inn informed her that Claverstone was located in Kent. She called for her carriage and demanded to be taken to Kent.

Her hired men informed her that their next engagement was at Salisbury and not Kent. They were very sorry, but the carriage was no longer available and could certainly not to go to Kent. If she cared to go to Salisbury…

Carrying her own bags back into the inn, Caroline again inquired at the desk. She was told that the post conveyance would be coming though in four days. She was welcome to take her room back and wait.

With no recourse, she mounted the stairs back to the disgusting room. She sat on the bed and just waited. Fuming. At times like these, she dearly wished she enjoyed reading. Often she pretended to read, but, truthfully, reading bored her very much. She went downstairs to the common room, to see if there were any guests worthy of conversation.

Chapter 9

"Celebrations are activities arranged to engage a select group to commemorate success and make the praise widespread."

-Anonymous

Elizabeth and Fitzwilliam had just reached the front steps as the first carriage arrived! It was a happy event. The occurrences of the morning had been left behind.

He could never remember ever being so happy welcoming guests into his home. After nearly five and twenty years, the mansion had become a home for him. In fact, it was his home now, or it would be June one. Yes, Pemberly, a real home, that he shared with his wonderful wife, Elizabeth. As owner, he was especially pleased to host his new family. He thought them all very precious and exceptional people.

There was another very real reason to celebrate such a family gathering. For the first time in his life, he felt he belonged to a real family. For so many years it had been only himself, his father and sister. Now, because of Elizabeth, he had three beautiful children as his nephews and a niece, three new sisters, a wonderful uncle and aunt, a father-in-law, and even a surrogate grandfather! One day, in the not too distant future, there would be more children.

His children. An heir and more. A home for him, at last. And this all because of his beloved, Elizabeth! Yes, Elizabeth. All that she is, and all that she is to him. His wonderful Liz-Beth.

He looked at his young wife. She was wearing the freshness of her youth and the grace of her classical beauty. He could look upon her for hours and continue to find new reasons to adore her. Knowing what she must be going through, even now, he stepped close to her, and holding onto her skirt, he whispered in her ear, "Darling, I have never had such joy in welcoming guests. And to watch them seeing our home for the first time is wonderful. Are you able to enjoy everything?"

She stopped in her tracks, threw her arms around his neck, and kissed him. She whispered back into his ear, "Oh, my love. I am so happy. What a perfect time to have our family about us!

"Thank you for being concerned about me and remembering me. Just please keep loving me. I need you, husband. The truth is, I would die without you. Surely you must know that, do you not?"

Seeing this spontaneous display of affection, Aunt Gardiner smiled at the couple. She whispered to Edward, "Do they remind you of any other couple you remember?"

Soon servants appeared and assisted them by taking guests to their assigned rooms. The Gardiner family had been shown to rooms on the ground floor. The governess was grateful.

A tea for the children had been set out for them, and the adults were to be offered tea upstairs in the large salon. Fitzwilliam himself would give a tour when everyone had arrived.

The Bennet and Bingley carriages arrived at the same time. Elizabeth smiled, and Darcy knew what she was thinking. "You are smiling because you know Charles has purposely followed Jane's carriage, are you not?" he teased.

"Maybe, my love? Is it wrong for me to hope your best friend may wish to be attached to a most beloved sister? And, pray, do not tease me about their rooms being next to each other. Remember love, three days and two nights in London harmed no one."

Kissing him quickly, she took his hand. He smiled and nodded his head. Putting his lips upon her ear, he whispered, "But remember, we were engaged."

"Yes!" she taunted, "Engaged in the most salacious and wonderful new activities! I remember, my darling." He smiled and lifted his eyebrows playfully. He remembered, too.

In moments they were all upon them. Mary and Kitty gapped at the painted ceiling fresco in the grand entry. Everything enthralled them. They could not stop the flow of praise and complete appreciation. It seemed there was so much to view at once. It was overwhelming as they had absolutely no idea what to expect nor could they have imagined such wealth.

How could this mansion be their sister's new home?

The Darcys worked to stifle giggles of joy at their family's obvious admiration of the grand home. Mr. Bennet seemed to be looking for the library, naturally expecting good things given the size and wealth of the mansion.

Jane and Charles did not look at the opulence which surrounded them, but continued to gaze upon each other. Jane, knowing she would look at the house later, kept her eyes on Charles as much as possible. Fitzwilliam winked at his wife. She returned the message with a smile and a nod; it was a very subtle message that no one else would see, and it filled him with a passion and covered him with a sudden warmth.

Fitzwilliam became concerned that his father's carriage had not yet arrived. He discretely called for Clovis.

The man appeared immediately and took him aside. He told him that the Darcy carriage was detained at the first checkpoint in order to inform him about the Wickham situation and give information concerning Roberts and Finch. Relieved that he would not be the one to so inform his father, he thanked the footman and returned to his wife.

"Darling, Father is detained by the footmen at our first checkpoint. I suggest we offer tea to our guests."

Happy and excited voices filled the salon with everyone enjoying the tea. Elizabeth used the opportunity to preview the coming events. She told of Georgiana's coming birthday and the celebration she had planned. When the fishing derby was announced, there was a great outburst from the men. She found it necessary to shush them in order to continue.

After an hour of taking tea, Elizabeth invited everyone to rest in their rooms. It seemed like a good idea to refresh themselves and settle into their surroundings.

Fitzwilliam wanted to have his wife for himself. He took her hand and led her to their rooms. He stretched his long legs out on the bed and patted the place next to him that he wished her to occupy. Compliantly, she took off her slippers and snuggled in beside him. "Are you well, Liz-Beth?"

"I think I am well. I hardly know. Perhaps I could answer you this way." She took a deep breath and began to explain herself. He watched her as closely as he listened.

"Suppose I gave you a gun as you became master of Pemberly. When you received it, I asked if you could use it to kill someone to defend yourself and to protect your family. What would your answer be?"

"Of course I would say yes."

"When you gave me a hunter's bow from America, you did not ask such a question of me. Possibly because I am a woman and because we have staff to protect us. Or, you may not have thought of such a bow being a lethal weapon. Yet, that is exactly why that type of bow is made. I put it to you, Fitzwilliam, is there really a difference?"

"No. And, I had never given it any thought. I just saw it with the arrows in a shop in London. It seemed a proper gift for my wife."

"Fitzwilliam, my darling husband, such a lethal weapon is a gift of power and authority. Is that how you saw me? How you see me now?"

"No. God, no, Liz-Beth! I just knew you loved archery and thought it good for you to have living on the estate with me."

"So, you saw such as being appropriate for my life on Pemberly?"

"Yes! I did, and I do. I am beginning to see what you are trying to tell me. I was used of God to provide you with what you would need. You preserved your life by taking action. I was that instrument used to equip you with what you needed to defend yourself. I know also that Wickham would have killed father had he kidnapped him."

"I think," she said, " I am feeling better and better with each passing moment. I fondly hope you are getting better, as well. I was so afraid you would feel, um, this is hard to say. I feared you would feel somewhat emasculated because I was forced to do what you felt was your job. Clearly, everything took place because our footmen failed. All actions spun from their lack of protection."

"Liz-Beth, truthfully, I was beginning to feel emasculated. I was feeling somewhat angry with you and did not know why. I feel I should apologize to you. I was angry with Jenkins and his cattle as well." He gave her a sweet little smile, to go along with his confession.

"You owe me no apology. I am just thankful we are at last talking it over. Fitzwilliam, this is communication. You are making me so happy right now. Thank you, Handsome Man."

She began again, "As our ride would not have taken us to the tree line, Wickham would still be at large. Think of all the events we have planned? The children playing outside. He could have skulked about, to do God knows what." She took his hand and said, "Do you not agree?"

"Precisely!" he added.

"I think it best if we can just put it behind us. I shall enter the archery contest. I shall enjoy my sport and think not one thought of him."

"Liz-Beth, you have helped me feel so much better. Oh, my darling. I have been so blessed with having you as my wife. You are such a gift. I am thankful that you shall be the mother of my children. They shall be fortunate to learn at your knee. Even I would have wanted to learn at your knee, but far better, I love learning between them!"

She smiled and batted him with a pillow. "You are incorrigible! Learn from my knee as a little child? I shall say this, you are a child! Little boy! And, between my knees? What a naughty little boy you are, at that! Such nasty thoughts in your mind!"

He grabbed her, pulled her under himself, and raised her hands above her head pinning them to the bed. Bending her knees, he put her feet flat to the bed. Then he pushed up her skirts and planted his face in her groin. He was indeed, between her knees! Laughing, he did not even look up as he asked, "Now, let us see, what to kiss first?"

Charlotte Collins held two letters in her hand. She had read both of them twice. Each was from a woman she loved and admired as dearly as a sister. Smiling, she sat at the desk in her very private sitting room and began to respond to the senders. Although they had never met, these two women needed each other. Charlotte could make that happen.

It was always bittersweet writing to her dear friend, whom she called Eliza. She knew they could not be together again, not now that she was married to Mr. Collins. But, she could bring her beloved Eliza, into the company of her dearly loved cousin, Shannon Colleen.

At age seven and twenty, Charlotte was pressured to marry. William Collins was present and willing. It was an opportunity she had to take, even though Lizzy had tried to warn her off the man. The practical needs of life had always driven Charlotte. Now, it seemed most logical to become the agent to introduce Miss Shannon Colleen to Mrs. Elizabeth Darcy.

The house was beginning to show signs of life. Three hours later, the guests began to reappear in the large salon. The Darcys were dressed for dinner and looked very refreshed. They made a striking couple and enjoyed dressing to please each other!

"You look very, very rested and ravishingly beautiful, Mrs. Darcy."

"And, may I say, you seem quite pleased with yourself, Mr. Darcy. Anyone would think you had something to do with my rested appearance," she nearly whispered her answer as she leaned into her husband.

"Indeed!" he smiled and pulled her next to him. Extending his hand to a chair, she was seated. He held on to her hand and continued his warm smile.

Someone cleared his throat from the doorway. It was George Darcy. Smiling, he slowly entered the room. The man absolutely could not quit his eavesdropping habit.

"Am I an unpleasant and untimely interruption, children?" he asked, fearing he was breaking up something very important.

"Not at all, Father!" Elizabeth was saying, as his son added, "You are very welcome, indeed. We are both delighted that you have come home."

"Elizabeth, Fitzwilliam. I am grateful to have this time alone with you. I have much for which to thank you. I learned of the events of the morning as I entered Pemberly." Walking toward Elizabeth, he continued telling them how he had heard the news. "I was told that Wickham was located on Pemberly land, quite near the house, and had been killed.

"My immediate reaction was to learn the man's name and insist that he be given a reward. Imagine my shock to be told that it was done at the hand of my daughter! I had to hear it twice to understand. All of the circumstances were then related to me. My darling, Elizabeth, are you quite well?"

She looked at the gentleman she had learned to love as a father. "Yes, I think I am quite well." Squeezing her husband's hand, she looked at him and added, "Yes, Father, we are both quite well. I am happy to tell you."

"You had no recourse, but to shoot the man," George said. "I am told that you understand the full impact upon our family. We are saved from the threats of an evil man. He continued to tempt fate with illegal actions. Daughter, I would visit my thanks upon any individual who served our family so faithfully. It gives me extreme joy and much satisfaction to so endow these upon you. To say my son married well, is an understatement."

"I must say, Father, the same is true for me. I lovingly adore your precious son. We were earlier discussing the irony of his wedding gift to me. He gave his little bride a lethal weapon, never thinking I would use it as such. Yet, the purpose of shooting such a weapon is to project a fatal assault. I would not have chosen this morning's events, yet given other possible outcomes, I am blessed. Father, I am thankful that your threat is gone. I know I shall be required to give a formal statement, yet, after that, I shall never feel the need to discuss this again."

"Children," he said, most seriously, "Clovis has just informed me that the work you did with Roberts and Finch proved to be most beneficial. He has just learned that the pair were masterminding a kidnap plot against Georgiana. They have been delivered to the magistrate in London, along with three other individuals from Lambton. I have inquired, these men are not known to me. They are new to our area, it may be that they have located here just for this evil."

Elizabeth turned white when she learned this news. Fitzwilliam worried she might faint. He rose to bring her a glass of wine. Returning he sat upon the arm of her chair, he held her hand as she asked her questions.

"This is shocking and more than disturbing, I cannot even think of it where our little Georgie is concerned. I cannot suffer to think such evil should ever be suggested against her. I should have put an arrow each into those malefactors when I had the opportunity."

Fitzwilliam asked, "Did they know when this was planned to occur, Father?"

George lowered his voice, "It was believed that her birthday was to be the date of the abduction."

Elizabeth gasped, "No! Thanks be to God for causing events to unfold as they did. We cannot know the end from the beginning, would you not agree?"

Both men nodded their heads and gave each other a look that said they would talk more on this matter.

"It is felt that the judges in London shall wield more power against those accused and impose heavier sentences for the heinous plot," George explained. "Georgie's age shall be a deciding factor in this case, but it is presumed they all shall be hanged."

Elizabeth nodded her head, and simply said, "Good, Father, that is good."

Georgiana's birthday arrived with a beautiful morning. Pemberly was prepared. The great lawn was set with all the games and festive tents dotting the landscape. All had been readied for the fishing derby and archery contest. Even the beautiful little ponies had been saddled.

"It seems Edward has done such a convincing job talking about the joys of fishing that our children have asked to fish today," Aunt was saying.

"Oh, dear, Aunt. I hope Fitzwilliam shall allow our children to select their own entertainment."

All the ladies laughed. Elizabeth felt a strange heat surge through her body at the thought of having children. It made her feel peculiar. She had no idea why.

Georgiana was looking forward to her birthday cake. She loved the German custom, for she dearly loved sweets. Elizabeth was attempting to get the ladies organized for the archery contest.

"Is there no one to shoot against me? Birthday girl, you are becoming very good, please tell me you shall shoot."

By this time, all were aware of the Wickham incident. It appeared that no one wanted to shoot, fearing that it might be difficult for Lizzy.

"Family, please allow me to say this. I take no joy in what I was forced to do; however, I also shall not allow that vile man to take joy from me. I delight in my sport, and I shall shoot, even if no one shall join me."

Elizabeth set her jaw and picked up her bow. She faced the target and began firing arrows very rapidly into the centre. The ladies stood with their mouths open and watched her. Mary moved next to her, put on her arm and finger gear, took up a bow and quiver. She walked to the nearest target and joined her sister in shooting.

Fitzwilliam and Rory rode up soon after they began. Seeing the cousins together, Elizabeth thought to say a word of caution.

"This is Georgie's day, Fitzwilliam. No fencing! Seeing you two cousins together with nothing better to do than ride around the lawn worries me. No swordplay, please!"

"Upon my honour, cousin, I shall not draw my blade against your husband today," Rory promised. "Why does that provide me no comfort?" she pertly replied.

Upon seeing them, Georgiana became excited to get Rory involved in the archery.

"Rory, come and shoot. You are the swordsman in the family. You should be good at this."

Rory looked at Fitzwilliam and laughed. "Did you hear that, cousin? I am the swordsman in the family?" He dismounted and picked up the equipment.

Fitzwilliam did not hear the remark. He was looking at his wife with intensity, hoping that she was enjoying her sport with no thought of Wickham.

Walking to the mark and preparing to shoot, Rory looked nervously at Elizabeth's target. He was never told that she was the mysterious archer in the little phaeton at Kent.

"Maybe we should have a men's tournament?" Georgie shouted, jumping up and down as her cousin took aim.

He frowned and asked for silence as he took his shot. Rory let the first arrow fly. It just missed the target and flew out into the lawn. He began to turn red. Fitzwilliam laughed and the ladies covered their mouths. They were afraid to embarrass the cavalry man.

"We do not fight with bows and arrows," he stated defensively, for Fitzwilliam's benefit. Then, looking sheepishly at the ladies, he blushed.

Fitzwilliam put up his hand and yelled, "Stop! Rory do not shoot! Somebody quickly move the innocent little ponies. God knows where this foolish man may send his next arrow!" Looking at the Shetlands, barely visible near the lane, everyone broke out into wild laughter.

On Rory's second arrow Georgiana was quiet, as her cousin took aim. He hit the edge of the target and the arrow bounced off sideways and skidded to a stop lying lengthwise upon the grass.

Before the third arrow, Rory looked at Fitzwilliam and boldly challenged, "Cousin, would you care to place a wager?"

"Cousin, I believe I would. Is this to hit the target anywhere?"

"Nay!"

"Well, either you are a ringer and you are fooling us with your rather comedic showing, or you are a novice, and the tiny bow string and small arrows are not well suited to your oversized and sausage-shaped hands. I shall take your bet if you are claiming a bull's eye."

"And, what shall be the prize?" Georgie squealed with delight.

Looking his cousin squarely in the eye, Rory straightened himself and offered: "Your wife has told me that there shall be an informal family dance after dinner. If I make a bull's eye, you, Fitzwilliam, shall play pianoforte for two songs. And, if I fail, I shall play violin for one!"

"Oh!" Georgie interrupted, "but I did not know either of you played. Do you play pianoforte, Brother? And you, Rory, the violin? Is this a jest? How long have you played? Wait! Only one?" Georgie asked, suddenly realising the terms of payment. She was so excited!

Georgiana had never heard either man play. This was a closely guarded secret, and now she was privy to the intelligence. She felt it was so amusing.

"Yes, birthday girl, only one!" Rory answered her, "I am so terrible on the violin, sitting through one song shall set everyone's teeth on edge!" Laughter rang out at this thought!

All eyes were upon Rory as he squared up facing the target. He stopped a moment, and asked in a loud voice the exact distance to the target. Then he wetted one finger and held it up to determine which way the wind was blowing. The crowd moaned with disapproval.

"Shoot! Shoot! Shoot!" They began to chant. Rory feigned disappointment. "Ah! The angry mob is turning against young Robin Hood. See, the Sheriff of Nottingham is so busy looking at Maid Marian that he fails to watch the tournament. He does not see my merry men in the trees waiting to free me! And, so I shoot and then, away to Sherwood Forest!"

"Look!" Mary shouted, "Did you see? His head was turned when he shot." The arrow's flight seemed to take minutes.

Everyone held their breath! With a swoop, and a strong vibration, it hit the line. Nearly a bull's eye, nearly not!

The Sheriff of Nottingham pretended to be the judge. The crowd protested.

"No! Aunt, your honest opinion and fairness makes you queen. Please call it, Queen Aunt Lucille!" Georgiana cried, trying to stifle the giggles.

Lucille entered into the impromptu comedy. She put her hands behind her back, bent her body downward, and walked straight to the target, nearly touching it with her nose. Acting as though her vision was poor, she groped the target, then her left hand found the base of the arrow, and she slowly pulled the shaft out with her right. Moving her head side to side so each eye could examine the hole, she turned her body slightly away from the crowd, as though they were not clearly visible to her either, and declared a line shot.

"I decree the pair shall play a duet. The same song, played at the same time. None of your tricks!" she affirmed, with the power and authority of a monarch. The crowd exploded in cheers.

Fitzwilliam signaled to Liz-Beth that he wanted to perform a rescue mount. She nodded agreement and walked toward the middle of the lawn.

Fitzwilliam shouted: "Look! The beautiful Maid Marian is trying to escape the Sheriff of Nottingham—I shall retrieve her thusly!" Even though they had never performed it with Percival, he kicked the horse into a gallop. He came next to her, and leaned down even lower than he had when he rode Marigold for the rescue. His speed was perfect, Elizabeth took his arm and he swooped her up behind him with no difficulty.

It worked as well as it had with Marigold. The pair were exhilarated, and the crowd went wild with cheers and laughter! It was an exciting moment for Georgiana and later she would say that it was as wonderful as a circus act!

"I had forgotten the thrill of this," he yelled to his wife, over his shoulder. "I wondered what you would do with your gown."

"Did I scandalise you, Mr. Darcy? As you know, I wear no undergarment."

He smiled, although she could not see it. Reaching back to touch her, he said, "Let us ride into the forest, and I shall make certain you wear no undergarment, Mrs. Darcy. It feels so good to do this again," he told her, "We must always do this, for I dearly love riding one horse with you." The two galloped off, to Georgie and everyone's delighted amazement.

"Shall I come in front of you, my love?" she asked him, reminding him of the first time she felt his arousal. They both laughed at the memory, and she pressed her breasts into his back, stretched her arms around him, and held on tightly to his thighs, next to his groin. She squeezed him, and pressed her cheek against his shoulder.

The lovers went to the opposite side of the house. They dismounted and engaged in wild kissing for several minutes before Rory discovered them and ruined their entertainment.

The ballroom was set up for the celebration. There was a birthday cake and a table with gifts. Musical instruments were set up, and ready to be played. Mary took her place at the pianoforte and happily played several jigs.

Pemberly bakers had created a masterpiece of a birthday cake. After everyone had indulged in at least one delicious piece, gifts were opened and appreciated. Everyone in the family danced, even the Gardiner children, who danced without partners. The crowd was happy and lively.

Lord Claverstone was given the dubious honour of introducing the cousins' duet. He laughed as he announced them. They selected "Loch Lomond," and tried to force poor Charles Bingley into singing a solo. Not having consumed sufficient ale, he respectfully declined.

Never had a performance contained as many technical errors and musical mistakes as the painful execution of this unfortunate duet. The music was horrid, yet the musicians were waggish, and the entire group was outrageously entertained!

Elizabeth was congratulated on a spectacular party. Slowly, each one parted, wishing happiness once again to Georgie. It had been a long day.

After the dance, Charles and Jane, Rory and Mary, and the Darcys went for a late walk in the gardens. The air was sweet and the sky clear, although just a bit chilly. The conversation was lively, and topics ranged from the constellations above to poetry. The group laughed often and easily. They obviously enjoyed each other's company. Rory escorted Mary to her rooms. Charles and Jane were going to be the last to leave. They lingered in the moonlight until Darcy said, "Bingley, do turn the stars out when you two go inside, shall you? Liz-Beth and I hate to leave them on all night!"

Elizabeth and Fitzwilliam walked side by side, up to their rooms. "He is going to ask her to marry him tonight. Do you not agree, my love?" she asked her husband. "Tonight is the night; I just feel it!"

"Liz-Beth, you romantic. I highly doubt it! Bingley does not make a move without discussing it with me first. He places a high value upon my opinion, and I have never ill advised him. He has hardly spoken to me of your sister. He is a kind man, to be sure, and respectful of her. But I cannot see that he has shown her any special attentions. Do not be disappointed, beloved. I cannot see that he has any special feelings for Jane."

"How about a wager, Handsome Man?" she invited him, with a sly smile.

"Absolutely, my Goddess of Horses! Prepare to lose, my love."

"I shall win." She laughed. " And when I do, what shall be my prize?"

"Well my lovely wife, I know you shall probably think of a prize I shall dislike. Any other woman would want jewels or furs. Nay, you shall want something of my flesh, no doubt."

"I have it!" she giggled, "I shall require to break my fast in bed, with you in delivery of my meal tray. Then, I shall have need of a nice warm bath with lavender soap. You shall bathe me, of course. After which, I shall need a lavender oil body massage, given to me by your hands, my husband. It shall be a very erotic massage, I should think." Instinctively, she tickled his ear, and whispered, "You shall also provide me with any other service I may require. Shall we just make it a day of such?"

"Liz-Beth, you make me wish to lose!"

Reaching their rooms, fatigue hit her. He could see exhaustion upon her beautiful face. Kissing Elizabeth good night, he thanked her for all she did to make Georgiana's birthday special.

Their room was sweetly quiet as both husband and wife fell asleep immediately. The house was dark and peaceful.

Suddenly Elizabeth sat up, sobbing without control. Her breathing was rapid and irregular and she began to hyperventilate.

A cold sweat covered her, and she became pale. Her eyes were wide with fear!

Fitzwilliam awoke in a frantic state. He had no idea what was wrong with his wife. He was just about to ring for Otis when his efforts to speak to her and awaken her seemed to help. Her eyes opened and stared at him blankly. Clutching the sheet to her bare bosom, she tried to get away from him as fast as she could. He reached out to grab her and pull her back, but she began to shout. "No!" She repeated the word, punctuated with body-wracking sobs.

This repetition continued with decreasing volume until she mouthed the two letter word in a grotesque pantomime. Her beautiful face contorted with obvious sorrow. Her fingers released the silk sheet, and it slid softly down to her lap. Now her breathing was shallow and swift. Her heart beat so fiercely; its rapid contractions pushed up into the wall of her chest as though it were trying to escape her body entirely. To her helplessly frightened husband, it was as if a foreign body was attacking her from within. After what seemed like an hour, Fitzwilliam finally got her to speak to him. He told her she had experienced a nightmare.

He had never witnessed anything like it in his life.

Presuming it to be about Wickham, he asked whilst holding her, "Liz-Beth, were you afraid in your dream?"

"Fitzwilliam, I am tired, please forgive me for this, and try to get some sleep. It only happened because I was exhausted. You need not worry about my fears."

"No. I shall not sleep until you tell me the dream. Do you always have the same dream?"

"No," she replied, "I just always have the same fear. This is the first time I have had such a dream."

"Please tell me, Liz-Beth. I am your husband. I share your daydreams, and it is only right that I share in your nightmare. Was it about Wickham?"

"No. I do not wish to tell you of whom I dreamt."

"Why? What are you afraid of, sweet girl?"

"Believe me, telling you shall do no good for either of us. Pray, let us forget this matter."

"No. I shall not," he insisted.

"Husband, my fear has been the same for a long time. I am afraid of being humiliated. Please pay me no mind and go back to sleep. You shall need your rest, love."

"Liz-Beth, this is obviously very important to you. You had a dream that must have seemed very real to you. You must share it, or I shall call for a physician from town."

"Faced with that choice, I shall tell you. It may not make sense to you without knowing my fear. I have lived with this particular fear since April."

"April, when we met?"

"Nearly."

"And what of that fear, Liz-Beth?"

"If you insist to know, I shall reveal the fear and the dream as well. You might as well know both, if I am forced to reveal part." She closed her eyes as she spoke.

"Fitzwilliam, you are an amazingly handsome man. You are intelligent and one of the ten wealthiest men under age thirty in the kingdom. Thousands of women have been in pursuit of you for all your adult life; probably hundreds have actually met or contacted you. I know you to be a man of very vigorous sexual needs and very strong desires. I love that about you, but I also have with that knowledge, the base of my fear. You have told me yourself that if God had told you not to fornicate, you probably would have anyway. Did you not say so?"

He stared at her in silence. He was fearful of where she was going with this. His fear turned to a brooding stare.

"You have performed acts with me that I did not know existed. I realise you enjoy my body and the way I love you. Yet, I fear the day you shall tire of me. We love daily. It is only a matter of time until I shall be with child. What if I have sickness, and you cannot make love to me? How long might it take, before you fall back to your former habits of promiscuity? You have plenty of opportunities and there are many willing girls. I have been tempted to ask your father how he did it, but as a woman I do not dare!"

Shocked into speaking to her, he demanded, "What? How he did what? I do not understand, Liz-Beth? What does he have to do with me and this crazy irrational fear of yours?"

"Your father is a very handsome man, Fitzwilliam. He has not always been six and fifty. He was once young and virile, just like you. He had a young wife. He had great wealth and good looks. I am sure he was tempted. How did he stay faithful? And what did he do after Anne died? He was only two and forty when he was left alone. He had needs. Have you not asked him for advice on the matter?"

"My God, Elizabeth! Once again you amaze me with the things your brain can think. That is an excellent point. I have never thought of my father having or needing sex. He is very open with me. As I told you, he was concerned about me having all my questions answered. I shall ask him, Liz-Beth. Does that calm you?" Her lashes rested upon her cheeks as she did not wish to look upon him. She nodded.

"Now, the dream please. I shall show you how unfounded your fears are, my love."

He put his arm around her. Looking into her green eyes, brimmed with tears, he listened as she poured out the scene that had taken her into torment.

"I dreamt I was in the stable with Marigold. It was me, myself, except that I was the daughter of Mr. Gram. I was wearing a plain gown. You came into the stall with me and took me into a corner, and made me lie down. As Miss Gram, I was shocked. You spoke not one word to me. Without any emotion, you pulled my skirt up around my neck and reached down with both hands and pulled my undergarment down around my ankles. Still without speaking to me, your hand grabbed my mound. You squeezed it and felt it all over. You were turning your head, as if trying to decide something. Your fingers probed me. One finger traced my—Miss Gram's ring, as if measuring it.

"You, looked outward, away from me, and you said to yourself, 'this shall do, I may come back.' You arose from your knees and walked away. You were trying to catch up with me, Mrs. Darcy. I was wearing a beautiful and expensive gown, like the one I shall wear tomorrow.

You called to me, but your cousin Rory stepped out of the shadows and got into your face. He yelled at you! 'What the devil are you about? Why can you not enjoy family dinners at home? I have seen Elizabeth. You are so blessed, and you do not even know it. Let me take you home. If you have that girl, Elizabeth shall know it. She shall know it when she looks at you. They know, Fitzwilliam, women always know, Cousin.'

"Then I woke up. I woke up crying because when I heard Rory, I knew I had heard you too, and I saw you. I was Miss Gram, your innocent victim, and I was myself, your wife, who knew you were considering a future tryst. You said she would do, and, 'I may be back.'

"I, as Miss Gram, felt humiliation and pain. And, I, as Mrs. Darcy, felt rejection and humiliation, jealousy, and the worst possible pain imaginable."

Here she broke down and wept as before. "She was what you wanted. You were pleased! Oh God, Fitzwilliam, I know from my past that I could not survive if you were unfaithful to me. I beg you, if you have been thinking about this, please get someone to help you resist it. I would die of humiliation. I would be stone cold to you and that would drive you further away. This fear is real to me; the dream horrified me."

She began to wring her hands, and frowning deeply she continued, "It is all my fault. I should have known better. I do not belong here. We married too quickly, did we not?"

Fitzwilliam's heart froze. He seemed to remember a similar conversation with Rory about Elizabeth. Sensing he should do something, he took her in his arms. "Liz-Beth, I promise with all my heart it was just a dream. I shall not let it come true. I promised before God I would keep myself only to you, for as long as we both shall live."

She laid back down between the sheets and wished for sleep. If only he were a poor wood cutter, and a homely one, at that.

Was I as horrible as the man in the dream? I fear I was, especially when drunk. Where did this dream come from, and what does it mean?

He closed his eyes, but sleep did not come. He put his hand gently upon Elizabeth's back.

She was sleeping sweetly. It was he, who was troubled. Greatly troubled. His wife was nearly at her end with fear. It was like that night in London, only worse. If only he had told her several of the names and gotten it all out in the open when she offered to discuss and forget.

Did her insecurities bred this fear, or was this dream a warning from God?

True to her word Elizabeth met Jeannette at five thirty in the dressing room. Her bath was ready, and everything had been prepared. Her maid whispered **en francais** to her, and she smiled, keeping her responses short as to keep the noise level down.

Jeannette had been her confidant. This was one of the circumstances that required a French-speaking maid. Her husband sometimes tried to listen in on their talks, but his French was not adequate.

This morning was special. It was June one. Jeannette was seeing to her mistress and her request for a depilate of her body. Other than the hair on her head and eyebrows and lashes, Elizabeth was to have no hair. She got the idea one day when Jeannette spoke of the women in Paris who decided to remove their hair to make them more sensual. She elected to wait for her husband's birthday, as a gift to him. Remembering Juliette Marie's admonishment to keep him interested, she thought to try it.

They had never discussed this; perhaps he liked the bush. She did not know. It was worth a chance. If he did not like it, it would regrow in a matter of time. If he did like it, she was willing to keep it this way, if it pleases him. After about half an hour, she was successful. Looking in the mirror, Elizabeth loved the look and the feel.

Elizabeth Darcy was having a spectacularly good morning. Her gown was perfect, her jewelry was just the right touch, her slippers felt so good she could wear them around the clock, and Jeannette performed a miracle upon her hair.

The day was a busy one. Wednesday, June one would begin with a family breakfast, then to church for communion and a special service for the master of Pemberly. Next was the picnic upon the lawn for the tenants, then the rooftop celebration for the five and twenty birthday!

Checking on Darcy before she met Mrs. Reynolds, she tiptoed to his bedside. He was sleeping soundly. She brushed her hand up and down his stomach and lingered a moment on his erection and then kissed his lips. "Happy Birthday!" Smiling sweetly, she pulled away slowly. "Oh, birthday. Yes. Thank you," he said. He was groggy as he had not slept well.

"Darling, Mrs. Reynolds is waiting for me. We have a very busy morning. Breakfast, church, the tenants' picnic. I am afraid the day shall fly past us."

As she started to quit the room, he looked so adorable, she violated her own new rule of enticement. 'Always pique his interest, then leave him wanting more...'

Walking back to him, she said, "Do you desire to see one of your birthday gifts, my love?"

"Yes, please," he answered with eagerness, which made him look even younger and more adorable.

"You may, but remember, it is just to look. Do not touch! You must not touch!"

Taking a deep breath, she walked near his face. He rose up onto one elbow, and she slowly, very slowly, lifted her skirt. Watching his face through the process of the skirt lifting, she saw a look of disbelief, then a very big smile. Quicker than she could think it possible, he grabbed her hips and pulled her to his eager mouth! He began kissing her, all the while punctuating his kisses with words to express his feelings...

"Oh Liz-Beth, YOU look fantastic! Amazing, so sensuous, voluptuous, enticing, beautiful, intoxicating, touchable, kissable, loveable, desirable, umm, so very ripe, and delicious—Oh, come to me my sweet girl, my Liz-Beth!"

He continued to kiss her *mons veneris* and had ambitions to delight himself in her *vulve*. Twice she had to tell him to quiet his moans. His commentary and the subsequent very personal remarks to her were so loud she feared that they would wake the house. "Oh God, Elizabeth! You did this for me? You are naked and so lovely. Oh, I wish we had nothing to do today, all day, and no people here. I could spend the entire day between your lovely legs."

At that, she put her foot on the bed, and he felt the smooth leg she offered. "Wife, I am in ecstasy. I love being five and twenty if this is what it gets me. Oh, for just five minutes more to kiss and lick you, please? Oh, my what a sensation just to touch you. How did you think of this? You amaze me. Thank you, thank you, my love."

"I am so sorry, Mr. Darcy, but I must leave you. Mrs. Reynolds shall scold me for being late. We have an agenda for the day, my darling. You must excuse me. I shall see you soon, in the family dining room."

Everyone one was on time for breakfast. Fitzwilliam was first to arrive, eager to see his wife again. He looked wonderful in his breeches and boots, linen shirt, plaid waistcoat, and blue jacket. Elizabeth thought it a good idea to dress as a reminder that his tenants would see him soon, on horseback.

The morning was wonderful, so the family decided to walk to the church. Mr. Whiteside offered this special service as a tribute to the Darcy family. He was grateful to the family for the living. Mr. Darcy never tried to influence sermons. Mr. Whiteside was a faithful servant of God in return.

The sermon was short, it was a talk about faithfulness. Faithfulness in marriage vows, faithfulness in business relationships. It was from the heart and very much appreciated. The Holy Communion followed and was a sacred service. Everyone was quiet on the walk home.

While walking back, Jane and Charles stayed back by Mr. Bennet. Elizabeth noticed and nudged her husband. The two of them fell back and listened. Charles was asking to see the man alone in the library as soon as they returned to the house.

Elizabeth turned to her husband and gave him her order for the breakfast he would deliver to her, as he had lost their wager! All that remained was Mr. Bennet's blessing.

The air was filled with the aroma of the venison, roasting over the fires. Sounds of the musicians from Lambton tuning their instruments and practicing their music were floating through the air.

Once the lawn was in view, eager tenants and their families could be seen arriving early for the picnic. The Darcy family went immediately out onto the lawn and began speaking with the people. This was what made them loved by their tenants and the people of Derbyshire.

Elizabeth looked around her and saw so many of the faces she knew. She was delighted to realise that she also knew many of their names. Leaning against her husband, she whispered in his ear, "Just think of the hardships many of these faithful people face every day. They are brave, and very hardworking, are they not, my love?" He took her hand, and they met with many tenants as husband and wife. Many attempted to speak to her. Since the news of her shooting Wickham, she had become a celebrity of sorts. Her good humour also served well in leading the tenants to admire her.

Just before the music started, Mr. and Mrs. Darcy, holding hands, stepped forward. He spoke for about four minutes, telling the crowd he intended to continue in the good name and the excellent business practices of his father. His wife had dedicated herself to the tenants on her father's estate and would continue to do so here at Pemberly.

Elizabeth spoke next and briefly said she wished to follow in the footsteps of Anne Darcy.

The music began and so did the dancing. Mr. and Mrs. Darcy led off the first dance, and then they retired to the family under a canopy. "Experiencing any drafts, Mrs. Darcy?" he asked as they rejoined their family. She smiled at him with her fine eyes showing her love for him.

Fitzwilliam excused himself and rose to disappear into the crowd. George leaned over to Elizabeth and inquired after his son, but she had no idea where he was headed or why he had left the family. She was not certain why Fitzwilliam's actions seemed so strange to her. Reflecting upon his recent behaviour, she thought several things seemed out of the ordinary. *Perhaps my precious husband is feeling the stress of becoming master of Pemberly. He has his moments of doubt and worry, even though Father has pledged his support.*

The Gardiner children had a most exciting day. They took in everything that happened in the rural setting. London had been all they had known until this trip. Mr. and Mrs. Gardiner were thankful for the experience.

Grandpapa was also impressed. As an estate owner, he had never once hosted his tenants. He was most interested in their response. To him, it was very impressive.

Mr. Gram received the message from Mrs. Darcy. He was ordered to put hands into the stalls of the horses during the fireworks. Marigold and Percival especially, along with the other horses of high value were to be steadied and calmed during the twenty minute display. Dogs also were to be secured inside the tack rooms. The celebration would seem life threatening and very frightening to all the animals. Groomsmen and all hands were to be told of the noisy display and warned to do all they could for the animals.

Gradually the Darcy party drifted back into the house. George and Fitzwilliam slipped quietly into Mr. Darcy's study. Father and son had a talk about their wives. George was so very worried to hear all that his son disclosed. He shared his life's experience gladly. He was happy to suggest some very good ideas that Fitzwilliam felt might be helpful.

Fitzwilliam told him everything that worried Elizabeth. He confessed that she was right to worry, he did not trust himself. Yes, he had promised fidelity, but his past had been so filled with promiscuity that he did not feel that he could promise faithfulness with certainty.

George found this disturbing and difficult to understand. At the same time, he realised that his son probably did not believe him regarding the parentage of Wickham. It grieved him that his son did not hold to the values he had been taught as a child. Was it his fault? Certainly it was not the fault of Mr. Whiteside. The cleric had been faithful in his service. Was it his friends at Cambridge? The influence of Wickham? He promised to pray for his son.

Not since their talks at Rosings had Fitzwilliam felt so close to his father. It had been a very emotional, honest and frank discussion. It was also just the first of many such talks. Fitzwilliam seemed to be more sure of himself, with concrete reasons to hope that he would be faithful to Elizabeth. She certainly did deserve a faithful husband. She was a good and faithful wife. The saddest part of the dilemma was that she satisfied and pleased him in every way sensually. He was happy and loved her very much.

In fact, he could hardly keep up with her. But still…

Charles Bingley was just leaving the library. Mr. Bennet was stern with him, and finally after many attempts, he agreed and gave his blessing. Charles had the idea the man was doing it just for a diversion. In the end, Mr. Bennet asked if he would be allowed to announce the engagement after Fitzwilliam's birthday dinner. Bingley was delighted. He was glad the ordeal was over! The old man could be mischievous!

At seven of the clock, each family member was led quietly to the rooftop by Mr. Fleming or Mr. Clovis. One by one, they went silently to join the others. Refreshments were being served as they awaited Fitzwilliam and Elizabeth.

Fitzwilliam expected a family dinner in the dining room. The couple was dressed and ready to go down when Clovis tapped on their door. Reporting that noises had been heard and perhaps some activity seen, he wished the master to accompany him to the roof.

"I see you are both dressed, sir. Perhaps Mrs. Darcy would go with us, as it is most likely raccoons," Mr. Clovis explained with an apology for disturbing them.

"I thank you, sir. I would much rather go along than to sit and wait here alone." Jumping to her feet, she took her husband's arm and walked out the door with him.

The couple reached the rooftop. The door was opened, and everyone with glasses raised shouted, "Here is a jolly good fellow! Happy birthday, Fitzwilliam." If ever in the history of Pemberly there was a surprise executed, it was this evening's event. Fitzwilliam was taken completely unawares. After the picnic, he had no expectations of any further special plans except a nice family dinner.

Mrs. Reynolds was given a glass of champagne and drank a toast to the five and twenty birthday fellow and congratulations to the new master of Pemberly.

Fitzwilliam and Rory raised their glasses to her and declared, "A toast to Mrs. Reynolds, who knew all along that two boys were sleeping on this roof, and she kept our secret. And, our hides from being tanned." She had tears in her eyes as she laughed with them, and remembered and thanked them.

"Father, thank you for this special dinner." Fitzwilliam's eyes filled with emotion.

George held him by the shoulders and looked him in the eyes. "Son, I had nothing to do with this. It was entirely Elizabeth's idea. The dinner and everything else for this evening's pleasure was her own doing. She is the one you should thank."

Dinner was served. It was simple, with one meat serving, two vegetables, and two types of bread. Ale, wine, and water were served as beverages. A new flavored cake was served for dessert. Georgie had cake twice in one day!

After dinner, Elizabeth gave Fitzwilliam a large box, with a simple card which stated, "For the master of Pemberly." He hastily opened the box and discovered a marvelous new invention from America. It had been purchased in London and was not intended for sale for perhaps the next five years. It was an experimental model, an early prototype. There were only three in existence, this one, the one retained by the inventor, and the third in the possession of the American president, Mr. Thomas Jefferson. That gentleman was reported to be somewhat of an inventor himself, and keenly interested in the work of others.

The remarkable gift was an American version of the English Baker rifle. It was invented by a man named Henry, who was working with his inventor son on developing firearms for the young country. Fitzwilliam was amazed; he had never owned anything like it.

All the men crowded around the new rifle. Apparently, it boasted several features which none of them had seen. Rory was especially interested. All the men agreed to test-fire it on the morrow.

Fitzwilliam asked his wife how she came by the rifle. She told him she had been in a London gun shop, where she purchased his hunting knife. She overheard two men working on a physics problem. Neither of them had the answer, and it seemed quite important that they solve it immediately. She told them it was very easy and wrote out the answer for them.

The shop owner heard her and offered to sell her anything in the shop at a ninety-nine per cent discount. She asked how much the rifle would cost. The man told her it was not for sale.

Then, the gentleman with the problem introduced himself. He was the younger Mr. Henry. He offered to sell her the rifle at his cost. He explained that the money she had saved them with the solving of the 'force' problem would more than pay for this prototype.

Everyone listening was amazed at her matter of fact answer which understated her accomplishment. Gerald, Edward, Lucille and even Thomas just looked at each other and smiled. They knew their girl and the workings of her amazing mind. Fitzwilliam was just beginning to learn.

Darkness had fallen, and Mr. Clovis nodded to Elizabeth. She asked everyone to stand and make their way to the ledge that overlooked the lake. The servants extinguished the lights, and they all stood in darkness. Some complained that they could not see the lake. The group stood quietly and waited. Suddenly, a loud whistle sounded. The white tail of a rocket blazed toward the heavens, and all went quiet. After a few seconds, there was an explosion, and the wide burst of brightly coloured lights flickered brilliantly against a black sky. The apparition burned very brightly, and then a wide displacement of the lights occurred as the fragments chased each other across the darkening sky and faded from sight. There were plenty of "ohs" and "ahs!"

Filled with joy, Fitzwilliam stood behind his wife, enfolding her in his arms. Overwhelmed with her generous gifts, the special planning, and the flawlessly covert execution of his private party, he was nearly speechless. He simply whispered, "Thank you so much, love of my life. I shall thank you again when we are alone and I am allowed to enjoy my very, very special gift!"

The fireworks were a twenty minute spectacular extravaganza, then the candles were lit again, and coffee was served along with a slice of birthday cake.

When all the candles were relit, Mr. Bennet tapped the side of his water glass.

As soon as he had everyone's attention, he said, "I cannot top fireworks, but allow the news of the engagement of my daughter Jane Bennet to Charles Bingley to create enough excitement to light up all of our lives! They have spoken to Mr. Whiteside and wish to marry here at the chapel."

Everyone stood to their feet and crowded around them to offer congratulations. Fitzwilliam was the last. He put his hand on Bingley's shoulder and told him he had lost a bet over the news. "I bet my wife that you would not become engaged without talking it over with me first. I did not even know you had any special interest in my sister, can you imagine that, my friend?"

Lord Claverstone and Mr. Bennet turned in at ten of the clock. It had been a long day.

Other guests quit at four in the morning. Eventually the final few filed down the stairs to their rooms. Each slowly bid the couple good morrow and promised to see them at about four in the afternoon for tea. Fitzwilliam signaled Clovis to leave them. He and Liz-Beth got out the blankets and pillows she ordered to be stored for their use in sleeping on the roof.

"At last! Come here, mistress of Pemberly and allow the master to remove all of these cumbersome garments you have been forced to wear all day."

"Elizabeth, you wore no stays. I knew you wore no underpants, but if I had only known you were naked under your gown, it would have driven me wild, all day! Look at you! You are a glorious!"

"From the waist down, I resemble myself at age ten. Tell me, Mr. Darcy, do you approve of me, *sans poils pubiens*, or do you wish an annulment?"

"That shall depend. Am I entitled to have my way with you for more than one minute this time? You drove me mad this morning, wife!"

He kept his eyes trained upon her apex while he disrobed. They found the blankets were more than comfortable. He briefly gave her a kiss, and descended upon her with the glee of a ten-year-old boy. Albeit, one who knew precisely what to do with a mature woman who only looked like a ten-year-old girl, from the waist down.

Elizabeth clearly was not prepared for the erotic attentions she was to receive from her enamored husband. Finding her completely tantalizing, he was insatiable. He unleashed so many pent up thoughts upon her. He had never seen anything like this look. He could not believe she would expose herself to him, but he was so happy that she did.

In the heat of passion he told her of the hundreds of women had had known, none of them compared to her.

Oh God, there is was. Hundreds. Multiples of one hundred? At what age did he begin? Help me, Lord. Do not let this ruin my time with him I do not want to be angry, jealous, and unhappy about his past. Help him to be faithful in the future. And, now.

He declared his love for her. He thanked her again for this gift, and he tried to relate how much it meant to him.

If I could only know I was his one and only, Lord.

Just then, he lifted up his head and said, "Liz-Beth, there is no one like you. I need you to know how special you are to me, my love. I do not deserve you, Liz-Beth. In fact, you are more than any man deserves."

This was the rescue she had prayed for, and it was a healing balm to her wounded heart. He had no idea the pain he had inflicted. His speech was without thinking and from the heat of the moment.

His thirsting tongue burst into her, desirously intent upon tasting that which he craved. Finding it and loving it, most ardently, he continued over and over again to lick, then pierce her most sensual spot. Running her hands through his hair, she told him how much she loved the velvety feel. He could now say the same of her!

She could barely endure the ecstasy he was delivering. His forays and his words, now only of adoration, kept her dangerously lost in the depths of his consuming passion. Tenderly he covered her inner thighs with kisses. Then, he passionately applied gentle bites all over her.

Again and again his mouth fed upon her. Most gently he applied his lips, tongue, and, ever so softly, his teeth to tease and delight her. Light and momentary contacts, were interspersed with fleeting seconds of firmly pressed dominance. All perfectly sublime sensations, creating a new and even stronger craving for his love and attentions. This was how he commanded complete control over her. She desired him, only him forever! She experienced so many heights that she began to wonder if she could endure his energy and the new found appetite he had for her.

He expressed his desire to tell his dearest friends what she had done, and how exquisitely she looked and felt! Yet, he kept assuring her he certainly would not!

Their passion replaced all their rational thoughts. Fitzwilliam had never had this stamina.

He wondered if it was the empowerment of his title or of turning five and twenty! He lifted his head to tell her afresh that these sensations were completely new to him. All of her anatomy was so optically available to him. It seemed to be important to let her know that this was his first time to see a woman in this state. He could not tell her thank you enough!

When the sun rose, bright rays of light shone on them. He delighted in seeing all of her in the full light of day. Over and over he told her of her perfection and beauty. He could not stop looking at her. At last he entered her, and they loved until he released his seed. Fully satisfied, he collapsed upon her. Sleep came immediately for both husband and wife. For the first time, he slept atop his wife's body.

Pemberly enjoyed a very subdued Thursday. The new master and mistress slept until three. Tea was at four. Everyone looked fatigued, if not elated, with the celebrations of the day and night. The topic of conversation was now the wedding of Jane and Charles. The couple had decided upon early September. Everyone pledged their attendance. No one planned to quit Pemberly before the wedding.

The news of the wedding date troubled the master of Pemberly. He began to experience great anxiety with the thought of his wife meeting Caroline Bingley at last. How he wished he had dealt with that name in London whilst Elizabeth offered amnesty of all the names of women in his past who might make trouble for them in the future. He was nearly bereft of all peace of mind. It drove him to make a dangerous decision.

Fitzwilliam felt he must let Elizabeth know about Caroline Bingley and her obsession with marriage to him. It would be a difficult conversation, but clearly unavoidable. The situation was bringing him more stress than he felt he could handle. He needed to find a way to relax. He needed to cope. So much responsibility, and now a new situation which could turn his wife against him... forever? Approaching Elizabeth, he said, "Beloved, I feel Charles and Jane should attend us as I inform you of a certain set of circumstances. It somewhat concerns Bingley." Elizabeth studied him with suspicious thoughts.

At that, the betroths came into the study and were seated upon the sofa. Charles and Jane had never been more uncomfortable. Both gazed at the floor. Darcy spoke first: "Bingley, have you told Jane about your sisters? And, most especially Caroline?"

"I have Darcy."

Elizabeth looked up and frowned at everyone in the room. She felt betrayed. Apparently everyone knew what she was just about to be told. She felt her husband's eyes upon her and heard him launch into the topic.

"I have not wished to distress my wife with this intelligence, but in view of your wedding, and realising I cannot very well ban your sister from attending, it would seem time to burden her with the sordid story. Bingley, feel free to add or to correct me as needed."

His eyes pled with his friend.

Bingley nodded to Darcy with a slight smile, then hung his head. He looked sympathetically at his future sister as Darcy began.

"Sweetheart, in light of what you are about to hear, I fear you shall jump to the false conclusion that Caroline and I were lovers. I assure you, nothing can be further from the truth. Bingley and I met and liked each other immediately. He sought acceptance in my circle, and I offered to mentor him, introduce and sponsor him at my club, and so forth. You and he followed the same curriculum," at this, Bingley's eyes bulged, and he looked questioningly at Jane.

"Excuse me, Darcy. What did you say about Oxford?"

"Oh, yes. Elizabeth completed an Oxford education. Without recognition, of course."

"Well, pardon me, Darcy, but I would certainly like to recognise it! Upon my word, Elizabeth, that is a monstrous feat! Congratulations! I salute you. Was this self-studied?"

She nodded and gave a slight smile. It seemed the subject at hand was of far greater interest to her than talk of her background.

"I thank you, Charles. You are very kind. Yes, I quite enjoyed all I learned."

Fitzwilliam had the audacity to look annoyed. "Well, back to my story. We had no alliance from school, but because he is admittedly an amiable fellow, it was not long before he began to flow into my social circle."

"Yes," Elizabeth reminded him, "so you said."

He cleared his throat, "Caroline, the eldest of his two sisters, is unmarried. She had always enjoyed the access to rather wealthy young colleagues of her brother. Unmarried, as he is, she served as mistress of his household in town, and hostess to his events. When Bingley is an invited guest, he never fails to bring his household; Caroline and Louisa, who is Mrs. Hurst, and of course, her husband, Mr. Hurst.

"Caroline is one of the Ton. Her sole purpose in life is to marry advantageously. When she realised that Bingley and I were becoming good friends, she kept obtaining invitations to be included at Darcy House, and then, God forbid, Pemberly. Once she saw the estate, she was convinced that she would marry me. Or, should I say, my fortune?"

With this last statement, Darcy hoped to put an end to the matter. Elizabeth seemed most unimpressed with his choice of words, and made no comment. With an open hand, he unfolded his arm outward toward Bingley, then followed it with his gaze. Bringing full attention to Charles, he hoped to draw him more completely into the discussion. But, Charles either missed the signal or wisely thought he should not speak.

"When I wrote to him," Fitzwilliam nodded, almost theatrically, toward Charles, "from Darcy House, inviting him to dinner, I was most specific in his coming alone.

"Once at Darcy House, I kept him over night as our guest and requested that he covertly obtain his carriage, and servant, and belongings; and mislead his sister as to his whereabouts. I absolutely feared what she might do to you, and our wedding plans."

Elizabeth stood up. She looked Fitzwilliam in the eye. "Well, that was going to some great lengths, was it not? You held him captive rather than risk Caroline learning of your plans? And, then directed his actions as to how he would away to Kent! What control you exercised over your friend!"

He tried to ignore her curt reference to his efforts to evade Caroline.

"No matter, London is done, and now we shall have a wedding to host. I suppose it is only fair to allow the poor fellow the opportunity to have his family attend."

Elizabeth interjected, "How very sporting of you, darling. How thoughtful to allow the couple to invite their own kin." Looking at her sister she asked, "Jane! Did you know of all this and tell me nothing?"

Looking at her shoes, her sister nodded.

"Unbelievable." Elizabeth threw her hands into the air. "Fitzwilliam, you put yourself and your best friend through an ordeal just to keep this information from me? You thought it best to tell me nothing of this in London, or here? And, as you prefaced this meeting, you would not be telling me now except for the coming nuptials. Do you not understand this makes me wonder—" she walked a few paces and frowned at him, "why on earth was I kept in the dark about this woman? Am I unreasonable? Does she mean this much to you?" she shook her head slowly, "and you could not figure out how to tell me of your love for her?"

"No. No. You are missing my point all together, Elizabeth!" He was so angry, he looked away from her. He looked at Bingley with disgust for his refusal to help him.

Seeing that he was now trying to protect himself by using anger against her, she shook her head. Slowly she continued. "Have we not spoken about the need to trust each other and to communicate all things? Am I unworthy of your trust? Or, am I to be treated as a servant?

"You telling me only what you feel I need to know? Oh for God's sake! Simply admit you are only protecting yourself, once again!" Saying that, she folded her arms around her waist.

"No," her husband protested strongly. "You are not unreasonable nor untrustworthy, but that is accurately spoken of Caroline. Her tenacity and boldness renders her not to be trusted nor believed. While we were in London, I feared she would have stopped at nothing to keep me from marrying you. I feared what she might have said to you in an effort to turn you away from me.

Truly, now that we are married, I almost fear what she might do next."

Elizabeth drew herself to her full height. "And, pray, how would she have ever accomplished that feat had you told me of her first?" she said, trying to illustrate her point on the importance of communication. "How can this woman make you fear her next move?"

"Sweetheart, I feared that you would think that her claims upon me were valid. She had indeed been a guest here, probably for a total of about twelve months. Is that correct, Bingley?"

"That would be correct," he agreed.

Elizabeth turned red in the face! "Well, since she practically lived here on the estate, I can see that even a judge might have ruled in her favour! What else?"

"I may have danced about two dances with her for each ball we mutually attended. And, we were frequently in each other's company," he ended, with some perspiration collecting upon his upper lip.

"My!" Elizabeth hastily remarked, "Did you not know that one dance fulfills an obligation, and the second is bestowed from the heart of choice." He had never seen her so angry, not even on that first day in the glade, that first time he had seen her ire!

"Well, good grief, Mr. Darcy! Had I an inkling of all this, I would have been put off, thinking she had a former claim upon you! Whatever were you thinking? Oh, upon my word, men are so moronic where women are concerned. It is amazing to me she did not get you to the alter! How could you ever have allowed such goings-on? Why did you not put a stop to it, just by telling her that you had no interest in her? Unless… were you physically attracted to her, and it was flattering on some level to have a beautiful woman seemingly fixated upon you?"

He made no answer and did not acknowledge that she had even dared to ask the question.

She related all this with her arms folded in front of her chest. He knew this was a very bad sign.

"Elizabeth, I just do not know what to say. I think that as a man, I felt that giving her no encouragement was the same as discouraging her." At saying this, he looked down at the floor. His words sounded weak and meaningless, even to him. It was too late to take them back, or say something more forceful to convince her, or to intimidate her into silencing that truth-seeking voice of hers.

Elizabeth was outraged. "What a novel approach to problem solving! I am chagrined that it did not occur to me when confronted by Wickham. I simply could have given him no encouragement, and that would have been the same as discouragement to him!" She squared her shoulders and shook her head.

"I believe I understand the situation. Upon my word, had Caroline Bingley talked to me at Darcy House and related the past, as you, yourself have just told me, I would have gone back to Kent in a flash! The story you have just told me in this room would have persuaded me that you and she had an attachment. She would have succeeded in keeping me from the alter.

"I just cannot but wonder why you felt it necessary to keep this from me. In light of a certain conversation in London, I cannot imagine why this name was never spoken to me. Had I heard it from you, as you were interacting with Charles, I would have tried to see your part.

"I told you so, when I asked if anyone could bring problems into our future. Now, it seems to me that you are concealing something else from me. Both in London and perhaps even now?"

She finished this argumentation and felt exhausted, empty, betrayed, and very much alone.

Looking at Charles, she asked Fitzwilliam, "All those many nights spent right here at Pemberly. Which rooms did you occupy? Yours only?"

Her husband threw his hands into the air. He shook his head violently and frowned at her.

"Your reluctance to tell me of her, simply deepens the old pain! When shall we learn to communicate with each other? Husband, I am deeply hurt. Shall this woman go to the courts and show any letters or other documentation that may be used to free you?"

"No, of course not! There is nothing of the kind. How could you ask that of me? Do you not know nor trust me at all?"

Elizabeth looked her husband in the eyes again. "I am sorry to have spoken all of this before our family, but you were the one who needed them as a shield. You invited them to witness us. When in God's name shall you stop protecting yourself, Fitzwilliam Darcy?"

Charles and Jane studied their shoes. They each felt they wanted to be anywhere else. However, Charles did understand why Darcy wanted them to be present.

"Liz-Beth, you are making too much of this. You need to understand that she really does not like me for myself. She merely loves my wealth and position."

"Yes. And what did you like of her, my husband? I am learning that 'liking' another may not necessarily be requisite for certain 'things' to happen. One year, here? All those nights with her fawning over you? Fitzwilliam, two hundred years from now, if women were to hear of her desires for you, they may wonder if you gave her any encouragement at the very least of it!"

At this, he was silent. He had no answer. He just leveled his brooding stare at her.

"Well," Elizabeth said, while standing, "I thank you Mr. Darcy. I can see you were feeling the press of the calendar and dreading the day I would meet you former, whatever she was to you—while she is yet again a guest in YOUR home! It shall be interesting to see if she presses you for an annulment so the two of you may be married after all. Never have I felt like more of an afterthought!

And the fact that all three of you knew this, even my dearest sister?"

Putting her hand upon the door, she turned and said, "I thank you, it has been most enlightening. Strangely, I am not sure exactly what I should have been learning." She quit the room to go to her desk in their private sitting room. She had a letter to write. A very important letter!

Darcy leaned his head back and groaned loudly. Jane flinched and looked away. Bingley shook his head slowly and said, "Once again, Darcy, I apologize for my sister."

Darcy went out to look for Gardiner. He wanted a private talk with the man. He needed a good relationship with his wife, and he knew they had some way to go to reach the 'good' stage.

At ten of the clock the following morning, Fitzwilliam, his wife, his father and Lord Claverstone assembled in their study. Sitting at his desk, Fitzwilliam saw the letter and knew at once it was from his wife. He put the letter in his pocket.

"Thank you for taking this meeting. Liz-Beth has presented me with a proposal for a business to be conducted here at Pemberly, using our stock. No doubt, you have had time to review it as well. She admits her figures are premature in that Lord Claverstone has not yet completed his book of our horses." Looking at his young wife, he invited her to speak.

"Yes. I thank you. It is no secret that I have much to learn. I wish to pursue this opportunity and learn from the very best.

Lord Claverstone has the finest selective horse breeding mind in the country. Of course, this does not guarantee my success. It simply means that it would provide me with quite a good foundation.

"As you see, we start with some initial changes to the existing stable properties. The projected costs for these is listed using the most recent quotations. Those improvements shall enhance the estate's value and certainly be meaningful for the stock already necessary to its success.

"Even if we should decide not to pursue due to lack of interest, these changes shall remain a positive for Pemberly. I would think then, gentlemen, it is simply a question of allowing Grandpapa and me to send our letter of inquiry to see if we are able to generate interest in our services.

"Fitzwilliam, you still have not answered as to your interest in Percival as our stud. Until funds allow additional purchase of stallions, he is our best offer to interest the likes of Sir John Standish.

"Should we be allowed to begin, and should God bless us with success, my goal is to hire a faithful manager and turn the business over to him. Unless Grandpapa wants to take control for himself. That would make me happy, of course!

"Shall I leave you to discuss or do you have questions for me? Oh, I must also say, with clarity, Fitzwilliam is my head. Before God I vowed to obey him. If the answer is no, or if he says no on his own, I shall obey him. I want it perfectly understood. I am a woman who keeps her vows. My marriage is sacred to me. I shall never allow anything to damage our marriage. I shall honour him, always. Gentlemen, thank you all."

With that, she quit the room, and set out to the Gardiner wing to take the children riding.

In the study, Lord Claverstone spoke, "Gentlemen, it seems to me that father and son have some considering to do. Pemberly is the work of many generations, just as is Claverstone. I understand something of the weight of this decision. Moving into what some might consider trade shall alter the concept of Pemberly forever. Feel at your total comfort to tell me, and of course, Elizabeth if no is your gut reaction to her proposal.

"One word of caution, young man, if I may? I have known Lizzy all her life. She is very astute. Do not say yes just to curry favor with her. She would find that an impertinence.

"However, if I may. One option you may wish to exercise is this. In her doodling, I found her writing over and over again, 'Pleasant Glade Horses.' Apparently she likes the name for some reason. It might be that if you license the two of us as lease holders for a portion of your stables, and allow us to employ our own hands, we might technically become your tenants. Very close tenants, I concede. Yet, as such you would not share in any profits should she become successful. You would forever be locked into whatever rents you would collect from Pleasant Glade Horses. Just something else to think on, gentlemen."

He started to leave, and George caught his arm. "Gerald, please stay a moment longer. I wish to state for the record, I dearly love your little granddaughter. I am aware that you think of her as your very own. As do I. In fact, my friend, I owe my very life to her, as she kept a kidnap plot against me from coming to fruition, and she was also responsible for saving Georgie from the same.

"It grieves me that I did nothing for her. I have given careful thought to the reward I might have bestowed upon one of my own footmen. What if I should escrow 100,000 pounds into the Bank of London? I know Elizabeth would not hear of it, but she shall never know. Let her think that you have set up such an account. You may use it for capital and as profits are realised simply put them back into the escrowed monies. Elizabeth is serious about wishing to have this business to start a university for women in England. She proudly says her daughters shall attend there. She also wishes to build an inheritance for her daughters and any sons who shall not inherit."

"Gerald, you would be so helpful in this line of credit. Are you willing? And, son, how does this sit with you?"

Both men agreed readily. Fitzwilliam saw it as a way to get back into his wife's good graces, and Lord Claverstone welcomed the opportunity to start their business.

The men quit the study, and once alone, Fitzwilliam sat down to read his letter.

Pemberly Park, Derbyshire

10 June 1803

My Dearest Husband,

I need you to understand some things that are important to me. You hold our felicity in the same hand that you hold your own fidelity. I feel you do not understand my position. I cannot morally care about women, even a lot of them, you have had before we wed. Only your behaviour following our vows is of concern to me. Yet, several factors of our marriage frighten me. Therefore, I propose: on the subject of faithfulness—Should you commit adultery, I shall also! If your vow to me means nothing to you, then I am dead to both our vows.

All I know of sensuality and acts of love, you taught me. You are an excellent teacher, and I made myself a devoted student! Would you agree I have applied myself? I know I satisfy you deeply and I please you. You taught me how to please a man. I am good at doing that, am I not?

If you commit adultery, I shall select a man you know and respect and seduce him with the knowledge you have given me. Think about me doing to him, what I do for you? I give you all Fitzwilliam. I shall give him all. How would that make you feel? Would you feel the same pain and humiliation that you would cause me to experience? Do not think my character shall keep me from this. If you are unfaithful, I shall not care. Until Wickham, I did not know that I could do something horrible and not care. I have had a lifetime of humiliation, I shall not live with it in my marriage. Your behaviour shall be my answer. It does not need to be this way. I pray for your faithfulness.

Yet, I have come to fear your actions. You do not communicate with me. You hide things from me. I am tired of hiding my tears from you and everyone else.

Why did you tell me that even if God told you not to fornicate, you probably would anyway. Were you expecting me to give you permission to chase skirts? Yes, that sounds ugly, does it not? I learned that term in London, when I overheard two of the Ton talking about you. That is what they said you were. I had to ask Juliette Marie what their words meant. I thought I knew your character, so I exonerated you from their claims. Because I believed your words of affection were for me only. I did not know it possible for someone to have passion for passion. I believed your passion was only for me, as mine is for you. You promised me before God, and I believed you.

I feel you are spoiled. You continue to protect yourself, as you recently confirmed to me the truth about a certain beautiful woman who was attracted to you. Yes, I understood your unspoken confession completely. I hope you shall share this letter with Father and Uncle. I wish them to understand perfectly my response to you. Do not take this as an attempt to control your faithfulness. I know you well enough to realise no one controls you. Just know that adultery shall kill me, and I shall act as I have stated. Pray for us, my darling. I would not have made this decision if I did not love you more than I love my own life. I desire above all, that our children may have the home they deserve. A father who loves their mother. Their mother having a faithful husband.

Your Elizabeth.

He read the letter twice. Uncertain as to what he should do, he folded it and took it to his father's study. Fortunately, Uncle was there. After asking for their time and advice, he read the letter to the men. When he finished he asked, "It is not good news. She does not feel safe, nor protected, nor welcome anymore, and I need to find a way to fix that."

His father's eyes filled with tears. "Son, the one good thing about being my age is that I have lived long enough to know what is important. Do you honestly think that women like Elizabeth come along every hour or so? It is a rare thing to find true love with a wonderful woman like Elizabeth."

He had not one word to answer his father. Turning to Uncle Edward he asked, "Uncle, tell me what to do."

"Fitzwilliam, you have already answered your own question. She needs to feel safe, protected, and welcome. Only you can do that for her, and it is a work that needs to be done every day from sun up to sun down. Every day of your lives."

"Do you think she means it? Would she then be unfaithful to me, if I slip? She is a good wife."

Both men agreed, but Uncle Edward spoke, "Elizabeth is not like other women. She likely would not take your infidelity lying down. She would hurt you and then leave you. She would likely teach the other woman a lesson as well. Lizzy does not care one bit about your wealth. She does not bow to position and power. If you saw Longbourn, you would understand. She attaches importance to other things in life. She loves you, your father and her father, her sisters, Lucille and me, our children, her Grandpapa, Marigold, horses, music, education, books, and nature. Do you think she cares for the expensive clothes and jewelry she now wears? No, those are costumes to her.

"A word of warning, do not rely upon thinking she is merely trying to influence your behaviour. I do not believe this is an empty threat. I think she would do it, as certainly as she shot Wickham. She would hate it, and then hate herself, but I fear she would do it, son."

Gardiner finished saying, "If you do not want to work on your marriage, it is probably best that you send her away today."

"No, Uncle, I am willing to work on our marriage, I just fear I cannot change. I shall try and see what happens." On so thin a conviction, Fitzwilliam set out to find his wife and work on his marriage.

Finding Liz-Beth at the stables as she was teaching the children to brush the ponies, he happily joined in their merriment. The little group then walked to the house for a tea in the children's quarters. The little ones loved their time and all the attention from their older cousins. They were sad when the couple left.

Fitzwilliam suggested a walk in the garden so he could tell her the happy news of their business decision. She was thrilled with the idea of starting Pleasant Glade Horses and thought the terms of Grandpapa's line of credit would be workable.

He did not mention the letter because he did not know what to say. Taking advantage of her good mood, he walked her into the nearest copse. After a few kisses, she allowed him to lift her skirt and enjoy touching her smoothness. Others may have been nearby, but soon the couple cared very little.

Fitzwilliam took off his jacket and placed it on the ground. He gestured enticingly, and she lowered her body down, smiling up at him. He joined her there and prepared with a slight adjustment to his clothing. Slowly her fears and anxious thoughts about him began to soften. They kissed. Passionately. Intimately.

Unbeknownst to her, a subdued moan escaped from her throat, and gave way to a series of delicate, deep sighs. Darcy smiled to himself as he exulted in her improving emotions toward him.

After a few minutes in the copse, a weightless mist sprayed over them, providing a finely spun coverage of tiny water particles.

In the now fading light, their faces seemed covered in a dusty, powdery sheen. This covering shimmered as they moved under the delicate falling moisture. Just as the mist's influence became familiar, a very soft shower was fabricated. They rejoiced in it. At first, it was sweetly refreshing. Then, more stimulating and thrilling as it absorbed them in the warmth of its increasing intensity. In an effort to expose more of her flesh, Elizabeth sat up and removed her gown. Her nude body began collecting a greater share of water and inspired her husband to disrobe. The warmth of the unexpected shower delighted them. Remarkably, they found their sensitivity increasing greatly. Their naked bodies, lying entwined in this heavenly shower, provided them with a provocative indulgence.

Nature began to amplify the shower into a driving rain. This evolution stimulated the lovers' heated emotional expressions into hot and deeply arousing kisses. It was as if the escalating precipitation was dictating their salacious activities. The downpour of rain was proving to be a very powerful aphrodisiac. Their grasping lips slid across each other's mouths as their bodies became slick. They were wet outside, but inside they were glowing, flaming, and hot blooded.

Each burned with a zeal to release their pent-up passions and further arouse their lover. All this was expressed through the surrender of their inhibitions.

Any movement caused them to slither across one another as they loved in the soupy ground of the copse. Pounding raindrops kept their actions lubricious and somewhat luxurious.

Her body was deliciously lustrous. Attentively he watched water gather into seductive pools upon her skin. He lapped it from the valley between her breasts and sucked it from her navel.

The recently depilated skin of her apex glistened. With much effort he found his way down to her most sensuous spot. His hungry mouth consumed all of her honey. Keeping with the rhythm of the rain, he coaxed more and more from her depths. And, her body willingly yielded to his devoted attentions for more. In an arousing performance, two enthusiastic actors played unyielding upon each other's stage and lured out long hidden desires from deep within their souls.

Fearlessly they shared, through their own bodies, their innermost feelings of love, devotion, and faithfulness. Simultaneously, two desired to be one, shutting out all others. One.

Rising up to unite with her, Fitzwilliam was forced to plant his hands within the mud. It was warm and oozed extravagantly within his fingers. Overcome with the moment's exuberance, and without thinking, he scooped a handful and massaged it onto her breasts.

To his complete delight, she laughed, loving the feel of it. She scooped her own handful and smeared it upon his shoulders. Delighted with the compound's ability to newly enhance their bodies' erotic affects upon each other, they rollicked in the stimulation! Elizabeth was enthralled with the vision of his wet back muscles. She watched the rain cleanse his shoulders and her hands. The mud was gone. Her hands and fingers became fickle, allowing her to touch but not to hold. Both hands skidded from his from his back to his firm buttocks, drenched from the spanking he took from the large rain drops.

Elizabeth held his piercing blue eyes. They were dilated and shimmered like liquid. From the first moment she looked deeply into them, she had loved his eyes. Beautiful. They were reassuring orbs of his persuasiveness, proving his affection for her. His soaked hair and wet face somehow made him look years younger, more innocent. She wanted to kiss his wet face and lick the water from it, but she could not control her body. The wetness both propelled and prohibited their movements. The rain's driving rhythm was now demanding them to pulsate their bodies to its beat. It was an earthy experience that insisted on its own various positions, and demanded compliance to its gyrating gratifications.

Huge drops of water were pelting them into submission. The rain above and the warm mud beneath was revitalizing their intimacy. Nature itself was forcing them into a collaboration of its own stimulus. His feet found no firm foundation. All efforts to support his thrusts were supplied only as he held onto his wife's hips. So dependent were they upon one another, each had to give way to the other. Even their irregular and harsh breathing came in concert, one with the other. Intending to kiss his alluring neck, her lips slipped on his wet flesh, causing her to suck him with great force. His lips skidded from her cheek to her collarbone. But, it was their undiscriminating love that each generously lavished upon the other, that finally gave them their mutual heights. Each one satiated the other in unison.

Finally recovering their breathing, they were able to speak words to one another.

"Liz-Beth, that was an amazing and wonderful gift. I shall remember this all my life. We could never have planned such a beautiful experience. It makes me realise that by a fragile chance of timing we may have never met. Or, you may not have accepted me. And, we would not be here, sliding in the mud together. You must know, you have bewitched me, body and soul. I have some very selfish and stupid behaviours in which I have indulged. But, I fervently hope and pray that you shall continue to persevere with me. Please do not let me go. I am a spoiled man. I have been dull and very slow in my communications with you. It is very difficult for me to assume responsibility and admit when I am wrong. I do not seem to know how to do the things you need me to do, and yet, I want desperately to do them. Honestly, I do. I love and adore you, my precious wife."

"Fitzwilliam, you have made me very happy. I just need to feel secure and protected. I need to be welcome. It is really very simple. If I can be assured your love is only for me, I shall be so blessed. I have been feeling so homesick for you, my love. You are my home; you are my life. You have all power over me. What if you tire of me? What shall become of me?"

"How could I grow tired of you, Elizabeth? Your very nature refreshes itself every day. You create such diversions constantly and all are excellent. Please. You must know, surely you must know, you are the light of my life. Please be assured of my love, always. Would that I could change my past. But, God help me I cannot undo the things I have done."

Edwin Wallet needed to return to London. He required two weeks to finish a forgery, and then he would be paid. He needed money. As soon as he could, he would return to Lambton. The Darcy payoff would be more than he could give up. He would take Mrs. Darcy for a high ransom.

He was certain that Mrs. Darcy would come to Lambton. He needed her to come alone.

Upon his return to the inn, he would spend his days outside the lobby and watch for her carriage. Then, he would act. He would approach and tell her that he had an urgent message for her. He knew he could get her to go willingly into his carriage.

Caroline Bingley felt defeated when she reached her brother's home in London. She had exhausted her finances and still was unable to stop the wedding or even learn of the location. Going as far as Kent, she had to accept her losses when she learned that Lord Claverstone was attending friends. His granddaughter had wed and was now Mrs. Fitzwilliam Darcy.

She sat in front of her mirror. Her money was gone as were several items of her own jewelry she had been forced to sell just to get back to London. Feeling dejected, she screamed at the person knocking upon her bed chamber door.

In response to her cruel words, a letter was silently slipped under her door. She picked it up and saw it was Charles' handwriting. Ripping it apart, she read rapidly.

Marry? He is to marry the sister of Mrs. Darcy? No! No! I shall not have it. Wait! This is an invitation to Pemberly! Of course, I must attend my brother's wedding. I shall go in the Hursts' carriage. What then? Think! Yes! Pemberly has so many steep staircases. I shall wait for Mrs. Darcy to descend, and I shall come silently behind her and give her a good push! Yes, that shall take care of Mrs. Darcy very nicely. Then, after his mourning period, of course, we shall wed.

Thinking her plan to be flawless, she sat happily down and wrote a lovely letter to her dear brother Charles. She would practice being very sweet and loving and kind. This would be good practice. She would use these kind and compassionate skills on Mr. Darcy at the death of his dear wife, Elizabeth.

Yes, she would start with a very loving letter to Charles. Then, she shall continue this practice by being kind and compassionate with her servants. No more temper! Her influence shall be the kindest and most loving. Everyone shall compliment her special affection for all…

Lord Claverstone and Elizabeth were elated. They had received a wonderfully encouraging letter from Sir John Standish. He would arrive at Pemberly one week before the Bingley wedding. He was bringing two mares, on the strength of Lord Claverstone's recommendation.

Upon hearing the good news of the financial arrangements, Gerald told his little Lizzy that he would arrange the purchase of four outstanding stallions. Percival would not be a part of their business plan. The new stallions' bloodlines were impeccable. He would arrange their purchase and transport immediately. These were horses well known to Gerald. His research had been done long ago. He had been biding his time until the right day arrived. The day was here!

Construction projects were started, and four new hires were completed before the week ended.

Gerald confessed to Lizzy that he had been working on all of this even before the arrangements were made at the Bank of London. But, he was thrilled at the financial agreements and certain that they would have success.

Before the week was out, they had responses from Mr. Weaver, Lord Stafford, Mr. Branch, Lord Burton, and Mr. Adams. The total number of mares was six and ten. All mares were currently en route to Pemberly. They would comprise Pleasant Glade Horses' first broodmare herd. They would be safe and protected.

The bloodlines and journals were completed for all the stock. The additions to the stables were finished. At last, Pleasant Glade Horses was in business and getting their opportunity. Gerald and Elizabeth were now selective horse breeders.

Fitzwilliam began to feel their excitement. Mr. Darcy was elated and enjoyed watching Elizabeth come into her own. Her love of horses finally allowed her to step into a business of her own creation. Her Grandpapa was a godsend. Nothing would have been possible without him. He was the guiding force and the inspiration for Elizabeth. For Gerald, it was the reason to rise every morning. There was just one person who was very unhappy about the success of the enterprise.

Georgiana was miserable. She watched her father grow more and more fond of Elizabeth daily. He doted upon her success. It was such a novelty to him that he did not realise he was talking about it practically hourly. His little Georgie, for the first time since they had made her acquaintance, felt anger and resentment and even jealousy toward her sister, Elizabeth.

Elizabeth loved Georgie more than ever. She tried to share her progress with the girl, but each day Georgie withdrew further away from Elizabeth. Fitzwilliam joined his wife in efforts to speak with Georgie. A little cart and pony race was scheduled on the new track just so Georgie could take part in the opening activities. Elizabeth introduced her to all the clients who came to Pemberly. Nothing worked, Elizabeth was growing despondent over her loss of Georgiana's affection and friendship.

※

As the days and weeks passed, Elizabeth hoped her letter had helped Fitzwilliam settle the issue of fidelity. However, as Charles and Jane's wedding grew near, she could feel the distance between her and her husband growing. Something was just not right between them.

All the ladies were on edge. There was much to be done in preparation. Even a small wedding required many hours of planning and labour. Elizabeth felt as if she had spent less than an hour with Fitzwilliam during the past week. He retired late and rose early. She missed him dearly.

The day before the nuptials, Elizabeth was just leaving the Gardiner wing. Turning toward the stairs, she saw her husband ascending with a girl who could nearly be her own twin. She stared.

He seemed to be in quite a hurry. The girl looked familiar with the house, as she did not gape and stare as with most first time entrants.

Her jealousy and anger piqued! Elizabeth took the stairs two at a time, and she reached the top just in time to see them go into their study which functioned now for both Pemberly and Pleasant Glade Horses.

Elizabeth put her hand on the study door. In complete disbelief she saw it was locked! Reaching into her pocket, she withdrew her key and opened the door. Her heart sank as she saw her own husband seated on the sofa, next to the girl. They were sitting very closely to each other and appeared in conversation.

Looking at Fitzwilliam from the doorway, Elizabeth asked in a calm voice, "Fitzwilliam, did you lock this door when you entered this room?"

"No, I did not." He answered her without emotion, but his face held an angry look.

She walked to them. Looking the girl in the face, Elizabeth commanded, "Stand up!"

The girl, about the same height as Elizabeth, stood boldly facing her. Elizabeth lifted her right hand up, bent the elbow, brought her hand back, and then soundly slapped the visitor across her left cheek! It left a mark immediately. The sound of the slap could be heard out in the hallway.

The girl reeled. Elizabeth collected her by her left ear and then, not gently, led her out of the study and into the hallway.

"You are trespassing on Pemberly property!" she advised the young woman.

"Mr. Clovis!" Elizabeth called the footman with a commanding voice, much like the one she had used in addressing Wickham.

"Pray, what is your name?" she demanded of the girl, even though Clovis was on hand and could have questioned her.

"Emily Cooke." The answer was delivered as if in defiance of Elizabeth as mistress.

"Be so kind as to take Miss Cooke down to your basement and prepare her for the magistrate. She must answer questions as to entering Pemberly property without benefit of an invitation. Mr. and Mrs. Darcy shall prefer charges." Elizabeth addressed Clovis, yet she did not take her eyes off the girl for one second.

The girl, hearing this, started yelling at Elizabeth. "You murder trespassers, do you not? Savage! I have heard about you."

Turning slowly to face her, Elizabeth spoke clearly. "No," she corrected her, again using her strong voice. "I kill men who threaten me and my family and also trespass. I only shoot and kill women who try to touch my husband! You received a slap for having the audacity to lock our study door and sit on the sofa beside him!"

She made to return to the study, but Fitzwilliam had followed her and was standing next to her in the hallway.

"May I have a word, please my love?" Elizabeth asked him kindly, but her arms were folded in front of her chest, and her shoulders were squared. He followed her into their study.

As soon as she shut the door, she turned to her husband and asked, "Is there any possible way you have an explanation for this, husband? If there is, I would dearly love to hear it."

Unfortunately, not knowing how to answer her, he made no response. He quietly leveled his brooding stare at his very angry wife. Her answer, once again, was his brooding silence.

Elizabeth was as white as a sheet. She looked sadder than he had ever seen her appear. Her green eyes, usually filled with love and affection for him, were filled with disappointment and unbelief. Saying not one more word to him, she turned to join the ladies for tea in the salon.

Entering, she saw Mrs. Reynolds personally delivering the tea to Aunt. She ran inside without benefit of closing the salon door.

"Oh!" Elizabeth began, "I hope you did not hear that exchange in the hallway." Her face was ashen, and her eyes brimmed with tears. Now that the pressure with the girl was over, she was shaking like a leaf and turning red. Elizabeth was ready to explode in sorrow and release her pain to her aunt. Both concerned women spoke at once.

"Yes, we unfortunately heard," they both responded with great concern.

Even though it was completely out of place, Mrs. Reynolds boldly spoke up, "Mrs. Darcy in your condition, you have no business getting so excited and upset. You must think of the child you carry, please!"

"Mrs. Reynolds," Elizabeth jerked up quickly and looked the older woman in the eye. "I adore you and cannot do without you, but I must ask you to remember that I am your mistress. You have been sworn to secrecy about the baby. I must ask you to honour your pledge to me."

Aunt Gardiner was by her side in a matter of moments, "Lizzy dear, I know you are tremendously upset right now. I would be so livid I would not be able to see straight. But, you handled it in the best way you knew how at the moment." She put her hands gently upon Lizzy's shoulders and looked into her eyes with compassion.

"I am afraid Mrs. Reynolds is correct, dear. At this stage, your emotional condition is vital to your health, and the wellbeing of your child. Please do not allow yourself such anger followed by sorrow and grief. It shall take its toll on both of you. Your health is so very important. Your baby's survival depends upon your wellness."

George Darcy appeared suddenly through the open door.

"Ladies, I am going to admit to eavesdropping. I not only saw what happened in the hallway just now, but I am sorry to tell you that your voices carried, and I helped myself to the intelligence you offered.

"Elizabeth, please take a seat and calm yourself. My heart is so heavy for you. This is the time when you should be the happiest and receiving only the best of care. Please forgive me for spying upon you. I am, however, so happy to hear your wonderful news."

"Father, is it indeed wonderful news? I have a husband who has grown tired of me. I fear that any day now he shall replace me, and I shall be without a home. Now that I am with child, where shall I go, and what shall become of us? I have long feared that your son was too young to marry. I gave myself to him without reservation and provided him with the opportunity to ruin my entire life, forever. He holds my happiness in his hands, and that means that he has all power over me.

"Did you see that girl? Is she not a twin for me in looks and in body shape? I wish to die. If I could just lie down and my life could be over, I would not suffer this pain and humiliation and rejection.

"He needed to be master of Pemberly before we wed. I fear he did not know his own mind when we met. I believed his affection for me was sincere and lasting. Yet I am proved incorrect.

"Oh, I should be spending my days with my dear Jane, who shall leave me soon. But I am too miserable and cannot hide it from her. She does not deserve to hear my sorrow. This is to be the happiest time of her life, as I well remember it to be so, and I cannot ruin her joy.

"Please excuse me, I need to be alone. I have some thinking and planning to do."

With that, she bolted out the door, leaving the three of them with tears in their eyes and shocked expressions on each concerned face.

Lucille spoke openly to George, "She swore she does not want him to know about their child. She says she wants him to live a happy life with the girl of his mature mind's choosing. She is planning to leave, I do believe. I think she must be out of her mind with jealousy. With what just happened, it is hard to say she is imagining things." George put his hand over his heart, "This is most tragic news. Would that I could help."

Mrs. Gardiner put her hand lovingly upon his arm and patted it gently. Saying not one more word, she and Mrs. Reynolds quit the room. Mr. Darcy sat alone on the sofa, put his head in his hands, and sobbed openly.

Elizabeth headed for Marigold. She needed to ride as fast as she could. She needed to forget. Climbing on her mare, her thoughts ran wild. She wished to ride back through time and see the man in the glade, but ride away from him. She would change everything by not speaking one word to him. She would not fall in love with him.

George Darcy cried until his eyes were dry. Then he slid to his knees and prayed. He prayed until he had a measure of faith, then a more positive feeling. He prayed until courage came into his heart. Rising from the floor, he went to the window. Looking out, he saw his daughter on her mare. She was riding bareback and running as fast as he had ever before observed. To his horror, they were headed straight for a tall hedge.

He could not breathe, and he did not want to watch that jump. "Yes, she is an expert rider, but the girl is not herself," he whispered to himself. With wild relief he saw them sail over the hedge and ride out of sight.

George set out to find his son. Fitzwilliam was not difficult to locate. His laughter sounded through the hallways and led his father into his study. It was a jolly scene. A scene he many times enjoyed while Fitzwilliam was at Cambridge. The lad would bring a friend or two to summer at Pemberly, and he would often find them relaxing in the library, enjoying a glass of port, and smoking cigars. But, today at age five and twenty, with an expectant mother as his neglected wife; George was not pleased with his son. It disgusted George to see his only son laughing with Rory and Charles as though he had not a care in the world. How dare the new master of Pemberly bring another woman into this house right in front of his wife and their family!

Clearing his throat, he entered the room. "Fitzwilliam, I must talk to you!"

"My God, Father! Who died?" he asked, "With all due respect, I am master of Pemberly now, sir, and you shall not insist that I listen to you. Is it not at my pleasure, sir. Can you not see that I am entertaining my brothers?"

George Darcy looked at the two men standing with him. "Gentlemen, please excuse us. We need a few moments."

"Father, I do believe I have suffered enough humiliation for one day. My wife just slapped my visitor, pulled her by the ear, and sent her to the magistrate. Enough. Please, let this go, whatever it may be." Fitzwilliam turned to face his companions and hoped his father would leave.

"Very well," George spat, as he stood as tall as possible, "if you refuse privacy, I shall speak in front of my nephew and your best friend. Fitzwilliam, do you pay enough attention to your wife to know that she is with child?"

At this, all three men looked stunned. However, Fitzwilliam did not speak.

"I observed everything that transpired in the hall. You gave no explanation. You forced your wife to deal with a situation you created. Do you think she wanted to be the one to resolve this issue? I honestly do not know what Anne would have done in her place. I thank God I never would have put the woman I love into a position such as that. As to what in bloody hell you were doing with that woman behind a locked door, is, I suppose, your business.

"However, I just looked out the salon window and saw Elizabeth running Marigold as fast as I have seen that horse move. She was riding bareback and jumped that tall hedge. I fear Elizabeth has a death wish.

"Now, if you do not give a care what happens to the woman you said you loved, then I wonder if you do care enough about your unborn son or daughter to go after her? She spoke to me after the incident with that girl. And, by the way, the fact that she looks like Elizabeth did not escape her. She was visibly shaken. I think her mind is set to leave you and Pemberly. She told me she has had a lifetime of rejection, shame, and humiliation, and she just shall not continue here under these circumstances."

Bingley put his glass on the table and quit the room. He kept his reddened face down and said not one word. He could not look upon his friend.

Rory put his glass down, took Fitzwilliam's glass, put it down next to his, and hit his cousin with his fist, striking his eye. Fitzwilliam staggered backward. Rory pulled him back by the waistcoat and hit him one more time. He shoved him into the nearest chair. Standing in front of his cousin, Rory looked at a man he no longer knew.

"Spoiled cousin! The first was for Elizabeth who has only been good to you! The second was for your child who deserves a better father! You, Fitzwilliam, make me sick!"

At that, he quit the house and went to the stables for his horse. He mounted and set out to look for his cousin. Hopefully he would find her before she broke her neck.

George stood looking at his son. His tears would not stop streaming from his eyes. He shook his head in disbelief. Silently, he turned his back and walked away. He went to his room to pray for his family.

Fitzwilliam stood in one place. He somehow felt anger toward Elizabeth, but he did not know why.

He had anger toward Rory, and, rubbing his face, he did know why. He felt anger toward his father, but he did not know why. His father was very angry with him, and he did not know why.

Standing by his desk he tried to focus his eyes, and tried to unscramble his tumbling thoughts. He needed to think, but he could not collect any thoughts long enough to think about anything. The room seemed to spin and his eyes would not focus, he needed to take a chair and rest.

Elizabeth's mind slowed enough to think about Marigold. She had been running her too fast for too long. Wisely, she slowed the mare to a lope, then a trot, and a walk, then a slow walk, in an attempt to cool her down. There was water nearby, but it was not safe for the horse to drink yet. Marigold was far too hot to drink.

Thinking only about her horse now, she dismounted and rubbed Marigold's face, and then she stroked the sweaty body and calmed the animal. Knowing that she came close to killing her friend, Elizabeth decided to straighten out her thinking. She must deal with things the way they were, rather than crying and carrying on like a little child. She would be a mother; she must start to be an adult. She could not go back in time. Nothing she had done could ever be undone. It was time to accept her life as it was and make the best of it. She must think now of protecting her unborn child, and begin to care more about his welfare than her own unhappiness.

Suddenly, she heard hoof beats. A horse in a dead run! "Fitzwilliam!" she called out as loud as she could.

"Grandpapa!" a voice bellowed back at her. "I saw you take off, Lizzy, what has happened?"

"I was acting like a foolish little girl, I am afraid. Look what I did to my Marigold!"

Getting off his mount, Gerald put his arm around his Lizzy. Then he took the saddle off his mount and used the blanket to rub Marigold down. Several minutes passed before they spoke.

"Lizzy, I know you. You are too kind, and you love this mare too much. This happened because you were either grieved or completely upset about something. Is it not time to tell your husband everything, and allow the man to grow up? He deserves an opportunity to do the right thing, does he not?"

"Grandpapa, I would rather go back to Claverstone and live there. We could take Pleasant Glade Horses with us, could we not?"

"No, child, your life is here. The man loves you. Whatever it is that is causing the trouble, you can work it out. Now we have guests tonight who cannot hide their admiration of you. Perhaps it would do no harm for the lad to be just a bit jealous of his beautiful wife.

"What say we go home, prepare for our dinner, and entertain our clients. Keep your husband next to you, and he shall see what I see in the faces of those men. It shall do him good."

"Brilliant!" she answered, trying to put on a brave face for her Grandpapa. They watered their horses. Gerald replaced the saddle on his mount, and the two headed for home. They walked their horses and talked along the way. Gerald was a wise man.

Reaching the house, Fitzwilliam was anxiously standing on the front stairs. Gerald laughed loudly and said, "Oh, Lizzy, you are a most amusing girl. Thank you for a wonderful ride.

"Fitzwilliam! We shall have a marvelous dinner tonight, shall we not? So generous of you to be with us as we say farewell to our clients." Gerald quit the pair, leaving them on the steps together. He began praying for the couple even before he reached his rooms. He had concerns for his Lizzy, great concerns.

Fitzwilliam took Elizabeth's hand. He knew he was waiting for her to return, but he could not remember where she had been. They walked up the stairs, and he could sense there was something he should be saying, but he did not know what it was. He was silent, although not hostile, toward her.

Jeannette sang a sweet melody while she prepared her mistress. She selected a fetching low-cut gown. Elizabeth's breasts were getting much larger, so it was an overwhelmingly attractive look.

Fitzwilliam arrived at the grand salon with Elizabeth on his arm. They entered and the visiting gentlemen rose to their feet. "Mrs. Darcy," they chorused followed by the usual civilities. Three bachelors wore broad smiles for her, and it was true that all of them hung upon her every little word. They were in the palm of her hand. Fitzwilliam saw it.

Sod off foot-lickers! What kind of men enter another man's home and cannot take their eyes off his wife. Their bloody eyes are locked on her bosom, and if they knew about her mons veneris, they would be pawing her. She is breathtaking though. She is the very best-looking woman I have ever bedded—God! What is wrong with me? She is my wife. I must be losing my bloody mind. Breathe. All shall be well.

Elizabeth and Gerald enjoyed the dinner with family and the clients. They took care to see that the gentlemen were pleased with the meal and the conversation. Bingley and Lucille could scarcely eat one bite. They too, kept their eyes upon Elizabeth.

At the evening's conclusion, the Darcys returned to their rooms. "Fitzwilliam would you be more comfortable if I slept on the sofa in the sitting room? It is obvious that you prefer others to me."

"No. I have no desire for you to sleep anywhere other than next to me. I would like to discuss your awful behaviour of this afternoon. What were you thinking?"

"Oh, I?" she retorted, throwing her hands onto her hips. "I was thinking that my husband looked more than a little guilty slinking up the stairs as fast as his long legs could carry him.

"And, by his side, walked my replacement. She looked enough like me, did she not?"

"She was just an old friend who did not know I was married," he responded.

"And she had to lock the door before she could learn that you had a wife. Where has she been, that she did not know Fitzwilliam Darcy married?" Elizabeth took a deep breath.

"Tomorrow my sister weds, you have until then to decide what you want. If you desire a life as a happy single man, then I shall leave. Sleep on it, and let me know what you wish. Good night."

As she set off for the sitting room, his hand held her arm. "So, that is your apology then, with so little attempt at civility?" he demanded.

"Excuse me? I am expected to say I am sorry? I do not need to seek your favour, sir. I am decidedly not sorry for my actions, but for yours, yes, one hundred times I am sorry you are acting in this manner. Whilst you may say you once married a fool, you shall never say I did not act within my pride. I held my head high today when you skulked inside with your friend.

"What a cozy conversation I interrupted as I saw you seated next to her upon the sofa, as if she had been your cousin Anne. Oh yes, I am so very sorry for your behaviour, sir."

For the first time since they went to London, she turned her back on him and quit their bed chamber. She did not kiss him, nor tell him she loved him. Leaving him with his thoughts, she headed for the sofa.

The Hurst carriage finally made it to Pemberly. The vehicle had broken down four times. It was well after dark. Three angry occupants were handed down from the carriage. Clovis had awakened Bingley and brought him outside. He had quickly collected a sleepy Jane and the two of them greeted his family.

Forgetting all about her new kindness campaign, Caroline Bingley was in rare form. She complained about the inconvenience of the carriage breaking down. She scoffed at the dusty conditions of the roads and the rough carriage ride. The Hursts were insulted and very tired of their sister's insufferable behaviour.

Charles tried to lift their spirits, "Allow me to introduce my wife-to-be. Jane Bennet, please meet my eldest sister, Miss Caroline Bingley, and my youngest sister, Louisa Hurst and her husband, my very fine brother, Mr. Hurst."

Jane curtseyed and smiled at each of them. Trying to welcome them, her voice sounded faint. It seemed these were the most intimidating faces she had ever seen! Servants appeared out of nowhere and assisted the new arrivals to their newly assigned rooms.

Fleming appeared also, and he announced that there would be a change in their accommodations. They would be situated on the ground floor. At hearing this, Caroline flew into a rage.

"No. This shall not do. Fleming, you know us quite well. Please see us to our usual rooms."

Fleming cleared his throat and stood his ground. "Mr. Darcy has increased his family size, and now all of the second floor rooms are appointed to his family. You shall be shown to your rooms, miss." Adding to this, Fleming turned to them once more. "Our kitchen staff has retired. We have the wedding breakfast to attend to, you know. Food has been laid out in your rooms. Please wait to be called upon in the morning. We shall offer a light fare before you go to the chapel. Thank you."

"Miss Bingley, James shall take your bags, kindly follow him." Caroline set off in a huff. Jane and Charles realised that she did not so much as say 'How do you do?" to the bride.

"Jane, dearest, I am afraid I must apologize for my sister. Be assured that she shall not be living with us when we return to London. I have made arrangements for her to move north. I have authorized my solicitor to confer the funds from her inheritance. I am no longer responsible for her care or comfort. Unfortunately, I never could influence her civility."

Jane looked into his eyes and offered her thanks for his reassurance. She knew it would be impossible to live with anyone displaying such a quick temper and bad disposition.

Caroline Bingley was too much like Mildred Bennet for Jane's comfort. The more she reflected upon the two women's behaviour, the more alike she saw them. Yes, it was true, Mildred Bennet and Caroline Bingley were exactly alike, she thought.

George Darcy heard a tap upon his door. He opened it eagerly hoping to find Fitzwilliam. "Rory! come in lad!

"Rory, she is home and she is safe. Gerald went after her. She entertained her clients tonight and has gone to bed. I shall hope to see her in the morning, she is an early riser.

"Thank you, Rory for all you did today. I was proud of you, son—"

Before he could continue, Rory asked him to take a seat. He needed to speak with him.

"Uncle, I think I might know something of Fitzwilliam's behaviour. I found this under his desk on the floor. I went there to see if my riding glove had fallen to the floor when I hit him. Looking slightly under the desk, I found this empty bottle."

He handed it to his uncle. "Laudanum! No. Can it be, Rory?"

"Uncle, it is the only thing I can think of that would make your son indifferent to his own wife and not even respond to the news that he is going to be a father."

"But, where? How?" his uncle asked him,

"I would think someone is selling it to him. I have no clue whom."

"Not Charles Bingley?" George offered.

"No! Definitely not," Rory was shocked that the man would mention Charles' name.

"We just need to watch and see," Rory had an urgent suggestion, "Uncle, in the meantime, we need to get a physician from town. Fitzwilliam may even need to be tied to a bed somewhere, so he can get off this junk. If he has just started there is a good chance he can overcome it. I have seen soldiers get over it, provided they have not been taking it for too long a period."

George pulled the cord for Fleming. He quickly sat at his desk and penned a message. In minutes the butler was at his desk. George requested their fastest rider to go for the physician. "Mr. White is a good man, and he lives this side of London. He shall not delay."

Rory interrupted, "Uncle what of the wedding? Should we alert Bingley to change his plans?"

"No. Let us not put the word out there. Charles has seen and heard too much already. Pity about all of us missing their wedding; charming people all of them. No. It cannot be helped. His life is more important."

"Uncle," Rory corrected him, "All three lives are more important."

Walking over to his nephew, George put his hand upon Rory's shoulder, "You are a good man, Rory, a very good man."

※

At first light, George Darcy was up and dressed for the day. He went to the breakfast room for coffee and the morning paper. As he had hoped, Elizabeth was the first one to join him.

"Lizzy, I must speak with you, immediately. Please join me in my study."

Reacting to her father, she looked grave. The two entered the study, and George handed her the empty bottle.

"I am sorry to tell you that Fitzwilliam has been taking this drug. I do not know how long he has been taking it, and I do not know how much he has taken. I do know that God shall help him get off it altogether. I know he shall recover his life from this poison."

"Father, I am shocked! Never in my entire life would I have thought him capable of doing such a thing. Where did he get it?"

"Elizabeth, I am beginning to have the strangest feeling that it was brought to him by that girl, yesterday. I shall send for Clovis to investigate. Rory found the bottle last night when he went into his study to see if his gloves were there on the floor."

"But, I do not understand, Father."

"She may well have brought it to him. It is possible that he took a dose immediately. I believe that to be the case. I went to speak with him about one half hour after Clovis took that girl. I told him about his child, and he had no reaction at all."

Elizabeth wrung her hands and looked up at him, questioning what she was being told.

"Daughter, that is just not normal, do you not agree?"

"Yes, of course," she replied, lost in thought. "That would mean he was not—do not misunderstand me—I hope he is not taking this..." She was still holding the bottle, and standing quickly she put it on the desk. "I also hope, the girl was not...Father, what if you and I call him into the room, and I tell him I am with child? He has had a good night's sleep. Perhaps he is no longer under the influence, and you can see if there is a difference from yesterday. Now that you mention it, he did seem like an entirely different person to me yesterday."

Mr. Fleming was sent to request Mr. Darcy to join his wife and his father. In just a few minutes, he entered the room. He greeted Elizabeth with a kiss and acted as if there was nothing whatsoever awry.

"Dearest, please sit down. I have news for you, and I think it would be wonderful to have Father hear it as well. Would you join us, please?"

"Oh, Liz-Beth, what is it my love? Are you well?" he asked with concern. His voice was clear.

"Yes, darling. I am quite well. I am blessed to tell you that you and I are going to be parents. We are going to have a baby on or about February five."

"Elizabeth, are you sure? This is wonderful, my darling wife! How do you feel?"

He sat closer to her and put his arms around her. Kissing her forehead, he asked, "Are you having any problems? You would tell me so, would you not?"

"No. I am having no problems at all," she smiled at him.

"Oh, my dearest Liz-Beth, you have made me so happy! But, are you sure there are no problems, I want all to be well with you and our child."

She shook her head, no. "It is a wonder but I feel better than I ever have, and Aunt says it must be beginners' luck! Are you not happy, Handsome Man?"

"My dearest, darling, Liz-Beth, I am happy. A million times, yes. You have made me so completely happy! A baby. I know nothing of babies, but I shall love ours so very much! Perhaps we shall welcome the heir to Pemberly? Do you know, now that we are to have a child, I find I truly do not wish for a boy? A beautiful little girl would be just as wonderful, would she not?

"Father, are you hearing this? You shall be Grandpapa! Elizabeth, where shall our child be born? In London, or here at home?"

"We have the finest midwife. She hails from County Cork and is now located in Lambton. She is Miss Shannon Colleen. She has all the modern equipment and has recommended a new birthing chair. Under her direction we are making the birthing room and nursery ready. She is pleased to hear you want to be with me, and she says you shall be an amazing help to me."

Fitzwilliam could not stop smiling at Elizabeth, and he could not take his hand from her stomach.

"Did you know that our child can hear you when you speak to me, or to him? Miss Shannon says it increases the baby's intelligence to talk or sing to him often. Fitzwilliam, you shall like Miss Shannon very much. It was she who calculated the approximate date of birth. We cannot know exactly."

He put Elizabeth upon his lap and asked, "Why have I not noticed changes in your body?"

Looking at George, he said, "Father, I am sorry. I do not wish to embarrass either of you, but I am sure you know we see each other's bodies daily." Not waiting for an answer, he was eager to settle his concerns about the use of a midwife.

"Darling, I feel you should have a physician, not just a midwife. Our baby should be born in the hospital in London."

Elizabeth set her jaw and squared her shoulders. He knew this posture, certainly a strong opinion would be forthcoming.

"No. Heavens no, Fitzwilliam. It is becoming well known that the London Hospital has a very high mortality rate. Many healthy new mothers and newborns die there. Miss Shannon says the reason is they fail to practice simple hygiene. The doctors put their hands into sick patients then, without the benefit of using soap and water to wash the hands, they transport the sickness into the bodies of healthy mothers. Infants are given the same filthy treatment. If they would just wash between patients, they could treat them safely. Horribly sad, is it not?"

He gently put her head against his chest and stroked her hair. She continued to speak.

"Pemberly is where our child should be born. He shall be a Darcy. It is only right that he be born here, on Pemberly soil. He shall be a man of the land, just like his father and his grandfather before him.

"Remember, it shall fall to us to teach him to love the land and to serve it all his life."

George had tears in his eyes as he listened to her telling his son about their responsibilities.

It was obvious to both of them that Fitzwilliam had absolutely no idea that he had been given this information on the previous day. He would be shocked and dismayed to know that he had been so indifferent as to not lift a hand to help his wife and child. It would be heartbreaking for him to learn that he had been the cause of Elizabeth's foolish ride that had put their lives (and also Marigold's) at risk. He had been more interested in that girl and perhaps, what she had to offer?

Clovis tapped on the door, George rose and left the room to meet with him. He gave instructions to call upon the Cooke girl. They would know the truth soon.

Elizabeth turned to face her husband. She laced her fingers behind his neck. She kissed him and sighed. It felt so good to have him hold her in his lap once more. She smiled. She was so happy to have him back, even if it was for a brief amount of time. Fitzwilliam began kissing her lips. He told her how much he loved her and that she was such a wonderful wife and would be a very special mother.

Lord, please let me keep this man. I do love him so very much and adore him. Show me what I can do to help him recover. Would you give us a child and then take my husband from me? I beg you to help my husband make a full recovery.

George Darcy returned to his study. He sat quietly while his son held his wife. They were such a beautiful couple, healthy and good looking. He knew it would be difficult for Fitzwilliam to get the drug out of his body and then keep it out of his life. He would pray earnestly for his son's full recovery.

About an hour later, Clovis tapped on the door. George joined him in the library. "Mr. Darcy, I am afraid your son has purchased laudanum from Miss Cooke who was here yesterday. I have the missive he sent to her requesting the purchase and delivery. He learned of her supply June one when the tenants were here." Giving Mr. Darcy the missive, he quit the room.

Fleming announced the arrival of the physician. He had been situated in the small salon on the first floor. Directing him to alert Otis and take the doctor to the Darcys' rooms, George set off to speak with Mr. White before he saw his patient.

It was thought that he had not been a long-time user. Apparently he had heard of the drug being used by friends in college and thought it would help him relax. Otis was asked about his knowledge of earlier use. He knew that Fitzwilliam had been using the drug from time to time. It was difficult to know how much he had used. No matter how long he had been using the liquid opium, it was imperative that he get off all drugs immediately.

At last, George called for Rory. He knew they might need muscle when Fitzwilliam's body demanded more drug. There were physicians in America who were just starting to write about keeping the body's system cleansed. Mr. White followed their plan.

Mr. White suggested breakfast for Fitzwilliam. Eventually he would have nausea, but he would need his strength as well. Elizabeth enjoyed just a few more minutes of her husband's company in a normal setting. Then they quit the dining room for their bed chambers.

It was early and the house was still quiet.

The confrontation with Mr. White was almost unbearable for Elizabeth. She could not endure seeing Fitzwilliam suffer this type of conversation. The man's words were hurtful, direct, and harsh. He did not believe one word Fitzwilliam told him. Fitzwilliam denied everything, and it was then that Mr. White put the missive into his hands. Finally he began to admit to his behaviour. Mr. White explained the dangers of using laudanum for diversion. He told them what is needed to overcome such addiction. Elizabeth wanted to be anywhere else, but she knew it was very important for her to understand.

Thus began a trial for Fitzwilliam Darcy and a test of endurance for Elizabeth. Before the fifty-one hours were completed, he would endure dry-mouth like cotton, body pains, profusion of sweat, aches, and stomach problems including pains, vomiting, and dry heaves.

Headaches would be a constant source of pain. No matter how much he would try, nor how much he would wish to feel normal, he could not.

Guests had been told that Fitzwilliam had the flu and Elizabeth was attending him. Mr. Darcy regretted that he also felt ill, and Rory sent his regrets without reason for his absence. Mary was most disappointed.

Elizabeth left her husband only once, to go to Jane and ask forgiveness for missing her wedding. She cried so hard that Jane could understand only a few words of what she said.

Returning to their rooms, Lizzy sent a note for Aunt. She trusted Jeannette to deliver it at a time when no one observed her.

Returning to the bed chamber, she looked to Mr. White. Fitzwilliam's eyes were closed, and he was calling for her, and not softly.

"Liz-Beth, please, lie next to me."

Mr. White nodded, and she climbed onto the bed and settled in beside her husband. She allowed herself to forget the presence of Father, Rory, Clovis, and Mr. White. Hours past and yet the men remained.

Fitzwilliam was a faint representation of himself. She knew he suffered greatly in his body.

He recounted things from childhood involving Wickham. George had never heard these accounts, and it was horrifying to him. Numerous times his son could have been killed by the wicked older boy. Elizabeth did not understand half his words until he spoke of Caroline Bingley.

He said he was sorry he did not give the name in London.

"Liz-Beth, I know I do not deserve you, but I need you so much."

She reminded him of their afternoon in the rain and the promise she made not to let him go. She would persevere with him. Rory watched in amazement. He had never heard such words of devotion. He wondered if Mary was of the same character. She resembled Elizabeth more than Jane or Kitty.

The chapel looked beautiful. Elizabeth had placed the fresh flowers only the day before. The groom waited with Hurst as a stand in for Darcy. Mary was taking Lizzy's place. Mr. Bennet was happy, yet he appeared worried over the absence of Lizzy.

Kitty held Georgiana's hand and whispered that her family would recover from the flu.

Caroline Bingley's head swiveled as she constantly watched the door for Fitzwilliam.

Jane looked wonderful, never more beautiful. She wore the jewels Lizzy had given her just the day before, when they all seemed so happy and carefree.

At the close of the service, the Gardiner children rose to sing. It was a wonderful wedding; however, the Darcys were greatly missed by all.

Caroline Bingley could hear the wedding party enter the dining room to begin the wedding breakfast. She knew the couple would leave immediately for the Lake District. She did not care; it was more important to look in Fitzwilliam's desk. She wanted to find anything with his signature. She had planned to find a forger. She was going to fabricate a letter confessing the times they had sex and offer a proposal. She would take it to the courts.

"May I help you, Miss Bingley?" Clovis asked as he towered over her. She had found letters which she held tightly in her hand. Clovis entered so quietly, she did not know he was there.

She knew his words meant, "Why are you in Mr. Darcy's study, and what are you doing snooping in his desk?"

Not waiting to hear her answer, the man commanded, "Miss Bingley, you are not authorized to be in Mr. George Darcy's study. I must insist you leave the Darcy property immediately." Clovis crossed the room and pried the letters from her hand.

As he spoke a servant appeared at the door holding her bags. She followed him without a word. They descended a back staircase, and she entered a waiting carriage, which she noticed had the Darcy crest upon the door.

No one spoke to her. Her family did not see her leave, and she was not allowed to write any messages.

<hr />

Edwin Wallet could not believe his eyes. He had just taken a seat outside the inn when the carriage pulled to a stop. The door bearing the Darcy crest opened, and Mrs. Darcy stepped out.

Approaching her quickly, as planned, he said, "Mrs. Darcy?"

"Well," she said, "who else would be stepping out of my husband's carriage?"

"Yes, Mrs. Darcy. I have just received an urgent message to return you to Pemberly. My carriage is here." He saw her bags, but did not take the time to think about them. She entered sweetly and was very happy for his assistance. He latched the doors and took her to his hideaway.

<hr />

Fitzwilliam held Elizabeth close and was now whispering his love into her ears. He made sense only to her. She loved the sound of his deep, sensuously masculine voice; it was music to her ears.

Their door opened quietly, and Aunt walked into the room. Her eyes filled with tears, but she approached the bed in silence. There lay the dear boy she had grown to love. He was tightly clutching his precious wife. Lizzy handed her a note. It was a simple prayer request for his total healing. She wanted the innocent children to pray, especially.

Lucille bent down and kissed Fitzwilliam on the forehead. He opened his eyes and said, "Mother! Thank you for the kiss; I love you so much." She answered, "I love you, too, son. Sleep well, my dear children." Then she quit the room and rushed down the hall to release her tears.

He slept. Elizabeth stoked his head. Clovis was called to an emergency. George napped, and Rory daydreamed about Mary.

Hours passed and Fitzwilliam seemed lost to sleep. Everyone jumped when he sat up in bed and shouted, "Liz-Beth, did you feel that? The baby kicked my hand and arm, very strongly. Can you feel it, love?"

"Yes," she laughed, "you should feel it from my side."

"I dare say, he is quite vigorous. This is the most amazing gift. I can feel *us*. That is you and I, living and thriving, growing inside you. It is *us*, is that not a miracle?"

George, Rory, and Mr. White listened with their mouths open. They had never heard a man speak so to his wife. George was ashamed that he could not remember ever having spoken so to Anne whilst they were expecting.

"Yes, my darling, Fitzwilliam. We have indeed become one flesh, have we not? One flesh in him or her. Through our child, we shall continue to live. There shall forever be a part of us, here at Pemberly, living, thriving, and growing from one generation to the next."

Looking at Fitzwilliam, she thought he was improved. She asked him. "What is that date of our child's arrival?"

"On or about February five," he said proudly.

Mr. White stood to his feet. He walked to his patient. "Look who is improving, I dare say. I think I shall have your man, Otis, show me to those delightful rooms. Food and rest are sounding good to this old man. Call if you need me."

George and Rory looked at each other. They knew they should not be hearing this conversation, but both were intent to listen.

"Darling, I need rest and sleep. Liz-Beth, shall you stay with me for a little while so I may sleep."

"I shall not leave you," she said, touching his cheek. "Sleep and rest and rid your body of that poison. You shall need to be a healthy and strong papa. Whatever the problems were at Pemberly, we shall fix them together, and you shall not need additional help to relax."

George cleared his throat. Rising, he stepped to Fitzwilliam and did something he had not done for about twenty years. He kissed his son on the forehead. "Son, I have as much confidence in you as I had on June one. Nothing has changed in my trust of you as master. We shall find a suitable transition, and I shall offer more help if you need me."

He kissed Elizabeth on her head and then said, "Rest well, children. I shall continue praying for the three of you."

He quietly shut the door, leaving Rory in his chair. The man stood to his feet. He made to quit the room without speaking, for he did not know what to say. When he opened the door, he heard a deep voice rumble through the room and envelope him. "Cousin, you are a real brother to me. We love you and thank you for all you do for us."

"Awe, go on now!" was Rory's only response. He left wondering if he could find Mary.

Chapter 10

"Sometimes it is important to allow your heart a chance to change your mind."

-Anonymous

Edwin Wallet was taken by Mrs. Darcy's beauty. He adored her red hair and pale white skin. He liked his women plump! She was so much more than a payday. He thought he would rather marry her. Yes, he would keep her for his very own.

He returned to his room at the inn and just thought about the ways he could marry Mrs. Darcy.

He had her; he would not give her up for money. Opening his chest, he withdrew a wedding certificate. Mr. Geoffrey Godfrey weds Millicent Murphy. Holding it up, he could see it was his best work. Next to purchase the laudanum from the apothecary. Taking coffee from the common rooms, he checked out of the inn, went to the hideaway, and prepared to consummate his marriage.

Finding Caroline nearly impossible to handle, let alone listen to, he pinned her to the cot and forced a large amount of the liquid down her throat. He would put it in her coffee once she was more agreeable. Soon she was sleeping, and he removed the gown she had just worn to her brother's wedding. The same dress she wore as she crouched by the stairs and waited to murder Elizabeth. The same one she had planned to wear to console Fitzwilliam.

Edwin was thrilled with her pink body. He enjoyed himself for quite some time before he entered her. He knew she would enjoy this too, if she were awake.

When completed, he dressed his wife and prepared her to travel. They would take a ship to New York and start over. He was an excellent forger on any continent. Experience had shown Wallet that there was no shortage of people who were looking for a man with his talents. Men and even women often sought his skills.

At Pemberly, Caroline was never missed. The following morning when the Hursts prepared to return to London, Mr. Hurst called for Caroline. Clovis answered that call. He told the couple that she had been taken to the inn at Lambton immediately following the ceremony. The driver remembered seeing a well-dressed man put her immediately into his carriage. She seemed happy to be with him. There was no note nor missive.

The couple discussed briefly whether they should return without her. Louisa felt her life was easier, if not happier, without the influence of her eldest sibling. Their carriage left within the next five minutes. The couple planned a second honeymoon for themselves. They would visit New York, New York in America.

※

Shannon Colleen took the letter from her assistant. It was from him. She opened the drawer and put it with the other unopened letters he had sent from County Cork. She was not going to read anything he had to say.

Sitting for a moment behind her desk, she considered herself fortunate to have escaped the scandal. Bless dear Charlotte. She was so kind to introduce her to Elizabeth Darcy by mail.

Mrs. Darcy, though young and very wealthy, impressed her as being highly intelligent and well educated. The rent-free use of the house and office that Mrs. Darcy furnished would be the payment for delivery of her first child. And the offer of an opportunity to write a health manual appealed greatly, although it could not be published under her surname, Sullivan.

Wondering what Mr. Darcy would be like when they meet in two weeks, Miss Shannon allowed herself to feel blessed. It was unusual that the wife conducted the business; however if the stories of his wealth were only half true, the man must be blessed with his wife taking some of the burden from him.

She would have wanted to help Hamilton in the same way, had he lived. He was gone, and it was the nasty work of her own brother, Ian. As a wealthy Englishman, Hamilton provided help to Irish Catholics. That is he did, until Ian heard he could win some gold from the Crown if he would give their spies the name and location of the man they sought. That man was William Hamilton.

Her brother denied this, but he did not know that moments before the pounding on the door, she herself, had been in bed with the man! Her father and brothers did not know that

Hamilton was her lover. He wanted to marry her, but she knew it could not be. Their marriage would have put him in too much danger.

Knowing they were coming for him, he lifted Shannon from the bed and carried her to the kitchen. Pulling up the hooked rug, he opened the trap door and allowed her to descend the steps to the cellar. She had clearly heard Ian's voice along with the Englishmen who captured her lover, and took him to Brighton for his mock trial and hanging. Shannon Colleen had wished to go with him that night, even to the scaffold. Without Hamilton, there may as well be no moon, nor stars, nor sun!

Gerald had never looked nor felt younger. The hard work agreed with him. Pleasant Glade Horses was returning a profit, but he worked for the fun.

George Darcy was learning the balance of admiring and enjoying Elizabeth's success and being an attentive father to Georgie. He was also spending much more time helping Fitzwilliam.

Remarkably, Elizabeth had time to assist with tenants and spend half-days with the horses. Things were going quite well at Pemberly.

The regular appearance of Colonel Rory Fitzwilliam was beginning to fascinate his cousin. Fitzwilliam could not fathom reason nor rationale for Rory's weekends at Pemberly.

"Rory, are you not back to your London encampment?" he wondered aloud at dinner one night.

"Indeed! It is my permanent assignment, cousin. I shall always work there. I have paid my dues in battle and recovered from numerous injuries. I am settled now and a regular resident."

"Aye!" The twinkle in her husband's eyes made Elizabeth nervous. "Pray, then why are you billeted here at Pemberly every weekend?"

Rory cleared his throat. "I feel I should check on the Pleasant Glade Horses project, cousin. I am the best judge of horseflesh in the family, after all."

"Sorry to disappoint," Elizabeth smugly corrected him, "my Grandpapa holds that title, Rory."

"Perhaps it is the fresh country air," Georgiana suggested with a giggle.

Kitty caught the giggles, and the two girls could not restrain themselves. Kitty looked at Mary.

"Sister Mary, could you not help us determine what brings our cousin to the countryside so often?"

Mary tried to cover the blush she felt rising from her chest to the top of her head. Rory gathered his courage and said, "I confess. I come so I can get better acquainted with my new family."

Mr. Bennet smiled. He enjoyed the diversion, "Perhaps we should have a chat, Rory. I might be the very one you should speak with on that account.

Fitzwilliam took pity, "Cousin, we are only playing with you. We are a motley mob of witless humorists! Tomorrow night you shall hear teasing and torment focused upon the poor expectant father. They laugh at me because I continue to ask my wife to tell me if the child is a boy or a girl. She keeps insisting she knows not! I trust her to care for and carry our child, and she troubles not herself to learn the gender? Amazing!"

Everyone laughed and Rory appreciated his deflection of the pressure, even if it had been Fitzwilliam himself who created the uncomfortable situation.

Elizabeth suggested a walk outdoors. The Gardiners made a short walk as they were leaving for town in the morning. The evening was balmy and pleasant. The stars were bright, reminding Elizabeth of the night Charles proposed to Jane.

Feeling frisky, she nudged her husband and whispered the similarities into his ear. He shook his head in firm denial of her idea. But to show he was sporting, he offered, "All right a wager, then?"

"Yes. Name your prize."

"The same as yours last time," he smiled with a wolfish grin on his face.

She giggled with amusement. "Oh, my toes are tingling already, my love."

Overhearing the last part of their conversation, Rory demanded, "Here, here! Would you like to share with the other boys and girls, Mr. and Mrs. Darcy?"

"As a matter of fact, yes, I dare say I would!" Fitzwilliam spouted, before his wife glared at him to stop. But, as they looked into each other's eyes, the couple suddenly burst into peals of laughter.

Rory's look censured them.

Elizabeth sighed, "Now I am starting to feel very tired. I think I am walking for two this evening. Would all of you excuse us, please?"

Everyone began to excuse themselves, leaving Rory and Mary alone.

At first light, Elizabeth was up, working with Jeannette to prepare for the day. She wished to see the Gardiners off to London and to be ready for the important interview in the afternoon.

Elizabeth and Grandpapa had suggested that they share an assistant with Fitzwilliam. Fitzwilliam had thought it a good idea to engage someone to help him.

Regis Bates was expected for an interview with the three of them at one of the clock. The two and forty year old man had recently lost his employment when His Excellency, the Honourable Edward Charles Chauncy, Ambassador to America retired from active service. Lord Matlock had written a letter to Gerald advising him of the professional gentleman's skills.

Entering the breakfast room, Elizabeth spotted her father enjoying a cup of coffee and reading the *London Topics*. They greeted each other. Mr. Bennet barely looked over the top of his paper. Both jolted, as Rory burst through the door!

He was acting rather peculiarly—nervously pacing the room. He halted only when Mr. Bennet complained of sea sickness.

After several minutes of hemming and hawing, he made an attempt to get to the point.

He led out with two false starts, and from there, made a rough beginning. Speaking too loudly, he was distracted by his own echo filling the room.

"Mr. Bennet, I wonder if you might have a few moments of my time, please?"

"Certainly my boy," he answered as if there had been no error. "What is it that you can do for me?" Bennet smirked through a very sincere smile.

Rory, still missing his original error, as well as the older man's attempt at a clever and humorous retort, rushed on.

"Well, sir, perhaps if Mrs. Elizabeth would take our leave, we could go anywhere else, away from here, and speak in the breakfast room, if you shall join me."

"Of course," Mr. Bennet calmly replied, holding his lips in a tight line, "Which is it you would most like to see happen? Whom shall go where, and are we not already in the breakfast room?"

At last, looking up at her, Rory threw his hands in the air, and pled, "Elizabeth, please?"

She giggled. "Certainly cousin. But I dare say, that until you spoke your last two words, you were making no sense whatsoever! Good luck, Father. Should you need an interpreter, Fitzwilliam shall be in shortly. He has been conversing with this gentleman all his life. He may be very helpful, indeed." Throwing back her head, she laughed with such gusto she brought a servant running to see if all was well.

One half hour later, Fitzwilliam and Elizabeth entered the breakfast room. Seeing Mary and Rory seated by Mr. Bennet, Fitzwilliam sighed and put his hands on his wife's shoulders.

"Are you clairvoyant? A mystic from the East? When shall I learn not to wager with you?"

Over breakfast the five of them conspired on the details of a Christmas wedding at Pemberly.

Upon breaking up the gathering, Fitzwilliam took Rory aside and asked him when he had a change of mind about marriage. The solider always said he would never marry.

"That is an easy question to answer. I had a change of heart when I watched you and your wife during your ordeal. I have never seen two people love and care for one another as do the two of you. She shall never leave you. I want that in my own life.

"I suppose, cousin, you could say that my heart changed my mind! Why should I let you have all the fun?"

Elizabeth caught Mary's hand and asked if she had finished the book she was writing on prayer.

"Yes, I have completed the volume. Do you desire to read it?"

"Of course, and I also desire to publish it so that others may read it as well."

"Oh Lizzy, do you think it might be possible? Oh, what a great joy to have it read by others!"

"When I receive word, I shall let you know. Please pray, Mary," she suggested.

The **HMS Sonnet** docked at last in New York Harbor. Mr. and Mrs. Godfrey looked forward to going to their new home. Millicent was dependent upon her daily coffee with her powders. Her headaches were no better.

She knew she would feel much improved after her coffee with the powders. Thankful that her husband took such good care of her, she felt he was her world. They were looking forward to living in their new home.

Mr. Bates was impressed with Pemberly and even more so with the three individuals who interviewed him for the position. He was happy for an opportunity like this. Splitting his work between the two concerns would be exciting and keep him from being bored.

When he was given a chance to speak of his own talents, he said he was flexible, the soul of discretion, and enjoyed children. The next thing he knew, he was being shown his rooms!

Mr. Bates felt it was his remark about children that tipped the scales in his favour. He was going to work very hard for Pemberly and Pleasant Glade Horses.

Fitzwilliam was a new man! Even the simple thought of someone else writing all those long letters freed his mind. He felt a great burden lifted from his life! He was thankful to his wife.

Walking down the hall, side by side, Fitzwilliam thanked Liz-Beth for the clever suggestion for a new hire. He needed this help, but never would have reached out for it on his own.

Now, sharing an assistant, was the perfect solution!

Suddenly he grabbed her, opened a door, and swept her inside an empty room.

"Come here, wife, and receive your reward for hiring that wonderful assistant. I wish to reward you for having a clever mind!"

"And, what shall my reward be, Handsome Man?"

"This—" he picked her up and put her upon the bed.

Lifting her skirt, he smiled. She was still beautiful, and as bare as ever, but her stomach put a much different accent on her *mon veneris*. Touching her gently, he squeezed her mound and smiled.

"You love doing that to me, do you not?" she asked raising her eyebrows.

"I cannot deny it, I do," he answered, proudly.

"Please do not deny it, husband. Pray, never deny me the thrill of having you perform it. I love it, too, my darling."

He inserted one finger and circled her ring. "You are ready, Mrs. Darcy. But because it is your reward, what is your pleasure?"

She looked confused momentarily. "Do you know what room we have entered?"

Kissing her neck, he hardly looked up. "I have no idea. Why do you ask?"

"Because, " she said slowly, "there are clothes on that chair."

The two arose from the bed and shook out their clothing, straightened their hair, and turned to quit the room.

Fitzwilliam turned the key, and they walked out, side by side.

They were just in time to greet Mr. Bennet as he returned to his room to prepare for dinner.

"Well, upon word, it is my host and hostess! Did you come to pay your papa a visit?" He smiled, hardly controlling the twitch that threatened his lips with laughter.

"Indeed," Fitzwilliam responded. "We wanted to see if the library was still to your liking or if there are any books we should acquire for your enjoyment."

"Perfectly wonderful. I am a very happy man, son. As I can clearly see, you are as well. See you both at dinner, then."

"My love, what did he mean?" she asked, then quickly placed her hand over her open mouth.

Looking down at her husband, she saw the answer.

"Oh…yes! I have always said that bulge does not tell even half the story!"

He answered her sheepishly, "Apparently, it tells enough…"

Charles called for his wife to join him in the study. Jane came in happily, and Charles showed her the letter. Smiling, he invited her to sit in his lap whilst he read it to her.

"'Tis a letter from Fitzwilliam, darling. Shall we see how they are doing?"

Jane nodded as she put her head against his shoulder.

Pemberly Park, Derbyshire

13 November 1803

My Dear Bingley,

How can I make amends for the poor treatment you and your beautiful wife received upon the most glorious day of your lives? There is nothing, I fear, so I must then go straight to the confession, old chap.

Did you surmise that I was more than ill with the flu? You are an Oxford grad, so the answer is probably 'yes.' Because you are my dearest friend, and I dare say, among the few, as well, I must tell you the entire of it.

Before your mind goes hither and yon, I should like it to be known that I am a poor, besotted man who dearly loves and is entirely devoted to his wife. If you knew the half of that statement, old man, you would indeed pray that I might survive her own devotions to me. (Might I assume Jane is reading at your elbow?)

Perhaps you heard references to a particular girl who entered our home shortly before your wedding? She unfortunately followed my request and brought a certain substance that we saw something of at Cambridge during final examinations. Going to Oxford you avoided that, I am sure.

I had no Cambridge difficulties, except to glean a subconscious awareness of what my chums claimed it did for them. It was later that I made the wrong decision and tried it for myself. I dare say, it is no remedy for boredom, and certainly not a cure for anxiety.

Falsely, I thought I had a panacea in that evil substance.

Inquiring in a large crowd was the easiest thing I did. Or, should I tell you the only easy thing about the entire sordid mess. Suffice it to confess, I self-prescribed, imbibed, and set myself upon a wild journey in which I became another person, and not of a good sort.

Here is where I must humble myself before you, Charles, and with my heart I say that I am sorry for that very poor decision. One cannot find the remedy for stress and anxiety in any sort of bottle, large or small. I deeply regret my behaviour and the fact that you were a witness to it. I caused you the loss of my friendship in that I was not able to stand up with you, and missed your wedding and the fellowship. I am most sorry, also, that I parted two sisters who dearly love each other and caused them both to miss each other, on the most important day of your lives.

Rory has told me some of what you witnessed, and I must only now ask that you forgive me as your brother, for my horrible behaviour.

A physician from town was called to help me through fifty-one hours of messy and very unpleasant business.

Just know that Elizabeth is a queen. I worship at her feet daily for all she is and all she has done for me. Speaking of her feet, it has been some time since she has seen hers whilst standing.

Our child shall join us, on or about February five. We are both beside ourselves with joy.

Are you hearing from your sister Mary? If yes, then you know that Rory has asked for her hand.

For reasons which I cannot determine, the girl said yes. We are to host their wedding at Pemberly on Christmas. We shall be totally unable to do so, old chap, if you and your beautiful bride are unable to join us, either for the nuptials or the season.

You and your wife are greatly missed. Elizabeth pines for Jane. Do say you shall come.

Come whenever you wish and stay as long as you desire.

Come and allow me to earn your friendship. I shall apply myself toward being your brother as well. I soon shall have Rory competing with me for the title of favourite brother.

See how your stock has risen by your connections with me?

Kindest and most affectionate regard to dearest Jane.

F.D.

Both readers had tears in their eyes. The letter brushed over the mental and emotional torments that Fitzwilliam and Elizabeth must have endured. They felt the humility and sorrow that inhabited each phrase of the letter.

"What a dear man," they both agreed.

Charles commented upon the tears in his wife's eyes. She admitted that she also missed her dearest sister each day. The Darcys seldom used their London home. If they were to be seen, it must be in the country.

Taking a file from his desk, Charles showed Jane papers for the Hazel Nut Farm he nearly bought one year earlier. They read the file. It was decided he would write to Darcy and see if the property was still available. If so, they would ask him to deposit earnest money for the purchase. Charles started the missive immediately.

Following Mrs. Darcy's dictations, Bates penned a missive to Mr. Gardiner. The purpose was an inquiry to ascertain the feasibility of exporting livestock to America.

Edward smiled as his assistant placed the morning's post on his desk. Knowing Lizzy's writing, he immediately relished the idea of hearing from Pemberly. He loved all his nieces, but Lizzy would always be his daughter. He enjoyed her personal letter before he read the business letter. She explained that she and Gerald were having such success they were forced to hire an assistant, and the business letter had been dictated.

Liking the ideas set forth in the business letter, he decided to take it home and answer it from his study. Lucille would wish to enclose a letter of her own.

It was early morning and the house was quiet. Fitzwilliam rose early and left without a sound. Elizabeth did not stir, and it was for the best. He did not want her to ask questions. He hoped she would sleep until he returned. He wanted no discussions.

Finding the clothes Otis set in the hall for him, he picked them up, along with the large towel.

He headed downstairs with the bundle under his arm. He was on time, Clovis had not yet arrived in the game room.

Fitzwilliam had just finished dressing in breeches and a linen shirt when Clovis entered. The men walked to the rack and selected their foils. Wordlessly, they began.

Working for about sixty minutes, both men were tired when they finished. Reaching for their towels, they wiped their faces and headed for the door.

Just before they quit the room, Clovis handed a thick envelope to Darcy. "This was delivered to me by Mrs. Reynolds. She caught one of the maids reading it as if it was the most interesting novel ever written. I interviewed the girl and determined she had told no one of the discovery. Mrs. Reynolds and I felt it was best to offer the girl one month's severance pay and send her to a job opportunity in Newcastle. She departed yesterday in the company of Foster. He shall see her safely installed. The girl is from that area, and she should settle in quite well."

"Well, in God's name, what the bloody hell could have cause so much inconvenience to my staff, and expense to me?" Darcy demanded.

"Sir, it is the diary of Miss Caroline Bingley. Your name and some details pertaining to you are in this journal. Also, a self-described plot to kill your wife is detailed. An account of her own, should I say, sins is also chronicled. It is information that should not be allowed to circulate. Upon hearing the plot to kill Elizabeth, Darcy put his hand over his heart. Stunned by the news, he asked Clovis to repeat the remark about a detailed plot to kill Elizabeth.

"Please read it, Mr. Darcy, and if I may be of further assistance, please call upon me."

Darcy turned the envelope over in his hands, as though the backside would reveal the answers to his questions.

"Clovis, other than the two of you, are you aware of any in the house who may know of this?"

"No, Mr. Darcy. I believe we have it under control. I warn you, the contents are quite shocking and more than a little disturbing."

"Thank you, Clovis."

Heading up the stairs, Darcy was met by Otis who escorted him into one of the guest rooms to enjoy a bath and dress in fresh clothing. Darcy felt guilty deceiving Elizabeth about his fencing. He knew she strongly disapproved, but she certainly did admire the muscles it developed.

Relaxing in the hot tub, he opened the envelope and began to read Caroline Bingley's diary. He was thankful to his loyal staff; he certainly did not want anyone reading this journal. Especially Elizabeth!

London's morning post brought two letters to Bingley House. The first was from Darcy, the second from Louisa writing from New York, where the couple was celebrating a second honeymoon. Both contained news of the highest order.

"Jane! The farm is available! We shall be less than seven miles from Pemberly. Darcy has checked on it twice, and he says it is pristine. The staff wishes to stay and serve us." The couple congratulated themselves. Darcy declared that the farm was such a good purchase, that he would buy it himself should Bingley change his mind.

The next missive from New York was news of Caroline. It seems the Hursts saw her, dining with a very wealthy-looking man. The couple got away before they could speak with her, but Hurst has engaged an investigator to locate the pair. Their next letter should give the details, but Louisa believed they are married, and the man looked very well to do.

Agreeing it would be interesting to hear if it is, indeed, Caroline, and why she left without word to her family, they awaited the next letter from America.

Mr. Bates went to the stables to deliver two important-looking letters to Mrs. Darcy. Deathly afraid of horses, he wanted to do the best for his employers. He defied his fears.

"Thank you so much, Mr. Bates. I shall read them in a few moments. Please feel free to return to the house. Your discomfort is making the horses nervous, sir." She was jesting, but the dear man was too fearful to notice her humour.

Stepping into a stall, she looked at both letters. Uncle's was most important. She eagerly opened it and read the good news. It included a prospectus she could share with Grandpapa. Aunt's letter told of their plans to join the Darcys for Christmas.

Secondly, there was a letter from Ellen Gates. As an employee of a nearly bankrupt London publishing company, Ellen was in a position to advise her on the opportunity to lease or purchase the business. Accounting figures were enclosed in Ellen's communication as well. Elizabeth would study these before tea.

Upstairs Elizabeth called for Jeannette and began her preparations for their tea. The maid smiled setting out a very appealing gown which would best show her bosom. The dress was large enough to accommodate her changing shape, yet flattering.

A special tea had been set out. She would serve sherry rather than tea, and sweets rather than cheeses and breads.

Grandpapa was first to join her. "We have received word from Uncle. He wants to partner with us in the America concern. He sends figures on costs and suggests North Carolina as our port of entry and Kentucky as our destination. He says that Kentucky is the state most like England with the use and love of sport horses. He sees a market for our ponies and an open-door opportunity for Pleasant Glade Horses.

"Demand for the Welsh and Shetland ponies is increasing in the United States. We should take advantage of this while there is an open door."

"Yes, Lizzy! What are Americans but disgruntled British men who had high ideals, lots of money, and George Washington?" he laughed at his own political humor.

"I congratulate you on your pursuit of the idea. I had no way of knowing that you were going to pursue this and contact Edward. I think it is a capital idea, my girl! However, in view of your condition, I never would have suggested it to you. I shall not wish to bother your brain at a time like this. Well done! Bravo!"

Fitzwilliam entered at the word 'Bravo.' Taking one look at the very appealing gown adorning his beloved, his thoughts went straight to her bosom.

"Yes, I should say, 'Bravo!' You look so *very* marvelous, my darling wife!"

"Thank you, love. You as always are so very handsome. I shall be distracted to a fault this afternoon."

"Ahem! Ahem!" Gerald cleared his throat to bring their thoughts back to the tea.

"Children, I would like to take a moment to say that Bates is a rare man. He has me so organized that I do not know my own work! I hope you both feel the same."

"Indeed!" they both agreed.

Taking a deep breath, Elizabeth launched into her letter from Uncle. She then presented the financial projections he sent with his letter. Thinking this to be the brainchild of Grandpapa, Fitzwilliam turned to Gerald, "Congratulations! It appears this shall yield quite a sum almost immediately. Shall you use the same men on both continents?"

Looking at Lizzy, Gerald answered, "Grandson, you shall need to ask your wife that question. This was entirely her idea."

"Liz-Beth!" he scolded, "I thought we agreed that Bates would help you slow down. You are still having a baby in two and one-half months, are you not?"

"You know I am," she answered, biting her lower lip and looking at him through her lashes.

"This was an idea I had some time ago, but I wanted to wait to speak with you because I lacked the financial reports. You can see we have them now. Uncle wants to be a full partner. He likes the idea very well." Here, she stopped and put one finger upon his lips to hush him. "Do not say another word, darling, pray, just think on it and read and reread the information. The ponies shall stay in their appropriate places until you have seen fit to approve the endeavor."

"And, why do you think I should approve another project?" he asked, impatiently.

"If you shall note, the net should be rather large. Uncle's share would be half, with Pleasant Glade taking the other half. In addition, this project would provide employment for one dozen men. That would put a lot of food on twelve family tables!

"Uncle also suggests that Kentucky shall be the next biggest horse racing interest in America. The ponies shall give us access to these gentlemen that possibly no other avenue shall present. It should give our letters a warmer reception than just sending inquiries."

"Oh, Elizabeth, when shall I learn?" he asked, smiling at his wife.

"Well, it is not like I am going to get the ponies and then take the ship to North Carolina. I shall be right here at home, happily growing fatter by the day and waiting for our baby to arrive."

"May God haste that day, my lovely girl. Oh! Wait, that was too easy. You would never give us these treats for tea unless you want something. It is not a holiday, nor a special occasion. Tell me what else is lurking to trip me up, like a snared rabbit!"

"Well, I had planned it to be private. I wanted to discuss some things of a very sensitive nature. May we wait on that until after dinner, please?" Her plea was somewhat seductive.

He agreed, keeping his eyes on her bosom.

Miss Shannon was counting her blessings. This week's income was larger than anything she had ever earned in Ireland in one week. She wanted to start work on the health book, but perhaps it was too soon. She should wait until the time is right. Her new life in England was beginning to feel like a success and she owed it all to Charlotte for acquainting her with Elizabeth Darcy.

Miss Shannon had a strong liking for Elizabeth and her kind husband. She was impressed with the close relationship the two had, and appreciated the support Mr. Darcy gave his wife. In fact, she could not remember seeing another couple so much in love as the Darcys.

There was just one thing about the pregnancy that concerned her. Elizabeth was young and healthy, and the father was healthy, yet he was such a large man. How big might the baby be? That was a question Miss Shannon asked herself almost daily. Knowing that the baby's weight gain was going to be greatest during the last month to six weeks, she had concerns. She was trying to remain optimistic. Time would tell the size of the newborn. Still, the mother was quite small…

Shopping in a small and fashionable boutique on Broadway, Louisa caught a glimpse of Caroline leaving a store just three doors down the street. Once again she and her wealthy-looking husband departed before the Hursts could reach them. Going into the store, they asked for information.

The manager was eager to provide the address for the Godfreys. One look at the Hurst woman told her the two were sisters. It would be difficult to match that colour of red hair. No doubt the Godfreys would appreciate the manager going to so much trouble to reunite a family.

Mr. Hurst suggested they return to their inn and send a message. Even though New Yorkers were not as formal as the British, a written request for a visit was still in demand. Americans may be casual, but the Godfreys were not really Americans, were they? A missive would request an opportunity to visit in the morning. If a return message came, they would go to the Park Avenue address and visit Caroline and meet her husband, Mr. Godfrey.

Chapter 11

"Dreams shared may become dreams realised."

-Anonymous

The late afternoon post brought a letter from the Bingleys. Jane and Charles would arrive at Pemberly within the week. They asked to stay with the Darcys for a month to prepare their new estate. This request thrilled Elizabeth and Fitzwilliam, and they were happy to oblige.

"Fitzwilliam, this shall be wonderful! Jane shall be such a help with Mary's wedding, and nothing shall prevent us from enjoying the festivities. Charles seems to be relying upon your wisdom once again. Did you notice how many issues he wants to clear with you before they move into their new home?"

"Yes, my love. It shall be a blessing for all of us. I am looking forward to spending some excellent time with my friend, now that I am no longer crazed."

"Oh, darling, please do not speak like that," she pled with him.

"No. I shall never allow myself to forget what a monster I became. I absolutely must keep all of that out of my life. I must remember how I totally lost control of myself. Our child deserves the very best parents God may provide."

Locking the door to their study, he embraced his young wife and placed his hands over her stomach. "Are you well, Liz-Beth? How fair you this evening?"

"Very well, only I feel you did not lock our door just to ask of my wellness."

Smiling at her, he began to run his hands all over her body. He whispered, "How well you know me, Liz-Beth."

"Um, I love the feel of your hands touching my curves. You seem quite amorous."

"Yes, I am ready to seduce my beautiful wife, so as to ascertain exactly what she wants me to bless and agree to this time."

"Fitzwilliam, could we sit on the sofa, please? I wish to take my slippers off, and perhaps you could lie down and put your head in my lap."

"Oh no! No. It shall not be that easy, expectant mother of my first child. I have your best interests at heart. We may sit, but if anyone puts their head in a lap, it shall be your head in my lap," he corrected her.

"Very well, that sounds wonderful. Let it be myself lying down and putting my head in your lap." With that, he sat, and she did lie down with her head in his lap.

"You are aware of conditions for women in this country, are you not? We have so few basic rights, and live our entire lives under the dictate—or, may I change that and say, under the rule—oh dear, I should say…well, I just cannot find a positive way to say that men rule the realm. Do you deny it?"

"No, but is this to be a debate, Elizabeth?"

"I should think not! You are already aware of the shocking denial of education for my gender. Look at the amazing authors who must publish under the anonymous nom de plume, 'A Gentlewoman.' Now that is an outrage, is it not?"

"I shall not disagree."

"Do you not recall that when you married me, a virgin, yet even though twenty years, I had no knowledge of my own body? I knew nothing of sexuality nor even of bride's disease?"

"But, my love, it was such a joy to teach you."

"I understand. What if I had been a shy girl, or one who listened to and believed the old wives' tales of painful joining? You would have had your work cut out for you, Mr. Darcy. She began kissing his neck and was nearly lost to her thoughts . . .

"Although, I admit you are so amazingly appealing …that I would have given you anything you asked me for at any time. You are so desirable, Mr. Darcy…Ahem! Oh, but I forget myself."

He bent down and kissed her. She nearly forgot what she was going to say once again.

"Miss Shannon says I am approaching the stage of my pregnancy where I shall desire intercourse constantly. I think I must be there, for I certainly am having a strong desire just remembering how you taught me certain things about my body.

"Oh, yes, I nearly forgot what I wanted to say. Fitzwilliam, I desire to have Miss Shannon write a book for women. I wish her to instruct about the female and male anatomy, sexuality, reproduction— simply symptoms and suggested remedies.

"Such a book would be a highly successful financial project for even men would buy it.

"From some of the tales I have heard, many men are also woefully ignorant on these important issues." She took a deep breath, looking into his amazing eyes.

"Liz-Beth, this would be a wonderful idea, but no publishing house in London would produce such a book. She would need to go to France for that type of freedom"

"Well, we know war shall make that impossible. Besides, this is for British girls. And it is, after all, not just about this one book. Not just this book, but any worthy book that a woman writes should be published upon its own merits. Would you not agree?"

"Certainly," he assured her.

"How is The Swan Creek Inn coming along, my husband?"

"Wonderfully successful, I thank you. We shall net a handsome profit this year."

"Yes, it 'tis wonderful to have an effective manager on site, is it not? One that may do all the work for you. Your need is just to overlook the business and make suggestions as needed," she smiled sweetly.

"Elizabeth stop this instant. I know when I have been snared! Have you purchased a publishing house?"

"Truly or in theory? Because if you are asking me if I own a publishing house I would say absolutely not! I would not do such a thing without the blessing and approval of my husband. Um, the one I find so irresistible at the moment. Give me a kiss, Mr. Darcy."

Sitting up, she began to kiss his neck. "Pray, what is it about your neck that weakens my knees and makes me desire you more than taking my next breath? Have I ever told you that the sight of your neck makes me wild with desire?"

"As much as this pains me to say, please stop right now. We need to finish this talk first. I promise you, I shall give full attention to your many physical demands as soon as we are finished with your fishing expedition," Darcy lectured his wife.

She sat up and moved away from him, just to be safe. "Very well, I have been writing letters to a very wonderful lady. She is British by way of South African heritage. An impressive young woman, willing to work very hard for a cause in which she believes.

"She has worked all her adult life for Knightly Publishing in London. She became upset when several lady authors were denied publishing of their books.

"It has come to my attention that the same company is verging on bankruptcy. Ellen Gates, their former employee, had determined that the bank and title holder shall either sell or lease the business.

"Now, I am fully aware that I personally know nothing about this business. Ellen Gates does. She has served as executive assistant to the publisher. She knows the editor and all of the printing and distribution personnel.

"Have I mentioned that I have an account with the Bank of London under my maiden name? Uncle opened it for me when I began to keep my father's accounts. I was paid only a small sum, but with compounded interest and with some modest investments, it has come to an amount that would provide a six-months start."

He interrupted her, "Liz-Beth, your monies shall remain your own. I can understand that the subject has never risen, but I feel you should keep your funds. I am happy for your enterprising youth, my darling."

Smiling at him, she sat beside him again, and kissed his lips. It was a long, very passionate kiss. Then, she said, in a whispery voice, "Thank you, my Love. What was I speaking about?"

"You wish to become England's first powerful female publisher," he prompted.

"Oh, thank you," she replied, rolling her eyes at him. "Quite.

"I feel strongly that Miss Shannon's book alone shall be a very popular seller. Who in the Kingdom does not want to read about sex? This book shall have a wide appeal. If we are successful, then I suggest we keep it with our holdings. Profits can go to our daughters and second or third sons, as well." She smiled at him again, "If I am wrong, then we are out of business in six months.

At least that is enough time to get the book out in the stores. Oh, and if the stores ban the book, we shall offer mail orders."

"Minx. You have thought of everything. Do you want the English girls to rival the French in amour?"

"*Oui*! Oh, I almost forgot, we shall have at least one book on prayer, as well."

"Very well, tomorrow we shall look into this together. It shall take some time to put such an arrangement together. You shall surely have a babe nursing at your breast when the papers are signed to take this business."

"Oh," she said, running her fingers through his hair, "do not forget that you promised to remove the excess milk from my breasts, so I shall have two of you nursing."

Sliding her gown down to her waist, he bent his head toward her breast. "I shall practice now…"

"Husband, I am always amazed at the speed in which you can disrobe me, before I know you have begun—"

The Gardiners were busy preparing for their trip to Pemberly. Edward was excited to meet in person with Gerald to complete the work on the ponies. Lucille was thrilled to visit with the Darcys again. The children were happily planning which song they would sing for the wedding.

Lucille and Edward planned the time they could afford to spend at Pemberly. Having Christmastide to include in their trip would extend it for a total of about two months. More, if absolutely necessary. The year of 1803 had been chiefly spent away from home for the couple, and they needed to look at the planning for 1804 with the consideration that more time should be spent in London.

Miss Shannon sat at her desk and read Elizabeth's letter for the third time. She had the nagging feeling that she should go to Pemberly early and take the rooms provided for her.

Looking at her calendar, she decided that the first day of the new year would be the appropriate date of arrival at Pemberly. This should put her in residence one month and one week ahead of the due date.

A feeling of unrest filled her mind. Perhaps she should go sooner? Mrs. Darcy was so small. There were some concerns which would not be laid to rest. When to go to Pemberly?

Mr. and Mrs. Hurst jolted at the firm knock upon their door. Mr. Hurst answered and found a page standing before him. He took the missive and tipped the boy.

Turning to Louisa, he said, "Here it is. Our answer from Park Avenue. Mr. and Mrs. Godfrey wish to invite us to tea on the morrow. It seems Caroline has suffered a mental breakdown of sorts. She has been quite ill and may or may not remember us. She is under a physician's care and is improving. Mr. Godfrey shall be very happy to meet his family.

"Let us go to bed early tonight. We may need our rest; with Caroline's condition, we may have a difficult day tomorrow."

"At least she is wealthy," Louisa said, "In her seven and twenty years she has not changed. She always wanted great wealth, did she not? It was really all she has ever wanted."

Night fell suddenly and deeply upon the mansion. They had just been in the study, and she went on to bed. The master, having a bit more work to do, stayed on for a few minutes. Leaving now to walk to their second-story set of rooms, he heard a shrill scream. Recognising the sound of his beloved's voice, he ran to her as swiftly as was in his power!

A servant came from out of nowhere, looking at the frantic master, and she waited for orders. "Call that midwife!" he screamed to the servant who had come into the hall.

All at once footsteps were heard in the second-floor halls. Doors opened and closed as everyone wanted to know the problem and be satisfied that a resolution to the scream was being sought. Running into their bed chamber, he groped around the bed.

"Beloved? Where are you?" he called, as he felt around the bed. It was so cold and dark in their room. He wondered who allowed the fire to burn so low. Reaching out, he touched her slender ankle. He followed it up her leg. A maid ran in, and he yelled once more, "Call that midwife and get some light in here—light the candles and build up that fire!" He was barking orders more harshly than he had ever done in his life.

He could not understand what had gone so wrong. They were just having a wonderful time in the study. She was so well! How could she be ill? No, she would be well.

"Oh my darling, do not worry. Help is on the way. Take it easy, my love. All is well with our baby, I promise."

To his dismay, she was not answering him. Perhaps she was just resting and saving her strength. He took her arm and tried to feel for the pulse as he had been taught, but he could not remember what he should be feeling.

Two maids rushed in and lit candles. His butler entered and brought one of their new coal-oil lamps. Looking at his precious wife, he could see blood.

In the hallway the sounds of an arrival were heard. Soon the midwife stepped in and ordered him out of the room.

"You do not understand, I promised her I would stay with her when the baby came. She needs me."

Alone in the hallway, he blindly paced the floors of his mansion. He was in such a state, no one dared approach him. He feared the worst possible outcome.

Pacing the floor, he suddenly stopped. A firm hand was being placed upon his arm. The midwife was talking to him. She was excited, and her foreign-sounding accent prevented his understanding. It was English, but spoken with such modification that the words were difficult to determine. Finally one word sunk in. Dead.

Tragically he was receiving the news he most feared. He shook in grief and disbelief as the midwife placed her compassionate hand upon his arm and led him into his bed chamber. As he slowly entered the room, he was understanding more of her conversation.

Yes. His wife and child were both gone. It appeared she did not suffer. The child had been a boy. It had been too early for the baby to survive. It was not clear why she had not cried for help. Perhaps it had all happened so quickly that there was no time beyond her first scream. It may have been that she fainted from pain, or the sight of the blood. No one knew for sure.

"NO! NO! NO! Do not tell me such things! How shall I live without her? What of my son? My heir? I do not wish to continue living, my life is over! Get out! Everyone get out of the house. Go. Get out now! I shall be alone with my beloved and our son!"

He walked through the second floor yelling at everyone and no one.

"Go, do you hear me! Go!" his tears filled his face. His vision was blurred, and his head was spinning.

Entering their bed chamber, his eyes fell upon the tiny bundle lying in his wife's arms.

Gently crawling into bed, he softly took the baby into his own arms. It was so small next to him. He had been wrapped in one of the blankets purchased to welcome him into the world. Now the dear child was gone. At least that worthless midwife had cleaned him up and wrapped him in a blanket.

He knew they should have gone to the hospital and had a physician, not a midwife.

Taking the lifeless infant and the body of his precious wife next to him, he settled down atop the pillows. He closed his eyes and imagined the happy conversations they would have been having now, and the plans they would have made for their family. If only they had lived!

Opening his eyes, he began to sing a little song he remembered from when he was a child.

Suddenly he stopped his singing. Catching the sight of their reflection in the mirror above the bed, the candlelight revealed the image of the three of them. He was captivated by just how much their son resembled his dear, sweet mother.

"Yes!" he declared aloud, "My son, you have your mother's bright red hair! You look just like your mama!

Remembering the missive of the afternoon, he said, "At least your Auntie and Uncle shall be here for your funerals."

He felt such fatigue. He was so tired, perhaps he would sleep just the one night with his family.

The grand salon had been turned into a winter wonderland. Remarkably there was no snow yet, and with such mild weather it did not feel like Christmas. Yet, everyone was happy just being in each other's company.

Rory and Fitzwilliam spent the afternoon in the study. The unlimited use of Darcy House was being discussed, and Rory was fighting the generosity off as best he could. Rory's pride would not allow him to accept extended residency. At last, he agreed that they would stay six months whilst they searched for a house within their means.

Plans for the wedding ceremony were on schedule. The addition of Lord and Lady Matlock and their son and daughter rounded out the guest list. No one insisted when Lady Catherine sent regrets. It was felt that she could not bear being at Pemberly without her daughter being mistress.

Fleming cleared his throat at the door of the study. He held a tray revealing a black-bordered envelope. The men knew at once it was reporting a death. Walking toward the man, he saw that it was addressed to Bingley.

"Shall I go and get him, cousin?"

" Yes, Rory, thank you, and perhaps Jane should accompany him." Darcy directed.

In moments, the Bingleys appeared with Elizabeth at their side. She wanted to be of help should they need her.

"I am so sorry, old man," Darcy said, as he put his hand upon his shoulder.

Charles, nodded his head toward Darcy, looked at Jane, and then opened the envelope.

It was from Louisa sent from New York. He read it quickly once, then told everyone the contents.

"Apparently Caroline was discovered in New York whilst the Hursts were there on their second honeymoon. She had married a very wealthy man from London by the name of Godfrey. It was he who met her at Lambton right after our wedding. They took passage on the *HMS Sonnet* and made immigration to America. They made their home in a mansion on Park Avenue in New York City. Mr. Godfrey made his fortune in banking. The Hursts had seen them twice before learning their whereabouts. It seems Caroline had nearly been sent to Bedlam at some point just before they left the Empire. She was under a doctor's care for mental problems. However, she was also with child. Mr. Godfrey learned that she had been taking laudanum for many months. Even during her confinement. They feel this may have caused their deaths. Caroline died a wealthy woman, that was her goal to marry well."

Condolences were expressed by everyone.

Charles and Jane discussed the situation and decided they would not wear black. Charles elected to wear an armband, but he would dance at the wedding. He forbade Jane to wear black.

The Darcys were well pleased with the wedding ceremony. Elizabeth was proud of Mary. For a very religious girl, she finally stopped spouting sermons. Elizabeth felt the Darcy influence had helped her become more accepting of others.

Mr. Bennet enjoyed coffee with three of his daughters the morning after the wedding. Georgie was also invited and told she was an honorary Bennet. Mr. Bennet spoke: "Perhaps it was being away from Longbourn that helped Mary relax. I dare say, I shall be fearful of returning to Mildred, myself."

"Then do not do it!" his daughters begged. He smiled at them, "You make me proud that you care about your papa."

"Papa, Fitzwilliam and I love having you here. We hope you shall never go back. Soon you shall have a little grandbaby to spoil."

Jane entered the conversation, "Papa, Charles and I have two homes. I am sure that when I ask him, he shall want you to spend some of your time with us, as well."

"We do not need to decide the future over one cup of coffee, would you not agree?" Mr. Bennet replied with a sincere smile. He was a man who was learning to parent rather late in life.

Elizabeth was sorry to see Charles and Jane leave. They promised to return for the birth of the baby, but they were eager to get to their farm. The house seemed so empty for they took Kitty and Mr. Bennet with them. Georgiana was as lonely as could be.

The carriage left at first light. Fitzwilliam and Elizabeth and Georgie stood on the steps and waved good bye. The Gardiner carriage was following along just to spend two weeks as Lucille wanted to help Jane settle in to her new home.

It was just a short seven miles to Pemberly. Practically a good ramble in the spring.

Returning to the house, Elizabeth tried to lighten the mood. She suggested that they should play games in the evening and enjoy hot chocolate next to the fireplace to welcome the new year.

"Kitty shall return in two weeks, Georgie. Then you shall have so much to tell each other."

"I do not understand why Father would not let me go." Georgie pouted, feeling sorry for herself.

The three kept busy during the day and adjusted as well as possible.

New Year's Day arrived. The attempt to ring out the old with hot chocolate did not accomplish the goal. All three were feeling somewhat bored and restless. Georgiana got out the almanac.

"Look, Brother, the weather for today, New Year's Day, is to be mild. Would not the new carriage provide a smooth trip for my sister and the baby? Could we not go and visit for a one hour tea? We could see the house and the almond trees."

"Fitzwilliam, it may be a very good idea. It would certainly be my final visit for quite some while. When our baby arrives, I shall be housebound.

"Miss Shannon is coming tomorrow and taking up residence in her assigned rooms. She shall hover over me, and should there be any ill from today, she could make it right with all that constant care." Liz-Beth looked up at him, adoringly. "But it 'tis your decision. You shall decide. No one may call for the carriage except yourself, my love."

"I cannot abide these long faces. It is against my better judgment, but we shall go for just a one hour tea. Am I to be understood?" he shook his head as he spoke. They had very little doubt they would heed his one hour time limit.

It was a beautiful day for a carriage ride, and remarkably all three were in high spirits.

Taking the back road off the property into Lambton, they had just climbed the final hill. The view from the top was exquisite. Lambton in the near distance looked picturesque.

All was going according to plan when on the downhill side, the carriage began listing to the right. Fitzwilliam heard a rubbing sound and tapped the top of the carriage to alert Clark, the driver. Either he did not hear, or he did not respond due to an emergency.

Elizabeth look frightened. She grabbed the side of the upholstered bench and held it tightly. Her husband's eyes were upon her. He put his arm around her and held onto her.

Fitzwilliam pulled Georgie onto the seat next to him and held her with his other arm.

As calmly as possible, he warned them that there may be a bumpy outcome or maybe even a crash. It did not look encouraging. The carriage was gaining speed, and there was a sharp curve in the road ahead. Within seconds his prediction came true.

The carriage veered off the roadway and plunged into a rather deep ravine. The fall was about twelve feet. The vehicle skidded onto its right side. This placed Elizabeth's head nearly out the window and upon the ground. She could still hear the screams of those poor horses as the coach slid to a dusty stop.

Georgiana screamed as they saw their driver, Mr. Clark, being thrown from his seat.

He flew helplessly through the air, right past their window. They would not know until they got out of the carriage that he landed upon the face of a large boulder about ten feet below them.

Fitzwilliam knew there would be no help for the man. He was in shock seeing the faithful Mr. Clark lose his life so quickly.

There was so much dust it was difficult to see inside the carriage. Breathing was hindered by all the dust particles. He looked at his wife. She was not bleeding as far as he could see. "Are you well, Liz-Beth?" he asked, trying to sound calm and in control.

Georgie declared herself to be unharmed and asked if she could climb up and get out of the carriage. Darcy told her to sit still until he could determine if the carriage was stable.

"Liz-Beth, are you well, and how is everything with our child?"

"I believe my arm to be stuck. My forearm appears to be wedged between the seat and the upholstery on the door. I do not think I can loose it myself," she explained.

"Georgie, can you move?" he asked.

"Yes, do you want me to climb out?" Georgie was eager to be out of the carriage.

Very carefully, he opened the left door next to Georgie. He had to reach up and push the door up, and then swing it outward. The door was heavy, and it took muscle to push it open. The left door was on top and the right upon the ground.

Fitzwilliam grabbed the doorjamb and pulled himself up and out of the coach. Thankfully the carriage did not move. He had been afraid it landed precariously, but it was solidly settled.

He walked around the carriage and looked up the hillside. There was no one in sight.

The horses were all dead. It was a mercy that none lingered and suffered. The four strong Warm-bloods were dead. He hoped Lizzy would not look at them.

Pulling Georgie out of the carriage, he told her where to stand and keep watch for vehicles or riders. He took the time to explain how voices are difficult to carry uphill, so if she saw someone she should alert him first, then shout "help" over and over. No screaming.

Back in the carriage, he checked on Elizabeth. "Sweetheart, are you certain you are well? Do you have pain anywhere? Can you move your right hand?"

"I honestly do not feel any pain. Of course, I may be in shock. My right hand seems to be in good stead. My right forearm does not hurt, but it is immobile. It is stuck."

"Yes, I know," he said, brushing his hand across her forehead. 'I am so very sorry, my darling. I am trying to think of a way to extricate your limb."

Suddenly she had a thought. "Darling, do you remember the hunting knife I gave you as a wedding present? Was it this particular carriage we were in when you were playing with it?"

"Yes, I believe it was," he said, thoughtfully. "At least I think it may have been."

"Remember you were making me so nervous with that blade; I feared you would cut yourself. I believe I asked you to put it in the compartment," she added, trying to remember.

"Yes, you did. I put it in this compartment, I think. I jolly well hope I did, anyway!" he answered her, feeling more optimistic by the moment.

Carefully moving around inside the carriage, he turned his head to the side and reached into the cabinet he hoped held the knife.

"Yes! Here it is!" he cried. "Now, be quite still, Liz-Beth. I shall just tear away at the door upholstery. Just a bit at a time until you are freed."

Slowly and very carefully he worked with the knife. He thought he could hear Georgie outside the carriage standing near to Liz-Beth.

Sternly he asked her to return to her position and keep a close watch. He reminded her not to scream. Just yell 'help.'

At length, the arm was freed! Reaching over her, he rubbed it and checked it for injury.

For some reason it reminded her of the day she killed Wickham. He had put her in the bath and checked her left arm for possible injury.

"Now, Liz-Beth, are you able to move? Do you think you could stand beneath the door and allow me to pull you up through the opening? Maybe I could climb into the driver's box and locate something you could put your feet upon. Or, I could possibly clasp my hand s together and hoist you up, as if mounting?"

"Please give me a moment to think about it, darling."

Before she could take a moment, she felt a very sharp pain! "OH, NO! Fitzwilliam, something is very wrong! Please. I have such pain. 'Tis in my thighs and the very small of my back, right here. Oh, God, I do not want to scream or yell. I shall frighten Georgie. Hold my hand, my love."

Darcy took her hand and allowed her to squeeze it as hard as she could. Her eyes brimmed with tears, and she bit her lip so hard she drew blood.

Concerned as he was about her labor, he could not get his thoughts off that steep hill just outside.

Please Lord, make a way out of here. Send help, and protect my sweet wife and our innocent little child. Let all be well with the birth.

He looked at Elizabeth. He could tell she was praying, as well. Suddenly Georgie screamed, "I see someone coming, I think."

"Darling, are you all right if I leave you for a few moments. If someone is coming, I shall need to shout to them. I do not think Georgie's voice could be heard."

"Yes, yes. Go, go. Please."

Grabbing the doorjamb, he lifted himself up quickly, and scrambled out toward the road. He looked up and saw a little phaeton and pony. A lone lady was driving. Georgie began to yell, "Help!"

Fitzwilliam joined her with his deep voice that easily carried up the hillside! The driver looked as if she would pass them by, but she pulled in at last and stopped. He could see her set the brake. Thankfully she knew how to drive well. Watching the woman disembark, he yelled again.

"We are down here. Can you see us?"

"Mr. Darcy? Is that you, sir? It is I, Miss Shannon Colleen."

"Thank God!" Elizabeth called. "You are an answer to prayer."

"Is that Elizabeth's voice I hear?" she shouted.

"Have you a rope?" Fitzwilliam asked.

"No, I have no rope I am afraid. However, I have a trunk full of clothing. Let me use a knife and cut my gowns. I can tie them together and build a makeshift rope," she answered.

"Please do take care to tie it tightly, Miss Shannon."

"Have no fear, Mr. Darcy. My father is a fisherman, and he had long taught his children to tie knots with skill."

Just then, Elizabeth called Fitzwilliam, "Husband, I have lost my waters."

"Not to worry, Liz-Beth, it is a common enough thing to pee when frightened."

"No, love, my bag of waters that holds our child. Please tell her I am in labor."

This news made him nearly panic. He yelled the intelligence up to Miss Shannon.

She took it calmly as though she expected as much. If she was concerned, she hid it from him.

Sweet Jesus, Mary and Joseph! Protect that fine lady and her wee one. Show me how to get down there and get her out of that carriage. And send help for anyone else injured here.

Georgie walked back to the side of the carriage Elizabeth occupied. She called to her, "Lizzy, I have been such a miserable little sister. You have been so kind and loving to me, and I returned evil to you. I was so jealous I could not see straight. I even prayed that God would punish you because my brother and father love you so much. But, I did not want to see you get hurt.

"Please do not die Lizzy. And do not let your baby die." By now the child was crying.

Fitzwilliam heard his sister and became very angry with her. The fact that she was a child did not calm his fears. Her words made him very fearful.

"Georgie stop talking this nonsense. No one is going to die today. Go and sit upon that log and watch for vehicles or riders. If you see anyone coming, call out 'help.' Do not scream."

Checking on Miss Shannon's progress, he was shocked to see her descending the rope rapidly.

Truthfully, she might have made it down safely without the rope, but to be certain it was a good thing to have. He made a mental note never to leave home without stocking the carriage for an emergency.

Darcy assisted Miss Shannon inside the coach by clasping hands together and giving her an upward lift.

Once inside, she had only a limited way to examine Elizabeth. Her patient could not lie down nor was there anyway the two of them would be able to get her out of the coach.

"Elizabeth you know you are in labor. Do not fret. Know that God is taking care of you."

Fitzwilliam was listening, although there was no room for him to go into the carriage. He was leaning against the left side and trying to listen to them through the open door at the top of the coach.

"Let us all trust in God. He shall safely deliver your baby," Miss Shannon's Irish accent was stronger due to the stress she was experiencing. Elizabeth and Darcy agreed.

"Tell me about your pains. When do you think you may have had your last one?"

Loud enough to be heard, she asked Fitzwilliam if he had a pocket watch. Elizabeth thought her last pain may have been about ten minutes ago. Ten minutes and still not another pain. Miss Shannon asked Fitzwilliam to time the pains.

Just as Elizabeth cried out in pain, Georgie yelled, "Help!"

Fitzwilliam apologised to his wife and ran out to see who was approaching. To his extreme relief, it was a wagon with a man and wife in the driver seat. The man, dressed as a farmer, was holding the reins, and the woman was holding a white box.

Fitzwilliam tried to pull himself up Miss Shannon's rope and yell at the same time. It was steeper than it looked. He certainly needed her 'rope' to assist his climb.

The wagon stopped. The driver set the brake, and he helped the woman down. Both hurried to the rim, and looking down, a familiar voice said, "Darcy, is that you?"

"Yes, Charles, it is! We crashed, and we are in dire need of assistance. Miss Shannon is here and Elizabeth is in labor. Have you a rope in your wagon?"

"Darcy, I do." He got the rope and was back in a flash. He tied the rope off and began to rapidly descent the hillside. Jane stayed above, praying for all of them. Reaching them, Charles asked what he could do to assist.

Darcy asked him to please take Georgie to Jane. She had no business witnessing Liz-Beth's labor.

Done is seconds, Charles was back at his side. Inside the carriage, poor Elizabeth was beginning to groan softly. She tried to suffer in relative silence. Pain and worry were starting to consume her. Thirst was a problem also; her mouth was very dry. Her lips were chapped, but remembering Mr. Clark's cruel fate, she felt blessed, indeed.

Climbing up to reach the open door, Fitzwilliam looked at Liz-Beth. He asked Miss Shannon the difficult question, "What is the best course to follow, Miss Shannon? Shall we bring her out?"

Was his wife well enough to allow the two men to lift her out of the carriage, take her up the hillside, and then home in the wagon? At least the wagon had a bed, and she could lie down. They were no more than five and forty minutes from home, going slowly.

Pulling herself up to look out of the carriage, Miss Shannon pondered the question. It would be night before the baby's birth. They must not be out there in the wreckage after dark.

Casting her eyes at the steep ravine again, and remembering its depth, she looked back at the carriage. There was no room to move about. It would be a difficult delivery. Taking a laboring woman, whose water had broken, up a steep, dusty bank was risky as well.

She nodded her head. "Aye, let us get your sweet wife out of this carriage and up yon hill. Her sister and a wagon await along with the promise of the luxury and comfort of her home and the cleanliness of the labor room she worked so hard to prepare."

Both men helped Miss Shannon out of the carriage. She told Elizabeth she would see her at the top of the hill. Then she made her ascent up to Jane and Georgie. It was agreed that Fitzwilliam would go inside the carriage and clasp his hands together for his wife. Hopefully, she could take it as a leg up, and both men would hold her steady. Then, Fitzwilliam would climb out, and both would lift her down. Time seemed to stand still as they worked this process. Both men were glad she was a slight girl, and even with the baby weight she was light. It also helped that she was athletic and had perfect balance. She was able to hold herself at the top of the carriage and await the four arms that would assist her gently to the ground. Once out of the carriage, Fitzwilliam followed instructions and tied Elizabeth's skirts through her legs, as if making bloomers from the gown. Miss Shannon called out her approval of the job he had done.

Charles tied the bottom end of the rope he had provided to a tree near the carriage. This made a taut, railing type of device the men could use to help pull themselves up the hillside.

Fitzwilliam used Miss Shannon's rope to place behind his wife, using it as a sling and keeping it off her stomach. He then tied the other end of Miss Shannon's rope around his waist. Going uphill backward, slowly and carefully he towed his wife.

Following his instructions, she paced herself slowly and sure-footedly up the hillside.

Charles helped Darcy put her into the back of the wagon. Then he slowly and safely drove them to Pemberly. Darcy rode with Elizabeth in the back of the wagon with the almonds, and hazel nuts. Georgiana sat beside Miss Shannon in the little phaeton.

Finally they reached the first checkpoint and told the guard of the accident. Mr. Gram was to be told about the need to rescue Mr. Clark and to see to the Warmbloods. A rider must be sent to Lambton to fetch the physician for Mr. Clark. A messenger was sent to the house to tell Mrs. Reynolds to make everything ready for Elizabeth. Several warm baths should be drawn as well.

Arriving at Pemberly, Miss Shannon was amazed at the skill level and preparations that were set in place for Mrs. Darcy. Elizabeth was in good shape considering all that she had endured. She was not in shock, and her spirits were good.

Fitzwilliam took a very quick bath, put on clean clothes, and went straight to Liz-Beth's side. It was the only time he left her. He needed to be with her, but not covered with dust and dirt. Sitting with his wife, he waited for instructions.

Quickly washing up, and changing clothes, Miss Shannon entered the birthing room and examined her patient.

Fitzwilliam stood by his wife and told her what an amazing job she did getting out of the carriage. He rubbed her back and said how proud he was of the way she handled herself at the accident. He thanked her for being such a wonderful sister to Georgie. He told her she was a woman of powerful influence and he was proud of her.

Soon, Miss Shannon asked him to sit behind his wife and support her back and encourage her.

At last, Liz-Beth was told to bear down and push as hard as she could. She did not want to cry out, but her midwife told her it would activate muscles she needed to push the baby out. This was a lengthy process and took so much longer than Fitzwilliam thought it would. His poor wife was so tired. He could scarcely believe she could work this hard after the energy the accident had taken away. Liz-Beth worked on and on, pushing as hard as she could. Her face and her entire body were covered in sweat. He tried to use a towel to keep her skin dry, but it did not help much. How he wished he could push for her.

Miss Shannon had to call him twice before he heard her. She motioned for him to stand beside her. He was shocked to see his wife's body stretched so far open. He could see a head with dark curly hair, and Miss Shannon wanted him to see this. "This is where we are, and we have got to get the wee lad out of there as soon as possible. I need her to push harder."

Suddenly he had an idea. Thinking of some horses giving birth whilst walking around, he asked if Elizabeth could stand up. Taking his wife by the hand, he said, "Liz-Beth, our child needs you to be very strong. Think about the mares you have seen that stand and walk around in an effort to drop their foals? Do you remember seeing that?" She nodded and immediately started standing up and moving to walk around the room.

"I know how strong you are my, love. You can do this. Push as hard as you can. Just this one last push, and we can meet our baby."

She walked and then stopped and said, "Oh, I can feel him dropping out—do not let him hit the floor—" Fitzwilliam picked her up and put her onto the chair, and Miss Shannon grabbed the babe and pulled him clear.

Fitzwilliam looked just in time to watch his son come out of the birth canal. "Liz-Beth, we have a son. He is beautiful, just like his mother!"

At that announcement, the baby's loud cry could be heard! His parent's laughed!

Mrs. Reynolds stepped forward and assisted as she was instructed. She helped clean the baby just as she had for Fitzwilliam and Georgie.

Soon the room was filled with the sounds of a baby crying his lungs out!

"There now, laddie, 'twas your Mama do'in all the work and feel'in all the pain. Sure and she is the one with the rights to be do'n the cry'in!" Miss Shannon's accent had slipped back with all the excitement!

Sweet Jesus, Mary, and Joseph, 'twas a miracle you did for these three folks. Thank all of ye.

"Papa, come and take your son. Your wife still has work to do. Lord bless her! Miss Shannon got busy delivering the afterbirth and completing the care of her patient.

When done she smiled at the healthy and very happy family. Elizabeth was now holding their son. Looking at her husband, she said, "My love, it occurs to me that we have not yet selected a name for our fine Darcy boy." Her husband laughed. "Liz-Beth, you and I are a bit lacking when it comes to meeting someone and learning their name. Would you not agree? We have just met our son and do not know his name!"

She laughed, "Well, we cannot call him Handsome Boy, because it is too much like his father's name. I do not want to call him George because of Wickham, and if we call him Thomas it may hurt your father's feelings. What shall we do, my love?"

"Liz-Beth, it seems to me that we would have been in so much trouble out there on that ravine without Charles' help. God sent him in an answer to prayer. I believe all three of us were praying." Miss Shannon nodded silently in agreement.

"I have often felt that Cousin Rory was an instrument in bringing you back to me from that terrible place that took you from me, my darling," she suggested, and he agreed.

Darcy said, "So, 'Charles Rory Darcy?" He looked at his wife.

"Well, when you think about it, he would not be here had we not both gone to Kent." Elizabeth added. "Might we add, Kent?"

"Charles Rory Kent Darcy," they said together, trying it on for size. Impressive.

Or, perhaps Charles Kent Rory Darcy. The uncles names divided by a neutral name?

"This way we can be diplomats and call him Kent. No one has preference," she smiled.

"Darling, you know our competitive brothers so well!"

Having named the boy, they now took him from his blanket and examined him closely. They inspected his fingers and toes, his tiny genitals, and even his mouth, though he had no teeth as yet. He was perfect. His hair matched his parents. His legs and arms were very long, and he looked like a baby born at exactly nine months.

"My, Miss Shannon, he is so big. How much bigger would he have grown if he were born on February five?"

"Mr. and Mrs. Darcy, I have been concerned about the lad's size since I met you, Mr. Darcy. I worried about such a wee mama. God worked it out. Now that you have had a large baby, Mrs. Darcy, even if your next is a full-term and large baby, even bigger than his older brother, all well be well. There is no doubt we had a miracle today. He could not have been bigger and allowed for you to deliver him."

Elizabeth remarked how quickly they seem to do things. They fell in love, quickly; married quickly; and even had a baby five weeks faster than the normal nine months!

After thanking Miss Shannon and Mrs. Reynolds, the little family rose to go to their bed.

"Come, dearest, we are going take our son to bed and sleep as long as he shall allow us."

Standing upon flimsy, shaky legs, Liz-Beth looked at her husband, "My gait is funny. I can feel it. My left foot is pointed decidedly to the left, and my right foot is straight ahead."

Her husband chuckled softly, "I have seen you walk worse than this, beloved. Believe me."

Kent was placed in his cradle next to the largest bed in the mansion. The three Darcys slept soundly.

Miss Shannon went to her rooms to sleep for about a week, she hoped!

Mrs. Reynolds was assigned the happy task of announcing the little heir's birth. She went merrily into the grand salon. Telling everything but the child's name, she relieved their minds when she said everyone was healthy, and all was well. On the morrow the new parents would come to the salon and show off their son. They would tell the baby's name then.

Mr. Gram approached Mrs. Reynolds with exciting news. Mr. Clark was recovered from the accident scene. He was at the physician's office in Lambton. His wife was with him. Miraculously, he had survived the accident with several broken bones, but the doctor assured them he would recover.

Mrs. Reynolds gave the message to Otis who took it quietly to Mr. Darcy, after determining the little family was awake. They rejoiced to hear such amazing and wonderful news.

Charles and Jane had been so happy that they decided to play farmer and take nuts to their neighbors! They'd had no idea the Darcys were even out on that road. They were just out living their dream when all of a sudden…

Chapter 12

"You might say, it pays to plan ahead."

-Anonymous

The Darcys had delayed their trip to town long enough. Ellen Gates insisted that the publisher meet with the staff. No one had expected the financial success of the first four titles. Darcy was glad to complete some business with his banker and spend time with Rory at their club. Fencing was still a love of his life.

Fitzwilliam had been known as one of the ten richest men under age thirty. His banker had just informed him that his complete profits for the past year alone had nearly doubled his net worth.

As Edward Gardiner could have told him, increased business means increased work and a greater investment of personal time. In an effort to reassign some of the labor, Darcy looked forward to giving additional duties to his personal banker. He was eager to spend time with the man and redistribute some of his responsibilities. Elizabeth had been partly responsible for his tremendous increase. She had good instincts and often saw opportunities early. Her own enterprises were going well. The horses were very profitable, and Uncle and Grandpapa parlayed their export project into a very good business.

The Knightly Press, now called Empowerment Publishing, was beginning to return a profit.

Resistance to the health book was stronger than imagined, and Elizabeth was forced to sell the volume by mail. Advertising was difficult to purchase as the *Topics* refused to sell space for the book. According to Elizabeth, this was an opportunity to start their own weekly paper. Printed on their Empowerment Press, the tabloid was delivered free of charge.

Keeping the publication in a quarter-page format helped lower the costs, but expenses were difficult to control. Especially with the owner out of town and management unfamiliar with the marketing and advertising concept. What began as a marketing tool, soon became a respectable vehicle for news, and to everyone's surprise, the little paper caught on and actually started returning a profit.

On their seventh night in town, Darcy had dinner served in their room. He wanted to speak privately with his wife.

Reluctantly, he asked her to sit beside him on the sofa. Slowly he began to speak, very carefully so as not to alarm her more than necessary. "Fitzwilliam, what in the world has gotten into you? Last night you wore a long-sleeve nightshirt to bed and refused to remove it when we loved. I cannot begin to think what you are about. I have never known the cold to bother you. It was an excuse. I insist you tell me now."

He stood to his feet, moving somewhat away from her. Lingering there for a few moments, he made eye contact. "Now, I do not want you to be alarmed and for God's sake, do not be angry with me. But, it does not seem any better, and I thought I should perhaps show you, my love."

At this, she stood to her feet and practically threw her hands upon his chest. Her eyes held a look of pure fear. "You have cut yourself. Have you not? Cut your arm? Which one? How deeply?" Her voice sounded more frightened than angry. "Did you do this yesterday morning when I thought you were with your banker?"

In clear avoidance of her questions, he slowly rolled up his right sleeve and began to unwind a makeshift bandage. She saw him gently uncover a deep gash in his forearm. It looked swollen and very red and smelled of pus even though she was two feet from him. She carefully touched the flesh near the wound. It was hot! He winced when she touched him.

"I started to send Otis for Mr. White after I left the club, but Rory warned me not to do it. He said physicians react poorly to infections, and if any pus results, he may even suggest amputation of my arm in order to preserve my life."

At this, his wife nearly swooned. She wanted to curse Rory for opening her husband's arm, but she realised it was as much Fitzwilliam's fault as his cousin's.

"This morning I was light headed, then a very strong headache started. My arm hurts so badly, I could not hold Kent when he came to me with his little hands up. The pain is worse, and I know it is starting to smell awful."

"Oh, Fitzwilliam Darcy, what am I going to do with you?" Putting her hand upon his forehead, she felt his fever. Elizabeth wasted no time in calling for a tepid bath. She went to her dressing room and withdrew her box of herbs. It was well known that Mrs. Darcy went nowhere without her 'medicine kit.' Looking through her bottles, she found the one containing yellow powder, marked 'Curcuma' it was Turmeric from India. Next, she found one of the large bottles of wild honey and a roll of wide, clean bandages tied with a thin strip of gauze.

She took Darcy into his bath and held his arm out of the water. Carefully pouring a small pitcher of water, she allowed it to gently cascade over the wound. He winced in pain, although he was careful to try to hide his discomfort. Getting out of the bath, he felt somewhat better. The cool water refreshed him a bit.

Elizabeth mixed some of the of the powders with the honey as a binder. Next, she sprinkled a good amount of the powder directly into the gash, then gently applied the paste into the wound.

At last, she wrapped the forearm with a clean bandage, and pulling a fresh nightshirt over his head, she put her husband to bed. His eyes were glazed, and she thought to keep water and a cloth nearby to bathe his forehead as needed.

Getting into bed with him, she felt his forehead again and noticed his fever was as strong as before. She prayed for his recovery, knowing that this type of wound could be fatal.

Her slumber was brief, as Darcy awakened her with a violent fit of tossing and turning. He was speaking frantically in his sleep. Verging on tears, his words were most earnest. She could not help but listen to him speak out the thoughts of his feverish dream. "Sorry, old man," he was repenting to someone, "I should have given you a chance to read it, but I burned it instead. I am not a good friend to you, nor a good brother. Please forgive me, old chap."

Not wanting to wake him, she reasoned that his words were due to the fever and the infection. She would tell him later if he wished to know his dream.

Rising early with Kent, Liz-Beth cared for their son, and both had breakfast. Fitzwilliam was sleeping late, and she thought it best to let his body have a chance to fight the infection and heal the wound.

When Darcy awakened, he was ill tempered and agitated. He called for his wife and insisted they look at the wound. Perhaps they should call Mr. White after all. He felt horrible, and the wound was even more painful than it had been last night. To make matters worse, it had a huge bump in the middle. Fitzwilliam was indignant when she explained that the bump was a good thing and the presence of additional pain was also a good sign. She suggested they call for another tepid bath, rinse the wound, repeat the application of the yellow powders, reapply the mixture of powder and honey, and then cover it with a fresh bandage.

A light breakfast of bouillon and toast was ordered, and he took it along with some comfrey tea. Immediately he went back to bed and slept until seven in the evening.

Rory paced the salon of their new home on Piper Street. He would not be still, and he would not tell Mary what was troubling him. He wanted to go to Darcy House but had a nagging feeling that he should stay far away from his sister. He could not face her anger.

"Rory, what on earth has troubled your spirit this morning?"
"I am just somewhat anxious, I suppose. What say you to a nice visit to Gracechurch Street? Uncle and Aunt are always entertaining. Perhaps a walk in the park would be good, as well."

Perhaps Uncle has heard how Darcy is recovering from his wound. If he does not have the intelligence I may prevail upon him to visit and discover the truth.

By five of the clock, Elizabeth awakened her husband. His son wanted to kiss papa good night. The three of them sat upon the bed. Whilst talking to Kent, Darcy suddenly told Liz-Beth that his head felt somewhat relieved.

Elizabeth immediately took Kent to his nanny. As she returned to their bed chamber, she requested a dinner tray for her husband to be delivered in one hour.

Returning to Darcy, she saw him sitting up in bed and beginning to unwrap his arm. He looked up at her peevishly, and without so much as a proper greeting, he snapped, "It is building up pressure. I believe it feels as if it is oozing something inside the wrapping," he complained fretfully.

Taking a shallow bowl from the table, she went to the bed, bent her leg at the knee and sat at an angle upon the bed, getting as close as she could. Placing the bowl under his arm, she began to slowly and carefully open the bandage. They saw that indeed it was oozing blood and pus.

The thing smelt as terrible as could be imagined! Instructed to sit still, Darcy sat quietly while his wife most carefully poured warm water over the wound. Gently, she pressed around the healthy flesh, up toward the wound itself. Darcy bent his head more fully over the wound to get a better look. She frowned a warning at him, "Now, Fitzwilliam, do be patient. You cannot rush healing." More blood and pus came rushing out. Remarkably, the patient claimed to feel relief. This process was repeated several times, each time with Darcy feeling improvement.

Repeating the process with the yellow powders, and the compound of powders and honey, another clean bandage was applied upon his arm.

"There now, you petulant, little boy of mine, I think we shall just keep you in bed for a while longer. Your body is working hard to recover, and you need to assist by staying quiet. Just lie back and let me take care of you."

Darcy actually enjoyed his sponge bath, although admittedly, he was not strong enough to show as much interest as his mind suggested. A clean nightshirt was put on, and the dinner tray was delivered. He ate with a hearty appetite. For the first time since seeing the wound, Liz-Beth was encouraged and felt optimistic for his recovery.

By the fourth day, Fitzwilliam was upset about the time being wasted in bed. His complaints were effective enough for his wife to allow him to dress and lounge about the house. His fever had left him, and his arm was beginning to look as though it had suffered only a deep cut rather than a life-threatening infection.

"If tomorrow it rinses clean and has no foulness, we can stitch up the wound. With a dressing, you should be able to go about normally—if you continue to improve," she declared with audible relief in her voice.

"I feel as though I have been away for a week. Kent looks so much bigger to me. Was I out of my head for a while, my love? What transpired during my absence? Have you made any major purchases? Do we now own a shipping company or a manufacturing plant?"

"Nothing at all. I have not been ten steps away from your bed the entire time. I would like to lecture you, but I know it shall do no good. I must learn that you cannot change all your habits. Fencing is a part of you, just as archery is a part of me."

"That sounds familiar. Who has said that?" he asked.

"What? Was it one of your fever dreams?" she asked. "I believe the first night you were speaking to Charles. He is the only one I have ever heard you call, 'old man' or 'old chap.'

"You were so very sorry for something or other. I could not make sense of it. You told him you had burned something, and you were sorry. I thought it was the heat from your fever and that of your arm which made you dream of burning something," she tried to bring reason from his fever dream.

"Fevers are always like that, are they not?" she said. "It is a horrible insult to the body."

"Elizabeth?" he asked as she got into bed beside him. "If I had access to certain information about Caroline Bingley, and it was of an unattractive nature, what do you think should be done with it?"

"I hardly know, is this actual information based upon good intelligence?" she inquired.

"The best authority of all. Her diary," he stated plainly.

"Excuse me, darling? Her diary?"

"Yes. Clovis brought it to me after its discovery. It seems it had been in the possession of one of our chamber maids. She had been reading it as though it were a novel. Apparently, it had been taking her weeks to read it through. Mrs. Reynolds caught her reading it whilst she should have been working, took it from her, and gave it to Clovis. He brought it to me.

"He had great concerns because we were both mentioned in it. It seems he questioned the girl and determined she had told no one. Then, he and Mrs. Reynolds, discussed what should be done. Because Caroline's obsession with me was the focus of the journal, they gave the girl severance pay, and a footman took her to Newcastle where she has family. They even placed her with new employment," he explained.

"My, what a lot of trouble," she said. "What in the world was in that book?"

"Among other things, my beloved, was a plan to come to Pemberly for the wedding, hide at the top of the stairs, and await you." Here he put his arms around her protectively and continued. "Her intent was to push you down the stairs and kill you. Then, ingratiate herself with me and after my mourning period, marry me.

"Clovis told me that he was with us that morning, sitting by my bedside when his men called him out for an emergency. One of his men actually saw her hiding in the hallway near the top of the second floor staircase. She was barefoot, and appeared to be waiting, crouching down, just out of sight. After the ceremony, she returned to the house and went into Father's study. She had been going through his desk and removed some letters.

"Apparently she thought it was my desk. She surrendered the letters, and a servant met her in the hall with her bags. She was escorted off property, driven to the inn at Lambton, and last seen getting into a carriage with a well-dressed gentleman."

"Oh, Fitzwilliam, I cannot tell you how horrible that makes me feel. You tried to tell me you feared what she might do, and I am sorry I did not believe you.

"I have chills when I think she would have killed Kent, too. She did not see me that morning because I was with you. Oh, how God protected all of us!

"But, husband, why did she want letters from your desk?"

"She wrote in her diary that she was looking for a forger to fabricate a letter, from me to her confessing our, ah, certain nighttime occurrences that transpired and an offer of marriage."

Fitzwilliam looked pale, for with this information, he had just confessed.

Ignoring that, she pressed on with another question. "Did she write about when she met Godfrey? Do we know anything of their wedding or when they were planning to go to America?"

"No," he said, shaking his head, "there was no mention of the man. However, there was a record of a man who was traveling through Devonshire and staying at the same inn. He was apparently wealthy, and she sold her body to him to finance her demented dream.

"Caroline was low on funds, for she had been spending money on hired carriages to track me down. She bribed individuals to learn our whereabouts. She wasted money buying clothes and jewels along the way."

"What a sick woman. Or at least I hope she was sick and not just evil." Elizabeth shivered as she made the comment, practically to herself.

"If no romance with Godfrey, who in the world was he? Had he been staying at the Lambton Inn? Was he the child's father?" she had many questions in her head.

"We have no clues as to Godfrey. It is more possible that her wealthy 'customer' in Devonshire fathered the child. Perhaps she did not yet know Godfrey when she left her diary behind.

"It is possible that she met him the first time in front of the Lambton Inn that same morning she was removed from Pemberly.

"Sweetheart, I hurried over a confession about Caroline. Perhaps you did not hear me say that she wrote of having relations with me. She recorded watching me drink, and when she could determine that I was drunk, she would follow me into my bed. This went on for quite some time. She wrote that she was hoping to become with child and force a marriage. When I was sober, she thought I did not remember because I was so good at denying everything, and Charles believed me," he looked into her eyes as he told her. "I am afraid I was very good at lying when needed."

"Oh, I see," she said, looking at him, "This explains why your staff put so much effort, time, and money into moving the maid to Newcastle. Obviously they also knew it to be true."

"Liz-Beth, it was my fault. I could have locked my door. I have been so troubled about telling you. This was exactly the type of situation you were wishing me to supply a name to when you directly requested it of me that second night here in London. I was so fearful all the while we were here, because I knew she was here. I knew the lengths she would go to, and I was nearly insane with worry over her talking to you. I sensed you would believe her, and greatly feared you would leave me forever.

"I am still very poor at communicating with my wife, but I draw your attention to the fact that I am telling you now.

"I have been miserable about that bloody diary. I could not let you read it, so I could not ask you what to do? I did not know if Charles should have read it, but if he did, he would know the rat I was, indeed. I need his friendship, Liz-Beth.

"What are your thoughts?"

Elizabeth took him by surprise. She kissed him. It was a serious kiss, the type that committed lovers bestow upon one another.

"Darling man, I adore you! Mr. Darcy, you are all sweetness to me. What would you want of Charles? Has he not perhaps suffered enough where his sister is concerned? She is dead and gone from him. What matters the how, when, where, what, and why of her story?"

"Then, there is one more thing I need to ask you. Please forgive me for not telling you all about Caroline in London when you asked me. I deeply regret that I did not respect and trust you enough to tell you then. Even though I did not know you during those years, I need you to forgive me for what I did with her."

Elizabeth smiled at him. His confession pleased her to the bone! She touched his cheek and said, "I am sorry I cannot forgive you what was not an offense against me. You had her, you can never change what you did with her. You failed to tell me when I asked, and I forgive you for that failure. You lied to me when I asked you again in front of Charles and Jane; I forgive you for that, but most importantly, you are telling me now, and I thank you for that!"

"About the diary, did I do the right thing by burning it?"

"Sad to say, I think Charles and Louisa are proud of Caroline, in thinking she married so well. What is the harm in letting them think she had an advantageous marriage?"

"So, you think it would be wrong to tell all of this to Charles?"

"Darling, there is a fine old saying, with which everyone is familiar, 'save your breath to cool your porridge.' She is gone. Your wife and son are still here on the earth with you! We should rejoiced in that and be thankful to God." Elizabeth smiled in relief.

"Come here wife! Let me show you how much I love and ardently adore you!"

"Oh, but your arm!" she protested.

"It must be improved, Liz-Beth. I hardly feel it is there!"

"Oh?" she smiled impishly and quickly stoked his enlarged *membre*, "Let me see if you feel 'this' is still there?"

Three days later the Darcys kept an appointment in a second floor office, just outside town. Women did not enter business offices, although that did not stop Elizabeth Darcy. Their appointment had been with a young woman engaged in raising money for a college. A very special college, intended to educate young British women.

"Just think, Handsome Man, that was our final contribution toward our goal…Our little girls shall have a college education.

The world shall open to them, and they shall reach out and achieve their dreams. They shall not need an advantageous marriage. Nothing shall stop them, my love. They shall obtain their own wealth! Our little sisters, Georgiana and Catherine shall gain an education as well, my darling!"

"Shall the school bear our name, Liz-Beth?"

"No! Heavens, it shall not! I want the world to appreciate that many men and women worked together to make this possible."

"Our contributions shall be without recognition. With some subtle exceptions. The library shall be called 'Handsome Man Library,' there shall always be a 'Percival Plaza,' and the dormitory shall be 'Goddess of Horses Hall,' and lastly, the administrator's quarters shall always be known as 'Marigold Manor.'"

Fitzwilliam liked the idea. He reached over and grabbed his wife. He kissed her with feeling and in public!

"Oh, one moment, my amorous husband. Kindly come with me, please." Taking him by the hand, she led him downstairs and across the property where the campus was about to be built. Using a key, they entered the one building standing upon the soon-to-be campus.

It was bare, except for one conference table and a few chairs.

"What is this," he asked with a sparkle in his eye.

"Handsome Man Library, of course! I thought it was only fitting for us to follow our own example, started at Pemberly. We shall need to return for the other buildings, but this is a good beginning, is it not?" A delightful smile spread across his face. He checked to see that they had locked the door. Then, moving toward his beautiful wife, he whispered, "Well, Liz-Beth, this is your prize, so what is your pleasure, my love?"

Made in the USA
Lexington, KY
29 May 2013